BRIAN JACQUES

A TALE OF REDWALL

MARLFOX

Illustrated by Fangorn

RED FOX

To the memory of a true Redwall friend and
talented illustrator, Allan Curless

MARLFOX
A RED FOX BOOK   978 1 782 95459 0

First published in Great Britain by Hutchinson,
an imprint of Random House Children's Publishers UK,
A Random House Group Company

Hutchinson edition published 1998
Red Fox edition published 1999
Red Fox edition reissued 2007

3 5 7 9 10 8 6 4

Red Fox Books are published by Random House Children's Publishers UK,
61–63 Uxbridge Road, London W5 5SA

www.**randomhousechildrens**.co.uk
www.**redwall.org**

Addresses for companies within The Random House Group Limited can be found at: www.
randomhouse.co.uk/offices.htm

THE RANDOM HOUSE GROUP Limited Reg. No. 954009

A CIP catalogue record for this book is available from the British Library.

The Random House Group Limited supports The Forest Stewardship
Council® (FSC®), the leading international forest-certification organisation.
Our books carrying the FSC label are printed on FSC®-certified paper.
FSC is the only forest-certification scheme supported by the leading
environmental organisations, including Greenpeace. Our
paper procurement policy can be found at
www.randomhouse.co.uk/environment

Printed and bound in Great Britain by Clays Ltd, St Ives plc

A Tale of Redwall

MARLFOX

THE TALES OF REDWALL

Click onto the Redwall website and find out more about
your favourite characters from the legendary world of Redwall,
and their creator, Brian Jacques!
www.redwall.org

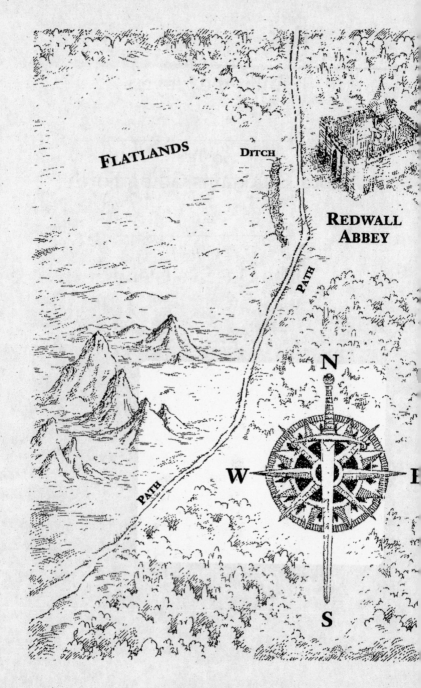

To where will they go,
This is a secret nobeast may know.

                              Marlfox!

Plundering murdering vulpine thieves,
Who blend with stone,
Or meld with leaves.

                              Marlfox!

See the pale eyes and swirling cloak,
Appear like nightmare,
Vanish like smoke.

                              Marlfox !

What steals upon the silent air,
Gleaming fangs, mottled fur,
A deadly axeblade lying there.

                              Marlfox!

Nobeast living can hide from thee,
O thou who treads invisibly,
Cross hill and vale, through woods and rocks.

                              Marlfox!
                                Marlfox!
                                  Marlfox!

PROLOGUE

Who are we but strolling players,
Wand'ring through the long ago,
Joys and sadness, hopes and longings,
Keep us travelling onward though
The laughter and applause of others,
Who view the passing cavalcade,
Leave echoes hovering some far summer,
Floating round a woodland glade.
'Twas but a tale for your amusement,
Like my small unworthy rhyme,
Gone, alas, into those realms,
The land of once upon a time.

Enter the Players

1

Eternally serene, the moon ruled over star-strewn vaults of cloudless sable night, like a round shield of flecked amber, casting pale light to the earth below. Vagrant breezes from the distant sea drifted idly through Mossflower Wood's southwest margins, cooling the heavy warmth a bright summer day had left in its wake.

Janglur Swifteye sat at the edge of a well-worn trail, his back against the broad trunk of a fallen elm, savouring the calm summer night. He was an unusual squirrel, half as tall again as most of his species, with dark terracotta fur, untypically long and thick. A huge bush of tail added to the impression of his size. Beneath the fur Janglur's limbs were hefty and robust, with a stomach of considerable girth, which his mother constantly chided him about. His eyes were hooded and long-lashed, giving the impression he was always half asleep. However, anybeast who knew Janglur Swifteye was careful not to be fooled by his air of easygoing idleness. He was renowned as a quick and dangerous warrior, immensely strong and wise in the ways of battle. But there was another side to him: he was also an obedient son, a dutiful husband and a fond father. In the woodlands behind him his family slept in their little travelling tent, his mother

Ellayo, his wife Rimrose and Songbreeze, the daughter who was the apple of her father's eye.

From beneath half-closed lids Janglur Swifteye watched, missing nothing. Clusters of flowering dock nodded lightly against gnarled oak trunks, orange-berried arums and spiking flowered sedge swayed lazily between elder, chestnut and sycamore trees, nocturnal insects trundled or winged their various ways through the darkened forest. From somewhere deep in the thickets a nightingale warbled its short rich trill. Janglur whistled a reply to it on his reed flute, aware that somebeast was creeping up behind him. The only move he made was to blink away a midge from his eyelashes. He knew who the intruder was by the way she approached. Janglur chuckled.

'I hear ye, missie. Couldn't sleep, eh?'

His daughter Songbreeze climbed slowly over the elm trunk and slid down beside him.

'Nobeast could ever surprise you, old Swifteye. Phew! It's far too hot t'sleep and Grandma's snoring like a score of hedgehogs after a feast.'

Janglur winked lazily at her. 'Huh, listen who's talkin'. Y'should hear yourself snorin' some nights, drowns yore grandma's poor efforts out completely.'

She shoved her father playfully. 'I do not! Young squirrelmaids don't snore, ask Mum.'

Janglur snorted softly. 'Y'mother's worse'n both of you put together.'

The nightingale warbled its short melody again. Janglur picked up his reed flute. 'Listen t'that feller, thinks he can sing. Come on, Song, show him.' No creature who knew the tall pretty squirrel ever used her full name.

Janglur played a brief introduction, then Song's voice rang out with such sweetness and clarity that a tear coursed its way down her father's cheek. Her voice never failed to move him.

'Flow'rs of the forest
Are bright in the spring,
Wake with the dawn
Hear a lone skylark sing.
Brooks gaily babble
O'er hillsides so green,
Streams ripple secrets
Of what they have seen,
Small birds give voice
Mid the leaves of great trees,
Which rustle softly
In time with the breeze.
I'll add my music
For what it is worth,
And sing just for you, love,
The song of the earth.'

As the last plaintive notes died away, Janglur put aside his flute and wiped a paw quickly across his eyes. Song nudged him gently.

'Big tough warrior, eh, crying again.'

Her father sniffed aloud, looking away from her. 'Don't be silly. 'Twas just a midge went in me eye, but I couldn't play for you an' wipe it out at the same time, had to wait till you were finished singin'.'

In another part of the woodland two foxes ceased their prowl through the undergrowth and listened to the sweet, plaintive melody floating faintly on the night air. Both beasts were identical; apart from the fact they were brother and sister they were alike in every other aspect. Ascrod and his sister Vannan were Marlfoxes, pale-eyed, with strange silver-white coats heavily mottled with patches of black and bluey grey. They wore swirling cloaks of drab brown and green weave. Ascrod's lips scarcely moved as he muttered to his sister: 'That singer warbles more sweetly than any bird I ever heard!'

Vannan's pale eyes glimmered in the moonlight. 'Aye, brother, and would trill even better at the court of our mother Queen Silth. Come on!'

In the space of a breath both Marlfoxes were gone, melted back into the night-shaded forest like tendrils of smoke on the wind.

Song plucked a blade of grass and tickled her father's eartip. 'Big old softie. Come on, play a lively tune and I'll put a smile back on your face, eh?'

But Janglur was not paying attention to her. He stiffened, both ears twitching as he sniffed the breeze. Song caught the urgency of his mood.

'What is it? Can you hear something?'

Janglur's hooded eyes flicked. He watched the trees on the opposite side of the path, talking quietly, not looking at his daughter as he continued scanning the woodlands. 'Go quick t'yore mamma, Song, an' tell 'em t'be silent. An' stay put! Hurry now!'

Song had seen her father like this before. She knew better than to stop and argue with him. Wordlessly, she slipped away to the tent.

Janglur took a dangerous-looking thorn dart, tufted with dried grass, from his belt pouch. Placing the missile in his mouth, he tucked it against one cheek, then sat back against the elm trunk. Idly he began playing his reed flute. Outwardly the big squirrel appeared calm, but inside he was poised like lightning ready to strike. In a short while he made out the two foxes moving expertly from a patch of fern to the cover of some bushes, coming closer to him by the moment. Janglur took the flute from his lips, calling out sternly, 'Quit sneakin' about an' walk on the path like decent creatures!'

Ascrod and Vannan had thought the squirrel was unaware of their approach. They hid their surprise by putting on a bold front, swaggering up to where Janglur sat. Ascrod kicked the squirrel's footpaw, just hard enough to warn him that he and his sister were well in charge of the situation.

'You there, who was that singing a short while ago?'

Janglur did not bother to look up at Ascrod, though his voice was menacingly low. 'None o' yore business, snipenose. Now get goin', an' take that other one with ye!'

Vannan winked at her brother and smiled nastily as her paw began to stray towards the single-bladed axe she carried beneath her cloak. Janglur appeared to ignore them, and went back to playing his flute. Ascrod leaned close to the squirrel, baring his teeth.

'You're very insolent for a fat lazy squirrel. Shall I show you what we do to beasts with insulting tongues?'

Pffutt!

Janglur Swifteye shot the dart from his flute, burying it deep in the tip of Ascrod's nose. As the fox shrieked out in agony, Janglur sprang upright. Whipping forth a loaded sling from round his waist, he hurled himself upon Vannan, who had her axe halfway out. She went down in an unconscious heap as the hard oval river pebble in the sling's tongue thwacked heavily across her skull. Ascrod was hopskipping about wildly, both paws clapped across his muzzle as he screeched with pain.

'Yeeeeeeek! Yaaaaarreeeeek!'

'Tails'n'scuts preserve us all! Who's kickin' up that awful din?'

Shaking with anger, Janglur turned to see his family dashing towards him, with Ellayo in the lead, brandishing a blackthorn stick.

Janglur stared accusingly at his daughter. 'Song, I thought I told you to stay put an' keep 'em quiet?'

Rimrose placed herself between them. ''Tweren't no fault o' Song's. You jus' try stoppin' that ole mamma of yours when she starts swingin' that stick!'

Janglur's paw shot out. He caught the tip of his mother's stick and held it tight.

11

Heaving on the blackthorn and stumbling on her long apron hem, the old squirrelwife berated her son. 'Leggo o' me stick, y'great boulder-bellied tree-walloper, leggo or I'll spank ten seasons' daylights out of ye!'

Song giggled and clapped her paws. 'That's the stuff, Grandma. You give him a good spankin'!'

Rimrose wagged a paw at her daughter. 'That'll be quite enough o' that, missie. Show some proper respect for yore elders!' Then, unable to prevent herself, she fell against Song, laughing helplessly. 'Oh, heeheehee! It'd be a funny sight to see yore grandma givin' that great lump a spank or two! Heehee!'

Grandma Ellayo let go of the stick and turned on Song and Rimrose, attempting to look fierce as she hid a smile. 'Hah! Don't you two think I couldn't tan his tail if'n I took a mind to do it. I'm still his mother, y'know!'

Janglur lifted his mother clear of the ground, hugging her fondly. 'You can skelp the fur off'n me any time ye wants to, my lovely ole barkbelter. Why, I'll bet y'could . . .'

Song interrupted suddenly. 'Look! The foxes are gone.'

All that remained of the Marlfoxes' visit was a few drops of blood from Ascrod's muzzle, glistening darkly amid the disturbed dust of the path. Janglur peered into the dark woodlands. 'Aye, they've got away somehow. Won't catch 'em now, they've vanished.' He put a paw about his daughter's shoulders. 'Mark what I say, Song. They're Marlfoxes, strange blood runs in their veins. They can disappear like no other livin' creature.'

'C'mon, ladies, we best break camp an' get travellin'.'

Janglur's family had been wanderers since he was in his infancy, and breaking camp was a simple affair to them. Once the canvas they used as a tent had been folded, their few cooking implements were rolled in it to form a backpack. In the pre-dawn light they breakfasted on clear streamwater and a travelling fruit and honey cake which Rimrose had baked two days before.

'Grandma, what's a Marlfox?' asked Song, between mouthfuls.

Ellayo tried to explain. 'The story goes back a long ways – 'tis far too long to tell in a short time. But I'll tell ye this much, missie. Somewhere there's a forgotten lake, a great stretch o' deep water, almost an inland sea somebeasts say. That's where the Marlfoxes live, an' the most cunning of 'em all, if'n she still lives, is Queen Silth. Aye, they call her the most powerful magic creature alive. 'Tis said her island is a place o' great riches an' beauty. I heard all this from a poor creature who was set upon by a bunch of magpies while fishing off the island.'

Ellayo fell silent, and Janglur said, 'Don't bother your grandma further, Song. If Marlfoxes are loose in the land y'may learn more than you bargained for. Pick up that linen now, we need t'be travellin'. North an' east a touch, I reckon.'

Song folded the small tablecloth, which she had embroidered herself. 'What lies in that direction, Father?'

Janglur shouldered the tentpack, settling it comfortably on his back. 'The Abbey of Redwall.'

The young squirrelmaid's eyes grew wide with delight. She had never visited there, though she had heard tales of the fabulous place. 'Redwall Abbey! How wonderful! Oh, Mamma, will it be as nice as you told me it was when I was little?'

Rimrose smiled at her daughter's excitement. 'Even nicer, I imagine. Words can't fully describe a place like Redwall.'

Song took Grandma Ellayo's paw, supporting her as they walked. With Janglur in the lead, they set off as dawn was breaking. It promised to be another hot summer day, but the tree canopy was thick and would shade them as the sun rose higher. Song could not resist a final question to her father. 'Why are we going to Redwall?'

Janglur tucked the reed flute into his broad belt. 'Because we must warn whoever rules at the Abbey that there are Marlfoxes roaming the land.'

2

Farther south, on the flatlands close to the woodland fringe, a gaily painted cart stood propped straight on its two large wheels. It had a single shaft, crosstreed at the end by a well-worn pushing bar. Stretched over willow hoops a canvas cover was copiously painted in once bright colours, now faded by sun and seasons, though the lettering still read clearly.

'The Sensational Wandering Noonvale Companions Troupe!'

On the nearby streambank a motley collection of creatures were preparing for a rehearsal. One of them, a theatrical-looking hare, stood forward. He was clad in a rumpled frock coat of lilac silk and a wide-brimmed straw hat, through which his enormous ears poked. He wore floppy yellow boots and carried a silver-tipped cane. The hare's outfit had obviously seen better seasons, as had the cart and the entire troupe. Nevertheless the hare twirled his cane and boomed out in fine dramatic fashion as if addressing a vast audience.

'Good morrow, one an' all. I am Florian Dugglewoof Wilffachop, h'impresario an' h'actor manager. I preesent to you the Sensational Wanderin' Noonvale Companions Troupe! Descendants of a talented tradition! Unrivalled throughout the entire land! Death-defyin' feats! Hilarious comical plays! Music an' magical virtuosity, jocular jigs an' deelightful dancin'! Come one, come all! Witness our mellifluously marvellous, perfectly pleasurable educational entertainment! Entirely free of charge!' He smiled winningly and continued in a loud stage whisper: 'Home-made cakes, pasties an' sundry comestibles, purely for the nourishment of the artistes, gladly accepted with profuse thanks. Ahem!'

From the cover of the cart a gruff voice interrupted Florian's speech impatiently. 'Oh, gerron wiv it afore us all falls asleep!'

The hare shot an outraged glance at the cart and snorted. Turning back to his imaginary audience, he beamed. 'H'anda now, my bucolic friends, goodwives an' rustic spouses – not forgettin' your charmin' young 'uns – we reach our fee-nah-lay! The very climax of our prodigious performance! Borrakul Ironchest an' Elachim Oakpaw, the two strongest h'otters h'ever born, will h'attempt a darin' display of muscle power, which H'i meself have seen kill ten h'other lesser beasts. If you are h'of a nervous nature, kindly look away, as swoonin' an' faintin' may distract the h'artistes' attention. These two mighty marvels will lift the h'entire, H'i repeat, the h'entire – disregardin' me goodself, of course – they will lift the h'entire Wanderin' Noonvale Companions Troupe . . . h'off thee gerround!'

Two burly otters, wearing tawdry gold-fringed pantaloons, skipped athletically forward, flexing their muscles and bowing. Puffing forth their chests and showing rows of white teeth in daredevil smiles, they performed a few limbering-up exercises and then went about their business. Seizing both ends of a long wooden bench, they started, with a great show of huffing and puffing, to lift. Standing on the bench were two moles, one dressed in spangled red bloomers, the other in a cloak and turban of jade green. Lying gracefully across

16

the heads of the two moles was a mouse wearing a coronet of imitation flowers and a flowing sky-blue gown. Skilfully perched on one paw placed upon the mouse's midriff, a hedgehog balanced precariously, his spikes tipped with a mass of pennants, small flags and bunting. Up, up went the bench, with all aboard it wobbling perilously. The hare, Florian, muttered encouragement in a loud stage whisper.

'Keep it goin' up, chaps, that's the ticket! Everybeast remain still now, hold y'positions. Up she goes, wot wot!'

Borrakul and Elachim grunted and strained artistically until they had finally lifted the bench over their heads. Suddenly Borrakul gave out a tremendous bellow.

'Yahwooooch!'

He released his hold on the bench and grabbed at his rear. Amid howls of dismay, the troupe and the bench came to earth in jumbled disarray. Florian dashed forward, furious. Down on all fours he berated Borrakul, who lay trapped by the bench, still clutching his bottom.

'Great seasons o' sausages, you blitherin' bangtailed buffoon! Why did y'let the bally bench drop?'

Crimson-faced, Borrakul gasped, 'Because that perishin' mousebabe shot me with a slingstone!'

Florian Dugglewoof Wilffachop drew himself to his full height, ears twitching, teeth grinding audibly. 'Oho, he did, did he! Well, 'tis high time I had a serious encounter with that blisterin' undersized miscreant. Dwopple! Come out o' that cart, front'n'centre, this instant. Out I say, sir!'

Florian strode resolutely forward, but the mouse in the blue gown suddenly flung herself dramatically in front of the cart. One paw outstretched, the other across her brow, she declaimed, 'Oh, mister Florian, I beseech you, sir, touch not a hair of that babe's tender head. Do nothing you will reproach yourself for in the sunlit seasons lying ahead. Hear a pitiful mother's plea, and punish not the harmless innocent. Spare him, I beg of you!'

Runktipp the hedgehog chortled bitterly as he removed the bunting from his spikes. 'Dwopple a harmless innocent? Huh, that 'un's about as harmless as a bucket o' serpents an' a sack o' stoats! An' you ain't his mother, Deesum, yore only his auntie!'

Deesum shot Runktipp a haughty glance. 'A mere detail. Do not quibble, sir. No mother could love a babe as I love Dwopple. Come to me, my precious little mite!'

Clambering into the cart, she grabbed a small fat mousebabe, who wore a stained oversized smock and a wicked scowl. Hanging from one of his grubby paws was a miniature slingshot. He wriggled and kicked desperately as Deesum smothered him with kisses.

'Garraaagh! Leggo a Dwopple, stoppa kissy me. Blurrgh!'

Elachim the otter massaged a bruised paw as he glared at the infant. 'You steamin' liddle nit, Dwopple, you ruined our re'earsal!'

Florian interrupted sternly. 'Indeed you have, ye young ripcurdle. Apologize to the entire troupe, this very flippin' instant! Say you're sorry, sir!'

From over Deesum's shoulder, Dwopple grinned fiendishly at the company. 'A soggy!'

The hare squinched his eyes at Dwopple. 'Beg pardon, what did y'say?'

Deesum stamped her paw impatiently. 'He said he's sorry, isn't that good enough for you? Would you like the little fellow to shed salt tears and roll in the dust? Isn't the word *sorry* satisfactory to a heartless, driving taskmaster like you?'

Florian threw up his paws in despair. 'Tchah! I suppose it'll have t'be, wot!'

Deesum patted the mousebabe's back reassuringly. 'There now, my little treasure, they've all forgiven you, isn't that nice. Will you give them all a big kiss?'

The hedgehog, Runktipp, backed off with a horrified face. 'Let that liddle savage kiss me? No thanks! He'd prob'ly bite the snout off'n me!'

Florian waggled his cane severely at Dwopple. 'Absolutely no need t'go kissin' an' huggin' everybeast. Just behave y'self in future, m'laddo, particularly at rehearsals, wot!'

Turning on his heel, the hare strode grandiloquently off, only to be hit sharply on his bobtail by a missile from Dwopple's sling.

'Yowhooch! Bandit, fiend, pollywoggle, scallywag! I'll have y'tail for breakfast, sah!'

The sight of Florian's enraged face set Dwopple crying in distress. 'Wahaaah! Nasty wabbit gonna eat Dwopple's tail. Boohoohoo! Me on'y a likka baybee. Wahaahaa!'

Deesum hugged the mousebabe closer to her as she rounded on Florian. 'You callous monster! Fancy frightening the poor little fellow like that!'

Florian flung his hat down and danced upon it. 'Madam, I'll have y'know that wretch shot me in the posterior, an' called me a rabbit t'boot!'

Deesum stamped her paw hard. 'Enough! One more word, sir, and I'll resign from your troupe and take baby Dwopple with me!'

Roop, the mole in the spangled bloomers, shook his head dolefully, grumbling in his curious molespeech. 'Hurr, no such lukk oi doan't surpose, burr no.'

Muggle, the other mole, gathered up a pail and trundled towards the stream. She wrinkled her velvety snout at her companions. 'Ee can stan' yurr arguin' all day. Oi'm goin' to get brekkist vittles readied. Bain't goin' to wurr moi jaws out a-shouten.'

Florian, who liked to issue all the orders, coughed officiously. 'Ahem, rather! Just what I was about to suggest m'self. Right, troupe, breakfast. Elachim, get a fire goin'. Runktipp, see to the larder, the rest of you make y'selves busy, wot. Quick's the word an' sharp's the action, wot wot!'

Runktipp spread the meagre rations on the bankside where Muggle was boiling water over the small fire Elachim had kindled. The hedgehog scratched his head spikes. 'Ain't enough grub left t'keep a fat bumblebee goin'.'

Deesum glanced at the two shrivelled apples, dandelion stalks, a stale loaf of ryebread which had crumbled into pieces and some half a dozen withered field mushrooms. 'Oh, seasons of mercy on us, the babe will starve!'

Ever the optimist, Florian began chopping the scanty provisions up and tossing them into the pail of bubbling water. 'Nonsense, marm. Fiddlesticks! Nature's bounty has provided us with sufficient food for a nourishin' broth. Let's all eat hearty an' look forward to better, more prosperous times, wot!'

The soup was dreadful, but knowing there was nothing else the Wandering Noonvale Companions spooned it down in stoic silence, until Runktipp began eulogizing on past dishes he had eaten, as hungry hedgehogs will invariably do. 'Crispy 'ot white bread, straight out o' the oven, that's the stuff. Goes down a treat with some good yellow nutcheese an' young onions fresh picked, all washed down with a foamy beaker of dark ale. Hoho! A feast fit fer a king, I say!'

Borrakul the otter closed his eyes dreamily.

'Pipin' 'ot scones, matey, spread wid meadowcream an' served wid fat juicy strawberries coated in honey, with a flagon of cold cider, o' course. Now *that's* a feast fit fer a king!'

Roop picked something dubious out of his soup bowl, wrinkling his nose as he flicked the offending item into the stream. 'Burr aye, well, seein' as 'ow you'm two bain't kings, whoi doan't ee use yore mouths furr eatin' an' not makin' us'n's 'ungrier?'

The mousebabe, Dwopple, picked up his bowl and began toddling off. Deesum chided her charge brusquely.

'Dwopple, come back here. Where are you taking that soup?'

Dwopple nodded to a rock-strewn knoll along the streambank. 'Diss soop not gudd for baybees. Gunna give 'im to the fosskers.'

Elachim stared at Dwopple quizzically. 'Fosskers?'

Deesum translated. 'He means foxes.'

Florian was immediately on the alert. 'Foxes, what foxes? Where?'

Another pair of Marlfoxes, identical to the two who had accosted Janglur, rose up from amid the rocks where they had lain watching the Companions since dawn. Their names were Gelltor and Predak, brother and sister. Seeing they had been spotted, the pair approached the camp boldly, their drab cloaks flapping slightly in the light morning breeze. Borrakul cautioned his friends, keeping an eye on the strange pair.

'Careful, mates, they're carryin' axes under those cloaks!'

Florian stood up. 'Steady in the ranks, chaps, leave this t'me. I'll do the talkin'. See those strange markin's? I reckon I heard about these creatures, but I never thought I'd ave the bad luck to see 'em for myself. Marlfoxes they're called – bad beasts!'

The foxes stopped a few paces short of the group. Florian walked cautiously out and greeted them. 'Good day, friends. Beautiful summer mornin', wot?'

Gelltor, the male fox, nodded slightly before speaking. 'Who are you and where do you go?'

Florian bowed eloquently, sweeping off his hat with a flourish. 'As you can see by our, ahem, cart, we are the Wandering Noonvale Companions, a purely theatrical group of talented creatures.'

Predak, the female, moved closer to the fire. 'What's in the pot?'

Deesum dipped a short curtsey. 'It's a sort of soupy broth. You're welcome to join us.'

Predak leaned over the pot and sniffed. She wrinkled her muzzle disgustedly. 'Slops!'

Borrakul picked up a large pebble and tossed it from paw to paw. 'Nobeast's forcin' ye to eat it an' you weren't asked to insult it either. Good manners don't cost much, fox.'

Predak's paw edged towards her cloak. 'Mayhap I'll teach you a few manners, riverdog!'

Florian was quickly between them. 'Tush an' pish, what's all this?'

Predak drew her paw away from the axe beneath her cloak. 'You've told us who you are, but you never said where you were goin'.'

The hare waved a paw airily. 'Oh, thither an' yon, y'know, thither an' yon. A travellin' show like ours doesn't actually *go* anywhere, we roam as the mood takes us. But you, friend, will you tell us your names, and where you are bound on this summer's day, wot?'

The Marlfox's pale eyes stared insolently at the hare. 'What we are called is not your concern, and where we go is nobeast's business.'

Florian Dugglewoof Wilffachop's ears quivered with indignation. 'Soho! It's bad manners an' insult time, is it? Well, listen t'me, you popbellied, pickle-nosed, lousebound patchquilts! You can both take a runnin' dive into that stream an' boil your fat heads, an' furthermore you can take your mange-ridden hides out of our camp before I assist you with a stout right boot. Good day to ye both!'

Gelltor had his axe half drawn when the otter Elachim picked up a thick pole used in a balancing act and flicked the air in front of the fox's face with it. 'I wouldn't draw that axe if'n I was you, matey. This pole cracks 'eads easier'n it does eggs!'

Predak found herself facing Borrakul holding his big pebble ready to throw and backed by the two moles brandishing burning sticks from the fire. Runktipp dashed across to the cart and dragged out a long shining sword, a stage prop which bent and flopped about comically.

'Now back off, both of ye, or get ready t'find out the colour of yore own insides. Move!'

The Marlfoxes knew they were outflanked and outnumbered, and backed off towards the rocks. Gelltor pointed at the troupe and snarled, 'We'll meet again, but 'twill be different next time!'

Florian threw the hem of his frock coat up across one shoulder and called back in an outrageously dramatic voice. 'Indeed it will be different! The land will be rid of two rogues when next we cross paths, mark m'words, you spotty villains!'

Predak pointed beyond the troupe and shouted, 'We're not the only two here. There are others behind you!'

The entire troupe turned and scanned the landscape. After a moment or two Florian scoffed, 'Not an earthly sight of anybeast. What do they think we are to fall for that one, a bunch of oafs, wot?'

When they turned back again the two Marlfoxes had vanished as if into thin air. Florian sighed. 'Wish we could learn that trick. Ah well, comrades, onward ever onward.'

Deesum was still looking about fearfully. 'Onward to where?'

With a great flourish the hare kicked the cooking pot over, letting the meagre broth spill into the stream. 'Why, onward to Redwall Abbey of course, m'dear, where else?'

Roop chuckled and rubbed his stomach gleefully. 'Hurr, oi dearly luvs ee vittles at Red'all h'Abbey.'

Florian issued the orders. 'Attention, troupe! Load up the cart. Borrakul, Elachim, in the shafts please. Runktipp, you and I will walk behind armed with poles to protect our rear. The rest of you ride in the cart. We must get the news to Redwall, there are Marlfoxes in the land!'

As late morning heat shimmered on the flatlands and grasshoppers chirruped dryly beneath a hot summer sun, the cart trundled off towards Mossflower Wood, with the entire company singing.

'Oh for the open road,
No dullard's life for me,
The world is my abode,
Performing endlessly.
I'm free I'm free, companions we,
Travel the highways happily,
Performing deeds of derring do,
And plays of heroes good and true,
Tumbling singing in merry attire,
Pray tell me, sir, what's your desire?
Come fiddle dum twiddle dum derrydownday,
A harum scarum hoopallahey,
Come one come all this day to see
The Wandering Noonvale Companeeeeeeeeeee!'

At the very heart of Mossflower country the fastness of lordly, wide-trunked trees gave way to an expansive watermeadow, formed in a wide shallow basin at the juncture of two streams. Mid-afternoon heat haze shimmered on the far margin as Log a Log, Chieftain of the Guosim, stood waist deep at the fringe of the tall reeds with his shrews. Though usually a loud argumentative band, the Guerilla Union of Shrews in Mossflower were unusually quiet. Each small scruffy furred fighter, equipped with varicoloured headband and short rapier, watched their leader as he parted bulrush and marshwort. Raising himself on tip-paw, Log a Log shaded his eyes, peering about over the reaches of waterlily, crowfoot and brookweed. A large striped dragonfly hovered near the shrew Chieftain's face, investigating him. He growled at it. 'Buzz off!' Surprisingly, it did. He watched a brown trout fin idly by him, just beneath the surface.

Log a Log wished that he could forget his tribe's troubles and go fishing. Behind him a young shrew chewed noisily at some watercress, and Log a Log turned and fixed him with a severe stare. The young Guosim shrew stopped chewing and swallowed guiltily. An older shrew pointed across Log a Log's shoulder.

'Over there, Chief!'

Log a Log's eyes narrowed as he turned and stared searchingly out over the sunstill reaches of the watermeadow. Over at the eastern edge, by a stand of weeping willows, an oar poked itself in the air, waving back and forth thrice. He cupped both paws around his mouth and let forth a long ululating call.

'Logalogalogalogaaaaaa!'

Immediately the shrews behind him relaxed and began chattering.

'That'll be Bargle an' the others!'

'Then the coast mebbe clear, eh?'

'Well, the Chief wouldn't have called if 'twasn't, stump'ead!'

Log a Log followed as they waded back on to dry ground, still disputing and debating.

'Stump'ead yerself, wobblesnout. 'Ow d'you know they ain't still around?'

'Wobblesnout? Lissen, matey, if I 'ad a snout like yores I'd keep me gob shut about others'.'

'Mebbe Bargle was alone. The others might've been ambushed.'

'Nah, Splikker was with 'em. He wouldn't let hisself get ambushed.'

'Oh, wouldn't 'e, then? Remember that time by the south rapids . . .'

'Stow the gab an' latch yore lips, mates. Mayon, see to the vittles!'

Log a Log stamped up on to the bank, shaking water from himself. The shrews were seated in a circle three deep when Bargle and his scouts came in. Log a Log motioned them to sit and help themselves to a beaker of rough cider each and some wedges of white celery cheese with shrewbread. When they were comfortably settled and eating, Bargle made his report.

'We saw the two Marlfoxes just afore noon, Chief, west of 'ere, over by widestream. Then they vanished, right in front of our eyes!'

Log a Log undid his shoulder belt and let his rapier fall to the ground, rubbing the back of a paw wearily across his eyes. 'No sign o' those rats or our logboats, I suppose?'

The shrew named Splikker shrugged. 'Never saw 'em, but we tracked their sign, an' they're bound west an' a point south, Chief. By the seasons, they can paddle boats as well as any shrew can, believe me.'

Log a Log shook his head despairingly. 'Stands to reason, doesn't it? They're water rats. West an' a point south, y'say?'

'Aye, Chief, but there's a lot of 'em, so the logboats'll be overloaded. I saw keel scrapin's in the shallows. They can't be travellin' very fast, weighted down as they are.'

Log a Log drained his beaker and sat awhile, gnawing worriedly at his lip. The Guosim watched him in silence, until a scuffle broke out behind his back. Log a Log whirled round in time to see a hulking shrew deal the young one who had been eating the watercress a hefty blow. As the young shrew fell back holding his face, the hefty one began to kick him, rumbling bad-temperedly, 'It was you, Dippler, sleepin' on guard while those foxes'n'rats stole the boats from under yer nose, yer worthless, tail-draggin' . . .'

Log a Log was up in a flash. Launching himself sideways, he caught the hefty one a flying double kick to the stomach, sending him sprawling. The Chieftain stood over him, quivering with anger. 'Lay a paw near Dippler again an' I'll boot yore guts through yer backbone, that's if you've got any!'

The hefty shrew, who was called Fenno, glared up at

his chief, his eyes filled with unspoken rage. Log a Log was older, smaller and lighter than him, but he was not Chieftain for nothing. Log a Log smiled, nodding back to his rapier on the ground. 'C'mon, Fenno, yer a fine big beast. Carryin' a blade, too. I'm not armed, but if y'figger yore brave enough t'carry out the beatin's in this tribe, then why not try me? Come on, mate, let's see what yore made of, eh?'

There was tension in the air as the Guosim watched both shrews. Then Fenno, still lying flat, placed a paw across his eyes, a sign of submission. A few chuckles broke out from the Guosim.

'Ole Fenno did the sensible thing there, mate!'

'Aye, so he did. Nobeast messes with Log a Log!'

'Leastways, nobeast that wants ter grow old in one piece!'

Log a Log helped Dippler up. Throwing a paw round the youngster's shoulders, he gestured for silence. 'Hearken now, I don't want any shrew complainin' about young Dippler, or tryin' to rough him up. We was all young once an' we all made mistakes, some of 'em worse'n others. Dippler slept on guard an' lost our logboats, all six of 'em – good craft too, they were. So the young 'un'll learn better, he'll try harder. You will, won't yer, matey?'

Dippler wiped mud from his bruised face, smiling through his tears. 'I won't let the Guosim down ever again, Chief. That's a promise!'

Log a Log patted Dippler's back heartily. 'Good feller! Now, Guosim, 'ere's the bad news. Those boats of ours can only go one way on widestream an' that way takes 'em too close to Redwall Abbey fer my likin'. I know we ain't used to walkin', but we've got to get to the Abbey an' warn 'em. I never saw water rats in Mossflower afore, but I know that their leaders, those Marlfoxes, are evil beasts. Magic, too. They've got tools, wood an' carpenters at the Abbey, so the sooner we're there the quicker we'll get new boats built. Right?'

The bass-voiced shrews roared back agreement gruffly. 'Right!'

Log a Log smiled as he buckled his rapier back on. 'So wot are you sittin' round like a crowd o' butterflies with wet wings for? Let's get trampin'!'

They formed up into six lines, one for the crew of each boat. As they marched away, Bargle called out to Log a Log. 'I know we ain't sailin', Chief, but could we sing a paddle song to 'elp us keep pawstep on the way?'

Log a Log nodded and roared out a fast paddle song with the rest as they stamped away through the dim tree aisles of Mossflower.

'Whum chakka um chakka chumchakka whum!
Guosim dig yore paddle deep,
Hurly-burly river wide'n'curly,
There's no time to sleep.
Whum chakka um chakka chumchakka whum!
Rapid wild and fast do go,
Hurly-burly river wide'n'curly,
Bend yore backs an' row.
Whum chakka um chakka chumchakka whum!
Keep her bows up in the foam,
Hurly-burly river wide'n'curly,
Logboat take us home.
Whum chakka um chakka chumchakka . . .'

The rousing boatsong echoed through wooded glades and grassy clearings as Log a Log and his Guosim shrews marched to Redwall.

3

Extract from the writings of Old Friar Butty, Squirrel Recorder of Redwall Abbey in Mossflower country.

I had a twinge in my left footpaw a moment back – I hope that's a sign of rain. We could certainly do with a good shower. Everything seems to be drooping or wilting. Badgermum Cregga says 'tis the dryest summer she's ever known, and she's seen more summers than the rest of us put together! Redwallers have had to form a chain from the Abbey pond to the orchard, bringing pails of water for the thirsty trees and vines that produce our fruits and berries. A pity we haven't more able-bodied creatures – Redwall Abbey seems to be populated by the elders or the very young these last few seasons. I can remember in the times when Abbess Tansy ruled, there seemed to be no end of willing otters, moles, mice, squirrels and hedgehogs to perform the daily chores of Redwall. But that was a long time back, when I served as an assistant cook in the kitchens under Old Mother Buscol. Who would have thought the days would arrive when I would be called old? Yes, Old Friar Butty, that's me, too old to cook and far too rheumaticky to serve as Abbot, even though there was a time when everybeast seemed to keep asking me to take up the position. 'Tis a sad reflection, Redwall Abbey without Abbot or Abbess, but that's the way things are this season. Poor old Arven, who was once Abbey Warrior, served as Abbot for three seasons, after Abbess Tansy had gone to her rest. Unfortunately he passed on to the sunlit pastures during the spring, having survived a rough winter. So now there is only myself and Badgermum Cregga, with the good mouse Sister Sloey running the Infirmary, Tragglo Spearback our hedgehog Cellarkeeper, Diggum and Gurrbowl, his mole helpers, and Gubbio, who is now Foremole. All that is left of our old friends. The sword of Martin, our Founder and first Abbey Warrior, hangs on the wall in Cregga's room. His brave guiding spirit is blended into the ancient red sandstone of our beautiful Abbey. Seasons have been kind and peace has reigned here many, many summers. I think it is thanks to the spirit of Martin. Oh, I forgot one other still here from the old days. In fact I can see him now, from the gatehouse window where I am sitting, Nutwing the owl. He was one of three born here at Redwall. His brother and sister have long flown off, but Nutwing has stayed and remained faithful to the Abbey. He is, how shall I put it, an unwise old owl, having great lapses of memory in his latter seasons. You will pardon me, I'm sure, but I feel I'm about to be lured away from my recording duties. I just hope 'tis nothing too strenuous.

The owl waddled right up to the gatehouse window and peered in through tiny thick crystal-lensed spectacles, perched on his beak curve. 'Hmm, mm. Is that you, Butty?'

The old squirrel poked his head out of the open window, facing Nutwing nose to beak. 'Who else would it be, pushing a quill pen, inkstained paws, buried among scrolls on a beautiful summer morn like this? Certainly not yourself, you feathered old fraud.'

Nutwing shook his head absently. 'Hmm, mm. No, it wouldn't be me. Don't like writing one little bit. D'you think it's likely to rain soon?'

Butty nodded towards the hot blue cloudless sky. 'I've had one paw twinge today, but that could mean nothing. Look up and tell me what you think.'

Nutwing flapped his wings resignedly. 'Hmm. Sky's too far up for me to see. I don't bother with it.'

Friar Butty came around outside the gatehouse to where the owl stood. 'Well, friend, I'm sure you didn't come this far just to chat about the weather. What d'you want?'

Nutwing thought long and hard, blinking and moving his head from side to side. 'Hmm, mm, er, let me see, was it something t'do with ... No, that wasn't it ... Perhaps it was ... Hmm, no, I'd forgotten about that ...'

Butty smiled indulgently. 'Was it anything to do with strawberries, perhaps?'

Nutwing looked astonished. 'How did you know?'

'Because when you flapped your wings a strawberry fell out on the grass. There it is.'

It was a giant of a fruit, shiny red, plump and speckled with seeds. Nutwing grinned happily. Retrieving the strawberry, he gave it to the squirrel. 'I brought this beauty over for you, friend. They're taking the berries to the kitchen, and your advice is needed.'

Friar Butty bit into the fruit, wiping juice from his whiskers as he chewed. 'Oh, delicious. I hope they're all the same quality as this'n. What a wonderful thing a strawberry is. It has a flavour and fragrance all of its own – the taste of a good summer. Right, let's go to the kitchens and see how I can be of help.'

Badgermum Cregga was totally blind, though it did not seem to hamper her greatly. She waited at the Abbey's main door to greet the pair. 'Ah, well done,

Nutwing, you remembered your errand. Come on, Butty, finish eating that strawberry and get along to the kitchens.'

The old Friar was amazed. 'But how did you . . .'

Redwall's blind Badgermum forestalled the question. 'I know 'tis you because you limp a bit on that rheumatic paw and any creature with half a nose and one ear can tell by the aroma and the sound of chomping when somebeast is enjoying a big strawberry. Now hurry along before the Dibbuns decide what to do with the entire crop.'

Gubbio Foremole and Sister Sloey had their paws full, trying to control the greedy Abbeybabes, the Dibbuns, from ravaging the baskets of fruit which were piled up everywhere around the kitchens.

'Yurr, you'm rarscal, git'n ee paws outen yon barsket!'

Foremole lifted a tiny mouse down from the shelftop, where she was rummaging in a basket to find the biggest berries. Sister Sloey menaced two small moles who were stained from ear to smock with crimson juice, shaking a wooden spoon at them as they stuffed strawberries into their mouths with both paws.

'Not another one, d'you hear me? Stop immediately!'

Through a mouthful of the fruit one of the molebabes explained patiently to the Infirmary Sister why they had to complete their self-appointed task. 'Nay, marm, us'n's be on'y h'eatin' ee ones that'll go bad soon. Hurr, it'n 'ard job furr ee loikes of uz h'infants!'

The Sister did not share their viewpoint. 'The only things that'll go bad are your tummies. You'll be sick as stuffed frogs the pair of you. Now stop it this instant!'

All the Dibbuns froze as Cregga's voice boomed severely through the kitchens. 'Just point out any Dibbuns who've been pinching strawberries an' I'll deal with them, by the thundering seasons of strife I will!'

The molebabe, Wugger, tugged Friar Butty's habit cord and whispered, 'Yurr, zurr Butty, doan't ee tell Badgermum oi bin pinchin' st'awbees an' oi woan't tell on ee!'

The old Friar winked secretly at Wugger and spoke out loud. 'Cregga, marm, how could you say such things? I'm sure none of the Dibbuns would be so villainous as to pinch strawberries. They're merely helpin' to carry them in and stack the baskets.'

A chorus of agreement burst from the Dibbuns.

'Yuss, Friar be right, marm!'

'Us'n's be gudd an' 'onest beasts!'

'Nono pincha st'awbees, not never!'

Cregga nodded solemnly. 'Well, I'm very glad to hear it, because once, many seasons before any of you were born, we had a Dibbun at Redwall who . . . D'you remember what happened to him, Sister Sloey?'

Sloey pursed her lips forbiddingly as she continued the tale. 'Oh, I recall that one right enough. He ate strawberries from dawn to dusk on the day of the harvest, never listened to a word when he was told to stop, kept on pinchin' and scoffin' all the biggest and juiciest ones. Guess what happened to him as he was on the stairs to the dormitory?' Sloey gazed around at the wide-eyed Dibbuns hanging on her every word. Suddenly she clapped her paws sharply and shouted out, 'He went . . . *Bang!* Just like that! Exploded! Was never seen again! Isn't that right, Friar Butty?'

The old squirrel nodded sadly. 'Aye, that's what happened, Sister. You can still see the red mark he left halfway up the stairs, poor greedy little mite!'

Shocked and horrified Dibbuns unloaded strawberries from their smock pockets back into the baskets, stunned by the fate of the gluttonous Dibbun in that far gone season. Then they rushed from the kitchens, squeaking and shouting as they headed for the dormitory stairs where the incident was reputed to have taken place.

When they had gone, Cregga popped a strawberry into her mouth, chuckling. 'Haha! That story works every summer. I wonder what that bright red mark on the stairs is, though? It feels quite smooth. Probably a lump of quartz in the stone.'

Nutwing watched Cregga feel around in the basket beside her for another large strawberry. 'Hmm, mm. I've seen it. A bit too big for a Dibbun. Must've been a greedy badger who wouldn't stop pinchin' strawberries, eh?'

Tragglo Spearback the Cellarkeeper, an immense hedgehog, lumbered in. Stuffing both paws in his wide canvas apron pocket, he grinned and winked at Nutwing. 'Aye, may'aps 'twere a badger. Now then, ole Butty, which ones are mine? Make sure they're good'n'juicy enough to brew into a barrel o' strawberry fizz.'

Friar Butty did his rounds of the baskets, sniffing and prodding gently at the fruit they contained, and marking certain ones with a charcoal stick.

'Those should be enough for you, Tragglo, a dozen good baskets. Sister Sloey, you take this one, to sweeten up those herb potions you give to sick Dibbuns. Brother Melilot?'

A fat dormouse emerged from an unlit oven with scrubbing brush and pail in his paws.

'Last time I let moles make damson jam in my oven. Sticks like glue when it bubbles over. Did y'want me, Friar?'

Butty indicated the unmarked baskets. 'These are all yours. What d'you plan on making? Strawberry tarts, obviously. I noticed a pot of redcurrant jelly cooling on the windowsill as I came in.'

Melilot took off his greasy apron and began tying on a freshly laundered one. 'Strawberry tarts for sure, with good shortcrust pastry and lots of whipped meadow-cream on top. I'll probably do some strawberry and pear flans too, and a big strawberry trifle if you'll be good enough to help me, Friar.'

Butty agreed willingly. 'Oh, yes, an extra big trifle, with plums and raspberries in it too.'

Everybeast began contributing their ideas of what

made the perfect trifle.

'An' lots o' flaked almonds an' hazelnuts sprinkled on top!'

'Aye, with a good beaker of elderberry wine poured in.'

'Be sure to set it in blackberry jelly.'

'With lots of honeysponge slices t'make it nice an' soggy!'

'Sweet arrowroot custard too, good'n'deep!'

'Burr hurr, an' gurt globbets o' clotted meadowcream atop o' that!'

The discussion was interrupted when a stocky older squirrel strode in, a younger one in his wake, both carrying pails in either paw. The older squirrel, Rusvul, was obviously hot and rather irritated.

'Anybeast interested in lendin' a paw to fetch water from the pond for that orchard out there? Seems there's only me an' my son left t'do it.'

Cregga placed a paw across her brow. 'Oh, I'm sorry, Rusvul. I meant to send Nutwing over to tell you the orchard's been watered enough for today.'

Nutwing smiled behind his pebble thick glasses. 'Hmm, mm. Glad I'm not the only creature who forgets things.'

Rusvul had been at Redwall less than three seasons. He had been a wanderer and a warrior, but when his wife died he'd come to stay at Redwall, bringing with him his son Dannflor, a quiet young squirrel. Both were strong and good workers, but Rusvul had changed since the death of his wife. He was no longer the happy-go-lucky creature of former days, but was often quick to take offence, and sometimes difficult to get on with.

He nodded at the creatures assembled in the kitchen, then turned to Dannflor. 'Let's put these pails away an' get washed up afore lunch, son.'

Outside, the Abbey pool seemed to cool Rusvul down a bit. Dannflor washed his paws in silence, watching his father sluice water across his face with both paws, blowing and snorting as it entered his nostrils. Dannflor glanced up at the sky. 'Wish it'd rain, then there'd be no need t'carry water, eh?'

Rusvul wriggled a paw in one ear to get the water out. 'Aye, son. Wouldn't have been a bad idea for somebeast to tell us the orchard had enough water, an' all.'

Dannflor shrugged good-naturedly. 'It's not the Badgermum's fault she forgot. She carried as much water as both of us earlier on.'

Rusvul nodded grudging agreement. 'Mebbe she did, but this place needs a leader, an Abbot or an Abbess. I liked ole Abbot Arven. When he was alive things seemed t'run smoother.'

Dannflor dried his paws on the grass. 'That's 'cos Arven was a warrior one time, just like you. Prob'ly the reason you got on so well together.'

Rusvul smiled one of his rare smiles, and flicked a pebble at his son. 'True enough, Dann. Me'n'you are the only warriors left in Redwall now, an' we get on well t'gether, don't we?'

Dannflor caught the pebble and skimmed it out over the pond. 'Of course we get on, 'cos I'm your son an' yore my dad. But I've never been in a fight or seen battle, so you couldn't really call me a warrior. I was only a Dibbun before we came here, y'know.'

Rusvul's eyes hardened. He took his son's paw and held it tight. 'But you are a warrior, Dannflor, I know it. The blood of warriors runs in yore veins. Never forget that, son!'

They rose together and walked towards the orchard, where lunch was being served in the shade of the trees. Dannflor paced easily beside his father. 'But Redwall Abbey's the most peaceful place a creature could wish to be. How will I know when I've become a warrior?'

Rusvul stopped and stared at him. 'Yore name is Dannflor Reguba. In ancient squirrel language the

Reguba was the greatest warrior in all the land. I am called Reguba, as my father was before me. When danger threatens an' you have to face the foebeast, then you will know you are Reguba, bravest of the brave!'

Lunch was a fairly simple one: sliced fruits – apple, pear, greengage and plum – some fresh-baked scones and damson jam, and dandelion and burdock cordial, foamy and cold from Tragglo Cellarhog's vaults. Rusvul sat chatting with Tragglo, while Dannflor chose to sit next to Cregga. The Badgermum reached out a huge paw and ran it gently over his face.

'You are troubled, Dann. What's going on in that mind of yours?'

The young squirrel sucked foam noisily from the top of his beaker. 'Not so much troubled as puzzled, marm. They say you were once a great warrior. My father likes the company of warriors, but he never seems to talk at any length with you. Why's that?'

Cregga shrugged lightly, her blind eyes facing straight ahead. 'Probably because I never talk about my seasons as a fighter. That is all in the dead past to me. Peace and this beautiful Abbey are what matter in my life now. Do you like Redwall, Dann?'

'Aye, I like it a lot. It's really home to me.'

Cregga smiled, nodding her great striped head. 'Good. 'Tis my home too, though I've never seen it with my eyes. I was blinded in battle before I ever arrived at Redwall. Do me a favour, Dann, look at it and tell me what you see. You can be my eyes. Go on. Let's see if we both live in the same place.'

Dannflor held the blind Badgermum's paw as he spoke. 'A path runs from north to south, and Redwall stands by the side of it. Mossflower Wood grows around the north and east walls and partially on the south. A big main threshold gate faces the path, with a little gatehouse just inside; the outer walls are high, thick and solid, built from old red sandstone, like the rest of the Abbey.

Battlements and a wide walltop run round the outer walls, making it like a safe fortress. Inside there are gardens and lawns, a pond and this orchard. But in the middle of it all stands the Abbey. It is a huge old building, very high, with a weathervane atop the great long roof, and marvellous stained-glass windows, great arches and columns. Built against one side is a belltower with two bells inside, which are tolled at dawn, midday, twilight and softly at midnight. I like the bells. They have a warm, friendly sound, as if they're watching over us.'

Cregga squeezed the young squirrel's paw gently. 'You have a good eye and a kind heart, Dannflor. Your picture of our Abbey is the same as the one I carry in my imagination.'

Whilst they had been talking the sky was starting to cloud over from the southeast, gradually at first, but the clouds increased as a breeze sprang up to drive them along, blotting out the blue summer noon. Friar Butty felt his footpaw twinge again.

'Hah! I knew it. We'll have rain before long, friends.'

Splot! Splack! Two large raindrops hit the leaves of a plum tree, one of them rolling down to burst on Foremole Gubbio's nose.

'Ee rain bain't awaitin' on yore word, Butty, et be yurr right naow!'

As the mole spoke, long-awaited rain came splattering and battering suddenly down, a proper summer storm, driven sideways on the wind. Thunder rumbled afar, with a distant lightning flash flaring briefly in the east. Dust turned immediately to mud, dry yellowed grass was flattened against the wet earth, and a tremendous din of countless large drops pattering against foliage and rapping upon treetrunks as it hissed around the Abbey virtually drowned out all other sound.

Brother Melilot and Rusvul swept the linen spread off the ground, and knotting it loosely into a large sack with foodstuffs and dishes inside they bore it off between them to the Abbey. Cregga Badgermum boomed out over the din, 'Everybeast inside!' Ambling sideways, she shielded many elders and young ones with her bulk. Sister Sloey tugged at Tragglo's apron, rain pouring down her face into her open mouth as she called to him.

'Mister Tragglo, there's two Dibbuns not here!'

Dannflor joined them, his fur plastered flat by the downpour. 'That'll be the two molebabes, marm, Wugger an' Blinny. They went off towards the gatehouse as my father an' I were comin' up from the pond.'

Tragglo Spearback shooed Sister Sloey off to the Abbey. 'You get yoreself indoors, marm. Me'n'young Dann'll find 'em!'

Dannflor and Tragglo dashed across the lawns, heads down, footpaws sloshing and slapping through the wet grass, as the thunder boomed closer and a great fork of jagged lightning rent the sky asunder. Both creatures were driven flat against the gatehouse wall by the wind, and stood there a moment regaining their breath before fighting their way round to the gatehouse door. It was flapping back and forth, for Butty had left it open, and they hurried inside out of the storm. Tragglo cast a quick eye about.

'Liddle rascals. They ain't 'ere, Dann, an' we never passed 'em on the way 'ere.'

The young squirrel wiped rain from his eyes on a window curtain. 'Let's think. I know! Maybe they're up on the walltop. Dibbuns are always being told not to go up there, so that's the likely place for them to be.'

Sheeting rain swept the ramparts, dancing across the stones and gurgling noisily out of small downspouts, so heavy that visibility was virtually nil. Tragglo and Dannflor were running almost doubled up past the north battlements when a peal of thunder exploded with frightening force directly overhead. In the crackle of chain lightning that followed the hedgehog pointed to the northeast gable end and the two small figures huddled there.

'Haharr, there they be!'

It was hard to imagine two more saturated and frightened little creatures. The molebabes wailed and threw themselves at their rescuers.

'Whhauhau! Us'n's be gurtly drownded, zurrs!'

Tragglo untied his stout canvas apron and placed it over the Dibbuns, then between them he and Dannflor picked them up and started down the east wallsteps, watching carefully where they trod as the steps were awash. Reaching the lawn, they skirted the rear of the Abbey, almost blown around the corner of the belltower by the increasing wind. Wugger and Blinny held tight to the canvas apron covering them as it ballooned and flapped. More thunder banged sharply overhead and lightning sheeted the scene, illuminating it momentarily in an eerie white flash.

Cregga and Sloey were waiting at the door, holding it open against the weather's onslaught, when the four of them rushed inside, breathless and bedraggled.

Sister Sloey gave Dannflor and Tragglo a towel apiece. 'You found them! Thank goodness. Where were they?'

The hedgehog rubbed vigorously at his face. 'Just where you'd expect the rogues t'be, Sister, top o' the bloomin' wall at the northeast corner, wetter'n water-weed an' yellin' to be saved from a drownin'. Anyways, they're safe now.'

As the little group passed through the Great Hall more lightning flashed outside, throwing cascades of bright pattern from the coloured stained glass on to the worn stone floor. A fire was burning in the Cavern Hole where all the Redwallers were gathered, towels flapping wetly about and steam rising from damp fur. Sister Sloey and Gurrbowl Cellarmole dried the two Dibbuns off, none too gently. Wugger's head shook from side to side as the Sister rubbed at it, scolding, 'Time and time again you've been told not to go up on that walltop to play. So what were you both doing up there, eh? Speak up!'

'Hurr, us'n's was on'y talkin' to they funnybeasts in ee woods, marm.'

'Funnybeasts? What funnybeasts?'

'Thurr wurr two of 'em, marm. They was whoit'n'blarck'n'blue, a-wurrin' gurt cloakers!'

Dannflor had trouble keeping a straight face. Wugger was obviously making up some kind of story to justify his visit to the walltop. 'Two funny creatures, all white and black and blue, wearing great cloaks? What did you say to them?'

'Us'n's din't say nowt. They'm arsked if oi'd cumm down an' open ee likkle wallgate furr 'em.'

'And what did you say?'

'Hurr, us'n's was a-goin' to, when ee rain cummed, then us'n's was too affrighted t'move.'

'So, what happened to the two funnybeasts?'

Wugger spread both paws and blinked. 'They'm gonned! Jus' vanished loik that, zurr!'

Dannflor smiled and winked at Tragglo, who nodded understandingly at the molebabe as if it all made sense.

'Ho, right you be, Wugger. The two funnybeasts just vanished, y'say?'

Wugger nodded, his little face completely serious. 'Aye, zurr, that's roight!'

Sister Sloey wagged a severe paw under his nose. 'You've eaten too many strawberries and made yourself ill. Straight up to bed for you, young mole – you too, Blinny. Both of you have had quite enough for one day, pinching strawberries, playing on the wall in that thunderstorm and telling a pack of fibs. Now not another peep out of either of you. Straight upstairs this instant!'

Looking the picture of dejection, the two tiny moles, fur still standing up from their towelling, were led off to the dormitories by Sister Sloey.

Friar Butty smiled at Nutwing. 'Black, white an' blue creatures with great cloaks that vanish into thin air. What'll they think of next?'

The owl dried his spectacles off on a towel corner. 'Hmm, mm. I blame their elders, telling tales of strawberry thieves who just went bang and were never seen again save for a red patch on the stairs. Little wonder that Dibbuns grow up telling fibs after hearing stories like that!'

Outside, the mid-afternoon resembled night as the storm roared around Redwall Abbey, lashing its ancient stones and causing the Mossflower treetops to sway wildly in its grip. Snug inside their comfortable Abbey, the creatures of Redwall, now warm and dry, took their ease in safety and calm.

4

Janglur Swifteye unfastened the tent canvas from his back and tossed it expertly across two rocks which stood a small distance apart on a knoll overlooking a storm-swollen stream. Rimrose and Song weighted the canvas down with flat slabs of sandstone placed on its edges where they lapped the ground, working quickly, their heads bowed against the pelting rain. Grandma Ellayo hurried into the covered space between the rocks and swept out the wet leaves, creating a dry floor inside the makeshift shelter. Janglur dropped the last large slab on the rear of the canvas, making sure it was stretched taut so that it would not fill up and belly inward upon them. Straightening up, he blew rainwater from the tip of his nose, blinking hard against the scything curtains of wind-driven wetness. Rimrose and Song were already inside under cover, and Ellayo called out urgently to her son. 'Git you in 'ere fast, afore that thunder bangs agin!'

Dropping on all fours, the big squirrel scrambled into the confined shelter space, the others moving aside to make room for him. Ellayo jumped instinctively as a thunderclap sounded overhead. Janglur put a paw about her comfortingly. 'There now, Mum, no need to be jumpin' about like a toad on a cinder. Thunder won't harm ye.'

43

But Grandma Ellayo was not to be placated. 'Mebbe thunder won't, but lightnin' will. Take that knife o' yourn an' bury it, son. Lightnin' has a way of findin' knives!'

Janglur knew there was a lot of truth in old wives' tales. Drawing the long blade he carried sheathed sideways across the back of his wide belt, he scratched a shallow trough, placed the knife inside and covered it. Lying flat on his stomach, he rested his chin on both paws, watching the stream being peppered with torrential rain as it pounded furiously on its course. Song joined him, while Rimrose and Ellayo snuggled down at the back of the shelter. Janglur nodded in their direction. 'Take a tip from them, Song, an' rest whilst y'can. Nought else t'do but sleep this storm out.'

The young squirrel watched the rain glumly. 'When's it going to stop so we can get to Redwall Abbey?'

Her father shrugged. 'It'll stop when 'tis ready to. Must be gettin' towards eventide now. If it ceases later on we may be able to travel by night. You have a good nap; I'll wake ye if it clears up.'

Song tried to sleep, but the longer the bad weather continued, the less she felt like sleeping. Twilight lent a strange aspect to woodland and stream, and a weird grey-yellow nimbus hovered over the banksides, cast through with a dull lilac glow. Gradually she began to drift towards slumber, lulled by sound of rainfall and swishing treetops, but then a sharp movement from her father brought her back to instant alertness.

'Be silent, Song, an' don't move. Look at the stream!'

A long logboat thundered by on the roiling current. Seated in the prow were two Marlfoxes, identical to the two they had encountered, and large scrawny water rats, some brown, others black or grey, packed the boat from stem to stern. The majority of the rats were paddling oars, skimming and sculling to keep the craft upright and on course, while the rest were kept busy baling out stream and rainwater with any implements they could lay claw to.

Janglur muttered to Song out of the side of his mouth, 'Just as well they can't hear yore grandma snorin' in this liddle lot. Be still now, here comes another!'

A second logboat forged along in the wake of the first. Janglur moved forward, poking his head out into the rain, peering upstream.

'There's more of 'em, another four if'n I ain't mistaken. Never seen aught like this afore. I'm goin' to take a look. You stay put, Song. Y'know where my dagger is if y'need it. Don't wake your mum or grandma, what they don't know can't 'urt 'em. Be back soon!'

Not far from the knoll where they had camped a big gnarled crack willow overhung part of the stream. Janglur Swifteye climbed it with surprising speed and grace for a squirrel of his size and weight. Skipping nimbly out along one of the main limbs that bent over the water, he tested it for firmness. Two more logboats had passed beneath the willow, their occupants unaware of the presence of a squirrel overhead. Janglur looped his tail and footpaws firmly round the sturdy bough, hanging downward almost as if he were part of the tree. Another logboat bobbed past on the turbulent waters. He let it sail by beneath him, noting that all the vessels were packed with water rats, but the only Marlfoxes were the two in the lead boat. Unwinding the sling from his waist, Janglur readied himself as the final craft shot towards the willow, a foaming bow wave curling either side as it plied the water. Three rats in the stern were baling busily. As the logboat sped past beneath the watching Janglur, the hindmost rat bent to scoop up a bowlful of water. Suddenly, a noose settled round his neck and a paw clamped round his mouth like a vice. The rat's footpaws were hauled swiftly clear of the scuppers and the logboat shot on without him, his companions not even noticing his departure.

Janglur flopped the water rat up over the willow limb like a landed fish, dealing him a sharp blow between ear

45

and jawside. Working efficiently, he sat him on the branch, whipped the sling from the stunned rodent's neck and bound his middle to the tree. A soft moan escaped the rat's lips as he began to come round. Janglur patted his cheek playfully. 'Hush a bye now, me ole cully, you sit there awhile until yore ready an' willin' t'do a bit o' talkin'!'

Song watched her father emerge out of the sheeting rain. He was carrying a bundle and whistling cheerfully between his two front teeth. One of the lazy hooded eyes winked slyly at her as he ducked to enter the shelter.

'Found some nice dry pinewood back there. Must be the only bit o' timber left in Mossflower that ain't wet this evenin'.'

Song unearthed the knife and took tinder and flint from their pack. Striking the flint against the spine of the blade, she blew softly on the bright sparks that fell on the dry mossy tinder. A thin blue column of smoke rewarded her efforts, followed by a glow and a tiny flame. Janglur began adding pine splinters until they had sufficient fire going to pile on some of the pine billets. Wakened by the smell of wood smoke, Rimrose held her paws out to the flame gratefully.

'A nice fire. Would you two like somethin' to eat?'

Grandma Ellayo's voice came from the back of the shelter. 'Aye, us three would like a bite if y'don't mind!'

The last of their provisions was made into an acceptable meal. Song sliced up the final piece of Rimrose's travelling fruit and honey cake, whilst her grandma brewed a kettle of mint and comfrey tea. Rimrose had saved four oatcakes and a small wedge of cheese. She toasted the cheese and oatcakes together. The family sat by the fire, staring out into the rainswept night as they ate. Later Janglur took out his flute and played, encouraging Song to sing.

'I once knew an ant and I knew him right well,
This ant he lived in a hazelnut shell,
He had relations to count by the score,
They used to come knocking on his tiny door.
One was called dist*ant*, he lived far away,
Another was pleas*ant*, he'd bid you good day,
A third was const*ant*, he was never away,
Then there was hesit*ant*, not sure he'd stay,
And poor old reluct*ant* not sure too,
And one called vali*ant* stout and true.
Now I'll tell you the reason they all came to call,
'Cos this ant was the most import*ant* of all!'

As the final echo of the ballad died away a gruff voice called from the streambank, causing Ellayo to jump with fright, 'Well sung, young missie. Y've got a fair pretty voice on yer!'

Song immediately grabbed for her father's knife, but Janglur stayed her paw, a smile flitting across his half-closed eyes as he replied, 'Aye, better'n any ole scrag-furred shrew could sing, I'll wager!'

Surrounded by a party of Guosim, Log a Log strode up to the shelter.

'Hah! Janglur Swifteye, ye great fat branchbounder, I heard you was dead three seasons back!'

Janglur shook his old friend's paw heartily. 'Log a Log Guosim, ye big-bellied brookbeast, I heard *you* died more'n four seasons ago!'

The shrew threw a paw about the squirrel's shoulders. 'Well, we must be the two healthiest ghosts in the woodlands.'

Introductions were made all round. The shrews joined their old logboat sails, which they carried with them, to Janglur's shelter. Using oars and dead branches, and taking advantage of nearby bushes, they soon extended the covered area. Log a Log sat by the fire, gratefully accepting a bowl of tea from Ellayo, whilst he told Janglur of what had befallen him and his tribe. The squirrel listened intently, then told Log a Log of his first encounter with the Marlfoxes. The shrew scratched his ear thoughtfully.

'D'you think the two you met are the same two who stole our boats?'

Janglur shook his head emphatically. 'Impossible. We were too far apart, but I saw the two foxes that took yore boats this very evenin'.'

Log a Log's paw grabbed his rapier hilt. 'You saw 'em? Where?'

'They sailed right by here, round about twilight, six boatloads of 'em, water rats, with the two foxes sittin' for'ard in the first boat that passed. So I went t'take a look.'

'So, tell me, what did y'see?'

The squirrel's long lashes flickered idly. 'Wasn't much to see. I figgered they wouldn't stop to chat with me, so I worked the ole rear ambush an' captured one.'

Log a Log leapt up and drew his rapier. 'You captured one? Why didn't you tell me this earlier?'

Janglur rose with a sigh. 'Because you called me fat an' said I was three seasons dead. Come on, stop lookin' so injured, an' I'll take you to him.'

The water rat was fully conscious, but his face showed little emotion as Janglur loosed the bonds and hauled him down from the crack willow. Log a Log's rapier point was swiftly at the rodent's throat. The shrew's voice dripped menace.

'Now, matey, yore goin' t'do a bit o' fast talkin'. Who are these Marlfoxes, how many of 'em is there, an' what are you doin' in these parts? Make it easy on yoreself an' speak!'

The rat's face was blank, his eyes devoid of either fear or hatred of his captors.

Janglur prodded the rat's chest with a hard paw. 'Where d'you come from? Are you from the same place as those foxes? I hear they come from a secret island at the centre of a great lake. Tell us about it. Who rules there?'

The rat's expression never changed, though Log a Log noticed that his paws were trembling visibly. The shrew leaned close to Janglur and spoke in a whisper so the water rat would not hear them. 'Wot d'yer make o' this one, mate? Mayhap he's a mute ... Look out!'

Before either creature could stop him, the rat dashed back a few paces and flung himself into the swift-flowing stream. Log a Log and Janglur rushed to the water's edge and stood helplessly, watching as the rodent was swept away on the wild racing surge. It was far too rough and speedy, even for a water rat, and his paws struggled feebly against the surging mass until a broken rowan tree came hurtling like an arrow on the current. It struck the unfortunate rat and he sank instantly. Log a Log screwed up his face in disgust.

'Tis always bad when a life's wasted for no reason, even the life of a vermin like that'n.'

Janglur fastened the sling back round his waist. 'I wouldn't say the rat's life was wasted fer no reason, mate. We mightn't know why he did it, but no creature could live in that current, so he knew what he was doin'. He must have been really terrified if he killed himself rather than betray any information.'

The shrew stood staring at the spot where the rat had gone down. 'Yore right, Swifteye. Let's go an' get some sleep. Mayhap we'll find the answer to all this when we reach the Abbey of Redwall.'

The Wandering Noonvale Companions' cart was stuck up to its axles in mud. Florian wrung rain from the hems of his frock coat and bellowed mournfully.

'Oh, calamity, folly and woe unto us! Abroad on a night like this in the midst of a hurricane, nay a typhoon, a veritable deluge! And now, to cap it all, we are sinking slowly into the muddy oblivion of a bottomless quagmire. Brave hearts and faithful friends, 'tis a night for lamentations. Ooooh, lack a bally day, wot!'

Runktipp tried unsuccessfully to block a rip in the canvas of the covered cart with a pennant he had plastered with mud. 'Aye, we could do with lackin' this day right enough. Pesky rain'll drive me off my spikes if it don't stop!'

Borrakul, who was caked in mud up to the waist from trying to get the cart unstuck, grinned mirthlessly. 'Cheer up, we're only lost, starvin' an' likely to be drowned by mornin'. At least there's plenty o' water t'drink out there.'

Roop twitched his nose at the otter. 'Oi bain't thursty, thenkee, zurr, tho' 'tain't ee weather oi'm wurried over, 'tis Dwopple. Ee young maister's gone vurry quiet, an' oi doan't loik et!'

Deesum instantly leapt to the defence of her charge. 'You're quite heartless, mister Roop. See, the dear little chap is slumbering innocently.'

Elachim, the other otter brother, who was trying to sleep at the same end of the cart as the mousebabe, shifted his position, muttering, 'Slumberin' innocently? The wretch is snorin' like thunder, an' he keeps tryin' to eat my tail in 'is dreams!'

Muggle flung her soggy turban at the otter. 'Gurr! Doan't ee menshun eatin' again. Moi pore stummick is a-growglin' an' a-rowglin' loik thunner an' loightnin'!'

Dejectedly, Florian pulled out his battered one-string fiddle and plucked at it experimentally. 'Tchah! Confounded wet weather's knocked it all out o' tune, wot!' Nevertheless, he scraped away at it with a tattered bow and began singing a song which he composed as he went along.

'Deah mothah I am hungry, hungry,
 An' starvin' as well to boot,
 Oh to be back home in your orchard,
 So full of delishowus froot.

50

If I perish'n'die before maaaawnin',
My last thought will be of yewww,
An' the smile on Father's whiskers,
An' a whackin' great bowl of stewwww!
Are Grandpa's teeth still missin',
The way I'm missin' yooooooou?
You're the nicest ma a son could have
An' I've had quite a feeeeeewwww.
Fare thee well my dearest parents,
For quite soon now I must die,
But if I get home before midnight,
Don't let Grandma eat all the pie!'

Florian's song was abruptly cut off when a soggy tunic flopped in his face. He removed the offending article, which had become tangled with his ears and whiskers, and held it up.

'Which rotter threw this? Own up immediately, wot?' he demanded with an air of injured dignity.

The troupe stared at him in blank innocence. Baby Dwopple shook with malicious mirth, but kept his eyes tight shut, pretending to be asleep. He even threw in a couple of lusty snores for good effect. Deesum stroked his head fondly, murmuring, 'So young, yet so talented. One day you will be a great actor!'

Night closed in around the little cart in the woodland as the rain continued to batter down.

5

The lake was so huge that nobeast standing on any part of
the shoreline could tell that its sweeping vastness held an
island at its centre. Not even birds, because they knew
better than to try to fly across the lake. Whipping up the
surface into a frenzy of crested waves, the storm raged
throughout the night hours. Rain howled like a wild
thing, driven by the winds. From the billowing masses of
black and purple-bruised cloud which obscured the
moon, thunder crashed and lightning ripped down in a
flickering dance across the heaving waters.

Inside Castle Marl a grim-faced band of brown-liveried
water rats were trying to drown out the storm noise with
music. They plucked at stringed instruments, struck
small gongs and played strange melodies on flutes and
pipes of varying sizes. From cellars to attics they paraded,
up and down the fortress's many ramps. There were no
stairs inside Castle Marl, just steeply sloping ramps,
winding or angled, everywhere. The odd group followed
a curtained palanquin, a long boxlike affair with silken
tasselled drapes round its sides, borne on four thick poles
running beneath its length and width. Over a score and a
half rats bore the odd conveyance, treading with carefully
measured paces, so that the box was kept perfectly steady

at all times, and by the side of the palanquin strode a Marlfox. When a sharp tapping noise issued from within the covered box, the carriers stopped moving instantly. A harsh rasping voice sounded from behind the silken curtains.

'Lantur! Tell them to play louder. I will not be disturbed by weather noises, for I am mightier, more powerful than storms! These fools must play louder. The storm stopped me sleeping, so they must outplay it. That is my command!'

The Marlfox, Lantur, strode back to the musicians, who had already heard the order. Nevertheless, she repeated it in the imperious tone of one used to commanding others.

'The High Queen Silth decrees that you play louder. If you disobey the royal word you will all answer to the Teeth of the Deeps. Play louder! You there, bring the Chanters so they may add to the music by singing the High Queen's praises!'

More water rats were quickly brought to join the band. At a nod from Lantur the procession continued, the Chanters droning along in time with the musicians.

'All powerful mighty Queen, whose beauty has ne'er
    been surpassed,
Far brighter than the sun, whose rays it will outlast,
We live to serve you truly, until our final breath,
Knowing you hold all secrets, the power of life and
    death,
Wisest of wise, greatness sublime,
Rules o'er our isle for all time.'

Rats with incense burners scurried ahead of the bearers, wafting sweet smoke into the air so that it would drift down between the curtains. Lantur drew close to the palanquin and spoke in a comforting, wheedling tone. 'You see, O Queen, whatever your heart desires is yours.'

The harsh rasping voice came back to her, childish and

53

complaining. 'I cannot bear not to be surrounded by beauty and calm. Oh, my head hurts with the noise of the thunder, lightning flashes through my brain! Tell them to play louder, Lantur. Louder!'

The Marlfox smiled as she bowed low. She resembled the four who had accosted Janglur Swifteye and the Noonvale Companions, but was slightly smaller, and finer-featured in a sinister way. Silkily, she said, 'Your wish is my command, All Powerful One!'

Outside Castle Marl the storm raged on, oblivious of the pathetic sounds from within as they strove to drown out the greatest sound of all: the power of the weather, combined with the forces of nature.

Below, in the rear courtyard, lines of manacled slavebeasts, squirrels, otters, hedgehogs and mice, stood with weary heads bowed in the downpour, waiting for the barred pens to be unlocked. The sadistic Slave Captain, the water rat Ullig, lounged under the protruding roof shelter, jangling a bunch of keys at his belt.

'So then, me lucky lot, yore gettin' off easy today. Darkness arrived early 'cos o' the storm an' I ain't standin' out in the fields gettin' drenched. But you'll work twice as hard tomorrer, or you'll feel my whip around yore backs!' Shrugging his heavy cloak closer about him, Ullig smiled wickedly at the tired, saturated slaves. 'Ain't that right? Come on, let's 'ear yer. Speak up!'

The wretched beasts were forced to call out in a chorus, 'Aye, right, Cap'n!'

Ullig tossed the bunch of keys to a water rat guard. 'You, open up an' get 'em under cover till dawn.'

Shuffling through the deepening puddles, the slaves crowded into the pens, throwing themselves down on the damp straw bedding, grateful to be under cover. Locking the pens, the guard returned the keys to Ullig. Two more guards staggered from the barracks nearby, carrying between them a cauldron of boiled maize porridge, which they placed close to the bars. Ullig watched the slaves thrusting their paws through and scooping the rapidly cooling mess into their mouths. He shook his head at the pitiful sight. 'I'm far too kind t'you lot. Must be gettin' soft with me long seasons.' Laughing to himself, he strode off to the cover of the barracks, where a warm fire and good food awaited him.

Song slept heavily. It was long past dawn when the young shrew called Dippler flicked rainwater at her head.

'Come on, dozychops, wake up or you'll snore until autumn!'

The squirrelmaid had chummed up with the Guosim shrew, who was roughly her own age, on the previous evening. Now Song opened one eye and lay unmoving as she threatened her newfound friend.

'You've just done three things that really annoy me. One, you flicked water on me while I was asleep. Two, you called me dozychops. Worst of all, though, is number three. You said I snore. For that, my friend, you're going to take an early bath in the stream!'

Leaping up, she dashed after Dippler, who was very agile and could duck and dodge with ease. They flew past Janglur and Log a Log, showering them with the wet banksand churned up by their paws.

'Aye aye, steady on there, you young rowdies!' The shrew Chieftain shook sand off himself, grinning at Janglur. 'Wish I had the energy o' them two. 'Tis good that your Song's palled up with Dippler. That young 'un ain't got many friends. He was the one doin' guard duty when our boats went missin'.'

Janglur dodged smartly aside as the pair chased by him again. 'Well, he won't go far wrong with Song. She's a good 'un, mate, an' she don't make friends lightly.'

Song and Dippler dodged about a bit more on the bank, then flopped down on the ground grinning at each other.

Dippler held up a paw, panting fitfully. 'Truce?'

Song nodded. 'Truce it is. Look, the rain's almost stopped!'

Last night's high wind was gone and the downpour had slacked off to a fine drizzle, though the skies were still slatey grey. Log a Log called out to his shrews, 'Break camp, mates, grub's all gone. We'll be headin' fer Redwall in comp'ny with Swifteye an' his family. Mayon, Bargle, stick with Gran'ma Ellayo, an' lend 'er a paw. Fenno, douse the fire. Splikker, take two scouts an' march ahead of us. Bit o' luck an' we should make the Abbey sometime in the late noon.'

The woodlands dripped water all morning as the party followed a trail left by Splikker and his scouts. Song and Dippler walked slightly ahead of the main group. Suddenly, a big otter emerged from the trees and approached Log a Log.

The shrew scarcely gave him a glance. 'Mornin', Skip.'

The big otter returned the greeting noncommittally. 'Mornin', Log.'

Log a Log nudged Janglur. 'This's Skipper of otters. Skip, meet Janglur Swifteye. We're goin' to Redwall.'

Janglur nodded at Skipper, who winked back in reply.

'So'm I, matey. Me an' the crew went over the waterfalls, three days from 'ere, 'cos of the hot dry weather. Huh! Hot'n'dry? Never expected this liddle lot. Any'ow, I've left the crew at the falls havin' fun. I decided to drop back this way an' see if everythin' was shipshape over at the Abbey after the storm. Where's yore boats, mate? 'Tisn't like the Guosim to be hoofin' it through the woods.'

Log a Log rolled his eyes skyward, making light of his misfortune. 'Oh, we lent 'em to a crowd o' water rats an' a couple o' Marlfoxes. Don't worry, though, we'll get 'em back an' make those vermin pay for the hire of six good logboats, take my word for it!'

The conversation was interrupted by Splikker, who

came trotting back on his own tracks, gesturing with a paw over his shoulder. 'Left the scouts further along the trail, Chief. There was all sorts o' noises comin' from the edge of the marshy area. Come an' see wot we've found. Y'won't believe yore eyes!'

He turned and ran off the way he had come. Their curiosity roused, the entire party hurried after him.

Florian Dugglewoof Wilffachop made a brave figure as he stood on the seat of the half-submerged cart like the captain of a sinking ship. In one paw he held the long sword with which Runktipp had menaced the Marlfoxes. It was only a trick stage prop and kept bending in the middle of its blade. Notwithstanding this drawback, Florian brandished it at the grinning shrews.

'Laugh all y'like, you scurvy villains, you'll not take me alive! By the cringe an' fur you won't, not while there's breath left in this poor body to defend the ladies an' the infant, wot!'

One of the shrews laid his rapier on the ground. 'We ain't gonna hurt ye, mate, ye've got my word on it . . . Yowch!'

Dwopple hung over the back of the cart. Loading another stone into his small sling, he announced with an innocent smile, 'I'm a h'infant. I shooted ya wi' me slinger. Heeheehee!'

The shrew rubbed furiously at his swelling nose. 'You liddle pot-scrapin', that ain't fair! We came 'ere in peace!'

Florian waved the flapping blade of the sword at him. 'A likely story, sah. Peace me flippin' whiskahs! I'll have y'know you are dealin' with a band of expert warriors, trained to slay with a single bally swipe, wot!'

Skipper, Log a Log and Janglur arrived on the scene at this point, closely followed by Song and Dippler. Song immediately went to the injured shrew and held a pawful of damp moss to his nose.

'What's going on here, may I ask?' she said.

At the sound of a sweet musical voice, Florian was

57

transformed. Sweeping off his straw hat, he bowed so low that he almost fell into the mud surrounding the cart. 'Faith, miss, your tones are music t'me ears, wot! Pray dissuade those small surly rogues from attacking us. We are innocents lost. A simple troupe of strolling players, ravaged by an unseasonable quirk of the weather and unjustly menaced by savage spikefurred persons.'

The shrew took the damp moss from his nose long enough to argue back. 'You flop-eared ole fraud, you was the one goin' to attack us!'

Deesum showed herself, wringing a large flowered kerchief anxiously. 'Oh, desist from bickering and help us, please!'

Gallantly Skipper and Janglur helped the troupe from the cart, taking care to swing them out clear of the mud. Introductions were made all round as the Guosim rolled their canvas sails into long bands, attaching them to the cart like tow ropes. Skipper and Janglur found a good stout yew limb to use as a lever. The cart rocked back and forth, making wet sucking noises, as the team of Guosim pulled and Skipper levered. Janglur found the shaft and the crosstree beneath the mud and hauled. With their combined efforts they soon had the cart back on firm ground. Skipper shook mud from himself as Florian thanked him.

'My my, what a stout feller you are – stout fellers all, in fact. Let us put on a performance for you in gratitude for your sterlin' services in recoverin' our jolly old transport, wot!'

Skipper could not help smiling at the effusive hare. 'Lucky y'never went any further afore ye got stuck, matey. That's a swamp out there, an' there wouldn't have been a trace of you creatures or yore cart in the middle of the marshes!'

'Oooooohhh!'

Deesum did a graceful swoon and fainted. Janglur indicated her prone form with a nod at Ellayo. 'Bring 'er round, Mum. Mister Florian, yore performance'll have to wait till another time. We've got to get to Redwall Abbey afore dark.'

Florian did a comical double take. 'Redwall Abbey, sah? Capital! The very place we are proceedin' to. Mayhap we can wend our way together – strength in unity, y'know. I can defend you from any blackguards, rogues or hardpaws we may encounter on the way. Lead on, my good fellow, lead on!'

Deesum gave a yowl and sprang upright. Borrakul looked in awe at Ellayo. 'You soon brought 'er outta that faint, marm. You must 'ave good medicine.'

Ellayo clambered up into the cart. 'Good medicine nothin'. I could tell she was fakin', so I just bit the tip of 'er tail. That brought 'er round all right. This's a good little cart, save my ole paws a bit. Move over, young 'un!'

Dwopple moved, scowling at the old squirrel. She scowled right back. 'Just put a paw near that slingshot o' yourn an' I'll bite yore tail clean off to teach ye good manners!'

Elachim the otter yelled, 'Here's the good ole sun come to chase the dull clouds away!'

After the prolonged rain, wind and dark skies, a bright summer sun set everybeast's spirits soaring. Cheering and laughing, they continued their journey to Redwall.

Late afternoon found Tragglo and Dannflor out on the path by the Abbey, gathering dandelions and the sticky-budded burdock. The Cellarkeeper explained the finer points of the plants as they culled them into a rush basket.

'Dannelions, now, you can use 'em fer brewin' or in salads. Pick the young 'uns with plenty o' buds on, they're the sweetest.'

Dannflor smelled the lemony fragrance of a young bud and nibbled it. 'Right, Tragglo, they do taste good. Which burdock do I pick?'

The hedgehog pointed them out. 'Those smaller ones.

They're the lesser burdock, much better'n the big 'uns, which're called greater burdock. Good juice in lesser burdock. Y'can use it fer treatin' burns an' bruises, or y'can take the whole plant fer brewin', or use the stalks in salads too. Hold 'ard there, young Dann, who be they comin' up yon path?'

Dannflor shaded his eyes against the sun, watching the strange assortment of creatures and the canvas-covered cart approaching the Abbey. An otter out in front raised his paws and called out, 'Redwaaaaaalll!'

Tragglo climbed out of the ditch where they had been gathering plants, wiping his paws on his apron. He chuckled. 'Me ole pal Skipper an' some friends by the look of 'em. Go an' give the bells a toll, Dann, let everybeast know we got company!'

The young squirrel scampered off, delighted to have the privilege of being bellringer. Hurrying into the ground floor of the belltower, he grabbed the two ropes, one in each paw, high up and pulled with all his might.

Bong! Boom!

Dannflor's footpaws shot off the floor. He dangled there a moment, then came down to the ground again as the bells tolled a second time. Releasing the ropes, he ran outside and joined the Redwallers who were hurrying towards the gate, eager to meet the visitors.

Dannflor's father recognized a friendly face instantly. Hugging and back-patting, they greeted one another.

'Janglur Swifteye, you haven't changed a hair since the old days!'

'Hahaha! Neither have you, Rusvul Reguba, you old warrior!'

'Ellayo, Rimrose, you look well. Hah! I'll wager that's yore daughter, Janglur. A lot prettier'n you but she's got yore long eyelashes. Come here, son, I want you to meet my ole pal Janglur an' his family. This is Dannflor Reguba, son of a warrior!'

Song shook Dannflor's paw. 'I'm Songbreeze Swifteye,

but they all call me Song.'

'Pleased to meet you, Song. I'm Dannflor, but they call me Dann.'

'Where's your mother, Dann? Is she here?'

Dannflor looked down awkwardly. 'She died when I was very small. I don't even remember her.'

There was a moment's embarrassed silence, then Dippler bounded up. 'Hello, you've found another pal for us, Song. Don't introduce him – I'll guess his name afore the season's done.'

Song gave the shrew a playful shove. 'This is Dippler, he throws water on squirrels when they're trying to sleep. Dippler, meet our new friend Dann!'

Brother Melilot had been holding a whispered conversation with Badgermum Cregga. She nodded in agreement with him. Melilot banged the main gate timbers with a copper ladle to get attention.

'Friends, guests, travellers, whoever ye be, welcome to the Abbey of Redwall. Now, d'you want to stand out here gossipin' an' back-slappin' until dark, or would you like to come along inside an' get somethin' to eat?'

Florian's voice rang out over the general chorus of approval. 'Eat, sah! Did my ears deceive me or did some-beast mention victuals? Lead me to the jolly old table an' I'll show you what a peckish thespian can accomplish armed only with mouth and appetite, wot!'

Foremole Gubbio murmured to Gurrbowl Cellarmole, 'Hurr, woe be us'n's, oi'll wager yon creature's gurtly 'ungered!'

Sister Sloey, who had heard the remark, nodded agreement. 'That hare looks as if he could strip the orchard bare on his way to clean out the kitchens!'

The visitors were seated on the lawn, close to the Abbey pond, whilst numerous Redwallers hurried off to the kitchens to prepare food for them. Log a Log, Janglur and Florian sat apart from the rest, and quietly reported the Marlfox sightings to Cregga, Friar Butty and

61

Nutwing. The blind badger listened carefully to what they had to say before giving her verdict.

'I'd always thought Marlfoxes were a legend, some kind of bogeybeast whose name is used to frighten naughty Dibbuns. But in the light of what you have told us I think there could be great danger in their presence around Mossflower.'

Nutwing preened his wing feathers thoughtfully. 'Hmm mm. What's to be done about them? Log a Log says that they've got a considerable number of water rats, and that means extra trouble.'

Friar Butty looked around the group. 'We need the advice of an Abbey Warrior. Trouble is, old Abbot Arven was the last Redwall Champion, but he's passed away. Er, I don't suppose any of you creatures would have a suggestion?'

Janglur's slitted eyes betrayed little as he spoke his piece. 'Here's what y'do. First you shut that Abbey gate tight. Nobeast leaves Redwall, except for scoutin' patrols. Our friend Log a Log can organize his Guosim shrews fer that. Meanwhile, we'll use what warriors we have to organize defences. Skipper, Rusvul an' myself.'

Cregga's heavy paw patted Janglur's shoulder. 'Thank the seasons we're not without sensible warriors. You arrived at Redwall not a moment too soon, friend. Friar Butty, what do we know of Marlfoxes? Is there anything in the Abbey recordings that might help us?'

'I'll take a look, marm. Mayhap you'll help me, Nutwing?'

The owl began polishing his spectacles on his breast feathers. 'Hmm mm, of course I will. I'll do my best to remember all you say.'

Janglur had another suggestion to make. 'If'n you want to know about Marlfoxes, I'd start by askin' my ole mum, Ellayo. She's never spoken too much about it, but I'm sure she's got a couple o' tales concernin' such beasts.'

Meanwhile, over by the pond, Dann scooted a flat

pebble out over the surface, counting the number of times it skipped. 'I make that five. Of course, I'm pretty used to this pond. See how many times yours bounces, Song.'

The flat brown pebble Song had found skimmed out while they watched it.

'Four, no, four and a little one. Oh, go on then, we'll call it five. Righto, Dippler, let's see if you can beat five!'

The young Guosim shrew picked up a pebble, not bothering about its shape or weight, and slung it almost haphazardly, turning to face his friends as the stone skipped on its journey across the water. 'Eight! But y'must remember that I was born around water, been skimmin' stones since afore I could speak.'

Dannflor was watching the main Abbey door from the corner of one eye, and now he noticed Brother Melilot emerge with a ladle and a flat pan. The young squirrel smiled slyly at his companions. 'Hmm, you two are pretty clever at most things, aren't you. Well, let's see how good you are at bein' first in for scoff!'

He took off from them at a dead run on the same instant that Melilot began banging the ladle against the pan and shouting, 'Vittles ready in Great Hall, come and get 'em one an' all!'

Song and Dippler pursued Dann, berating him.

'You crafty rotter, wait for us!'

'Treewalloper! Least you could've done was give us a level start!'

Mokkan the Marlfox pointed to a sheltered creek at the streamside, raising his voice.

'This should do. Pull in here, and hide the boats under those trees.'

The female Marlfox, Ziral, leapt ashore and watched until the last logboat had turned into the inlet. When the water rats had disembarked she called two of them. 'Allag, Ruheb, take six trackers apiece, spread out and go separate ways. Find our brothers and sisters and bring them back here.'

Mokkan stretched wearily out beneath a spreading sycamore, glad to be free from the confines of a logboat's prow. He snapped out orders to the water rats standing to attention along the bank. 'Get the nets, find fish. Archers, bring down some birds. You four, collect wood and get a fire going. Dry wood, mind – we want as little smoke as possible. Bring fruit and berries, only the ripest ones. You, spread my cloak carefully over that bush to dry out.'

As the rats scurried to do his bidding, Ziral sat down beside him, nibbling at a juicy grass blade. 'The Abbey of Redwall is not far west of here.'

Mokkan closed his eyes, savouring the sun's warmth. 'I know that, but we don't make a move until the trackers find Vannan, Ascrod, Gelltor and Predak and bring them back here. Relax, vixen, there's no hurry.'

However, Ziral was unable to rest. She paced the bank, honing her axe blade on a sliver of shale. 'I'll relax when we're back on the island with that mother of ours. Halfwitted old fool, you'd think she has enough possessions, but no, all she does is witter on from morn till night, "I must be surrounded by beauty, I must be surrounded by beauty!" I don't know how our sister Lantur stands it. I'd like to surround her with a couple of boulders tied to her neck and drop her in the lake, then she could be surrounded by fishes!'

Mokkan opened one eye. 'It's treason to speak about the High Queen in such a manner, you know that?'

Ziral snorted contemptuously and flung her axe. It buried its blade deep in the sycamore trunk.

Mokkan sniggered dryly. 'Temper, temper, sister of mine! That sort of behaviour won't do you any good.'

Ziral's pale eyes blazed. She pushed aside a water rat, sending the creature staggering into the shallows as he tried to hold on to the bundle of kindling wood he was carrying. The vixen Marlfox jerked her axeblade viciously from the sycamore trunk. 'High Queen? Silth is nought but a doddering old wreck who hides behind silken curtains. Why doesn't she die and leave the island to us, her own brood?'

Mokkan raised himself on one paw, smiling. 'That's when the trouble will really start. There're seven of us, we'd never be able to share all that wealth and rule the island together from Castle Marl. Not without killing each other off. Remember, we're Marlfoxes, born to stealth and deceit. Only one of us could ever rule the island.'

Ziral made as if to sheathe her axeblade beneath her cloak, then instead she suddenly brought it about in a scything swipe, only to find it locked against the curve of her brother's axe. Mokkan forced the vixen's axe to the ground and trapped it beneath his footpaw. He continued smiling at Ziral.

'You see what I mean, sister!'

6

Janglur Swifteye gazed in awe and admiration at the tapestry hanging on the west wall of the Abbey's Great Hall. It depicted vermin fleeing in all directions from the figure standing boldly at its centre, Martin the Warrior. The armour-clad mouse leaned upon the hilt of his fabulous sword, a friendly reckless smile on his striking features.

Janglur whistled softly. 'Now there stands a warrior among warriors, by the seasons! He looks so confident an' strong, small wonder those vermin are fleein' for their lives, mate!'

Rusvul pointed to the name embroidered on the border. 'Aye, that's Martin the Warrior. He was the creature who freed Mossflower from tyranny an' helped to found this Abbey of Redwall. I felt just as you do, when I first saw him. This tapestry means a great deal to any creature calling itself a Redwaller. But come an' join the company at vittles afore that hare an' his performin' troupe do a vanishin' act with all the food. Twist me tail! Those actors can put it away!'

Florian Dugglewoof Wilffachop was on his fourth bowl of summer salad with celery cheese and barley bread. Between salads he had demolished a number of strawberry cream tarts, a mushroom and leek pasty with gravy and a portion of woodland trifle topped with meadowcream that would have fed four Dibbuns for two days. The hare waggled his ears appreciatively. 'I say, you chaps, this spread is absojollylutely enscrunchable! My compliments to the cook, Lady Cregga, marm!'

The Badgermum put aside her apple turnover with maple syrup. 'Tell him yourself, mister Florian. He's just resigned at the thought of having to cater for you again!'

The entire table of guests fell about with laughter. Florian looked slightly baffled, and attacked a wedge of plum pudding pensively.

'Flippin' strange feller. You'd think a cook'd enjoy servin' up dinner to a chap who enjoys his tuck, wot?'

Dannflor sat between Song and Dippler, advising them on the fare. 'Here, Dipp, try some o' this candied fruit sponge, you'll like it. Song, here's some deeper'n ever turnip'n'tater'n'beetroot pie.'

Foremole winked broadly at the pretty young squirrel. 'Hurr, you'm gonna loik et, missie, us'n's h'eat et noight'n'day. 'Tis ee moles' fayvurrt grub, burr aye!'

Rusvul treated Janglur to a tankard of October Ale and a thick slab of yellow cheese studded with hazelnuts and carrot, with a small farl of hot brown bread. 'Git that down yore famine-fed chops, mate. 'Twill make yer feel like a real warrior!'

Janglur's hooded eyes gazed around at the scene. 'I came here once when I was but a mite. Have y'ever seen a more cheery an' welcomin' bunch than these Redwallers? No wonder travellers tell tales an' legends of this Abbey!'

Dwopple was sitting on Skipper's lap, in company with Blinny and Wugger. The otter Chieftain allowed them to sample his soup.

'Eat 'earty, mateys. 'Tis called watershrimp an' 'otroot soup, full o' dried watershrimps, bulrush tips, ransoms, watercress an' special spices. Otters like it 'cos it makes 'em big'n'strong!'

Sister Sloey rapped Skipper's paw with her fork. 'You are naughty, Skipper. Those Dibbuns won't be able to cope with your dreadful hot spicy soup.'

The big otter chortled as he saw the Dibbuns ladle soup from his bowl. 'Marm, beggin' yore pardon, but I'm a great believer in lettin' young 'uns find out things for theirselves. This'll learn 'em a lesson.'

However, contrary to expectations Dwopple and the molebabes thoroughly enjoyed the fiery concoction.

'Burr, ee soop be luvly an' warm. Oi dearly loiks gudd soop!'

'Mmmm! Dwopple 'ave more a diss soop, tasty nice!'

The delicious repast continued into late evening, when candles and lanterns were lit in Great Hall. During a lull in the proceedings, Log a Log hailed Florian.

'Ahoy there, matey, how's about you an' yore troupe puttin' on that show you promised when we rescued yer cart from the swamp?'

The hare stood and bowed to the assemblage. 'Why not indeed? The Wandering Noonvale Companions would be churlish in the extreme not to return the compliment of such fabulous fare. But I know that seated here at table this evenin' is one among us who possesses a voice of pure gold. Janglur's daughter, who is aptly named Song. Mayhap she would honour us? In anticipation of this, I meself scribed a small ballad.' Florian produced a scroll with a resounding flourish. 'Ahem, a few simple lines I recorded whilst in the paws of the muse, wot wot! Goes to the tune of "Breeze in the Meadow". D'you know that one, Song?'

The young squirrel took the scroll and studied the lines. 'I'd be pleased to, sir. These words fit the tune nicely. Father?'

Janglur smiled proudly as he played the introduction on his reed flute. Song clasped her paws in front of herself and took a deep breath. All eyes were riveted on her as the first heartbreakingly sweet notes poured forth, echoing slightly through the ancient hall.

'Our thanks to you friends, our thanks to one and all,
For kindly asking us to join you at Redwall,
We saw from afar, just as we thought we should,
Your Abbey like a gem, set in Mossflow'r's green
    wood.
The welcome you gave us was like we'd never
    known,
Like family you treat us, as if we were your own,
The bells tolled so pretty, out o'er the countryside,
A message of friendship, it echoed far and wide,
The food and drink you gave us was wonderful and
    yet,
'Tis you and your friendship that we'll never forget!'

Song's parents and Grandma Ellayo congratulated her heartily as the rafters rang with admiring cheers and applause for her singing.

Florian and the two otters, Borrakul and Elachim, took the floor next. The hare reversed his frock coat and tied the sleeves about his neck so that it hung down behind like a cloak, stuck a golden twirling moustache to his upper lip and struck a noble pose. The otters fitted brass rings to their ears, put on ragged breechclouts and brandished a pair of floppy stage swords. Florian explained the scenario to his audience.

'H'andaaa now, good creatures of this awesome edifice, we wish to present a historical h'entertainment ... the Duel of Insults! This was a h'actual h'incident, involvin' my great ancestor one Ballaw De Quincewold an' two vermin, ferrets, who would not let him pass. Picture the scene then, a narrow trail runnin' through a woodland glade, an' here comes I, the gallant hare Ballaw!'

Florian strode breezily across the floor, stopping short of the two otters, who were trying their best to resemble a pair of evil ferrets. The hare greeted them civilly enough. 'Good morrow to ye both, sirs. Pray stand aside an' let me pass through the woodlands, for I am but a travellin' gentlebeast, wot!'

The two otters paced towards him, waving their swords savagely.

'Haharr, nobeast passes 'ere an' lives ter tell the tale!'

'Aye, to pass safe y'must first defeat us in combat. Draw yer sword!'

The hare spread both paws dramatically wide. 'Alas, I am unarmed, but stay, I shall defeat ye both, though not with any mere weapon. Nay, I will use only my thunderous voice an' sparklin' wit, an' they will suffice to vanquish you both. In short, I challenge you to a duel of insults, you foul an' feckless ferrets!'

Elachim and Borrakul scowled wickedly and began their insulting.

'Yew rotten rip-eared rabbit!'

'Yah lanky lopsided lettuce leaf!'

Florian appeared to sway slightly, but stood his ground, jaw outthrust. 'Hoho! Is that the best ye can do? Well, let a champion show ye a thing or two!'

Wugger shouted out encouragingly, 'Goo on, zurr, you'm show ee vermints!'

Others began egging him on. He held up a paw for silence, then launched into his tirade. 'You misbegotten muddleheaded mudmuckers! Slop-pawed, fiddlefaced bottlenosed baggybottomed bucketbellied beetlebrained beasts!'

The two make-believe ferrets looked aghast, falling back several paces under the onslaught, then they recovered and retaliated.

'Stinky stringpawed snaggletoothed slopswiller!'

'Aye, filthy frogfaced flippin' foozlebacked fop!'

The hare threw a paw across his brow and reeled about as if wounded by the barbed words. Excitement broke out among the onlookers as Elachim and Borrakul swaggered

70

about triumphantly.

'Fight back! Don't let vermin shout things at y'like that!'

Dwopple shook a clenched paw at the ferrets. 'Nutnose nokkykneed smellypaws!'

Deesum covered his mouth, shocked. 'My dear, where did you learn such horrid expressions?'

Florian, alias Ballaw, was back insulting gallantly. 'Toothless twoggletongued twitterin' tripehounds! Slackgutted slimesided sludgehearted spiritless spit-spatterers . . .'

The ferrets began to sink to the floor under the weight of insults. Redwallers rose, clapping and cheering as they urged the heroic hare on to greater efforts.

'Don't stop, you've got 'em now!'

'Aye, carry on, sir, give it to 'em hot'n'heavy!'

'Show the villains who's boss!'

'Burr hurr, you'm tell umm wot you'm think of umm, zurr!'

Florian strode bravely forward, cloak swirling as he finished off the retreating foebeasts with resounding phrases. 'Addletongued applenecked amateur animals! Baldybacked bumptious birdbrained bootlickers! Craventailed crumpetfaced curs! Despicable dungeon-eared doodlebugs! Entrail-eatin' eggheaded eyesores! Foulfurred frog-fearin' felons! Nitnosed chopcheeked dishwater-drinkers! Loppylugged laggards! Begone! Fatuous ferrets!'

As Elachim and Borrakul dropped their tails and scrabbled off on all fours, the hare swaggered victoriously through the imaginary woodland glade. Every creature in Great Hall cheered him to the echo, leaping up on the tables and applauding wildly.

Florian took a jug of strawberry fizz from a passing mole server and drained it at a single draught. He bowed deeply, trying modestly to prevent himself belching from the large quantity of fizzy liquid. The Dibbuns thought it

71

great sport to dash about the tables, trying out new-found insults on their elders.

'You'm a gurt baggybum beetle, zurr, hurr, an' a foozleface too!'

'Heehee! An' you a flittynose an' a doogleduck figgleface, so there!'

Stifling a smile, Cregga rapped on the table for silence. 'That's quite enough for one night. Up to your beds, Dibbuns!'

Grandma Ellayo agreed wholeheartedly. 'Aye, an' bed for you too, mister Florian. Shame on you, teachin' liddle 'uns language like that. Go wash yore mouth out!'

Florian protested volubly. 'But madam, 'twas only an entertainment, a historical play. What about the two otters? They said some jolly dreadful things.'

Elachim and Borrakul sipped cold mint tea innocently.

'What, us? Oh, marm, mister Florian beats us if the insults don't sound bad enough!'

'So he does. We never used words like that afore we joined up with mister Florian's troop. We were brought up t'be gentlebeasts.'

Sister Sloey shook her paw reprovingly at the bewildered hare. 'Double shame on you, sir, for teaching these poor creatures dreadful things. What would their mother say if she could hear them?'

Gathering his cloak about him, Florian strode off in a huff towards the dormitory stairs. He turned and paused on the bottom step, his voice quavering with emotion. 'Culture is wasted upon such as you. I am injured, marm, deeply and sorely injured. I bid you goodnight!'

He tripped upon his coat hem and fell flat on the stone stairs. The Redwallers were in hoots of laughter as Runktipp called out, 'Which is the most deeply injured, sir, yore feelin's or yore bottom?'

Skipper of otters' face was almost purple. The hedge-hog had made the remark as Skipper was downing a beaker of cider, and now he spluttered and choked as he tried to stop laughing. Rusvul pounded his back. 'I think we'd all be better goin' to bed afore anybeast else injures theirselves too deeply!'

Badgermum Cregga never slept in bed, but propped herself up with pillows on the armchair in her room. Redwall Abbey was peaceful and quiet after the feast and entertainment, but the blind badger could not prevent her thoughts from straying. With Marlfoxes and water rats roaming Mossflower, how long was the peace and quiet destined to last?

Janglur and Rusvul, like the instinctive warriors they were, were light sleepers, and both squirrels were up and about in the hour before dawn. They met in the kitchens, where Janglur found his friend lifting a few hot scones from under the noses of three slumbering night cooks. Rusvul was armed with his favourite short javelin, which he tipped towards Janglur, who crept over to join him.

'G'mornin', mate. What're you up to?'

Janglur quietly lifted a small flask of elderflower cordial from the stone cooling cupboard. 'Just a feelin' I had. Thought I'd take a bite o' breakfast an' a stroll around the grounds, y'know, a sort o' patrol.'

Rusvul added a few scones to the ones he already had stowed in a clean napkin. He winked knowingly. 'Shows how a warrior thinks, eh? I had exactly the same idea. Well, I've got the scones an' you've got the cordial, so what are we waitin' for?'

The three night cooks, who were taking an early nap on a heap of empty sacks, slept on, unaware that the squirrels had been and gone.

Starting at the gatehouse Janglur checked the main gate bars, ensuring the heavy oak bolsters were secure in their slots. He joined Rusvul at the gatehouse window. 'Main gates well locked. All quiet here?'

His companion peered through a gap in the curtained windowpanes. 'Not exactly quiet. Ole Friar Butty an'

Nutwing are in there snorin' like thunder in the middle of all those scrolls an' volumes.'

Janglur shook his head disapprovingly. 'Should have at least one able-bodied beast who can stay awake in charge of this entrance. Shall we go up on the battlements?'

Rusvul swept the inner grounds with a wave of his javelin. 'Best cover the inside first, then we'll take a turn around the walltops.'

They headed towards the southwest corner, Janglur munching away at a scone. 'Mmm! Hot'n'fresh, like a good scone oughter be. I never tasted anythin' nicer'n Redwall Abbey vittles in all me life, mate.'

Rusvul passed him the cordial flask. 'Then why don't you stay? There's always a place for a useful squirrel like yoreself 'ere. I gave up wanderin' when I lost me pore dear wife. Redwall's home t'me an' Dannflor now.'

Janglur gave the matter serious consideration. 'Aye, I've still got my family about me, though my mum's gettin' too old t'be travellin' these days. I know Rimrose likes the Abbey. She said so last night, hinted that it'd be a good place to bring our Songbreeze up in, an' I agree with her. Pretty young maid like Song shouldn't spend 'er seasons roamin' the woodlands an' dales. Redwall's a place she can meet nice friends an' grow up good.'

They continued in this vein, strolling along the south grounds, conversing quietly, but checking carefully around bushes and shrubbery, their keen eyes constantly searching for things otherbeasts would miss, disturbed dew on the grass, or a freshly broken stem. Everything was in order. As they approached the small wallgate set in the centre of the east wall, both stopped talking and stood still.

Janglur's heavy-lidded eyes fixed themselves on the wallgate. He whispered, 'Listen, can you hear that scratchin' noise?'

Rusvul nodded, pointing his javelin tip at the

doorjamb. 'Look!'

The door was a solid little affair made from close-jointed elm planks painted green. It had a single heavy iron bolt securing it. The scraping noise started up again, and a narrow strip of soft metal, hooked at one end, poked through a fresh gap made in the doorjamb by a knife. Janglur looked at the wood shavings on the ground, and took in the full situation at a glance.

'Somebeast tryin' to push the bolt back an' open the wallgate!'

Now they could hear gasping and muttering from outside.

'Mmff! Grmmf! Should've cut a wider gap fer this t'go through!'

'Owch! Y've trapped me paw. Leggo, I can do it!'

Rusvul pointed silently to the walltop. Careful to make no noise, they hurried back and dashed up the southeast wallsteps. Dropping flat on the ramparts, both squirrels wriggled swiftly towards the centre of the east wall. Straightening cautiously, they peered down between the battlements.

Four water rats were at the gate, one with his body flattened sideways against the door as he strove to hook the metal device over the bolt and push it open. The others were either urging him on, or telling him to let them try to do it. Mouth close to Janglur's ear, Rusvul whispered, 'Four of 'em!'

Janglur scoured the scene thoroughly, eyes flicking from side to side. 'Rusvul, wait. There's five. See the Marlfox leanin' on that rowan!'

The Marlfox, Gelltor, unaware that he was being watched, struck the treetrunk impatiently. 'Hurry it up, Fatchur. What's the matter? I thought you were supposed to be good at opening locks.'

A rattle of metal upon metal sounded out. The rat, Fatchur, straightened up confidently, assuring his master, 'I think I've got it, sire. The hook's over the bolt end!'

Janglur nudged Rusvul urgently. 'Best put a stop t'this afore they're in. I'll take Fatchur, you pick off the Marlfox. Now!'

Janglur leaned out over the battlements whirling his sling. *Thwok!* Fatchur was slain instantly as the big round river pebble struck him square between the eyes. Rusvul threw his javelin.

It was only Gelltor's swiftness that saved his life. He saw the rat fall as the slingstone struck, and glancing up at the walltop he could see Janglur, sling in paw at the battlement, with Rusvul to one side of him launching the javelin. The Marlfox threw himself to one side, but not fast enough. The javelin, which was aimed at his chest, missed any vital spot, but took a chunk of flesh from his shoulder, pinning his cloak to the rowan. Stifling a shriek of pain, Gelltor ripped the cloak free as he fell on all fours. Not waiting to see what fate befell the other three rats, he took off through the undergrowth, crouching low and clasping his wounded shoulder. Instantly the remaining rats fled, sent on their way by another stone from Janglur's sling, which cracked the tail of the last one stumbling into the cover of the trees.

The squirrels immediately hurried from the walltop back down to the gate. Janglur unlatched the metal hook from the protruding bolt end and inspected the device. 'That rat knew what he was doin'. A good shove or two an' they would've been in. Let's see if'n he's still alive.'

They unlocked the gate and stepped out into Mossflower Wood. Rusvul turned the rat over, placing a paw on the creature's heart. 'Hmph! Won't get anythin' out o' this 'un. Dead as a doornail!'

The rat was long and thin. He wore a grey tunic with a wide belt in which were stuck a dagger and curved sword, the only other item he possessed being a half-length black cape. Rusvul rolled the carcass into some deep loam beneath a spreading buckthorn bush. Janglur heaved on the javelin, tugging it from the rowan trunk.

'Y'had tough luck there, mate. He moved a bit too fast for ye!'

Rusvul cleaned his javelin tip by jabbing it in the earth. 'Maybe, but one thing I'm sure of now, Marlfoxes ain't magic. They're quick, but they can't vanish like some say they do. Don't worry, I'll get 'im next time!'

Dawn was up now, rosy and clear. They strode back to the Abbey finishing the last drop of cordial. Janglur licked his lips. 'I'm ready for a proper breakfast now. Don't mention what happened back there to any save those who have t'know. Oh, an' we'll have t'see if'n those wallgates can be locked up more secure.'

Mokkan, the self-appointed leader of his brother and sister Marlfoxes, sat eating a meal of trout, cooked over the fire. Gelltor plastered stream mud on his wound, binding it with dockleaves and sorrel. Mokkan spat a fishbone at him, curling his lip scornfully.

'Blitherin' oaf! You made a right mess of that plan. Now the Redwallers are sure to know we're about!'

The vixen, Predak, helped herself to a portion of the trout. 'They probably already knew we were in Mossflower if they have half a brain between them. Don't blame Gelltor. I don't think you could have done any better.'

Mokkan wiped his paws on the grass, taunting his wounded brother. 'A Marlfox getting himself wounded by a squirrel, and losing a good water rat into the bargain. Tell me, Gelltor, d'you think I could have done better?'

Gelltor winced as he tied the dressing with green reeds. 'They'll get back more than they gave when I start on them. I'll slay ten for killing Fatchur and twenty for injuring me!'

Mokkan shook his head in disbelief. 'You don't understand, stupid. We came to steal, not to start a war. Where's the profit in that?'

Gelltor whipped out his axe and gripped the haft tightly. 'Blood for blood, I say. Who's with me?'

77

Ziral raised her voice. 'It's not blood for blood unless somebeast kills a Marlfox. That's our law, brother. Mokkan's right. We came for plunder and Redwall Abbey is the only place worth thieving from. You messed things up, got yourself wounded and lost Fatchur. None of us is with you!'

Mokkan picked his teeth with a fishbone, sneering at Gelltor. 'See, for the moment we're robbers, not killers. Haven't you got it into that thick skull of yours? High Queen Silth must be surrounded by beauty. Rich, wonderful things, that's what we need to bring back to the island. Imagine what she'd do if we staggered back to Castle Marl with half our number dead because we'd started an all-out war with the beasts of Redwall?'

Gelltor slumped against a tree, nursing his wound. 'Aarh! I don't see the sense to it, trampin' round the woodlands just to rob stuff to please that crazy old relic. It's daft!'

Ascrod, who had remained silent until now, spoke up. 'Listen, brother, we're storing up these valuables for ourselves. Remember, one day our mother will be dead – maybe sooner than we think, considering her age. When that day comes we will rule the island together. Castle Marl, everything, will be all ours!'

Ziral chuckled mirthlessly. 'Not according to Mokkan. He says we'll kill each other off until there's only one left to rule, right, Mokkan?'

Mokkan shrugged. 'Who can tell? I say let the future look after itself, and for now we concentrate on that Abbey. Listen, I've got a plan that's a lot wiser and less warlike than Gelltor's was. Let's get the rats on the march to Redwall. I'll explain to you as we go.'

Mokkan was the toughest and most resourceful of all the brothers and sisters. Even Gelltor went along with the scheme when he heard it.

7

Tragglo Spearback and his cellar helpers were good
carpenters. By midday they were fitting hingelocks to the
wallgates, bolts that doubly secured the doors and could
only be opened from inside. Rusvul and Janglur were in
conference with Log a Log, Skipper and Cregga, deciding
what the next move should be in the light of that
morning's attempted break-in. The Wandering Noonvale
Companions were rehearsing out by the pond, watched
by the Abbey Dibbuns. Dann was strolling in the grounds
with Song and Dippler when Grandma Ellayo passed
them, hobbling towards the gatehouse. Song and her
friends took the old squirrel's paws to assist her.

'You're in a bit of a hurry, Grandma. Where are you off
to?'

'I'm goin' to the gate'ouse, Song m'dear. Yore dad said
Friar Butty needs me t'tell him all I know about those
Marlfoxes.'

'Oh, can we come too? I love to hear you telling tales!'

The old squirrel looked at the three eager young
friends. She paused a moment as if undecided, then gave
in to the request. 'Oh, if'n y'wish, but y'must sit still an'
don't fidget, I can't abide fidgety beasts. Oh, one of you
nip back an' tell that nice Brother Melilot that we'll all be

takin' lunch in the gate'ouse!'

Dippler sped off, calling back, 'Leave it t'me, marm. I'll go!'

A few minutes later, seated comfortably on an old sofa, Ellayo faced Nutwing, who was perched on an armchair opposite her. Butty sat at the desk with quill, ink and parchment. Song and Dann settled themselves on the arms of the sofa. Friar Butty began.

'Now, marm, I want you to speak slowly and clearly. Address my friend Nutwing as if you were telling him a story. I'll sit over here and record all you say. You may begin if you're ready, marm.'

Ellayo stroked the smooth top of her blackthorn stick. 'Hmm, Marlfoxes, now let me see. When I was a maid, young as Song here, my father told me of a secret island at the centre of a great lake somewhere. Foxes had discovered the island and claimed it for their own – of course, that was after the lake monster was slain and the white ghost left the island . . .'

Friar Butty cut in on the narrative. 'Excuse me, marm, what lake monster and what white ghost?'

Grandma Ellayo sniffed at him irritably. 'How should I know? I'm just telling you what was told to me. Can you remember everything from your early seasons?'

Butty held up his paw respectfully. 'My apologies, marm. Please continue.'

'Where was I? Oh yes! Father said that a tribe of foxes, with water rats to serve them, took over the island and built a big castle there. Then the story went that there was a war. Y.'see, most of the tribe were ordinary vermin, save for two, a male an' a vixen, who were Marlfoxes. It was them who were magic. They could make theirselves invisible, 'twas said. Anyhow, the Marlfoxes got the water rats on their side an' wiped out the other foxes, slew 'em all. Then nothin' more was heard of, or from, that island. Now when I was a bit older, I had a mate, Gawjo, an' a liddle 'un too. That was Song's daddy

Janglur. Gawjo was a real adventurer an' a great wanderer, an' one day he went off in search of the Marlfoxes' island an' that was the last anybeast ever seen of him. I was left t'bring Janglur up. We became wanderers, always hopin' we'd find Gawjo again someday, but we never did.'

Song took in every word. She felt sorry for Grandma Ellayo, bringing up Janglur alone, always searching for her lost husband; it must have been a hard life. She put a paw around her grandma's shoulder as the old squirrel continued.

'One winter, when Janglur was still only a liddle 'un, we were camped in a hole on a streambank, with nought to eat but a few roots an' late berries an' a fire to warm ourselves by. Then one night a young kingfisher, half alive an' freezin', crawls out o' the stream an' up the bank to our dugout hole. Pore liddle bird, I took him in an' shared our fire an' wot vittles we had. This kingfisher told me he'd come from the great lake. He lived on the island an' was fishin' off it when he was set on by a bunch o' magpies. They chased him far, an' left the liddle bird fer dead in the lake shallows. But he wasn't dead, y'see, an' one way or t'other he managed to get away an' survive. I tell ye true, I owed me'n'Janglur's life to that kingfisher. When he got well an' could fly again, he brought food to us all winter long. At night we'd all three of us sit together by the fire to keep warm, an' he told me wot he knew of the island, said it was ruled by one Marlfox now, a murderous vixen callin' 'erself Queen Silth. The kingfisher said that she had a brood of seven cubs, all Marlfoxes, an' she slew her mate 'cos he wanted to call 'imself king. So then, wot d'yer think o' that?'

Old Friar Butty shook his head to think that such wickedness existed. Song crept down off the sofa arm to sit beside Ellayo. 'What happened to the little kingfisher, Grandma?'

Ellayo stared into the dust motes swirling in a shaft of

81

golden sunlight from the window, remembering that winter, long seasons ago. 'I recall one mornin', 'twas spring, me'n'liddle Janglur woke up an' the kingfisher was gone. I never set eyes on 'im again, but I always hoped that good bird had a happy life, 'cos we owed 'im a lot.'

Dippler breezed in with Roop, the mole from the troupe, pushing a trolley laden with food between them. The Guosim shrew bowed. 'Lunch is served. Summer veggible soup, leek an' mushroom turnover, an' apple an' blackcurrant flan, with a nice flagon o' rosehip tea to wash it all down. I 'ope you ain't started tellin' the story yet, marm. Nothin' better'n eatin' lunch an' lissenin' to a good yarn!'

Ellayo heaved herself up with a groan and began dishing out the food. 'Started? I've done all the tale-tellin' I'm doing for today, young feller m'shrew. Yore too late!'

Friar Butty put aside his quill. 'So that's all you know about Marlfoxes, marm, you can't tell us more?'

Ellayo passed him a plate of food. 'Aye, right enough, 'tis all. You'd best wash those inky paws afore you eat lunch, Friar.'

Nutwing, who had dozed off halfway through the narrative, awoke with a start, blinking repeatedly. 'Hmm mm, lunch? Did somebeast mention lunch?'

The mousebabe Dwopple and his two new friends Wugger and Blinny, young Redwall moles, were making thorough nuisances of themselves at the Wandering Noonvale Companions' rehearsal. Runktipp was going through his conjuring act in spite of their constant barracking and interruptions. The hedgehog spread both paws wide, a pebble had vanished, and Florian announced the trick's next stage.

'H'anda now, before your very eyes, the great Runktippo Magicspike will turn the pebble into a long string of flags which he will produce from his magical mouth whilst I give a roll of the drum!'

Most of the Dibbuns were silent, gazing awestruck at the performance, but Dwopple sniggered villainously as he called out, 'Well 'urry up, gerra h'on wid it!'

Florian shot him a glare that would have shrivelled lettuce. 'Silence, please. This is an extremely delicate an' dangerous illusion. Kindly refrain from shouting aloud!'

Dwopple whispered something to Wugger, who immediately yelled out, 'Runktippo dropped ee pebble onna ground. 'Tis unner 'is footpaw!'

Florian picked up the drumsticks, eyeing Wugger icily. 'Any more interruptions, sah, an' I will eject you from the audience! Great Magic Runktippo, are you ready?'

The hedgehog nodded as Blinny announced what Dwopple had told her. 'Ee can't talk 'cos 'is mouth be gurtly full o' flags'n'string!'

The final straw came when Florian tried a drum roll, only to find that the drum head merely gave forth a dull sticky thud. 'Sabotage! Some rotten cad's poured honey over me drum. Dwopple!'

The mousebabe and his companions sensed the game was up. They took to their paws and fled, with Florian hurling dire threats after them. 'Fiends! Show-wreckers! I'll have y'roasted with turnips, I'll chop off y'tails with a rusty saw! I'll . . . I'll . . . !'

Deesum twitched her nose at the furious hare. 'Mister Florian, you'll stop this unprofessional behaviour in front of your audience and continue with the rehearsal!'

Behind the bushes by the north wallgate, Dwopple sat with the molebabes, wondering what mischief they could accomplish next. He pointed to the battlements. 'We go play up onna wall.'

But Wugger and Blinny would not hear of it.

'Burr! Nay, zurr, us'n's bain't a-goin' up thurr agin, ho no!'

They contented themselves with banging on an old

cooking pot which Blinny kept hidden in the bushes. The molebabes whacked it gleefully with sticks, as Dwopple mimicked the troupe's act.

'I'm a magic Dwoppo, pulla lotsa flags out me nose, heeheehee!'

They marched about behind the shrubbery, banging and yelling.

'Us want cake and st'awbee fizz! Lotsa lotsa cake or we don't gerra wash!'

On the other side of the wallgate the vixen Ziral had no need to press her ear against the wood. She turned to Mokkan. 'You were right, the young ones are there. Allag, bring the others round here from the south and east wallgates.'

Gelltor winced as Mokkan patted his injured shoulder. 'I told you, sooner or later they play by the gates or on the walltops. Now, we only need to snare one and we won't have to worry about thieving. Those Redwallers will give us what we want when they hear what we could do to a little hostage.'

Gelltor moved out of range of Mokkan's paw. 'Well, let's see you get one of 'em on this side of the wall.'

Mokkan loosed the drawstring on a bag he carried beneath his cloak. 'Easy, just watch me!'

Dwopple and his friends eventually grew tired of marching and shouting. They were about to run off and see if there was any fun to be had around the gatehouse, when several loud knocks sounded on the wallgate door. The little ones went to the door, listening curiously as the knocking continued. Dwopple picked up a stick and knocked in reply. 'Who's derr? Wot you knock for?'

The answer came back in a soothing homely voice. 'Who do you think I am, little friend?'

The mousebabe pondered a moment, then made up a fictitious name that he liked the sound of. 'Stickabee!'

A slice of preserved apple, thick with crystallized honey, slid under the narrow gap at the bottom of the door. The voice chuckled. 'How did you know my name is Stickabee? Well done!'

Dwopple stuffed the delicacy into his mouth. Wugger crouched down and called under the gap, 'Summ furr Wugger. Oi wants some Stickybee, zurr!'

'Of course you do, Wugger, but you must open the door so that I can give you the whole bagful.'

Mokkan listened to the sound of tiny paws scraping on the door, followed by the voices of disappointed Dibbuns.

'Us can't open d'locks, mista Stickabee, they's too tight!'

Gelltor smiled mockingly at the Marlfox leader. 'Oh dear, what are you goin' t'do now, mister Stickabee?'

Mokkan's paw strayed beneath his cloak. 'One more word from you and I'll introduce you to mister axehead!' He turned back to the door, his voice cajoling the Dibbuns. 'Oh, come on now, I'm sure you can open one little lock?'

Dwopple sounded impatient at the Marlfox's ignorance. 'It not one liddle lock, there be's two. One's too stiff an' the nuther one be too far up t'reach. Pusha more candyfruit unner d'door, Stickabee!'

'But I can't, my little friend. The fruit slices are too thick to fit under the door, they'd get all dirty and squashed. Look, why don't you come up to the walltop and we'll think of a way to get the whole bag up to you. Good idea, eh?'

Dwopple jumped up and down with excitement. 'Aye, good idea, good idea, we go up onna wall!'

Wugger and Blinny backed off, shaking their heads vigorously.

'Hurr no, us'n's bain't goin' on ee wall!'

'You'm catch gurt trubble if'n ee go up thurr, D'opple!'

The mousebabe headed boldly for the north wallsteps. 'Yah, you two 'fraidyfrogs!'

The moles trundled off to the gatehouse. They had

learned their lesson about walltops.

Dwopple looked down at the assembly of rats and Marlfoxes below on the ground. 'Where mista Stickabee?'

Mokkan held up the bag of crystallized fruit. 'Gone to his house to get more candysweets like this. Are you the friend he was telling us about?'

'Aye, my name Dwopple, I mista Stickabee's friend.'

'Oh, good. He said I had to give these to you. Here, catch!' Mokkan tossed the bag, which rose only a short way before falling on the ground. The Marlfox shook his head sadly. 'I can't throw them high enough for you to catch, little friend.'

Dwopple spread his paws expressively. 'So whatta we do?'

Mokkan paced back and forth, as if deep in thought. Suddenly he clapped his paws and smiled broadly. 'Of course, you can come down and get them, Dwopple!'

'Yah, silly, Dwopple no can climb downa wall!'

Mokkan took off his cloak, gesturing to several rats to get round and hold the edges. They held it high, stretched tight in a great triangle. The Marlfox pointed to it, grinning brightly. 'Now you can, Dwopple. It'll be great fun. Just jump and all my friends here will catch you safely!'

The mousebabe clambered on to the battlements and looked down doubtfully, not sure whether he would enjoy the experience. Mokkan leapt on to the cloak, bounced on the taut material once and jumped back off nimbly.

'Hoho! That was great! I wish I were up there with you, Dwopple, I'd really enjoy jumping down on to the cloak. That's unless you don't want the candysweets and you're a 'fraidyfrog!'

That did it. Dwopple swelled his fat little tummy out and scowled. 'Me norra 'fraidyfrog, Dwopple jump high, higher'n dat, right offa top o' mister Florian's cart! You watch me. Yeeeeeeeeee!'

86

Dwopple launched himself off the ramparts. He landed in the centre of the cloak, bouncing twice. Mokkan deliberately trod on Gelltor's footpaw as he passed. 'What've you got to say for yourself now, mister oafhead?'

The water rats had Dwopple wrapped and bundled in the cloak before he could make another move.

8

Cregga Badgermum and Rimrose completed their after-lunch stroll by calling in at the gatehouse. Grandma Ellayo and the owl, Nutwing, sprawled on the old sofa, fast asleep after the amount of food they had eaten. Song, Dann and Dippler had joined Friar Butty at the table, searching through ancient scrolls and dusty volumes of Abbey records. Rimrose guided Cregga to the armchair and seated her.

'Whew, 'tis warm out there today!'

Song filled two beakers with rosehip tea. 'This is nice and cool. Where's Dad?'

Cregga sipped her tea, the beaker almost lost within her huge paw. 'Taking up a new career, I think. He's with Tragglo and the cellarmoles, learning all about October Ale and such. When your mum and I passed there earlier he seemed t'be enjoying himself.'

Rimrose glanced at the books and documents on the table. 'And what are you up to, missie?'

Song flicked idly through the pages of a hefty tome. 'We're helping Friar Butty to look for more information about Marlfoxes. Grandma told us all she knew, but it's not enough.'

The blind badger held out her beaker for more rosehip

tea. 'But she did tell you a few things that you didn't know before?'

Friar Butty rerolled a scroll neatly. 'Indeed she did, although at first her story was a bit muddled. She began talking of a white ghost and a lake monster that lived in a great lake until it was slain. Then she said that the white ghost left the hidden island, but she said she didn't remember much about it. I think it was probably some figment of Ellayo's imagination from her young days.'

Cregga sat up straight. 'Maybe not. I was once Badger Ruler of the hollow mountain by the sea called Salamandastron. Badgers always rule there. I recall seeing some rock carvings in a chamber on the mountain. I never really paid them much attention. Strange how it comes back to one at the mention of certain words. A lake monster means nought to me, but a white ghost, I remember that. You see, those wall carvings told of all the great Badger Lords who had held sway on Salamandastron. Two of these were twins, Urthstripe and Urthwyte. I think the tale goes that they were separated at birth and lost to each other. However, Urthstripe discovered his brother, Urthwyte, on an island in the middle of a vast lake. There, Urthwyte, who was born completely white of fur, became known as the White Ghost. They both travelled from the island to Salamandastron, where Urthstripe was Badger Lord. There was a great battle against vermin hordes and Urthstripe was slain. Urthwyte became Badger Lord in his stead and was often known to the hares that serve the mountain as Whiteghost. That's all I can tell you, but it may prove Ellayo wasn't imagining things.'

Cregga stopped talking. Holding up a paw for silence, she listened, and after a while she smiled. 'Come out, you two. Blinny and Wugger, if I'm not mistaken.'

The two molebabes crawled from behind the sofa.

'Hurr, you'm surrpintly bain't mistaken, 'tis us' 'n's.'

'Burr, 'ow did ee knowed 'twas us'n's, mum?'

Cregga judged they were within paw range and swept both Dibbuns up on to her lap. 'I just knowed, that's all. Now what are you two after in Friar Butty's gatehouse?'

'We'm horful thursty, marm. Ee sun be 'ot out thurr!'

Song poured them a beaker each of the cool rosehip tea, smiling as she watched them noisily sucking it up.

'Been playing hard, I suppose. Where's your pal got to, that rascally mousebabe Dwopple?'

Blinny drained the last of her drink, wiping a paw across her mouth. 'Us'n's never goed on ee walltop, miz, 'onest we'm din't!'

Butty wagged his quill pen at the molebabes. 'But Dwopple did, eh? What was he doing up there?'

'Ee'm talkin' to mista Stickybee. We'm tol' 'im not to go oop thurr, but D'opple a likkle naughtybeast, hurr aye.'

Friar Butty shook his head wearily. 'He certainly is. Song, would you and your friends like to go and get that little wretch down off the ramparts before he does something silly and injures himself? Which wall was it, Blinny?'

'Norff wall, zurr. Ee'm oop thurr a-talkin' wi' mista Stickybee.'

Dannflor patted the molebabe's velvety head. 'Don't you fret, young 'un, we'll get mister Stickybee down too, whoever he is. Come on, Dipp.'

The three chums mounted the walltop by the gatehouse steps and trotted along the north wall. Song searched carefully around the angle of each battlement, whilst Dippler and Dann covered the east wall adjoining.

'There's no sign of 'im 'ere, Song.'

'No, he's not here either, Dipp. What d'you think, Dann?'

'Oh, the little wretch prob'ly got fed up and got down by himself. Perhaps he's by the pond. Let's take a look over that way.'

Florian and the troupe were singing a comic song for

their audience, who were not just Dibbuns, but many Redwallers who had finished their chores. The onlookers were in pleats laughing at the antics of the Noonvale Companions as they performed funny walks in time to their song, encouraging the Dibbuns to get up and join in with them. The little creatures needed no second urging and paraded joyfully with the troupe.

'Oh come along dearies follow me,
I'll take ye down t'the sycamore tree,
Plum pudden an' turnover, apple pie.
Beneath its spreadin' boughs we'll lie,
With veggible pasty an' damson tart,
We'll wheel it along in a little cart,
The birds will sing "Give us some do."
Oh the food's for us an' the crumbs for you,
So empty the cupboard out what d'you see,
A fruitcake for you an' trifle for me,
There's bread'n'cheese an' what d'you think,
A jugful o' raspberry cordial to drink.
A rowtle tee towtle an' toora lie ay,
What do you think our old mother will say,
Riddle dum diddle dum derrydown dare,
When she comes home to find her cupboard all bare?'

Dann caught up with Florian, who leaned against the cart wheezing after the performance.

'My word! Not as young as I was last season, wot!'

'Sir, have you seen baby Dwopple lately?'

Florian mopped his brow with a red spotted kerchief. 'That scutterbug! Can't say I have, young laddo, but with a bit o' luck an eagle may've flown off with the blighter!'

Deesum was immediately in the midst of things. 'Eagle, what eagle, where? Oh, my poor little treasure, he's been carried off in the talons of a huge eagle!'

The hare rolled his eyes skyward and sighed. 'Dwopple was not borne off by an eagle, marm, 'twas merely wishful thinkin' on my part. Huh, pity the poor eagle that had the nerve to try an' make off with *that* miniature rotter, wot!'

Song reassured her. 'I'm sure Dwopple is safe, miz Deesum, somewhere within Redwall, but we can't find him. Blinny and Wugger, the molebabes, were the last to see him, on the north walltop. We've looked but he's not there.'

Deesum snatched the kerchief from Florian and wrung it distractedly. 'Then we must search until we find the sweet little mite. Everybeast, stop what you are doing and search the entire place. Look high and low, drag the pond and scour the cellars!'

Florian could not resist a dig at the mouse's dramatics. 'Right y'are. I'll turn out m'pockets an' comb my fur!'

He wilted as the tough-looking Rusvul caught him tight by the paw. 'A babe is missin'. 'Tis no jokin' matter, an' you'd do well to quit playactin' an' join the search!'

Janglur and Tragglo searched the cellars, Brother Melilot and Foremole Gubbio checked the kitchens. Song and her friends accompanied Sister Sloey through the Infirmary and dormitories. The three otters, Borrakul, Elachim and Skipper, waited until the coast was clear before diving in the Abbey pond and covering every fraction of it carefully. Skipper thwacked his wet rudder on the bank, sending droplets cascading wide. 'Thank the seasons the liddle feller ain't in there!'

Runktipp and the two moles, Roop and Muggle, had patrolled the orchard twice. They tried to comfort Deesum, who wept pitifully.

'There there now, miz Deesum, don't go gittin' yoreself all of a tizzy, that mousebabe's bound to be somewheres in the Abbey or the grounds. Stands to reason, don't it?'

'Burr aye, all ee gates be well locked oop, an' ee walls be too 'igh furr maister Dwopple to clamber o'er. Doan't ee fret, marm, us'll foind 'im afore long.'

Evening came and still they searched, finding no trace of the mousebabe. Badgermum Cregga and Friar Butty questioned Wugger and Blinny patiently.

'What time of day was it when you last saw Dwopple?'

'Urr, just afore lunch, zurr, on ee norff walltop.'

'Right, now what about this mister Stickybee? Did you see him?'

'Ho no, marm, us'n's din't see 'im!'

'Then how do you know there is such a creature?'

'Ee'm talked to uz an' gived D'opple a candysweet.'

Friar Butty scratched his ear distractedly with the quill pen. 'But how could he do all that and you still didn't see him?'

"Cos ee wurr outside, zurr, back o' ee likkle wallgate. Stickybee slided D'opple a candyfruit unner d'door. Stickybee say ee give us'n's a gurt bag o' candyfruits if'n uz go oop to walltops.'

'But you two never went up there, only Dwopple did, right?'

Both molebabes nodded. Butty tried to hold his patience. 'Why did you not tell us all this before?'

"Cos you'm never axed uz, zurr.'

Cregga could not help smiling, despite her anxiety. 'Well, Friar, there's a bit of true mole logic. Wugger's right, though, we should have thought to ask them a lot earlier. Come on, you two, 'tis dark out and way past your bedtime.'

Friar Butty walked back to the Abbey with them. 'Cregga, marm, I don't like the sound of this. Sounds like the Marlfoxes to me. Remember the night of the storm? These two practically described Marlfoxes to us, but nobeast believed them.'

Cregga felt for the Abbey door handle. 'Aye, that's true, Friar. But I want no mention of what they've told us made to anybeast yet. There's no need to cause alarm. Dwopple may be found hiding somewhere before morning. We'll just have to keep searching.'

'But what if we can't find him?'

'Then we'll just have to search the whole of Mossflower.'

Mokkan and the other Marlfoxes sat round a fire on the creek edge, roasting a couple of plump waterfowl. The rats sat further away, cooking fish over their own fires. Mokkan blew a feather from his muzzle tip and watched it float off into the night.

'Plenty of good vittles in this part of Mossflower. Nothing like a roasted bird after a good day's work, eh!'

The cloak, with its top tied securely, hung from the bough of a beech tree close by, bobbing about as Dwopple kicked and protested from inside his prison. 'You fibba liars, where mista Stickabee? Lemme go, I wanna bag o' candysweets, you let Dwopple go!'

Gelltor slapped the bag lightly. 'Quiet in there, or I'll give you something to shout about!'

The mousebabe did a dance of rage inside the cloak. 'Rottin fosskers, toucha Dwopple an' I get you wirra me slinger!'

One of the vixens, Predak, stared across the flames at Mokkan. 'You're very confident this is going to work, brother?'

Mokkan tested the roasting bird with a knifetip. 'Why d'you say that? No reason it shouldn't work. You'll see, those Abbeybeasts would part with anything rather than have one of their babes hurt. But speak up if you have a better idea.'

Predak watched a moth shrivel as it ventured too near the firelight. 'Oh, your idea's a good one, but wouldn't it be better if we had another plan to fall back on in case anything goes wrong?'

Mokkan's pale eyes glimmered as they reflected the flames. 'Tell me. I'm not like our brother Gelltor, I'm always ready to listen to other schemes.'

On the island, two rat guards marched up a ramp towards the main chamber. One of them whispered irately, 'Well, what is it tonight? There's no storm to disturb 'er.'

The other rat's eyes flickered from side to side among the gloomy recesses and curves of the winding stone passage. 'Keep yer voice down, mate. Y'never know who might be lissenin'. Queen Silth'll let us know wot's on 'er mind soon enough, an' you can bet yer tail it won't be good news. It never is!'

Outside, the great lake was calm and the island quiet in dim peaceful summer night. But the main chamber was lit like noontide, with banks upon banks of thick tallow candles ranged from floor to ceiling, their light reflecting amber and gold against the long brass wallplates the Marlfoxes used as mirrors.

Threescore rats of the Guard Command stood stiffly to attention, their black livery marking them apart from the brown of lower ranks. Each carried a leaf-bladed short spear and a small round buckler shield. Above in the crisscrossed roofbeams more than fifty magpies swaggered and strutted, hopping boldly about, some even venturing to perch on the big circular candle-laden wheels which served as chandeliers. These were the tribe of Athrak, feared favourites of the High Queen. The two water rats from the shoreline patrol hurried to stand in formation with their fellow Guard Commanders, flinching as drops of hot wax from the ceiling fell on them each time a magpie caused one of the wheels to sway. After a while, even the magpies became still and silent, and an uneasy quiet fell over the chamber as Silth made her entrance.

The carriers bore their burden with exquisite care, setting the silken-curtained palanquin slowly down on a raised block of speckled marble at the chamber's far end. All eyes were now centred on the stone, though they had seen it many times before. A gasp went up from the onlookers as the vixen Lantur seemed to materialize from the speckled marble block. She had been standing there since the first rat entered, completely undetected, camouflaged by the stone's pattern. Lantur held her paws wide as two water rats hurried forward and draped the brown-green cloak about her shoulders. At a nod from her the Guard Commanders raised their spears, calling out as in one mighty voice: 'O eternal Silth! High Queen, live for ever! Beauty be yours alone!'

The harsh rasping voice that issued from behind the curtains held a petulant note, like that of a spoiled young one. 'Noise! All night long. Noise! I hear the waters of that lake, trying to eat away the rocks of my island! I hear the night breeze whispering like death, swirling about my castle, trying to find me! But what have you done about these things . . . Nothing! Sleep will not come, it flies away from me on dark wings, I cannot catch it. Why?'

The water rat Commanders stood rigid, not daring to move a muscle, watched by the bright searching eyes of the magpies above them. Lantur strode up and down between the ranks, chastising the hapless rodents with her tongue. 'You are growing fat and idle whilst your Queen suffers. There are no excuses for your stupidity. At night, whilst you are shirking your duties, the White Ghost wanders the rooms and corridors of Castle Marl!'

The Queen's voice interrupted Lantur, shrill with fear. 'Fools! I know what you are thinking, but I have seen it!'

At that point one of the unfortunate Guard Commanders dropped his shield. The clang of metal upon stone echoed through the chamber. Athrak launched himself from a crossbeam, calling his tribe.

'Rakkarakkarakka! Gerrimclaw!'

The magpies zoomed down like lightning upon the wretched creature. Talons and beaks gripped fur, paws, tail and tunic cruelly, lifting him bodily from the floor. Knocking other rats aside, the magpies rushed their prisoner forward, chattering gleefully as they dropped him in front of the marble block and stood surrounding him. The water rat lay cringing on the floorstones. Silth's voice was harsh and accusing. 'Have you seen the White Ghost?'

A thin smile played about Lantur's features. She adopted a tone of reasonable enquiry. 'Well, friend, have you seen the White Ghost or haven't you? Answer your Queen.'

The rat was in a quandary. If he said he had seen the White Ghost Silth would make him describe it. If his description did not ring true, then what? His only hope was to tell the truth.

'O High Queen, I have not seen the White Ghost, I swear it!'

It was the wrong answer. The tasselled silk curtains shook as Silth raged insanely.

'Of course you haven't, because you've been sleeping on duty and idling your time away! Athrak, tell my protectors of the skies to remove this worthless heap of offal from Castle Marl! He shall answer for his laziness to the Teeth of the Deeps!' The rat gave a pitiful moan as Athrak's magpies seized him with wicked joy and bore him off.

At an upstairs window the curtains of the palanquin parted slightly. Silth watched the scene below on the lakeshore. Blazing torches had been spiked in a semi-circle into the rock at the water's edge. The head of the Guard Command chopped a dead fish into chunks and hurled them into the dark waters. There were no shallows; the island was a massive, steep-sided mountain, its bottom resting on the lake bed, unfathomable depths below. The water rats stood watching the surface, their stomachs knotted in terror, mouths dry with fear, as the waters began to thrash and churn. Dorsal fins and gold-green scales, hooked jaws and curved sets of ripping teeth flashed in the torchlights. Pike! The great freshwater predators set up bow waves as they stormed to the spot, whipping themselves into a feeding frenzy as they fought for gobbets of the dead fish. The condemned water rat screeched as Athrak's ruthless birds lifted him out over the depths. 'No, no, I lied. I've seen the White Ghost! Eeeeeyaaaagh!'

Silth listened to the splash as the rat's body was dropped to the waiting pike shoal. She shut the curtains with a triumphant chuckle. 'I knew he was lying all along. If I've seen the White Ghost then others have. Right, Lantur?'

The vixen Marlfox smiled slyly. 'It is as you say, O Great One!'

Two water rat Guard Commanders unspiked the torches and extinguished them, sizzling, in the lake.

'Is she still up at the window watchin'?'

'I dunno. Keep yer eyes front, mate, unless you wants ter feed the fish. You know 'tis death to look upon the Queen.'

'Huh, 'tis death to do anythin' on this cursed rock. In fact ye can get slain fer nothin'. Lookit pore ole Rigglent, all he did was drop his shield. That ole Queen was just lookin' for a chance to pick on somebeast. This place gets worse!'

The other rat finished stacking the torches in a pile. 'Don't tell me, cully. Why don't yer leave? Lake full o' pike an' the sky guarded by magpies, wot's to stop yer, eh?'

In the slave pens there was speculation over what had taken place at the lakeside. An ancient mouse rubbed the area above his footpaw, where the manacles had worn through his fur, causing a sore. 'Sounded like one o' the water rats bein' fed to the Teeth o' the Deeps. Better one o' them than a slave, that's what I say.'

A lean, tired-looking otter stared longingly through the bars at the water rat barracks. 'Aye, yore right there, matey. I don't suppose there's any chance that the one who got slung in the lake was Ullig?'

Sitting up in the straw, a sturdy hedgehog maid muttered, 'No such luck, friend. Y'best keep quiet, 'ere comes the bully hisself.'

Slave Captain Ullig rattled the bars with his whip butt. 'Silence in there or I'll pick a few of you lot out to feed the Teeth o' the Deeps. Those pike ain't fussy wot they eat. Even a couple of scrawny slaves would taste good to 'em.'

Ullig sauntered off back to the barracks, watched by the silent slaves. When he had gone a gaunt-eyed squirrel smashed his chains against the bars in helpless rage. 'Swaggerin' scum! I'd teach Ullig a lesson if I was free of these chains just fer a moment!'

The ancient mouse shook his head in despair. 'Free? There ain't no such word for a slave. I've been on this island so long I've forgotten wot free means.'

'An' you've never seen any slave break free in all that time?'

The old mouse smiled grimly at the young hedgehog who had asked the question. 'I saw lots o' slaves break free, like that'n in the corner.' He pointed to an emaciated vole, lying in a huddle shivering so hard that his chains rattled constantly. Two other slaves were bathing his feverish brow with damp rags. The vole's eyes rolled wildly, and he whimpered and coughed as another tried to force water between his trembling lips. The old mouse nodded knowingly as he explained to the hedgehog maid, 'That pore beast'll be free afore dawn – dead free. That's the only way you'll leave the Marlfoxes an' Slave Cap'ns an' this island, matey, tail first!'

9

Florian Dugglewoof Wilffachop walked along the west walltop, calling out for Dwopple at the top of his voice. They had searched all morning but not a trace of the little one could be found. Stopping briefly at the threshold over the main gate, the hare breathed deeply. Despite his constant chastisement of the mousebabe, he was secretly very fond of him. He did not notice the Marlfox emerge from the ditch until the creature hailed him.

'Hey, rabbit!'

Florian stared regally down his nose at the Marlfox. 'Huh! Rabbit y'self, you speckled scrap o' jetsam. I'd come down there an' drub some manners into y'hide if I had me bally stick with me, wot. Count y'self lucky, measle-features!'

Rusvul, who had just emerged from the gatehouse, heard Florian's voice and called up to him. 'Hi there, mister Florian, who are ye talkin' to, yoreself?'

The hare was in no mood to be bandied with. 'M'self? Pish tush, sah, never! Actually I'm exchangin' insults with one of those Marlfox types down on the path, doncha know.'

Rusvul dashed off, roaring at the top of his lungs, 'Marlfox out on the path! Marlfox outside the gate!'

The Abbey bells boomed out an alarm. In a short time most of Redwall was atop the wall, armed with anything that came to paw: ladles, shovels, curtain poles and sundry everyday implements. Mokkan the Marlfox leader backed off to the ditch edge on the path's far side, ready to flee if things got more dangerous. Cregga's voice was low and menacing, but quite clear as the exchange took place.

'You've got a mousebabe, one of our young 'uns.'

'Aye, that's right, had him since yesterday noon.'

'Clever of you, and now you've come to bargain. What do you want?'

'Oh, I don't know yet. What've you got in there? A rich Abbey like yours, should be something valuable enough to save a life.'

'We do not hoard treasure at Redwall. If you need victuals we can give you a supply of the best food prepared anywhere.'

Mokkan shook his head, almost pityingly at the simple offer. 'No, no, food doesn't interest us, there's plenty in Mossflower. Let me gather my brothers and sisters, we'll come into your Abbey and take a look around. I'll wager Marlfoxes could find something of value as a ransom for your babe.'

Skipper of otters wiggled a paw in one ear. 'Did I 'ear that right? You want t'bring a pack o' your kind inside Redwall an' take a root about? Lissen, snotnose, 'tis only the grass that's green round 'ere, not the Abbeybeasts!'

Mokkan drew his axe and tested the blade edge. 'You have until midnight. After that you won't see Dwopple again!'

Shouts of indignation rang from the walltops.

'Don't you dare touch that Dibbun!'

'You stinkin' coward!'

'Hurr, big bravebeast loik ee, slayin' liddle 'uns, you'm nought but sloim'n'mud!'

'Harm not my precious mite, sir, I beg you. Take my life instead!'

'For shame! You, sir, are nought but a scum-wallower!'

Janglur Swifteye held up his paws for silence. 'Save yore breath, friends. 'Tis wasted on the likes of that 'un. Lissen, fox, we'll meet you at the southwest corner of this wall at midnight. I'll see these Redwallers bring lots o' pretty things to trade for Dwopple. Agreed?'

Mokkan smiled up at the squirrel. 'I'm glad there's one creature at Redwall with a bit of sense. I accept your offer, squirrel, but make sure whoever comes is unarmed. One false trick will cost the mousebabe his life!'

As the Marlfox vanished into the ditch the Abbey gates burst open. Log a Log and his Guosim shrews came pouring out, rapiers drawn. They leapt into the ditch, but there was not a trace of the Marlfox. Rusvul patted the shrew's back as he returned through the gate. 'Tough luck, matey. You was just a smidgen too slow there.'

The shrew Chieftain sheathed his rapier and helped to bar the gate. 'The fox just disappeared. Vanished.'

Rusvul snorted. 'They ain't magic. I know 'cos I pierced one of 'em through the shoulder with my javelin. Hah! That'n didn't look too magic, scrabblin' off on all fours!'

Janglur bounded down the wallsteps. 'Let's go to Cavern Hole. I've got a plan!'

Rusvul called Dann, Song and Dippler to him. 'Right, 'tis about time you three started to grow up a bit. I've got a meetin' with Janglur an' the others in Cavern Hole, so that means we need to mount a guard on the ramparts, in case Marlfoxes or water rats come back. How d'you feel about some sentry duty?'

The three friends were proud to accept. Dann spoke for them. 'You can trust us, we won't let Redwall down!'

Rusvul nodded approvingly at his son. 'Spoken like a Reguba! See what ole Butty has at the gatehouse in the way of weaponry an' arm yoreselves. Keep a sharp eye on the woodlands an' don't be afraid to yell for help if'n you needs it.'

In the gatehouse, Friar Butty was poring through old record books. He indicated a long, narrow corner cupboard. 'There's weapons in there, I think, though they've not seen the light o' day in many a season. Help yourselves. Personally, I could have done with your assistance in my researches, but if you three are needed on the walltops then so be it. I'll come up and let you know if I discover anything about the Marlfoxes or their hidden island.'

Hardly a breeze stirred the treetops of Mossflower Wood. Grasshoppers chirruped and butterflies winged placidly in the shimmering midday heat on the western plains and flatlands. Beneath Dann's footpaws the broad sandstone walkway was pleasantly warm as he paced back to the threshold from the east walltop. The young squirrel had outfitted himself with a long spear and a dented copper helmet, which he had dusted off and polished. Song had found something that fitted her paw as if it were made for her: a short solid stick, with a ball of green stone mounted on one end. She twirled it skilfully, feeling its balance as she returned from her patrol of the south battlements. Dippler was waiting at the threshold for them. The young shrew looked comical. He had found a chainmail tunic and a crested helmet complete with visor, and was practically staggering under their weight. Beside his shrew rapier Dippler carried an immense halberd, the heavy long-poled weapon which is both spear and battleaxe combined. He threw up a clanking salute at his friends. 'Anythin' to report, mates?'

Dann took off his helmet and mopped his brow. 'Whew! All I've got t'report is that 'tis roastin' under this helmet. Aren't you hot under that lot, Dipp?'

Dippler was, but he would not admit it. 'Oh no, matey, I'm just fine, fine!'

Song could not resist laughing at the small overdressed

shrew. 'Hahaha! There's a little cloud o' steam comin' from under your helmet, Dipp. Are you cookin' a stew in there?'

Dann joined in the laughter. Dippler gave them both a haughty glare from beneath his rusty visor and clanked off, calling back, 'Laugh all y'like, outfits like this'n have saved many a warrior's life. Hi! Who goes there, friend or foebeast?'

Sister Sloey clambered up the gatehouse wallsteps, lugging a basket covered with a white cloth. She snorted at the challenge. 'Foebeast, indeed! Do I look like a foebeast? Cregga and Brother Melilot decided that you guards had best take lunch up here on the walltops. Here, take this basket, Song, my paws are old'n'tired.'

The three friends felt very grown-up and privileged to have lunch sent out to them as they spread the cloth and laid out the food. Dippler even removed his helmet.

'Well, this's the stuff to give the troops. Good ole Melilot! That dandelion an' burdock cordial looks nice'n' cool. Pour me a beaker, Dann. Look at this, mushroom'n'celery turnover, leek pasty, apple'n'blackberry crumble an' a bowl of nutcream. They certainly know 'ow t'feed us wallguards at this Abbey, mates!'

Friar Butty joined them, carrying a big ancient volume. 'Dearie me, Song, I wish you'd have a word with that grandma of yours. She's turned my gatehouse into a dormitory, and she and Nutwing have taken to coming there for their afternoon nap. Between them they've driven me out with their snoring and snuffling!'

Song poured the old squirrel a beaker of cordial. 'Never mind, fresh air's better for you than a dusty old gatehouse, Friar. What's that book you've brought up here?'

The Redwall Recorder opened the volume at a place he had marked. 'This is a chronicle from the time of Abbess Vale. I couldn't even begin to guess how many long seasons ago it was written, but it seems that two

Redwallers, a squirrel named Samkim and a mole called Arula, actually found the great inland lake and knew of the lost island.'

Dann cut himself a slice of pasty. 'Is there anything in the book about Marlfoxes?'

Friar Butty flicked a few pages, indicating the state of them. 'I wouldn't know, Dann. Somebeast left this volume outdoors and open in the rain during bygone seasons. The chapters that are of interest to us have been ruined by water. Parchment's flaked and the ink has run – 'tis a real mess.'

Dippler pawed through the spoiled pages. 'Bit of a shame, Friar mate. So you didn't find out anythin'?'

Butty stared pensively at the book. 'Maybe not about the foxes, but I think there's directions to the lake. Bit of a puzzle, though.'

Song was intrigued. She loved nothing better than solving mysteries. 'Here, let's all take a close look at it. We've eight sharp eyes and four good brains between us. Friar Butty, get ready with your pen an' parchment to record whatever we find!'

In Cavern Hole a desperate plan, calling for deception and daring, was being outlined by Janglur Swifteye. The squirrel warrior drew a square on the tabletop with charcoal. 'This is the outer walls, this mark here's the main gate. Tonight we meet the foxes and water rats outside at the southwest corner by the path. Make no mistake, mates, they'll come in force – well armed, too. Show 'em one sign o' weakness an' we'll all be slain!'

Cregga's blind eyes seemed to stare straight at him. 'You're right of course, Janglur. Treachery is the pawmark of foxes and vermin. So what do you propose we do?'

The squirrel's hooded eyes flicked idly round the table. 'We take everybeast who can wield a weapon. Remember I said to the fox this mornin' that we'd bring a selection of valuables to trade for liddle Dwopple. Well, we'll be carryin' four or five bundles, though only one'll contain trinkets. The rest will be bundles of weapons. Me an' Rusvul will open the bundle o' trinkets an' when we gives the word you'll all pull out the arms an' attack. Me an' Rusvul will snatch Dwopple an' pass 'im to Cregga, she'll protect 'im. Log a Log, some o' yore Guosim shrews will be with us, but as soon as it goes dark tonight, I wants you t'take half yore tribe out quiet like. Go straight out onto the flatlands an' sweep back so that yore well below the Abbey to the south. Then get in the fields an' woodland fringe. When you see the attack's started I want you to charge their rear an' take 'em by surprise.'

Tragglo Cellarhog scratched his headspikes. 'But why, Janglur? If we get the babe back, wot's the point o' fightin' further? We'd be best gettin' back inside o' the Abbey quick an' safe as possible. Why stay an' fight with 'em?'

Murmurs of agreement with Tragglo's reasoning came from all round the table. Janglur sighed and tossed down his charcoal stick. 'Tell 'em why, Rusvul.'

Rusvul Reguba pounded the tabletop slowly as he spoke, as if driving every word home. 'Because they'll slaughter us if we don't get 'em first! To fight vermin you gotta think the same way they do. If they lose the babe an' don't git no ransom fer 'im, then believe me, they won't just pack up an' go away. Oh no, mates, they'll be out fer revenge on Redwall, an' they won't rest till they gets it!'

Rusvul's paw rested on the table. Skipper's closed over it. 'He's right. Take my affidavit on it, mates!'

Cregga Badgermum nodded her huge striped head. 'It's a perilous plan, but I trust our warriors. All in favour say aye.'

Every creature in Cavern Hole gave their answer without hesitation.

'Aye!'

Mokkan had one hundred and ninety water rats and five

other Marlfoxes under his command, and he planned to use them well. They sat about on the creek bank as he issued final orders.

'You all know what to do. Anybeast who does not do it right answers to me. We move out at twilight. Rest now, but see that your weapons are attended to, make sure those blades are sharp and ready to serve the High Queen's brood. Ascrod, Vannan, which two do you need?'

Ascrod sought out the two they wanted. 'Dakkle and Beelu, you will accompany me and my sister.'

The two rats in question saluted. Mokkan went and sat next to Gelltor, who was changing the dressing on his shoulder. 'How goes it with your wound now, brother?'

Gelltor bit his lip as he peeled off a dockleaf which had stuck to the fur around his injury. 'None the better for your asking!'

Mokkan lay back and closed his eyes, the sunlight making him almost invisible as it dappled leaf patterns down upon his body. 'Don't worry, you'll have your revenge tonight on the Redwallers, a much quicker vengeance than your idea of all-out war.'

10

Florian Dugglewoof Wilffachop had decided that the best thing for creatures going into action was to inspire them with a stirring ballad. Accordingly he kitted himself out in a heroic toga, brandished a floppy sword and glared at his audience ferociously through a monocle with no glass in it. The Redwallers sat about in a semicircle by the Abbey pond, whilst Florian pranced about on the water's edge and treated them to a rendition of 'The battle for the final crumpet'. Roop, the mole, accompanied him on a small accordion and Runktipp sang the refrain. Florian scowled savagely at a few tittering Dibbuns as he launched into the opening lines of the song.

'Oh 'twas on the umpty-ninth of spring,
When a duck blew on a trumpet,
I led me army from behind,
To the battle of the final crumpet.
Some wore boots an' some wore clogs,
An' some wore big long faces,
An' two fat moles fell down with colds,
Before we'd marched ten paces.
At the battle of the final crumpet,
I very near lost me life,

When I got punched upon the nose,
By a big bad hedgehog's wife.
Then all broke out in mutiny,
When a mouse with a moustache said,
"Lie down me lads afore they charge,
So they'll all think we're dead!"
Well there we sat whilst all around,
The spears an' shafts were thuddin',
A-drinkin' goosegog cordial wine,
An' eatin' cabbage puddin'.
We finally defeated them,
When the duck tripped on his trumpet,
An' I got a feather in me cap,
'Cos I ate the final crumpet!'

Florian sang the final two lines whilst waving his sword and dancing energetically backwards for effect. He stumbled on one of his outsized boots and fell into the pond, to riotous applause. Skipper shook tears of helpless mirth from his eyes. 'Sink me rudder, mates, we're in fer a lively time if'n that 'un's defendin' the Abbey tonight!'

On the walltop there was great hilarity. Song, Dann and Dippler chuckled aloud, watching the two moles, Roop and Muggle, trying to haul the ungainly hare from the pond. Friar Butty tapped the tattered volume with his quill. 'Can we get back to our work, please?'

Still smiling, the three friends turned to the parchment the old Recorder had translated from the washed out, inkstained journal of Abbess Vale, a wise creature who had ruled Redwall in the far-off seasons. Dippler was no great scholar, and he stared at the Friar's neat rows of writing blankly. 'What does it all mean?'

Friar Butty flicked the pages of the ancient book. 'As far as I can make out it was written by a squirrel called Samkim in his latter seasons. He must have been a tricky creature, though – he wrote directions to the Great Lake in the form of a riddling rhyme. Listen to this.

'At the rear of redstone wall,
Find me o'er where breaks the day,
You cannot, shall not walk at all,
Just follow as I run away.
Discover the speechless hidden mouth,
Alas, my friends, our ways part there,
Go down green tunnel, bounden south,
Through trees with blossoms in their hair.
Then when the sky shows blue and light,
And clear down to the bed you gaze,
Be not deceived by rainbows bright,
Beware tall stones and misted haze.
Leaping boiling, stealing breath,
None can stand against this might,
Which sweeps the traveller down to death,
In caves of grim eternal night.
And should you live to seek the lake,
Watch for the fish of blue and grey,
Betwixt those two's the path you take,
Good fortune wend you on your way!'

Dippler scratched his fur beneath the weighty chainmail suit. The young Guosim shrew was still puzzled by the cryptic words. 'Sounds pretty enough, but I still ain't got a clue, mates.'

Friar Butty smiled at Dippler's inexperience. 'Fiddley dee, young feller, you'd be the wisest creature around if you did. Riddling poems are not written so that we may solve them at a glance, right, Song?'

The pretty young squirrel nodded as she scanned the verse. 'That's correct, Friar. We need to study this thing hard, take it a line at a time and concentrate upon the words.'

Dann settled his chin on both paws, staring hard at the puzzle. 'Hmm. By the look of it this doesn't mention anythin' about Marlfoxes.'

Dippler struggled out of the chainmail, which had

finally become too uncomfortable for him. 'Maybe it doesn't, Dann, but it might lead us to know 'em better – where they come from, why they made such a journey, an' so on.'

Friar Butty patted his young friend's back heartily. 'Well said, Dippler! I think you've the makings of a great scholar.'

Accompanied by Log a Log and some of his shrews, Janglur and Rusvul were collecting together all the serviceable weapons they could lay paws upon. Carrying bags made from old curtain drapes they approached the gatehouse, where Cregga had told them there was a cupboard full of disused armaments. Suddenly, Rusvul stopped so sharply that Janglur almost collided with him. Log a Log looked at the warrior squirrel, who was glaring grim-faced at the walltop.

'Rusvul, wot's the matter, matey?'

Ignoring the shrew Chieftain's question, Rusvul shouted angrily, 'Dannflor Reguba, what'n the name o' blazes d'you think yore playin' at up there?'

Still sitting poring over the writings, Dann waved cheerily down to his father. 'We're tryin' to solve a riddle. 'Tis all about that isle on the great lake an' how t'get there.'

Rusvul slammed his javelin point hard into the ground. 'A warrior who's put on guard duty should be doin' just that, guardin' the walltops! Not foolin' about with games!'

Janglur cautioned his friend in a quiet voice. 'Go easy, mate, Dann's still only a young 'un.'

But Rusvul's unpredictable temper allowed no margin for reason. 'Supposin' the foebeast launched an attack on the east wall while yore sittin' foolin' about on the west wall, what then?'

Friar Butty hastily bundled up the rhyme and passed it to Song, who stowed it in her tunic as all four stood up.

The Friar spread his paws wide, bowing slightly to the party below. 'You mustn't blame them, friends, 'twas all my idea. I thought that young fresh minds would help me with my investigations.'

The burly shrew Fenno pointed an accusing paw at Dippler. 'Hah! Might o' known he'd be part o' this. Remember wot 'appened to our logboats when he was supposed t'be guardin' 'em, eh?'

Fenno found that he could say no more, because Log a Log's rapier point was beneath his chin, forcing his head back. The shrew Chieftain spoke calmly. 'Who asked yore opinion, loudmouth? Keep out o' this or I'll pin yore big tongue t'that liddle thing y'call a brain!'

Song tried to calm things down by addressing her father. 'We really were guarding the walls. It was only when lunch arrived that we took a little break and had a look at the Friar's rhyme.'

Janglur Swifteye winked lazily at his daughter. 'I ain't complainin', missie. I felt good'n'safe down below in Cavern 'Ole whilst you an' yore pals stood sentry up there.' He shrugged and nudged Rusvul playfully. 'Wasn't you ever young yoreself, mate? Come on, let it be. Dann's a fine son, just like my Song's a good daughter. We should be proud of 'em.'

But Rusvul would not let it be. He pointed an accusing paw at Dann. 'A guard's a guard an' a warrior's a warrior, not some kind o' dusty scholar. More so if yore name is Reguba. That's a title to live up to, son, always remember that!'

A voice boomed out behind them. 'Stop all this! I will not have arguing and bad feeling within these Abbey walls!' Cregga Badgermum strode up, with Skipper at her side. The big otter stood forward and spoke for her.

'Log a Log, put up yore blade, mate. 'Tis against Redwall's rules of 'ospitality to draw steel agin' another whilst yore a guest 'ere. An' the rest of you, 'ear this. If you got any grievances whilst yore at Redwall Abbey, then the council of elders'll sort 'em out. All must live in peace 'ere without arguin' or fightin'. So settle any differences or ferget 'em. Show an example t'the young 'uns, eh?'

Log a Log sheathed his rapier and shook Skipper's paw. 'Sounds like good sense t'me, messmate. Right, let's get on with gatherin' weapons so we can show a liddle good manners to those Marlfoxes an' water rats tonight!'

The dispute broke up amid chuckles and laughter. Cregga reached out a paw and halted Rusvul as he moved off. The good badger spoke to him out of earshot of the rest. 'You have not been here many seasons, Rusvul, and I know you had a hard life. But you should not have shamed your son by shouting at him in front of otherbeasts like that. Dann is a fine young creature, but like us all he is bound to make mistakes. It's part of growing up. I know you honour your title of Reguba, and the way of the warrior is not an easy one. However, it is no bad thing for a warrior to have a scholar's knowledge. It can bring wisdom to his judgement and shrewdness to his thinking.'

Rusvul patted the badger's wide paw. 'Yore right, of course, marm, but 'tis no easy thing t'be both father an' mother to a young 'un. I'm more used to fightin' than to parentin'.'

Cregga turned her eyes towards him as if she could see him. 'Good. Then show us what you are made of out there tonight.'

Five sacks of weapons had been collected, blades and short arms which were easily concealed within the curtain bags. Supper was taken early in Great Hall, and before it was served Skipper gave final orders.

'Log a Log, straight after you've eaten, take some Guosim out. Go from the main gate across into the ditch, follow it north a bit then sweep out an' come back down t'the south woodland fringe. We'll give you a shout when we're ready for yore lot to attack from the rear. Janglur an' Rusvul, you'll lead the party carryin' the sacks of arms. Tragglo an' Gubbio, you'll be in charge of our own Redwallers an' the rest o' the shrews. When you see Janglur'n'Rusvul open the sack o' trinkets, that's when you grab the weapons out of the sacks an' attack. Make sure you shout'n'yell plenty to confuse 'em. I'll grab Dwopple an' pass the liddle 'un safe to Cregga, an' we'll get 'im back to the Abbey. Friar Butty, 'ave the gate ready, an' soon as Cregga an' Dwopple are inside, lock it! I'll come back an' join the rest of ye. 'Tis a scrap I'd 'ate to miss! If all goes well we should be soon bangin' on the gate to get back in, so lissen for us, Friar. Now, Sister Sloey, Melilot an' Nutwing, you take all the elders an' Dibbuns down to the wine cellars. Stay there safe an' silent, you'll be fine. Dann, Song an' Dippler, you three'll stay guard 'ere in Great Hall. Make sure none enters here save Redwallers. The safety of our Abbey's in yore paws. So that's the plan. Good luck to all an' blood'n'vinegar to our foes!'

Ellayo looked uncertainly at Skipper. 'But they are so young, Skip. Are you sure they are ready for such a great task?'

'Don't worry yourself, marm. With our plan no rat or fox will find its way inside these walls.'

Everybeast pounded the tables and roared approval, though none more than Dann, Song, and Dippler, who were flushed with pride at the enormous responsibility Skipper had bestowed upon them. Badgermum Cregga spoke when the din had died down. 'I think a warriors' grace is in order before we eat.

'Fate and fortunes, seasons fair,
Be kind to us this day,
Let nobeast here whom we hold dear,
See comrades borne away.
May the strong defend the weak,

Protect those who take part,
Grant victory of truth and right,
To warriors brave of heart.
Banish the foebeast from our land,
And when new seasons fall,
Leave not an empty space of grief,
Amongst us at Redwall!'

There was silence for a moment, then Florian Duggle-woof Wilffachop added a few lines in a stage whisper that could be heard by all.

'An' if on an empty tummy I'm slain,
Then I'll jolly well never get killed again,
So pass the pudden an' fetch the pies,
An' I'll give the foebeast a rotten surprise!'

Deesum rapped the hare's paw sharply with a spoon. 'Mister Florian, what a dreadful thing to say!'

Florian wrung his paw and blew upon it. 'Owooch! Save your aggression for the enemy, marm! I say, what a super pasty. Is that all for me, wot?'

Gurrbowl the cellarmole sliced off a wedge of pasty and presented it to the gluttonous hare. 'This yurr pasty be's full o' woild garlic, maister. You'm may not loik et, 'tis powerful strong, ho urr!'

Much to the amusement of everybeast, Florian ate a double helping with great relish. 'Exceedingly tasty, my good mole. Garlic, y'say? Well, at least I won't have much trouble bowlin' the enemy over. I'll just shout in their faces like this. Whoooooo are yoooooooooou!'

Deesum fell back, clutching a serviette to her nose. 'Really, sir, do you have to do that?'

Rimrose helped herself to some mint wafers and maple sauce. 'Were you ever in a battle, mister Florian?'

Borrakul the otter paused, a ladle half in and half out of a bowl of summer vegetable soup. 'Oh, don't start him, marm, please!'

But Florian was on fine form. Piling his plate high with woodland trifle and plum tart, he put on a brave face. 'Battle did y'say, marm? I once frightened off a thousand flippin' frogs armed with nought but a pail o' wet blackberries!'

Tragglo Spearback swirled the October Ale in his tankard. 'Don't tell such whackin' fibs, you great furry fraud!'

Deesum looked up from a slice of strawberry flan she was nibbling. 'Oh, but he did. Let me tell you how it happened. We'd been picking blackberries and had collected a small pailful, but unfortunately baby Dwopple upset them in some mud. Mister Florian took them down to the stream to wash them clean while we set up camp. It was in deep woodlands down southwest. While he was away we were suddenly surrounded by masses of frogs. There must have been a thousand of the dreadful things, and they looked very aggressive and pretty angry with us. I think it was because we had done our washing in a poolful of their tadpoles. Anyhow, they had us captured and looked as if they were planning something ugly as a punishment for the whole troupe. Go on, you tell them what happened next, sir.'

Florian smiled modestly from behind his heaped platter. 'Oh, 'twas nothin' really. Y'see, I'd spotted what was goin' on. Those frog chaps looked rather peeved an' I thought they might harm my troupe. I had the jolly old pail full of water, with the blackberries in it – they'd gotten messed up a bit an' looked rather mushy, but still jolly tasty, wot. So I comes trundlin' up, pullin' the drippin' blackberries out o' the water pail an' scoffin' 'em by the pawful, shoutin' out loud in a fearsome voice. Tadpoles! Haharr, tadpoles (says I), nothin' nicer for lunch than a perishin' pailful o' tadpoles except a nice juicy green frog or two! I say, you chaps, hello there! Saved some frogs for me, wot wot?'

Elachim shook with laughter as he recalled the

incident. 'Hohoho! You should've seen those frogs scatter. Some of 'em leapt clear over big bushes. They thought ole Florian was comin' to scoff 'em! Hahaha! An' there he stood, cool as y'like, shovin' wet blackberries down 'is face an' pretendin' they was tadpoles!'

Florian mused around a spoonful of trifle. 'Hmm, maybe some of 'em were. That stream was full of all manner of small black wriggly things, blackberries, tadpoles, who could jolly well tell? Silly bloomin' frogs. Fancy takin' a perfectly respectable cove like m'self for a cannibal frogscoffer. Tchah!'

Winking broadly at Nutwing, Friar Butty shook his head sympathetically. 'Indeed, how could they have made such a dreadful error?'

The lively meal progressed into the evening, with the Wandering Noonvale Companions Troupe rendering one of the songs from their repertoire in three-part harmony, with the hedgehog Runktipp acting as conductor. Log a Log watched Abbey lamplighters illuminating the candles and lanterns around Great Hall as daylight's last gleam deserted long stained-glass windows. Rising silently from the table, he nodded to his chosen group of Guosim. Quietly they checked their rapiers, slings and stone pouches, then slipped off into the gathering night, with the melodious strains of the singers echoing around the hall after them.

'I paint my face or wear a mask,
For I'll be anybeast you ask,
As I wander on my way.
A skilful tumbler bounding high,
A pitiful mope who'll make you cry,
My actor's part I play.
And what care you if I am sad,
Or if ill fortune I have had,
'Tis just a clown, you say.
Aye, just a droll who plays a part,

Who travels in a painted cart,
From dawn to dusk each day.
An actor can be young or old,
Figure of fun or hero bold,
From tears to laughter without pause,
I strut the stage to your applause,
Then I look in my mirror and say, "Hey,
What fool shall I play today?" '

11

Mokkan glanced up at the waning moon settling itself behind a rambling cloudbank. Somewhere off in the woodland a lone nightjar warbled, while a warm breeze stirred sedge and rye grasses on the ditch top. It was a night perfect for ambush. The water rats and Marlfoxes crouched in the ditch bed, spears and blades blackened by firesmoke so they would not betray a glimmer. The vixen Predak moved silent as night shadow down the ditch to where the main force waited with Mokkan. She gestured back towards the main Abbey gate. 'Ascrod and Vannan are in place with their two rats.'

Mokkan ventured a swift peek over the ditch top. 'No sign of the Redwallers yet?'

Predak scratched her muzzle, betraying a slight nervousness. 'Maybe 'tis a trick, perhaps they won't come?'

The Marlfox leader's teeth gleamed in the darkness. He kicked the bundle containing Dwopple, who had been fed a potion of herbs to keep him in a drugged sleep. 'Oh, they'll come, take my word on it. Those Abbeybeasts are far too honest and dull to risk any tricks. This mousebabe is their main concern. Being the virtuous fools they are, they'll expect us to play by their rules and return the babe in exchange for a few trinkets. Oafs! They'll learn that dealing with Marlfoxes is like trying to hold a pawful of smoke.'

Log a Log stood with his Guosim shrews, well hidden by the bushy southeast fringe of Mossflower. Dodging from fern clump to long grass, the scout Bargle arrived and nodded over towards the ditch. 'Vermin are still there, Chief, they ain't made a move back or for'ard. Couldn't get close enough to 'ear wot they was sayin'.'

The shrew Chieftain peered through the night towards the ditch. 'It doesn't make any difference, mate. We never came to chat with 'em!'

Bargle pawed his rapier hilt thoughtfully. 'Y'know, they don't know we're 'ere, but we know exac'ly where they are. May'ap 'twouldn't be a bad idea t'sneak up be'ind 'em an' pick off a few to thin their ranks, eh?'

Log a Log sighed regretfully. 'I was thinkin' the same thing meself, matey, but we'd best stick t'the plan an' wait for the signal.'

Bargle was weighing the land up. 'That's a fair distance to charge, from 'ere across open ground to the sou'west wallcorner. We could become targets in plain view.'

Log a Log ruffled his scout's ears fondly. 'Then we'll just 'ave t'spread out an' duck'n'weave.'

'Aye, an' get ourselves killed fer creatures who ain't even shrews!'

Log a Log turned to the speaker. 'I knowed it wouldn't take long fer you to pipe up, Fenno. When all this is over me'n'you are goin' t'take a stroll in the forest, outside where we won't be abusin' Redwall's rules.'

Fenno glared at the smaller and older figure. 'I'll look forward to it. I'm sick o' you pushin' me around!'

Log a Log's paw shot out and dragged Fenno forward by his ear. 'So be it, but until then y'can stay in front where I can see yer. I don't want you be'ind me when the action starts!'

*

Dann, Song and Dippler watched as Sister Sloey and Brother Melilot guided elders and Dibbuns downstairs to the wine cellars. Melilot waved to them from the stairwell. 'They're all accounted for, you can leave them to us now.'

Song saluted him with her greenstone-tipped stick. 'Thanks, Brother. We'll be up here if you need us.'

Dippler crossed Great Hall to where the main party were assembled. Skipper hid a smile as the small chainmail-laden figure trundled up. 'Yer a fearsome sight, matey. Now don't forget an' bar the door soon as we leave, an' don't lift that bar to anybeast except us when we gets back. Clear?'

Dippler tried a fancy salute and almost tripped over the huge halberd he was toting. 'Clear, Skip. I won't even let an ant pass!'

Cregga placed her paw on the wonderful tapestry, touching the spot where stood the likeness of Martin the Warrior. 'Guide us to victory this night and let us bring the mousebabe back to Redwall unharmed. Rusvul, Janglur, lead on.'

They passed through the main wallgate, treading carefully to stop the weapons clanking in their sacks. Friar Butty and Nutwing held the gates open, wishing the rescuers good luck as they went.

'Let's hope all goes well, Tragglo!'

'Oh, it'll be all right. Just make sure you stay awake, Nutwing.'

'Hmm mm, stay awake yourself. You'll need your wits about you out there tonight.'

'Aye, we will that. See you later, eh, Friar.'

'I certainly hope so, my friend, with all my heart!'

Standing out on the path the old squirrel Recorder and his owl companion watched the procession start south down the path. They did not even feel the draught from the swirling cloaks of Ascrod and Vannan as the two

Marlfoxes, accompanied by the rats Dakkle and Beelu, slipped into Redwall like four dark wraiths. From the shadows of the wallsteps the vermin intruders watched whilst Butty and Nutwing secured the gates, chunnering away at each other as old friends always do.

'Come on, you ancient featherbag, lift your end of the bar!'

'Hmm mm, I am lifting. Phwaw! This bar gets heavier every day. Are you sure you're lifting your end, old bushtail?'

'Of course I am! Right, hup, two, three! There, that does it. What's the matter now? You've got a face on you like a squashed pie.'

'Hmm mm, got something sticking in my leg.'

'Let me see. Oh, 'tis only a splinter. Come in the gatehouse and I'll get it out. Stop hoppin' about like a one-legged duck!'

'Hmm. Only a splinter, he says. Feels more like a log to me!'

The trespassers waited until the gatehouse door closed before making their way across the silent lawns towards the Abbey.

Cregga was not too familiar with the outside path, and allowed Skipper to guide her towards the southwest corner where the rendezvous was to take place. 'Are they there as they said they'd be, Skip?'

Rusvul's voice murmured low to one side of Cregga. 'I see the scum. They're lyin' in the ditch, speartops pokin' up.'

Janglur's eyes shifted under their heavy lids. 'Right, mate, I sees them meself now. There's that Marlfox climbin' out, two rats be'ind him. They're carryin' somethin', looks like the mousebabe done up in a sack.'

The Redwallers halted at the southwest corner. As Mokkan walked forward the other three Marlfoxes led the water rats out of the ditch in a pincer movement to form a semicircle in front of the Redwallers, standing with their backs to the wall. Janglur nodded curtly to Mokkan. 'Well, fox, got a liddle 'un with yer?'

At a signal from Mokkan two rats dumped the sack containing Dwopple in front of the Marlfox. He placed a footpaw on it. 'He's right here. Brought the valuables with you?'

Janglur indicated the Redwallers bearing the curtain bags. 'We've brought 'em, but y'don't get to see one trinket until you show us the mousebabe unharmed.'

Mokkan smiled thinly and bowed slightly to his adversary. 'My compliments, you show good sense. Show them the mousebabe.'

One of the water rats sprang forward and slit the sack expertly with a small thin dagger. Baby Dwopple rolled out, curled in a ball and snoring uproariously. Mokkan pointed at the curtain bags. 'Now let's see the ransom!'

Janglur winked at Rusvul. 'Open 'er up, mate!'

Between them the two squirrel warriors ripped aside the ties on the bag of trinkets they were carrying, smashing it in the faces of Mokkan and his companions with a mighty roar.

'Redwaaaaaaallll!'

Then the action began at an alarming rate.

Skipper hurled himself headlong at the ground, snatching Dwopple and laying flat two rats with flailing footpaws and thwacking tailrudder. Redwallers tore open the bags of weapons and went straight at it. Skipper placed Dwopple in the paws of Cregga, and between them they battled their way through a sea of water rats, regardless of slashing blades and stabbing spears. Cregga, who had once been the mightiest of badger Warriors, roared like thunder splitting the skies. With Dwopple's tunic gripped in her teeth she lashed out with both paws, ripping, wounding and slaying everybeast that came within the range of her frightening destructive power, snapping spears like matchwood and bending blades like green twigs. Tragglo Spearback had a large bunghammer, which he swung with both paws, and the rest grabbed what they could, yelling wildly.

'Redwaaaaaaalllll! Blood'n'vinegaaaaaar!'

Marlfox axes slashed the air and spears bristled in the night as the vermin pressed in. Anybeast unfortunate enough to fall was trampled flat in the mêlée. Though they were heavily outnumbered, the Noonvale Troupe were giving a splendid account of themselves. Florian had formed them into a tight circle. Standing at its centre wielding a long grass rake, dealing out devastating blows over the heads of his companions to the rats who pressed them in on all sides, the lanky hare boomed out his challenge. 'C'mon, babe-stealers, try me for size, wot! I'm the son of the rip-snortin' rat-tippin' Wilffachop, try stealin' me away in a sack an' I'll peel your hides to th'bone an' feed y'to each other!'

As soon as he heard the warcry of Redwall being shouted over by the southwest corner, Log a Log drew his rapier and roared out the battle call of the Guosim shrews.

'Logalogalogalogaloooooog! Chaaaaarge!'

The shrews took off at a dead run across the open land, whirling slings and slashing the air with their short rapiers. Gripped by the heat of the charge, Log a Log sped past Fenno, who had conveniently stumbled and tripped. The brave shrew Chieftain had made a fatal error, and the coward seized his chance. Jumping up, he threw his rapier like a spear, straight into the unprotected back of his Chief.

Log a Log staggered on a few paces then fell, unnoticed in the night by the other shrews who were running eagerly into battle. Sudden panic at the ruthless murder he had committed gripped Fenno. Turning, he fled back into the cover of Mossflower Wood.

Meanwhile, Skipper pounded on the main Abbey wallgate, calling urgently to the gatekeepers. 'Open up, mates, we got the liddle 'un. Hurry now, Cregga marm's wounded!'

It took a moment or two for Butty and Nutwing to lift the heavy crossbeam out of its holders, then the gates creaked open. Skipper pushed Cregga and Dwopple inside, baring his teeth in a ferocious grin at the two elders. 'Take care of 'em. I'm off back to the fightin'!'

Mokkan knew that his side had the upper paw. Triumphantly he was shouting orders to his Marlfoxes. 'Predak, keep 'em pinned to the wall! Gelltor, attack those two squirrel warriors, keep them busy. Ziral, take more rats, stop that hare and his creatures breaking through the cordon!' Swinging his double-headed axe, Mokkan pressed forward savagely, fully intent on inflicting total retribution on the Redwallers, whose courageous but foolish ruse had gone awry.

12

The water rat, Beelu, stood on the lawn at the back of Redwall Abbey. His keen eyes soon spotted what he was after, a small dormitory window, below which was a protuberance in the shape of a gargoyle head carved on to a thick spur of sandstone. Beelu unwound a plaited hide rope from round his waist, freeing the three-pronged grapnel hook hanging from it. The water rat gave the tough thin rope a few swings, paying it out as he whirled the grapnel in a wide circle. When he was ready, he released the rope at the crucial point, allowing the hook to soar upward and latch over the gargoyle with a dull clank of metal striking stone. Beelu stood stock still and waited for several moments, listening intently. When he was sure nobeast had heard the noise he began to climb swiftly, hauling himself up, paw over paw, with both footpaws braced firmly against the wall. Once up to the window he chose a tiny pane. Opening his belt pouch, he drew forth a piece of bark, plastered with a thick compound of honey and soil, which he stuck to the window pane. There was virtually no sound as he dealt the bark a sharp tap with his dagger handle, but still he paused and waited. After a short time he peeled the bark from the thin glass, shards of broken window sticking to it like crystal. Cautiously the rat loosened more broken pieces from the pane, dropping them to the grass below. When he had enough space to work, Beelu put his paw through the hole he had made and undid the catch. A moment later he was inside the Abbey and on the dormitory staircase.

Dippler sat in the big ornate chair which had been used by all the Abbots and Abbesses of Redwall. The young shrew impudently placed both footpaws on the table and leaned back, lifting the visor of his heavy crested helmet. 'Wonder 'ow 'tis goin' out at the southwest corner?'

Dann had his old copper helmet full of hazelnuts, which he was lining up on the floorstones and cracking with light taps of his spearbutt. He winked confidently at the shrew. 'I'll wager those Marlfoxes an' their water rats are sorry they ever captured Dwopple. Our side'll be givin' 'em blood'n'vinegar an' their own tails for supper. What d'you think, Song?'

The young squirrel was standing in front of the tapestry, admiring the heroic figure of Martin the Warrior. 'Oh, there's no doubt that the vermin are on to a good hiding and a lesson they won't forget. With warriors like your father an' mine, an' Skipper, we can't lose. Just look at this picture of Martin. I'll wager he could have cleared the lot up single-pawed!'

Dann stooped to gather the hazelnuts. 'Nobeast could stand against Martin. D'you know, his sword hangs in Cregga Badgermum's room? Funny, though. The elders say that he often appears in dreams to Redwallers, to give advice and warn us if the Abbey's in danger. Wonder why he never appeared this time?'

Dippler tried unsuccessfully to straighten the rusty fold of his chainmail as he sprawled in the big chair. 'Oh, I suppose Martin knows we can take care of ourselves. Don't forget, besides yore fathers there's my Chieftain Log a Log an' a fewscore o' Guosim fighters t'deal with.

What's that?'

Song turned from the tapestry. 'What's the matter, Dipp?'

'Did you 'ear a noise?'

Dann tossed a hazelnut and caught it in his mouth. 'No. What sort o' noise was it?'

Dippler struggled out of the big chair. 'Sort of like a clanky sound.'

Song stole a pawful of Dann's hazelnut kernels. 'Hahaha! That'd be yourself, Dipp. You make clanky sounds every time y'move in all that old armour!'

Beelu passed by the three young friends, hugging the shadows at the north end of Great Hall. When he reached the Abbey door he stood still awhile. Song and her companions had their backs to him, but there was no sense in taking chances. Pulling a small flask of vegetable oil from his pouch he dripped it on to the bolts and hinges, and then, ever cautious, he gave it another couple of moments, listening to the gossip and laughter of the three youngsters out at the hall's centre. The locks slid back smoothly, with scarce a sound or scrape. Beelu held his breath as he swung the door slowly open to admit the two Marlfoxes, Ascrod and Vannan, who had been waiting outside with the other rat Dakkle. Beelu placed a paw on his lips, indicating the three youngsters who had been left to guard the Abbey. Dakkle nodded, but Ascrod and Vannan were not paying any attention to Beelu. Their eyes were riveted on the wondrous tapestry which graced the west wall.

Friar Butty inspected the ugly gashes which had slashed through Cregga's paws when she had been grabbing sword and spearblades. He dabbed at them with a cloth which he was dipping in a water pail. 'Be still now, marm, please. You'll have to stay here in the gatehouse awhile yet. There's no question of moving you, I'm afraid.'

Nutwing spread a curtain across the mousebabe, who was still snoring in the armchair. 'Hmm mm. Been given lots of motherwort and a smidgen of valerian, I suspect. He'll probably sleep a good while. Mm, nasty! It looks like our badger has lost an ear.'

Friar Butty took a peek, drawing in his breath sharply. 'Great seasons, so she has, and will you look at this broken arrowhead sunk into her shoulder near the neck? Gracious me, Cregga marm, didn't it hurt you at the time?'

Spread out on the couch the huge badger snorted wearily. 'I never felt a thing. In the old days, when I could see, they called me Cregga Rose Eyes, you know. My rage was so great in battle that nothing could stop me. I was possessed by a thing called the Bloodwrath, like most badger Warriors.'

The Friar shook his head worriedly. 'I'll have to go up to the Abbey. 'Twill take Sister Sloey's herb satchel, sewing twine and clean dressings to patch you up right. Now stay there and don't move!'

Nutwing ambled out of the gatehouse, muttering as he went. 'I'll go, hmm, mm, I can still flap these stiff old wings a bit. You stay here, Butty, in case anybeast of ours comes knocking on the gate. I won't be long!'

The old owl hopped and flapped, sometimes touching the ground, other times with the grasstops brushing his talons. Faintly upon the night air he could hear the sounds of conflict from over the outer wall at the southwest corner. Surprised to find the main Abbey door half open, he shuffled in, blinking his eyes against the lantern and candle lights, and walked straight into the backs of Dakkle and Beelu. Still blinking, he called out, 'Hmm mm, who's there? Is that Melilot?'

'Nutwing! Look out! Get away!'

At the sound of the owl's voice Song had looked up. She saw the four vermin in plain view, creeping towards them. Ascrod grabbed Nutwing. Using the flapping owl as a shield, he and his cohorts rushed the three young guards.

Song was dashing towards the Marlfoxes, her green-stone stick raised. Dann and Dippler seized their spears and charged after her. Dippler's helmet fell over his eyes, and the monstrous halberd he was lugging slipped sideways. Both he and Dann tripped on the shaft and went sprawling on the floor. Song was almost upon the Marlfoxes, her eyes glinting with the light of battle. Ascrod swung his double-headed axe, slaying Nutwing with a single blow. He pushed the owl's still flapping body at Song, bringing her down. The young squirrel's scream of horror was cut short as the axe handle cracked down on her head. Vannan and the two rats were upon Dann and Dippler before they could rise. Vannan's axe crashed down on the young shrew's helmet, leaving a long dent in it. Dann struggled to get up but both rats jumped on him, cracking his head back hard upon the floorstones.

Ascrod sped across to the tapestry and began pulling it from the wall. A hubbub came from somewhere below, and the Marlfoxes heard the sounds of Redwallers on the wine cellar stairs. Vannan glanced about at the three fallen friends. 'What about these? Shall I finish 'em off?'

Ascrod had pulled a chair across to the tapestry so he could reach the top hooks that held it to the wall. He snarled at his sister. 'Idiot, what concern are they to us? This is the most valuable thing we've come on in many a season. Help me with it. Beelu, get outside and open the small east wallgate. Dakkle, lend a paw over here. Move, you fools, those Abbeybeasts will be on our heels in a moment. Hurry!'

At the southwest corner the fortunes of war had changed. Mokkan fought his way back through his own ranks until he was close to the ditch. It was the Guosim shrews who had saved the day. Charging wildly in at the rear of their foes' left flank, they swept all before them. As the enemy turned to intercept the Guosim attack, Skipper, Janglur and Rusvul led a push away from the wall into the ranks of the water rats. Mokkan was shouting now, realizing he had lost. 'Retreat! Get across the ditch onto the flatlands! Retreat!'

Rusvul went down with a spear in his side, but Janglur stood over him, swinging his loaded sling. Rusvul was half up when he cried out, 'Behind yer, mate, quick!'

Janglur spun like lightning, his whirling sling wrapping itself around the handle of the killing axe that the vixen Ziral was swinging at his head. He pulled sharply, dragging the short double-headed axe from her paws. Quick as a flash, the warrior squirrel caught the axe and swung at Ziral with all his might. That single blow finished the battle completely. The water rats who saw the beheaded Ziral lying on the path set up a wailing scream.

'A Marlfox is slain! A Marlfox is slaaaaaaiiiiinnn!'

In the blink of an eye the remaining Marlfoxes and water rats had abandoned the fight, leaping over the ditch and dashing headlong across the flatlands. Florian Dugglewoof Wilffachop waved his garden rake and started after the routed enemy, haranguing loudly. 'Villains! Fiends! Pollywogglin' babe-snatchers! You shall feel our wrath, we will pursue you to the very cracks of doom! Come on, you chaps. Chaaaaaarge!'

Skipper grabbed Florian's frock-coat tails and hauled him back. 'Leave it, matey, they still outnumber us two t'one. Let 'em go. We got our own to tend back 'ere.'

Victory over the foebeast had been won, but at a terrible price. The Noonvale otter Borrakul sat wounded, cradling Elachim's head in his lap, repeating over and over, 'My brother won't wake up. Wake up, Elachim, please!'

Runktipp took the slain otter gently from his grieving brother. 'He ain't goin' t'wake up, friend Borrakul. Leave 'im t'me.'

Janglur hauled Rusvul upright and supported him. 'You all right, cully? That's a spear you got growin' out o' yore side!'

Rusvul gasped and winced as Janglur removed the weapon. 'Never went in too deep. I'll live, mate. But that's more'n I can say for some who weren't so lucky!'

Skipper stooped over Tragglo Spearback, patting the Cellarhog's face and talking gently to him. 'Tragg, come on, ole lad, don't go sleepin' there. We'll get y'back 'ome to a nice soft bed. Wake up now.'

The old hedgehog's eyes fluttered open and he smiled weakly. 'Slingshot. Must o' been a bit o' metal. It's still stuck in my 'ead.'

A heart-piercing cry came from out on the open ground to the south.

'Logalogalogalogalog! Our Chieftain's doooooown!'

Florian, who was helping Runktipp to carry Elachim's body, looked round at the sound of the voice. 'Wot'n the name o' seasons is that?'

The Guosim shrew Mayon strode up, ashen-faced. ''Tis the Guosim death cry. Log a Log is slain. Bargle found 'im.'

Surprisingly enough it was Florian who restored order and got things moving. 'Now there's been terrible battle done here this night, y'know, chaps, but we must attend the livin' first. Right, pick up the wounded an' let's get 'em inside the Abbey. When that's taken jolly good care of I'll organize a party to return for our fallen comrades. Come on now, please, can't sit about here weepin' all night, wot?'

Skipper shouldered Tragglo Spearback, regardless of his spikes. 'Mister Florian's right, mates. Come on, let's git inside. There'll be elders an' young 'uns waitin' t'hear whether we won or not.'

Emerging from the cloud shadow, a pale moon cast its soft radiance over the dusty path at Redwall's southwest corner, where so much had been won and lost that night.

13

Song felt a cool damp cloth bathing her brow as Grandma Ellayo soothed away at the red-hot hammers of pain pounding inside her temples. From somewhere above she could hear her mother's worried voice calling her back to consciousness.

Gradually her eyelids flickered open. She was lying on the floor of Great Hall with her head resting on Rimrose's lap. Janglur hovered anxiously in the background, pacing to and fro. When she spoke, Song's voice came from far off, as if it belonged to some other creature. 'Unnhhh! Marlfoxes . . . where are they . . . Nutwing!'

Janglur breathed a sigh of relief. He knelt by his daughter. 'My liddle Songbreeze, thank the seasons you got a head as 'ard as yore ole dad's!'

Groggily Song allowed herself to be led to a chair. She sipped a potion which Sister Sloey pressed upon her, gazing over the beaker rim at her two friends. Dippler's head was swathed in bandages, and Foremole Gubbio was showing the dazed Guosim shrew a massive dent in the big helmet he had been wearing.

'Hurr hurr, maister, you'm lucky yon 'emlet saved ee. Yore 'ead was loik to 'ave bin sliced in two. Burr aye!'

Dippler touched his bandaged pate gingerly. 'Ooh! It

feels like this 'ere lump is another 'ead growin' atop my own. Aye aye, Song, you awake at last? Where's Dann?'

The young squirrel was sitting hunched on a form, bent forward as Brother Melilot tended an ugly swelling at the back of his head. He winced silently as a compress was applied. The good Brother finished binding the damp herbs and patted Dann. 'Pity 'tisn't winter. Ice would have worked well on that bump, but there you are, Dann, good as new. You'll live, young 'un!'

Dann stood shakily and stared about, seemingly unable to remember. 'Phew! I feel terrible. What happened?'

Rusvul pushed aside two helpers who were dressing the wound in his side. Pulling himself upright on his javelin, the warrior squirrel glared contemptuously at his son. 'What happened? I'll tell yer wot happened! You were left to guard the Abbey an' you let yoreself get knocked silly by a couple o' vermin! Nutwing was slain, aye, an' the great Redwall tapestry was stolen from the wall, that's wot happened! Were you playin' more games, solvin' puzzles, was it? No, 'twas crackin' nuts, I see by the shells all over the floor. Well, while you were doin' that the foebeast got in 'ere, cracked yore nut, murdered an Abbeybird an' robbed the very symbol of Redwall. Call yoreself a Reguba. Hah!' Quivering with rage, Rusvul snapped his javelin in two pieces and flung them from him, tears of anger glittering in his eyes. 'I wish that spear'd gone right through an' slain me, rather than stand 'ere an' see the Reguba blood shamed by a son o' mine. Coward!' Turning his face from Dann, Rusvul limped off, out to the orchard to sit and brood whilst he tended his own injury.

Brother Melilot put a paw about Dann, shaking his head in disgust at Rusvul's outburst. 'How could a creature say that about his own son?'

Dann tried to keep his face straight as tears poured unchecked down his cheeks. Janglur hurried across and threw a comforting paw around the young squirrel's shoulder.

'Shush now, Dann mate, yore dad didn't mean it. You couldn't 'ave done any more'n you did, all three of yer!'

The Guosim shrew Mayon marched in and threw a salute to Bargle, who was acting temporary Log a Log. 'They left by the east wallgate, Chief. I made shore it was all locked an' secure. Ahoy there, Dipp! Still alive, eh, mate?'

Dippler smiled sheepishly and held up his battered headgear. 'Aye, but they killed this 'elmet. Was there any sign of 'em, Mayon?'

The shrew poured himself a beaker of October Ale and blew off the froth before drinking. 'No, not a hair. They're long gone. All's quiet out there now, 'cept for mister Florian an' the others. They're puttin' our lost ones t'rest all together, just by the sou'west wallcorner inside the Abbey grounds. 'Tis a sad business, mates, very sad!'

Dippler looked away, scrubbing at his eyes with a spare bandage. 'Ah, poor Nutwing. If only we'd been faster . . .'

'You mustn't blame yourself,' said Mayon. 'Three young ones against that evil scum – you didn't stand a chance. And you've heard that Log a Log is gone?'

'The Log a Log was like a father t'me. That ole shrew'll live fer ever in my memory. Wish I could get me paws on the vermin who slayed 'im. I'd make the scum pay, matey!'

Bargle looked up, surprised that Dippler did not know the truth. ''Tweren't no vermin that killed Log a Log. He never made it as far as the battle, Dipp. The scum that murdered 'im was Fenno. We found that'n's rapier buried in the Chief's back!'

Despite his injury the young shrew's teeth ground together hard. 'Fenno, that big bully, where is 'e?'

Bargle accepted the beaker from Mayon and took a swig. 'Nobeast knows. Fenno ran off like the slime that he is.'

Dippler drew his rapier and licked the blade as a true Guosim warrior does before making a solemn oath. 'Then I'll find Fenno someday, an' when I do this blade'll be wetted with somethin' else. My name is Dippler an' my word is as true as my sword!'

Gurrbowl Cellarmole came bustling down from the dormitories, shaking her head as she counted off bedspaces for the wounded on both paws. 'You young 'uns, Dannflo', Dippler an' miz Songer, you'm all in marm Cregga's room whoile she'm a-layin' in ee gate'ouse. Though, dearie oi, oi doan't know 'ow she's goin' to go on when she yurrs about poor Nutwing.'

Song's mother took charge. 'Right. Come on, you three, upstairs with you and rest those heads.'

Janglur took a stroll out to the orchard where he seated himself beneath a pear tree, next to Rusvul. 'So, me ole mate, you reckon yore son shamed the name Reguba?'

Rusvul stared straight ahead into the moonshadowed stillness. 'Well, what d'you think?'

Reaching up, Janglur plucked a pear and rubbed it on his jerkin. 'For wot 'tis worth, I think yore a great warrior, strong in paw an' brave in war. We carved a few paths in our younger seasons, you'n'me; we're still good pals an' always will be. But let me say this t'you, Rusvul Reguba. I never knew you was a foolish beast until tonight. Our young 'uns are the hope o' the future. They need t'be 'elped, not 'umiliated. It took no bravery to call Dann a coward – he loves you too much to answer back. So all you did was to bring shame on yoreself by the way you talked to Dann. No, don't answer or argue, jus' think about it, matey. An' that's the advice of a friend.' Without further comment Janglur Swifteye arose and walked off, leaving Rusvul to wrestle with the problems of his own stubbornness.

The three friends lay on Cregga Badgermum's big sofa.

All three felt terrible about Nutwing. Dann felt it most. It was clear his father's onslaught had hurt him deeply. They sat awhile in silence, heads still throbbing, unable to sleep. Dann's eyes wandered to the sword of Martin the Warrior hanging upon the wall, and suddenly he sat bolt upright.

'Yes! Now I remember!'

Dippler cringed, putting paws to his ears. 'Well, you don't 'ave t'shout about it, mate. Wot d'you remember?'

Dann got up and went to the sword, as if drawn to it by a magnet. 'When I was knocked senseless, he spoke to me, Martin the Warrior!'

Song was curious. She watched Dann attentively. 'Well, don't stand there gawping at the sword, tell us. What did he say to you?'

Dann automatically spoke the words triggered by the sight of the marvellous blade which Martin had once wielded.

'Four Chieftains going forth,
To bring back Redwall's heart,
Vengeance, honour, friendship,
Each will play their part.
The flower bears my blade,
And greenstick, Warrior's daughter,
Join with the shortsword bearer,
And one who lives by water.
Before the herald lark,
Ere night's last teardrop falls,
With none to bid you fond farewell,
Go! Leave these old red walls.'

Dippler stared at his two friends. 'Sounds great, but what does it mean?'

Song shook her head in despair at the young shrew. 'Honestly, Dipp, you're the blinkin' limit. It means we three are going to go out there and bring back the tapestry!'

Dippler thought about this a moment. 'But we're not four Chieftains?'

The pretty squirrelmaid shrugged. 'Well, I can't help that. If Martin has spoken we must obey. Though you're right, Dipp, there are one or two things about the verse that puzzle me. For instance, Dann said, the flower bears my blade. Who in the name of acorns is the flower?'

'Well, don't go shoutin' it all around the Abbey, but it's me.'

Song stifled a giggle at Dann's reluctant confession. 'You? I never knew you were called flower?'

Dann looked defiant. ''Twas my mother's idea. Dad wanted me named Dannblood, said it was a proper warrior's name, but Mum wouldn't hear of it, she insisted I be called Dannflower. So that's my real name, but Dad an' me shortened it to Dannflor after my mother died. Well, Song, you carry the greenstick an' yore a warrior's daughter. Dipp, you got the rapier, that's a shortsword, so that's the three of us, even though we ain't Chieftains. Who the fourth is, the one who lives by water, huh, who knows? But 'tis plain we three must go!'

Dippler brightened up as the poem's meaning began to sink in. 'Aye, Redwall's heart is the tapestry. I understand now, mates. We've got to leave the Abbey before dawn!'

Song interrupted the young Guosim excitedly. 'Of course! Listen, here's the first few lines from an old song, one of the first I ever learned, called "Daybreak".

'Before the herald lark,
Ere night's last teardrop falls,
Like dewdrop from a rose,
The rising Minstrel calls . . .

'That's the first bit. Oh dear, I wonder why we've got to go with none to bid us farewell?'

Dann snorted mirthlessly at his friend's innocence. ' 'Tis obvious. 'Cos they'd stop us, that's why. Huh, imagine my father, he'd say we were off to play some silly games. Then there's yore mum'n'dad an' Grandma Ellayo – d'you think they'd be pleased to see you wanderin' off into a woodland full o' water rats, Marlfoxes an' who knows wot else?'

Song nodded ruefully. 'They'd stop us for sure!'

Dann reached up carefully and took down the sword from its pins on the wall. Martin the Warrior's weapon felt like wildfire in his paws. He held the black-bound grip with its red pommel stone and crosstree hilt, feeling the perfect balance of the lethally sharp blade. Double-edged, strangely chased and patterned down to the perilous tip, keen as an icicle honed by midwinter gales.

Song and Dippler touched their paws to the sword as Dann's voice sounded firm and resolute. 'We bring the tapestry back to Redwall Abbey!'

Dippler looked from one to the other. 'An' if I can I'll avenge my Chieftain Log a Log!'

Song smiled at them both. 'I go with you because you are my friends!'

Dann picked up a broad old belt from the shelf and fastened it across one shoulder to his waistbelt. He thrust the sword through the broad belt, so that it was flat across his back, the hilt showing above his other shoulder.

'Well, what are we waitin' for, mates? 'Twill be dawn soon. Come on!'

Four Chieftains
Going Forth

14

Camouflaged by the morning suntinged leaves of a horse chestnut tree, the Marlfox Mokkan sat in a fork amid the high branches, watching the scene below on the stream-bank, listening carefully to all that was said. He was cunning and highly intelligent, always cautious to know which way the wind was blowing among his brothers and sisters. Accordingly Mokkan had made it back to the camp shortly after dawn, and finding that he was first to return he hid in the tree and watched the reactions as the rest filtered back to the camp in small groups. First to arrive were Ascrod and Vannan with the rats Dakkle and Beelu. They draped the tapestry over some bushes, prepared a scratch meal and sat back to gloat over their plunder. Predak the vixen came next, heading a group of rats, followed by her brother Gelltor at the head of a second band. Cooking fires were lit, and some prepared food whilst others tended their wounds. By the time the sun was fully up the final few had returned. Ascrod and Vannan with their two rats were the stars of the day, proudly showing off the wondrous tapestry.

'How's that for a nice bit o' thievin', eh?'

'Aye, we were right inside that Abbey for a good while, wounded three, killed one, an' trotted off with this beauty!'

'Pity we never had time for a proper look around. I reckon Redwall's stuffed with treasures.'

'They're not so tough. I slew a big owl, stupid creature!'

'Huh, the three we laid out are prob'ly dead by now too. I whacked a shrew wearin' armour so hard that my axe paw still tingles.'

Ascrod stood over Gelltor, smiling whimsically. 'So, how did the attack go? Not too well by the look of you lot.'

Gelltor flexed his shoulder to get the movement back in it. Grim-faced, he spat viciously into the fire. 'Allag, what's the head count?'

Further down the streambank the water rat called back to Gelltor. 'A hundred an' seventy-three, sire. I'm just numberin' the wounded.'

Gelltor lay back, watching the blue-grey campfire smoke wreathing among the shafts of sunlight between the trees. 'That's nearly a score of rats lost. Then there was Ziral too!'

Vannan tossed aside her food and stood upright. 'What? You mean our sister Ziral was slain?'

'Oh, she was slain sure enough. I saw her head lyin' on the ground. The one who did it was a big squirrel, looked as if he was half asleep. Janglur, they called him. I'll remember that one's name!'

Ascrod stroked the tasselled tapestry border thoughtfully. 'A Marlfox slain. High Queen Silth won't be well pleased to hear that. What about our glorious leader Mokkan and his grand plan?'

Gelltor kicked a branch hanging from the fire, sending sparks showering as the dead pine crackled. 'Mokkan! Don't talk t'me about him. He left it too late for a quick ambush, wanted to stand round chattin' with the Redwallers. It was them who attacked us. There's no doubt about it, they got some fierce warriors an' they were quick too. For a while there we thought we had 'em, they were outnumbered. But then we were hit from behind by gangs of those Guosim shrews, don't know where they came from. That was when we lost the advantage. Next thing Mokkan's yelling for everybeast to retreat, and we had to run for it like a ragtailed bunch of amateurs. I'm not surprised Mokkan hasn't shown his face around camp yet. Bungler!'

As Gelltor finished speaking, Mokkan hobbled into camp, bent almost double and limping badly, his face creased with pain. He held up a paw for silence before any creature could speak further. 'All right, all right, 'twas all my fault. I messed it up, by taking those Redwallers for fools, which they weren't. But hear me! You all fought a gallant fight. I couldn't ask for braver beasts in my command, particularly you, brother Gelltor, and you, sister Predak . . .' Here he paused for effect, shaking his head sadly. 'And our dear sister Ziral, so treacherously slain after I had called retreat. How can I go back to our mother Queen Silth and tell her that poor Ziral is with us no more? Gelltor, you were right, brother. I should have listened to you.'

The Marlfoxes were slightly bewildered. Mokkan had never spoken like this before, but had always been arrogant and imperious. Vannan tapped the handle of her axe against the tapestry. 'It wasn't a total loss. Look what we took from the Abbey.'

Mokkan had been looking at the thing for over an hour from the tree limb. But he put on an expression of awed astonishment and approached the object reverently. 'You stole this? Wondrous, beautiful, it must be beyond price! Well, congratulations to you. Our mother will be overjoyed to see such a splendid and magnificent prize. At least poor Ziral didn't give her life in vain. But remember what she said here only a day ago. Blood calls for blood. It is the code of Marlfoxes, our law. Redwall and its creatures must pay dearly for our sister!'

Gelltor drew his axe and brandished it in Mokkan's face. 'Like I said at first, we should have gone to war!'

Mokkan sat down by the fire with agonizing slowness, biting his lip. 'Aye, brother, you were right, I was the fool. Now I am sorely wounded and unfit to lead. Leave a few good rats here with me so that we may guard your plunder. I need rest, I may never walk again with these injuries. Split our forces up between the four of you and take vengeance upon those Redwall scum. Go quickly, before they become confident and begin combing the woodlands for our blood. Surround Redwall Abbey, kill them one by one, with the cunning that is the pawmark of a Marlfox. Snipe at them, starve them by keeping them penned up inside their Abbey, make them prisoners inside their own home!'

Gelltor's eyes lit up, fired by plans of conquest. 'We'll besiege them until they crawl out begging to be spared! Then I'll execute the one that wounded me and we'll take revenge on the squirrel Janglur for Ziral's death. Those whom we spare can be dragged back to our island in chains, to serve us!'

Mokkan clasped his brother's paw with feigned fervour. 'Ah, ever the wise warrior, Gelltor. But you must hurry and set up your siege whilst they are unaware of your brilliant plan!'

Within a short time the army was ready to march again, each of the Marlfoxes commanding two score water rats apiece, while Mokkan stayed behind to recover and protect the tapestry with a guard comprising the thirteen remaining rats. Mokkan lay back as if he had fainted away, listening keenly to Vannan murmuring instructions to the water rat Beelu. 'I leave you here to guard our prize with your life. If Mokkan recovers and tries anything odd, you must hide the tapestry and make your way to Redwall, where you will report to me only!'

As the army marched out of camp, Mokkan turned on his side, chuckling under his breath. 'Never trust a vixen.'

It was close to noontide when Song called a halt at a

shady glade in the Mossflower depths. 'This looks like a good spot for our lunch. There's some fat juicy berries on those blackberry brambles round the dead oak.'

Dippler unshouldered the pack he had loaded from the kitchens. 'Lunch? What 'appened to brekkfist, miss? An' jus' one other thing, when d'we sleep? Last time I closed me lids was when I was knocked unconscious. We missed a full night's shut-eye, y'know!'

Song threw her haversack down and began picking blackberries. 'Oh, give your little face a rest, Dipp, stop moaning!'

Dann took off his sword and foodpack and sat down gratefully. 'Dipp's not moanin', Song, he's arguing. Guosim shrews aren't happy unless they've got something to argue about, right, Dipp?'

The young shrew opened his haversack, fishing out three of Brother Melilot's newbaked scones and a slab of cheese, which he cut into three pieces with his rapier. 'I'm not arguin' *or* moanin'. It's called debatin'. That's 'ow us Guosim get t'be so wise, by debatin'.'

Song aimed a berry at him, but Dippler ducked it. 'You greedy little hog, I notice you've given yourself the biggest slice o' cheese an' the largest scone!'

Dippler grinned, popping the blackberry Song had thrown into his mouth. 'But I need extra vittles, so I can grow big'n'strong'n'stronger, like you two. If I gave you the big bits then you'd both grow bigger'n'stronger an' I'd be liddle'n'thin!'

Song prodded his small round stomach as she passed. 'Thin, huh? You're about as thin as a hedgehog who's been locked in a larder for two seasons!'

Dann opened a flask of pennycloud cordial. 'Will you two pack in debatin' an' let me have lunch in peace?'

Song watched Dippler split open his scone. He packed the inside with blackberries, closed it and bit into the whole thing so enthusiastically that juice squirted out from either side.

Dann flicked drops of it from his nose. 'You greedy savage, you'll never grow any taller, just rounder an' fatter. Don't you Guosim have any table manners?'

Dippler shrugged as he crammed cheese into his mouth. 'Mm mm. Course we don't, 'cos Guosim never use tables. How'd y'get a table on a logboat? We got shrew manners, though.'

Song wiped her lips daintily on a dockleaf. 'And what pray are shrew manners?'

Dippler glugged down cordial to clear his voice. 'Simple, 'tis one o' the first things a shrewbabe learns. Listen.

'If you eat too much you'll sink the boat,
Burst yore boots an' split yore coat,
Just scoff enough so you stay afloat,
'Tis manners, good manners!
If you pinch the vittles from another's plate,
Wait till he's lookin' the other way, mate,
An' when fish are bitin', don't eat the bait,
'Tis manners, good manners!
If yore a shrew o' the Guosim clan,
You must be sure to think of a plan,
To share yore matey's pudden or flan,
'Tis manners, good manners!
Remember to chew everythin' in sight,
If it don't bite back, then get first bite,
An' always take a basinful to bed each night,
'Tis manners, good manners!'

Song was chuckling so hard she nearly choked on a bite of scone. Dann sent Dippler sprawling with a playful shove. 'Away, you rogue, your mother never taught you that lot!'

Dippler stole a piece of Song's cheese as he patted her back to restore her breath. He winked cheekily at Dann. 'I don't dispute that, mate, I made it up meself!'

'Ssshh! What's that? Get down!'

At Dann's urgent whisper the three friends dropped down behind the fallen oak trunk. There they stayed, silent and motionless, for several moments, after which Song stood up slowly. 'What was it you heard, Dann?'

The young squirrel rose, turning his head this way and that as he tried to pick up a trace of the sound he had heard. 'I don't know, I heard something, but 'tis gone now.'

Not much further out from where the three were sitting, Gelltor, Predak, Ascrod and Vannan passed with the army of water rats, travelling in the opposite direction, towards Redwall Abbey, to begin their assault.

Dippler finished up the remains of any food his friends had not eaten. Dann shouldered his pack and sword, weighing up the woodland surrounding them. 'Which way now, Song?'

The young squirrelmaid walked to the east end of the glade where they had camped. Using the knowledge her father had passed on during their wanderings, she cast about carefully. 'This way, I think. The ferns have been disturbed, see, one or two are broken – grass looks flattened too. Ha! Look at this.'

Hanging from a broken hornbeam spur was a strand of red thread. Dippler and Dann studied it as Song voiced her thoughts. 'That's from the tapestry. At a guess I'd say it was being carried shoulder high by two or more creatures. See here amid the grass, one of them stumbled on this blackberry creeper and narrowly missed walking into the hornbeam tree, but the heavy roll of tapestry they were carrying snagged on that broken branch. They've gone this way.'

Dippler wrapped the thread around his paw. 'Stupid vermin, they're leavin' a trail a blind moth could follow!'

Dann pressed forward, calling back to the shrew. 'Marlfokes aren't stupid, Dipp. Y'must remember that they were running with a weighty object, it was still dark, an' maybe they thought Redwallers might give chase.

149

Stands t'reason they'd want to put as much space between themselves an' the Abbey as possible.'

Dippler pushed the bushes aside roughly. 'Murderin' thieves. They won't get away from me, matey!'

Song cautioned her friends. 'I suggest from now on that we keep our voices down, don't talk unless 'tis necessary, an' tread quietly. Best not leave a trail – goodness knows who might follow it.'

The vast woodland was unusually still and silent, even the sporadic birdsong sounding as if it came from far away. Moving quietly eastward through the dense undergrowth, Song and her companions became cautious, realizing that behind the beauty of stately trees and summer-flowering bushes, danger might lurk in the shape of the foebeast.

At Redwall Abbey a brief ceremony had been held over the resting place within the southwest wallcorner. Four shrews, Elachim the Noonvale otter, Nutwing and Log a Log were honoured with small gifts, flowers and verses. Friar Butty sighed heavily, wiping his eyes on a spotted kerchief as they walked back to the Abbey, where Deesum and Brother Melilot were preparing lunch. Skipper spoke loud enough for all to hear.

'When we get time, there'll be a good stone marker carved for our pore mates back there, so they'll never be forgot by Redwallers. But fer now, messmates, let's git back t'the business of livin' an' survivin'. Janglur, Borrakul, mister Florian an' meself will move Cregga Badgermum out o' the gate'ouse an' up to 'er room. Bargle, will you an' yore Guosim guard the walls? Arm yoreselves with slings an' bows'n'arrers. Runktipp, stow yoreself in the belltower, an' if the shrews tip y'the signal that vermin are about, be ready to toll the alarm bells. Roop an' Muggle, will yer be kind enough to 'elp Gubbio Foremole an' Sister Sloey check on the wounded.'

Sloey fussed with her apron distractedly. 'Oh dear,

what with lookin' after the Dibbuns an' gettin' things tidy I almost forgot about our injured ones. Still, a good quiet rest's what they need most. We'll take them up some lunch soon as 'tis ready.'

A few minutes later, Florian entered the gatehouse and swept off his big floppy hat with a double flourish at the wounded badger. The friends were determined to cheer Cregga and not let her dwell on her sadness, or her injury.

'Ahem, marm, 'tis only m'goodself Wilffachop come to inform ye that your carriage waits without!'

Cregga turned her face in his direction. She was not in the best of moods after an uncomfortable night. 'I know 'tis you, hare, and stop waving that hat about, you'll disturb the dust an' have me sneezin'. Now, what's all this about a carriage outside? D'you think I'm a helpless Dibbun?'

Janglur nudged Skipper gleefully as he popped his head round the door. He announced in a loud officious voice, as if talking to nobeast in particular, 'One actors' cart waitin' to transport a wounded Abbeybeast. Er, is there a passenger in 'ere?'

The big badger struggled upright from the couch, grabbing a broken spearshaft, which she waved threateningly. 'Just let anybeast try to get me into a rickety actors' cart an' I'll give 'em a headache they won't get over for ten seasons!'

Janglur clapped a paw to his mouth to stifle laughter, while Skipper called out in a voice dripping with sincerity, 'Ho, marm, 'ow can you say such things? All's we're thinkin' of is yore 'ealth. After you've 'ad a nice ride in the cart we'll carry you up to yore room an' let Sister Sloey feed yer on a nourishin' lunch of 'erb broth an' elderflower water.'

That was enough for Cregga. A deep rumble of anger burst forth from the mighty badger. Grabbing Florian and lifting him as if he were a babe, she stumped resolutely out of the gatehouse, with the helpless hare protesting volubly.

'I say, marm, bad form, put me down, wot! Don't stand there grinnin' like ticks at a tea party, you chaps, help me!'

Cregga almost walked straight into the cart, which was drawn up just outside the gatehouse door. Feeling its contours with her paw, she dumped Florian unceremoniously into the seat and gave the cart a mighty shove. It flew off across the lawn, with the hare still yelling.

'Most uncharitable of ye, marm! I'll make a note of this peevish behaviour, you can jolly well bet I will! Yowch! Heeeeeelp!'

His pleas went unheard as Cregga raised a threatening paw at the other helpers. 'If you've got any sense you'll stay clear o' me. I'll walk back to the Abbey alone. Oh, an' you can tell Sloey if she wants to see another season she'd better not mention herb broth an' elderflower water while I'm around. I need proper food an' the comfort of my own room for a day or two!'

Skipper fled past her, tugging Janglur with him. 'Put a move on, matey. Dann an' Dippler an' yore Song 'ave taken over Cregga marm's room, so we'd better git there afore she does an' shift those young 'uns out sharpish like!'

Baby Dwopple was wide awake and none the worse after his ordeal. He elbowed his way in between Blinny the molebabe and Florian at the dining table for lunch. 'Where a vikkles? I starven!'

The hare rescued his summer salad and apple pie, scowling at Dwopple. 'Have a care there, young wretchlet, I need all the nourishment I can lay me flippin' paws on. Recoverin' from a nasty cart accident, y'know. I say, is that beechnut sponge I see? Chuck it this way, will you, m'good mole, wot!'

'I needs feedin' too. I 'scaped! I fighted off those

badbeasts! I frighted mista Stickabee . . .'

Cregga felt her way up the stairwell and gave the unlatched door of her room a light push. As it swung open, the badger entered, feeling about with outstretched paws. 'Somebeast's there. Come on, who is it?'

Janglur's reply was tinged with foreboding. 'Only me'n' Skipper, marm, but I ain't certain wot's goin' on.'

Cregga lowered herself into her favourite armchair as he continued.

'Last night my Song was put in 'ere with young Dann an' the shrew Dippler. You 'eard about wot 'appened to 'em, they was injured. But they ain't 'ere no more, an' Skipper sez that Martin's sword is missin' from the wall yonder.'

The badger mused over this information for a moment before replying. 'Hmm. It sounds a bit strange, but let's not dash into anything. They must be about somewhere, probably still within the Abbey.'

Janglur was not convinced. 'But wot if they ain't?'

The door behind them began creaking slowly shut before a slight draught. Skipper pointed to it. 'There's some markin's scratched on that door!'

Janglur inspected it closely, telling Cregga what he could see. 'Fairly fresh scratches, marm, done quick like with a sharp point. 'Tis only four letters. G an' T an' G an' T.'

Skipper opened the door. 'I'll go down an' see if they're at lunch, or they might be in the orchard. You two try an' figger those letters out.'

Cregga rose from her armchair. 'Wait!' Crossing to the door, she pressed her muzzle gently against the scratches, sniffing as she moved over the markings. 'G . . . T . . . G . . . T! I've a feeling those marks were made hastily by the last one to leave this room, carrying Martin's sword. He or she scratched them. G . . . T . . . G . . . T!'

Janglur nodded as the solution dawned on him. 'Aye, that'd be young Dann, tryin' to prove hisself after Rusvul shouted at 'im last night, and the other two've gone with 'im. We'd better get searchers out, Skip, find 'em an' get 'em back inside this Abbey before anythin' bad 'appens to Song an' her pals. I just figgered it out. Those four letters mean Gone To Get Tapestry!'

Skipper stared at the letters. 'Of course, that's wot they've done, taken Martin the Warrior's sword an' gone to get our tapestry back. Only beasts with not many seasons under their belts would try a thing like that. Young, brave'n'fool'ardy. Wish my otters was 'ere, we'd get 'em back afore y'could blink. Trouble is that I think my tribe's left the falls an' gone north on the stream down to the seaside. Lots o' good vittles there durin' summer.'

Janglur untied the sling from his waist. 'Can't stand 'ere jawin' all day. They might be in danger. Come on!'

Bong! Boom! Bong! Boom! Bong!

Skipper dashed past Janglur down the stairs.

'Foebeasts at the gate!'

15

By mid-noon Mokkan seemed well on the road to recovery. He had sat up after a long nap and eaten food. The water rats did not stray far from the camp, but sat awaiting his orders. Mokkan made a great pretence of trying to stand, but sank back down again grimacing. He beckoned to the rat Beelu. 'You're a good strong beast. Help me up and walk along the streambank with me while I get these paws working properly again.'

Beelu helped the Marlfox to stand upright, and Mokkan leaned heavily on him, smiling his satisfaction. 'Ah, that's better. Let's try a short stroll downstream, shall we?'

Silently the water rat obeyed, trying hard not to stumble as he guided his charge along the bank, close to the water. It was not long before they were out of sight of the others.

From behind the trunk of a crack willow, Fenno the shrew watched them. Weary, hungry and red-eyed from lack of sleep, he had blundered round Mossflower until he was hopelessly lost. The shrew grovelled down in the earth at the base of the willow and tried to meld himself with the tree, not knowing what to make of the incident that followed. He saw the paw which Mokkan had about

Beelu suddenly lock round the rat's neck and tighten. Mokkan spoke gently, soothingly, as he slowly throttled the life from his victim. 'What'll you tell my sister Vannan now, rat? This is the last lesson you'll ever learn, never try to outsmart a Marlfox!'

Beelu's paws kicked wildly, then his struggles lessened until he finally went limp. Mokkan hurled him into the stream and stood watching the rat's carcass being swept away. He chuckled. 'Never learned how to swim, eh? Typical water rat, they're not much use at learning anything!'

Fenno drew in his breath sharply with fear. The Marlfox melted back into the trees and was gone. The shrew scrambled out of his hiding place and threw himself flat on the bank. Thrusting his head into the stream, he drank, sucking in water greedily. Then, to his horror, a strong paw pressed itself down hard on the back of his neck. Fenno tried to lift his head clear of the water, but he could not. His limbs thrashed about helplessly as water rushed into his ears and eyes and up his nostrils. Just before he blacked out he was dragged clear of the stream and smashed up against the trunk of the willow. Fenno found himself staring into the pale, ruthless eyes of Mokkan.

'Where are the rest of your tribe?'

Fenno shook his head as he coughed up water and streambed sand. 'Gaaargh! I dunno. Kwaargh! B'lieve me, I dunno!'

Mokkan's double-bladed axe pressed none too lightly between the gagging shrew's eyes. 'Oh, I believe you, only a complete fool would dare lie to Mokkan. Now listen carefully to my next question, your life depends on the answer. Are you good at steering and guiding a logboat?'

Not daring to nod with the axe so close, Fenno managed to gasp out, 'Aye, Chief, I'm good at it!'

Mokkan's paw was like a clawed vice. It dug savagely

into the back of Fenno's neck as he was propelled forward. 'Good! I have work for you!'

The twelve remaining water rats rose to attention as Mokkan strode into camp, apparently fully recovered and thrusting a terrified shrew before him. He nodded to a rat. 'Keep your spear on this shrew, if he moves gut him! The rest of you, take your weapons to those logboats, but save the stoutest one. Here, shrew, which is the best of these craft?'

Fenno scrabbled across and laid his paw on a boat without hesitation. 'This'n, Chief. 'Twas Log a Log's boat – belonged to a Guosim leader.'

The Marlfox inspected the fine craft, nodding his approval. 'I'll keep this one. You rats, chop the rest to splinters!'

Swords, spears and daggers hacked and slashed at the other five vessels. Mokkan took a braided thong and noosed it about the neck of Fenno, locking off the knot so it could not be removed quickly. He dragged the bewildered and trembling shrew down to the boat he had chosen, bidding him sit in the stern. The Marlfox prised a towing staple from one of the wrecked logboats, knotted the thong end to the staple and drove it into the thick beechwood stern until the curve was embedded level with the wood. Fenno sat with his neck pulled to one side by the short thong. Mokkan smiled.

'If the boat sinks, then so do you. Right, rats, gather up all the supplies and stow that tapestry carefully amidships. High Queen Silth will be happy to see us when we bring Redwall's treasure to her.'

Dann went first along the trail, leading his friends in the direction of the noise.

'Sounds like an army of woodpeckers havin' a mid-season feast!' Dippler panted as he ran.

Song wielded her greenstone-tipped stick. 'Hardly likely, Dipp. Slow down, Dann, we don't want to rush into the middle of something we can't back out of!'

Dann slowed until they were travelling abreast. 'It's stopped! Listen, is that a stream I can hear?'

They skirted the wide pool formed by the end of the inlet. Stooping low and taking advantage of the bush cover, the three friends pressed forward along the deserted streambank. Dippler saw the wreckage of his tribe's logboats first. With a sob of dismay he threw himself down by the shattered prow of the first one.

'*Waterfly*! 'Tis me ole boat. I paddled that'n many a long day. Wot filthy villain'd wreck a good craft like 'er?'

Song had run ahead to where the main broadstream flowed. She called back to Dippler and Dann. 'Hurry, come and see this!' They both dashed up in time to see the surviving logboat speeding out of sight round a distant bend on the fast-flowing current. 'A Marlfox and some other beasts, with one bent over in the stern. I'll wager the tapestry's aboard that boat!'

Dippler scrambled up a pine tree as far as he could climb. Clinging on with one paw, shading his eyes with the other, he watched until the vessel was lost to sight. Climbing back down, the Guosim shrew stamped his paws angrily. 'We jus' missed the scum. Guess who the otherbeast was? I'd know that stinkin' bully anywhere. It was Fenno!'

'The one that murdered Log a Log?'

Dippler slashed the air with his rapier. 'Aye, the very one!'

Dann undid his sword and pack and flung them down moodily. 'Not much we can do about it now, mates. They've wrecked the other boats an' left us stranded 'ere. Besides, who knows where they're bound? They could be sailin' anywhere.'

Song drew Friar Butty's parchment from her tunic. 'That's where you're wrong, Dann. I'll wager an acorn to an oak they're away to the island in the lost lake. We can too. I've got the route right here, listen.

'At the rear of redstone wall,
Find me o'er where breaks the day,
You cannot, shall not walk at all,
Just follow as I run away.'

Dippler shrugged and sat beside Dann on the bank.
'You've lost me again, Song. You'll 'ave to explain.'

Song translated the lines she had read. 'The rear of the
redstone wall is the back of the Abbey, where we left
from. Now, we travelled east, through Mossflower, and
day breaks in the east, so we've found it, the river.
Obviously we cannot walk on water and the last line tells
us to follow whichever way the water runs. That's the
way Fenno and the Marlfox have gone, don't you see?'

Dann jabbed his swordpoint into the shallows. 'Of
course I see, but how d'we do that, Song, eh? The Marlfox
wasn't stupid, he smashed the other boats to pieces so
nobeast could follow him. 'Tis like I said, we're stranded!'

Song glanced hopefully at Dippler. 'No way we could
knock up a boat from the bits of broken ones, Dipp? You
know about boat-building.'

The young shrew shook his head mournfully. 'All you
could make o' that lot now is a good fire. It'd take me
days an' days to make the roughest ole boat, an' that's
always providin' we could find the right log an' drag it
down t'the waterside 'ere. No, we're stranded, matey.'

Song looked amazed at her disheartened friends. 'Hah,
so you give it all up, just like that? Well, not me, I can
follow a riverbank whichever way it flows.' She dashed
off down the water's edge, shouting, 'I'm not letting them
get away from me. Oh no!'

After a moment the young squirrelmaid chanced a
backward glance. There were Dann and Dippler, running
after her.

'Wait for us, mate, wait for us!'

Gelltor stood on the flatlands outside Redwall Abbey, out

of range of arrows or missiles. Skipper jumped up on to the battlemented threshold top above the gatehouse and called out to the figure on the sun-shimmered plain. 'Well, wot is it today, snipenose? What're you after?'

Gelltor had to cup both paws around his mouth to be heard. 'Blood for blood. The one you call Janglur killed a Marlfox. Give him to us, and after that we'll talk.'

Skipper scratched his tail in amazement, and winked at Janglur. 'Hoho! 'Ear that, matey? They want yer!'

The warrior squirrel's heavily lidded eyes flickered but once. Grabbing the otter's javelin, Janglur leapt on the battlement top above Skipper and threw out a challenge to the Marlfox. 'Are you the beast who wants t'meet me? Stay right there, patchbottom, I'll come down an' sort it out with yer, jus' me'n'you!'

Jumping from the wall he made for the wallstairs, only to be stopped by Brother Melilot. 'I know 'tis hard for a warrior to resist a challenge, Janglur, but only a fool rushes into an ambush. You'd be slain as soon as you stepped outside our gates. Let Skipper do the talking.'

Rusvul Reguba patted Janglur's back. 'He's right, mate.'

Skipper called out to Gelltor, 'Sorry, mate, you can't 'ave ole Janglur. We need 'im at Redwall, to slay any more Marlfoxes who come callin'. So wot now?'

Gelltor pointed dramatically, letting his paw sweep the walls. 'So now you must all die as a penalty for the death of a Marlfox!'

As Gelltor let his paw fall there was a brief pause, followed by a loud whirring noise. Skipper flung himself down onto the parapet. 'Lay low, 'tis archers!'

A flight of arrows, like angry wasps, buzzed viciously over from all points, most of their shafts thudding into the lawn inside the Abbey walls. Gelltor waved his axe aloft. 'Now 'tis war. Your Abbey is surrounded, and we will stay here for as long as it takes to slay you all or make you surrender!'

Skipper reappeared on the wall, holding an arrow. The otter Chieftain's face was a fearsome sight to see. He snapped the arrow contemptuously, tossing the pieces down on to the path. 'Hearken, fox, you want war? Then by the thunder you'll get it! Redwallers are peace-lovin' creatures, until they're attacked. Start diggin' yore graves now, 'cos we ain't goin' t'dig 'em for ye!'

Bargle detailed his Guosim back to their wallguard, then followed Skipper and the others down to the gatehouse. Rimrose and Ellayo were waiting for them.

'Did they mention our daughter or her friends?' Song's mother enquired anxiously.

The lazy-lidded eyes smiled comfortingly at her. 'No, me pretty one, course they didn't. They don't even know Song an' 'er pals are away from the Abbey, or they would've used 'em to try an' draw us out, ain't that right, Skip?'

'Correct, mate. Those young 'uns 'ave got the sense not to get theirselves captured. They know wot they're doin'.'

Rusvul went out. Sitting on the wallsteps, he buried his head into his paws. Ellayo came and sat by him. 'No good frettin', Rusvul Reguba, you can't do nothin' about yore son now. We're stuck in 'ere for better or worse, surrounded.'

The squirrel warrior wiped a paw across his eyes. ''Twas me drove Dann to it. D'you think he'll ever forgive me for the things I said to 'im?'

Ellayo took Rusvul's paw and squeezed it. 'Course he will. Dann's a good young creature, like our Song, he ain't stubborn an' unmovin' like his father. But it takes all kinds, friend, and wot we're goin' to need in the days that lie ahead are warriors, stubborn unmovin' warriors, like yoreself!'

For the first time since the battle at the southwest corner, Rusvul smiled. He stood up and bowed courteously to the old squirrel. 'I thank ye for those kind words, marm. When there's fightin' to be done an' warriors need to stand firm, you'll find me the most stubborn an' unmovin' of all. 'Tis just the way I am.'

Because of the danger from further volleys of arrows, Skipper requested that anybeast not on wallguard stay inside the Abbey. Florian decided that the time need not be wasted. If the Redwallers were to defend themselves from outside attack they needed drill and weapon training. Knowing nothing whatsoever about either matter, the hare made it all up as he went along. Armed with a motley selection of ladles, window poles, brooms and any domestic item that came to paw, elders and Dibbuns were lined up in Great Hall, together with the Noonvale troupe, and Florian swaggered about in what he imagined was true parade-ground manner.

'Right ho, troops, let's see if we can't knock you into shape, wot! Form y'selves up in four ranks here. Jump to it now!'

Brother Melilot and Diggum Cellarmole were edging away when the hare challenged them. 'I say, you two chaps, where d'you think you're jolly well off to? Back in line this very instant!'

Melilot put down the feather duster he had been shouldering. 'Excuse us, but you'll have to let us go, that's if you want dinner tonight. We're on kitchen duty.'

Florian waved them away hastily. 'Oh, right you are. Can't have starvin' troops, wot, wot?'

Sister Sloey and Gurrbowl grounded dustpan and window pole.

'Sorry, 'fraid we've got to tend t'the wounded in the Infirmary.'

Florian blew a sigh of frustration. 'Off y'pop then, you two, excused drill. You there, Dwopple, I said form four blinkin' ranks, not five. Come up front here, sir, where I can keep my beady eye on you!'

Saluting furiously, the mousebabe charged up front, dragging behind him a long-handled oven paddle, which cracked against footpaws and tripped all who came in contact with it, causing widespread chaos.

'Yowch! Go easy with that paddle, you wretch!'

'Oof! An' you watch that ladle, near put me eye out!'

'Aagh! Me footpaw! Get away, y'villain!'

Florian grabbed the paddle and tried to wrestle it away from the mousebabe, who was quite proud of his weapon and not prepared to give it up without a struggle. As he fought for possession of the paddle, the hare kept shouting orders.

'Steady in the ranks there! Stan' up straight, you chaps, pick up those weapons! No squabblin' at the back, that's an order! Where'n the name o' seasons are you three goin', eh?'

'Hurr, us'n's got to set ee tables furr vittles, zurr!'

'Oh, quite. Gimme that paddle before you lay everybeast low, you fiend!'

'You lerra paddle go, mista Florey. It mine!'

'Mutiny is it? I'll have ye locked up in the vegetable cupboard!'

'Mister Florian, how can you shout so heartlessly at a tender babe after all he's been through? Fie an' shame on you, sir!'

'Deesum marm, don't interfere or you'll be locked up with the blighter. Stand fast there, you lot, I haven't told you to move!'

'Dormitory duty. Beds won't make themselves y'know!'

'Dishwashing. Brother Melilot needs clean pots'n' pans!'

'Ale an' cordials to be brought up from wine cellar.'

'Candles and lamps need attendin' before evenin'.'

Dropping their makeshift weapons, Redwallers scurried off, left, right and centre. Florian managed to drag the paddle from Dwopple, who threw himself on the floor, kicking all four paws and howling inconsolably at the loss of his beloved weapon.

'Wahaaaah! Rotten ole rabbit pincha Dwopple's

paggle. Wahaahaahaa!'

Deesum picked him up, comforting Dwopple and castigating Florian in the same breath. 'There there now, my little soldier, did the cruel rabbit steal your paddle, nasty wicked beast!'

'Madam! Cruel, nasty an' jolly well wicked I may be, but I am a hare, marm, not a rabbit!'

'Indeed, sir? Well, you show all the sense of a rabbit, a two-day-old one. You are not fit to command that paddle you have stolen!'

Florian sat down dispiritedly upon the floorstones, staring about at the empty hall. 'Huh! Bloomin' paddle's about all I've got left to command, wot!'

Evening shades were stealing over the western horizon, scarlet sunrays reflecting off the undersides of heavy dark clouds drifting eastward. Skipper ducked low as he led a party of Redwallers along the ramparts. Meeting Bargle, the otter beckoned at the group he was heading. 'Evenin', mate. Brought the rest o' yore Guosim an' some Redwallers to relieve the sentries. Wot's 'appenin' out there?'

Bargle took a quick final glance over the parapet. 'Oh, nothin' much. They're shootin' off the odd arrow t'keep our heads down, but apart from that 'tis fairly quiet. Wot's for vittles?'

Skipper grinned at the tough little shrew, whose stomach was growling thunderously. 'Sorry I never sent any tucker out to ye, but I couldn't chance no pore kitchenbeast gettin' hit by an arrer. Don't worry though, messmate, there's food aplenty for you an' yore shrews: leek'n'celery soup, tater'n'mushroom turnover, sweet cider an' plum duff.'

Bargle grimaced longingly as he tightened his belt another notch to quiet his rumbling gut. 'Did I 'ear you mention plum duff, mate?'

Skipper winked. 'Aye, with sweet arrowroot sauce.'

Bargle grabbed the otter's paw fiercely. 'Plum duff'n'sweet arrowroot sauce. Don't say another word, Skip, or me stummick'll perish afore I make it t'the table!'

Each shrew who left the wall was replaced by a relief sentry. Skipper did the rounds of the walltop, whispering words of advice and encouragement. He gave special attention to Friar Butty, who was positioned at the centre of the north wall.

'Are ye sure y'can keep yore eyes open all night, Friar? Y'won't drop off t'sleep, will you, sir?'

The old squirrel patted his friend's sturdy paw. 'I'll be fine, Skip, you just leave me here. Funny, but I don't feel the least bit sleepy tonight. I couldn't face a night alone in the gatehouse without Nutwing. His snores always lulled me into a slumber. Ah, lack a day, I miss the feathery old rascal.'

Skipper looked away and blinked. 'So do I, Friar. We all miss 'im.'

He was distracted by Florian, waving from the battlements over the south wallgate. Skipper scurried across to the hare. 'Keep yore ears down, mister Florian sir, or they'll spot yer.'

The hare ducked and seated himself, gesturing over the wall. 'Somethin' rather odd goin' on down there. Vermin chaps dashin' back an' forth, carryin' bits'n'pieces an' whatnot.'

Skipper crouched, alert. 'Bits'n'pieces o' wot, sir?'

'Oh, I dunno, twigs, brush, wood an' what have you. Must be out o' their bally minds. They're dumpin' the stuff in front o' the wallgate an' scamperin' off. What'd they want to do that for?' Florian looked round, but Skipper was gone, rushing along the ramparts and down the wallsteps to the small wicker gate in the centre of the south wall.

Janglur and Rusvul were already there. The two warrior squirrels had been carrying out their usual patrol of the inner grounds. Skipper joined them, keeping his voice down to a whisper. 'What're those vermin up to, mates?'

Janglur watched the door through half-closed eyes as he replied, 'Me'n'Rusvul were passin' here when we smelled vegetable oil and pine resin, then we 'eard those rats pushin' dry brush an' wood up against the door. You know wot that means, Skip?'

The big otter nodded grimly. 'Fire. They're goin' to try an' burn their way in 'ere! Janglur, go to the wine cellars. Over the door there you'll see three great longbows an' quivers o' big clothyard shafts. Bring 'em 'ere quick. Rusvul, get Gubbio Foremole an' some of 'is crew, fetch buckets too, start fillin' 'em from the pond. We'll put a spoke in their wheel if they wanna play with fire, mates!'

16

Night had fallen along the fast-flowing river. Dippler sat at the water's edge, bathing his footpaws. Dann trotted back and tweaked the shrew's ear lightly. 'Come on, Dipp, you can't stop here.'

The young Guosim shrew let the cold water flow over his weary paws. 'Why not? They've got to rest too, y'know – don't suppose they could travel far on fast water like this at night, too dangerous.'

Song walked back to join them. 'He's right, Dann. Perhaps we'd better find someplace where we can take a bite to eat and sleep till dawn.'

They continued walking along the riverbank until they found a likely spot. Song was loosing her pack when Dann called to her. 'Song, come an' look at this. What d'ye make of it?' He was standing in the shallows, hanging on to the trailing branches of a willow and gazing downriver. Song waded in by him. 'See, further down the bank. Looks like firelight t'me.'

Song peered at the glow in the far darkness. 'Aye, 'tis fire right enough. Dipp said they've got to rest too, maybe it's them. Let's go and take a look. Best go armed!'

Steering back from the bank a bit they stole swiftly through the woodland, Dippler and Dann with drawn swords and Song with her greenstone-topped club. Drawing near to the light, they could make out a warm glow, but no sign of the flames which made it. Careful now, they measured each pace, avoiding dead twigs, dry ferns, or anything that might make a noise and betray their presence to the enemy. Song gripped her weapon tightly, whispering to Dann, 'What d'you think, is it them?'

A huge, bushy, brown-furred mouselike creature popped up in front of them and began chattering in a shrill voice. 'Ah yiss yiss, it could be them, though t'be shore 'tis not. Why, it's only ourselves an' we're not them, unless by them y'mean us, an' if 'tis ourselves yer after, then we're them yiss yiss!'

The three friends were taken aback. Dann was first to recover. Menacing the creature with his sword, he backed it up to a tree, only to have Dippler jump in and place himself between them. 'Leave 'im alone, mate. 'Tis a watervole. They're friendly!' The shrew held both paws out and wiggled his nose in a strange greeting to the newcomer. Grinning cheerily, the watervole returned the salute and continued chattering.

'Oh yiss yiss, an' you'll be one o' the Guosim, knew it as soon as I saw yer spiky little 'ead. Up'n'down, up'n'down this river yore tribe used to go alla time, oh yiss yiss. Don't see many Guosim these seasons though, no no, river's too fast for shrews I think. Whoo! Aren't I the terrible one fer gabbin' though. Yiss yiss, y'can spit in the river an' not make much difference to it, that's wot I always say. Yiss yiss!'

Dippler thrust his chin out aggressively at the watervole. 'Who d'ye think yore talkin' to, bush'ead? No river's too fast for a Guosim shrew, an' we should know 'cos we've sailed 'em all!'

Still grinning, the vole rattled on. 'Ah well yiss yiss, I see what y'mean, so I do, an' yer a fine figure of a shrew so y'are an' I take back any lie I uttered about yer, yiss yiss, so I do, 'cos an egg in a duck's belly is neither under

168

nor over the water an' that's a fact so 'tis, yiss yiss . . .' All through his ceaseless babble, the watervole's eyes were fixed greedily on Song's greenstone stick. He was making her uncomfortable, so she quickly hid it behind her back.

'Excuse me, but could I fit in a word sideways? I'm Song, this is Dann and the shrew's Dippler. We're just looking for someplace to eat and spend the night. We don't wish to stand here and be talked to death, if you'll forgive my saying so.'

Springing forward, the watervole began shaking Song's paw vigorously. 'Oh yiss yiss, yer well forgiven, missie. I'm called Burble. Me muther had a sense o' humour, y'see, yiss yiss. Food'n'rest, is that all y'll be needin'? Well, foller me, the Riverheads can supply that, y'can be sure as an onion's a sour apple with too many coats, yiss yiss!'

Song had great difficulty extricating her paw from Burble's ceaseless pawshaking, but the moment she did the vole shot off like an arrow. They had to follow him at a headlong run.

Why they could only see the firelight's glow soon became clear. It emanated from a great cave hewn deep into the riverbank slightly above water level. Burble bowed to them as they stood panting outside.

'Ah yiss yiss, 'tis only an ould bit of a hole, but 'tis home to me an' has been to my father an' his father before him an' his father before him an' his father before him and his mmffff!'

A big old grey-furred watervole had come out and clamped a paw over Burble's mouth. He nodded at the newcomers. 'Y'know, sometimes us Riverheads say that the river'll stop babblin' before young Burble does. Do you all come in now, an' welcome!'

Inside the cave, there were upward of twelve or more watervoles seated round an enormous fire eating bowls of stew. The old one called to them. 'Our Burble's brought some travellers for a bite o' supper, so he has.'

A fat, motherly-looking vole in a woven rush apron bobbed a curtsey. 'Yiss yiss, so he has, sit ye down an' a thousand welcomes to ye!'

Song touched the greenstick to her forehead in a salute. 'And a thousand thanks for your kindness, marm!'

Suddenly all the watervoles threw themselves face down. Paws outstretched, they set up a wailing din.

'Whooooaaaah! Gorramahooogly! D'Leafwood! D'Leafwood!'

'Did I say something wrong?'

Dann looked perplexed at the prostrate Riverhead tribe. 'I don't think so, Song. Wonder what a Leafwood is?'

Burble was only too willing to explain. 'Do ye not know what a Leafwood is? Ah 'tis a wunnerful thing, yiss yiss, so 'tis. D'Leafwood is carried only by the highest Chiefs an' greatest vole Warriors who live on the waters. Dippler, yore a water creature, shame on yer for not knowin' of the marvellous Leafwood. Why, meself has known of it since I was born, an' my father an' his father before him an' his father before him an' . . .'

Burble caught the look in Song's eye as she raised her Leafwood. He went silent with a meek grin, but only after having the last word. 'An' so on an' so on!'

The old grey watervole's voice trembled as he addressed Song. 'Ah, a Leafwood could surely make the Riverhead tribe famed an' feared by all. We would give anythin' to be ownin' such a marvellous thing.'

The young squirrel's reply was instant. 'I would trade it for a good boat, sir.'

The old one's face lit up with joy. 'Now isn't that a wonderful thing t'be sayin', for 'tis meself who owns the greatest boat ever t'sail on water!'

Dippler gave Song a warning glance, then stepped in to take charge of the trade himself. 'Let's take a look at yore boat first, sir. No offence given, I hope.'

The grey vole's stomach wobbled as he chuckled. 'Yiss yiss, an' none taken I'm sure, for who better t'look at a vessel than the grand Guosim himself? Foller me, young travellers.'

Taking them out on to the bank, he passed a lantern to Dann. 'Here now, great sword-bearer, hold on to that whilst I show y'me boat.'

Pulling aside clumps of bog willow and saxifrage, the oldster heaved forth a type of oblong coracle, fashioned from osier boughs covered with rowan bark and held together by layers of pine resin. He tapped a paw alongside his snout, winking slyly. 'Never leave boats moored out on water for allbeasts t'see, like the dreaded ould Marlfox an' his water rats who passed here t'day. Oh yiss yiss, it pays to keep yer boats hidden!'

Song glanced down the fast nightdark river reaches. 'So, they passed here. Where d'you think they went, sir?'

The oldster scratched his chubby cheeks and shrugged. 'Hah! They could've bin sailin' t'the moon for all I know, missie. Well, Guosim, wot d'ye think of me boat? A splendid craft, eh?'

Dippler had been inspecting the vessel, and now he said, 'Oh, it's not bad. Not good, but not bad, but seen too many seasons' service on this river for my likin', sir. Ah, here we are! This's the boat fer us. My friend'll trade the Leafwood for this 'un!'

The young shrew dragged forth another vessel, far newer than the first, which shone like a honey globule from the many coats of pine resin which had been melted down and applied to its sleek sides. Unlike the other, this craft had a proper pointed bow and butted stern, and patterns and symbols had been painted beneath the resin with coloured dyes, giving it the look of a very special boat. The old water vole shook his head and waved his paws furiously.

'Ah no, ah no, y'can't be havin' dat one, sure an' 'tis never the sort o' boat you'd be goin' after Marlfoxes with. No, me bold Guosim, I'm afraid I can't be lettin' y'have that one!'

Song twirled the Leafwood idly. Lantern light gleamed off the round, shiny green stone implanted at its end. She nodded to Dann and Dippler, and all three sauntered off, Dippler smiling back regretfully at the grey watervole. 'Pity. We'll just have to trade the Leafwood with some other tribe.'

The vole dodged in front of them, hopping back and forth to stop them wandering off. 'Whoa now, young buckoes, I've got other boats y'know, yiss yiss, good ones too, let me show yer them!'

Song shook her head. Feigning boredom, she wagged the Leafwood under the old vole's nose. 'No, I'm sorry, sir, no other boat will do. That's the one for us, same as this Leafwood is the thing you want. Here, hold it.'

The vole took hold of the object reverently, covetousness shining in his eyes at the symbol of power. Song judged the moment right.

'Now, d'you want to give it back to me so that when we're gone you'll never see it again? You look to me like a skilled creature, well able to build a boat, probably far finer than that one. What's it to be?'

The grey watervole looked from the Leafwood to the boat, from the boat to the Leafwood and repeated the performance. 'Ah, singe me whiskers an' sink me tail . . . 'Tis a bargain done!' He threw banksoil in the air, stamped his footpaw down thrice and spat on his outstretched right paw. Spitting on their paws, the three friends shook heartily with him. He grinned ruefully.

'A true trade, though you do strike a turrible hard bargain, yiss yiss. That's a Riverhead Volechief's boat y've got there. Light as a feather, true as an arrow, an' faster than a brown trout, there's not a craft on any water that can keep up wid it, let alone try t'beat it. 'Tis sorry I am to part with yonder vessel!'

Dann whacked him heartily on the back. 'But now you own the Leafwood, sir, the power is all yours!'

The vole did a little jig of delight. 'Yiss yiss, so I do.

Every good trade calls for a Comallyeh. So here goes.' He raised his head and called in a loud piercing yell, 'Comallyeeeeeeeh!'

Startled, the three companions jumped back, as watervoles materialized from seemingly everywhere, all crying aloud, 'Comallyeeeeeeh!'

Dippler took their haversacks and tossed them into the boat. 'Looks like we're invited to some kind o' celebration, pals!'

Later, the big cave on the bank was packed tight with watervoles, nearly every one of them holding either a little fiddle or a small pawdrum. Song and her friends sat by the fire spooning down thick delicious riverstew comprising cress, watershrimp, turnip, carrot, mushrooms and several other vegetables and herbs which they could not identify. Voles made sure that their beakers of honey and blackberry cordial were never empty. Soon every paw in the place was tapping to a lively jig, well played and heartily sung by the Riverhead tribe.

'Oh there's some fools take a bath each day,
By rollin' in the mornin' dew,
An' others who won't wash at all,
But that ain't me nor you.
Othersome take dry dust baths,
An' reckon that they're clean,
But if a watervole you be,
Well you know wot I mean.
Hoho, yiss yiss, ho hooooooo!

Don't sit'n'shiver beside the river,
Dive right in with a splosh,
Grab hold of a good ole soapwort root,
An' give yoreself a wash.
Scrub hard scrub soft scrub lively, mate,
Good health you'll never lack,
An' if yore paws can't reach around,
A fish'll scrub yore back.

173

Hoho, yiss yiss, ho hoooooo!'

The ditty finished amid great merriment, with the old watervole acting as master of ceremonies, pointing the Leafwood at the three. 'C'mon now, travellers, sing for yore supper!'

Dann flushed with embarrassment. 'Singin' isn't a thing I do best. You have a go, Song.'

Dippler helped himself to another bowl of stew. 'Aye, yore a good singer, missie. If they 'ear my voice that ole feller's liable to cancel the bargain.'

Song stood up and called out to the musicians, 'D'you know the one called "Green Rushes an' Lilies so pale"?'

Several of the old volewives threw their rush aprons up over their faces, calling out warnings to the pretty young squirrel.

'Ah sure, don't try it, missie, 'tis too fast!'

'They'll leave yer verses behind, pretty maid, watervoles play speedy!'

Song took a sip of cordial to wet her lips. 'Oh, they will, will they? Well, let's see 'em try. Ready, one, two, three!'

Watervole fiddles and drums started the music at a cracking pace. But Song was right up there with them, her sweet voice ringing out.

'Green rushes green rushes an' lilies so pale,
Pray sit ye down friend now an' list' to my tale,
For the rivers flow fast an' the mountains are tall,
An' across the wide moorlands the curlews do call,
Dirry wallaker williker doddle rum day!

Green rushes green rushes an' lilies so pale,
Bring me bread'n'cheese an' some dandelion ale,
An' light up a fire now to warm my cold paws,
I'll sit here all winter till that river thaws,
Skither riddle aye fiddle aye rumbletum hey!

Green rushes green rushes an' lilies so pale,

I've travelled so far over valley an' dale,
Stale bread'n'hard cheese an' the ale isn't here,
An' the fire isn't lit so 'tis goodbye, me dear.
Rowtle dowtle rye tootle I go on me way!

Green rushes pale lilies I'll bid ye good day!
For where I'm not welcome I never would stay!
An' to all you musicians I'd just like to say,
If I've sung out too fast yore indulgence I pray!'

Amid wild cheers and resounding whoops, Song was carried shoulder high around the cave. An old volewife shook a ladle at the pawsore, panting musicians, some of whom had stowed their fiddles and drums away, having been left far behind by the final verse, with Song completing the last four lines unaccompanied. The volewife cackled.

'Haharr, you lot'd better learn t'play proper, yiss yiss. The squirrelmaid sang the paws off'n yer, right sweet and clear too!'

Burble raised his beaker aloft: 'Yiss yiss, let's drink the 'ealth of the best bargainer an' finest singer, the bravest lookin' sword-bearer an' the starvin'est Guosim ever t'come inside Riverhead Cave. Good luck an' fine fortune be theirs wherever they travel. Yiss yiss?'

The watervoles raised their drinks and roared out, 'Yiss yiss! Yiss yiss!'

Dippler licked the rim of his bowl. 'Any more o' that stew left, matey? No point in lettin' it go t'waste!'

Mokkan lay back in the stern of the logboat, trailing a paw in the water as he issued orders. 'Ship those oars an' let her drift, an' pass some vittles back there. Fenno, my friend, keep our boat out in the middle, away from the banks.'

The shrew sobbed miserably as he manoeuvred a paddle oar in the stern behind the Marlfox. 'This noose is stranglin' me. I can 'ardly keep me eyes open, sir.'

Stern-faced, Mokkan tested the double-headed axe blade on his paw. 'You'd better keep your eyes open, shrew, or I'll shut them for good!'

The logboat drifted on into the calm summer night.

17

A luminous white figure, with black pits for eyes and a gaping bloodstained mouth, drifted spectrally around the bedchamber of the High Queen Silth. Its voice seemed to come from afar, like the spirit of one lost upon a dark and distant shore.

'Siiiilth! I see you, I hear you, I will not rest until you are dead. Die, Siiiiilth!'

From within the curtained palanquin, which served her every purpose, Queen Silth's voice screeched hoarse with terror. 'Go away! Leave me in peace, White Ghost! Guards! Guards!'

Immediately the bedchamber door started to open, the figure vanished upward. Water rat guards bearing torches dashed into the already brightly lit room. Obediently, they searched every corner as the Queen ranted on. 'It was here again, the White Ghost! Where's my daughter Lantur? I want her here right now! Lantur, Lantur!'

In the room directly overhead, the vixen Lantur hauled up a sheet through the wide floorboard joints. It was heavily flecked with fish scales to make it appear luminous, with black charcoal and red dye marking out the face. Folding the sheet carefully, Lantur stowed it in a corner cupboard. The vixen replaced some loose boards in the cupboard's bottom, but before doing so she directed a final spine-chilling moan into the bottom section, which connected with a similar cupboard in the Queen's bedchamber below.

'Ooooohhhhuuuuurrrrrhhhhh!'

Closing the cupboard carefully, Lantur listened to the commotion set up by her mother as it echoed upwards.

'There it goes again! I told you, fools, the White Ghost has been in this room, not a moment back. Find it! Lantur! I want Lantur!'

A moment later the vixen strolled calmly into the Queen's bedchamber. She dismissed the guards, who were only too glad to get out of Silth's presence. 'Now what is it, Mother? Bad dreams again?'

'Don't talk to me like that. How can I have dreams if I don't sleep? The White Ghost was here again, just before you came in.'

'If you say so, Mother.'

'I am Queen here, you will address me as Queen! It was here, I saw it through the gauze curtain. You don't believe me, do you?'

'O Queen, if you say it was here then it must have been. But where is it now? Why does nobeast save yourself see this White Ghost?'

'I don't know! Do you?'

'Perhaps, O Queen, it is something from your memory, some enemy you slew long seasons ago, a restless spirit coming back for vengeance upon its killer . . .' Lantur narrowly dodged a drinking chalice that was hurled out at her from between the curtains. Silth's voice was shrill with rage.

'Get out! Out! I won't have you talking to me like that!' The vixen bowed and turned to go. Silth subdued her voice to a whine. 'No, stay with me, daughter, stay. I fear being alone here. This room is far too ugly. It needs more light, more beautiful things in it.'

Lantur bowed again and continued towards the door. 'I will stay, Majesty. With me you need have no fear. Wait while I dismiss those fools who are supposed to be guarding your door.'

Lantur stepped outside and dismissed the guards. When they had gone she tapped lightly on the far wall. A female water rat emerged from the shadows of the upper stairs. Lantur nodded at her. 'Wilce, keep an ear to the floor of my room. When you hear me snore as if I'm asleep, then send down the White Ghost and start moaning. When you hear the Queen scream, pull it back up again.'

The rat Wilce bowed to her mistress. 'I know what to do, my lady.'

Lantur re-entered the bedchamber and installed herself in a chair. 'Rest, O Queen, I am here to protect you.'

Janglur and Rusvul stood in the battlement shadows, watching the moonpatched landscape of open field which skirted half the south wall. Each of the squirrel warriors gripped a massive yew longbow, with a grey-feathered arrow on its string, half as long and heavy again as a normal shaft. Something moved near the woodland fringe.

'Here they come, mate, two of 'em,' Rusvul murmured. 'Over by that high sycamore.'

Janglur followed his friend's direction, sighting the enemy. 'Aye, I've spotted 'em now, water rat an' a Marlfox. See the liddle glow? They're carryin' a piece of smoulderin' rope. Let 'em get closer afore we take a shot.'

The vixen Vannan bent double, taking advantage of every bracken patch and groundswell. Beside her the rat Dakkle kept pace, blowing lightly on the glowing end of towrope to rid it of ash.

'Don't blow too hard,' Vannan cautioned him, ''twill burst into flame. Leave it now until we're at the wallgate.'

Dakkle uncrouched slightly as they moved forward,

raising his head a fraction to survey the walltop. 'Looks fairly quiet up there, marm. We'll warm things up a bit for them soo . . .'

As soon as the long shaft struck Dakkle between his eyes, Vannan was off, rolling to one side into a patch of fern. *Thunk!* Another arrow embedded itself in the spot where she had crouched a moment before. Flattening herself, she wriggled away through the ferns. Two more arrows followed, the last grazing her footpaw. Vannan sprang up then and ran for the trees in a zigzagging rush, tripping and falling flat by the sycamore as a clothyard shaft buzzed overhead like an angry wasp into the woodlands.

Gelltor grabbed the vixen and dragged her to safety behind the tree. 'We'll have to think of another way to burn that door down.'

Vannan tried to regulate her panting breath. 'What about using fire arrows?'

Gelltor looked at her pityingly. 'Fire arrows? Did you see the length of those shafts the Redwallers are shooting? You need a great longbow to fire such a shaft. We don't have anything like that. Our bows aren't powerful enough – we'd be well within their range long before we could loose off a shot.'

The vixen settled her back against the sycamore, pouting sulkily. 'Well, why don't you think of something, brother? You're supposed to be the one with all the good ideas.'

With a wave, Gelltor summoned his rats from the underbush. 'No need to look so smug, sister. As it happens I do have an idea, a good one!'

The otter Borrakul made his way over to Skipper from the north wall. 'Bargle says that they're rainin' stones an' arrows heavy on the north side, Skip. He thinks they're plannin' some kind o' move over that way, usin' their firepower t'keep our heads down.'

From his position by the south wallgate, Skipper called

up to Janglur, 'Y'hear that, mate? What d'ye think they're up to?'

The warrior squirrel called back confidently, 'Hah! That's the oldest trick in the book, Skip. They're tryin' to decoy us away from 'ere so they can burn the wallgate. Borrakul, tell Bargle to sit tight there an' keep low.'

Rusvul had spotted movement at the woodland edges. Notching a shaft to his bowstring, he murmured calmly to Janglur, 'Here they come again, matey. Spread out this time, about eight o' them, I count. They're goin' to take some stoppin' this time!'

Janglur called to the otter on the ground below. 'Best make yore move now, Skip, whilst they're still far enough away.'

Skipper gave the nod to Gubbio Foremole and his crew, half of whom were carrying pails of water. 'You ready, Gubb?'

'Say ee word, zurr, us'n's be's never readier, hurr aye!'

Skipper unbolted the wallgate and swung it open. 'Go!'

Those moles not carrying pails scuttled outside and cleared the gateway of inflammable wood and brush, heaving it inside, whilst the rest doused the outside of the gate down with pails of water. Skipper stood out in front of them, his longbow bent with a big arrow resting on its taut string, protecting the moles from attack. Now vermin were about halfway across the open ground. Janglur watched them pause, spread wide in a half-circle. Suddenly the night blossomed with orange flame, as the water rats set burning tow to speartops bound with oily rags and charged for the gate.

'Front'n'centre, Skip!'

The otter heard Janglur's warning. Gritting his teeth he strained the longbow to its limit, letting the middle rat run straight at him. So strong was Skipper's shot that the arrow passed clean through the charging rat, who fell forward upon the burning spear. When the door was clear of brush and soaked well with water and all the moles were inside, Skipper jumped back in and slammed the bolts home. Janglur let his bow drop, unwrapping the sling from about his waist.

'They're close enough for stones now, Rus. Don't need these longbows.' He had already dropped one rat before Rusvul could load his sling.

'Come on, scum, my name's Regubaaaaaa!'

Another rat fell to Rusvul's whirling sling. The rest broke and ran back to the tree cover, all except one who carried on charging forward. Seconds before both the squirrels' slingstones laid him low he threw his spear. It thudded, blazing, into the wallgate door. 'Pail o' water on a rope, quick!' Rusvul yelled out.

Skipper hurled the rope end up. Rusvul hauled the water pail to the battlements, and then lowered it over the top until it struck the outstretched spear haft, upsetting its contents over it. Rewarded by the hissing sound of extinguished flames, Rusvul winked at Janglur. 'No sense takin' chances, even if the door is soaked.'

Janglur Swifteye retrieved his longbow and loosed off an arrow. It thudded into the far sycamore trunk, quivering. 'Aye, yore right there. Let's turn the tables on 'em an' keep *their* 'eads down for the night!'

Foremole gathered pawfuls of the bracken and wood which had been intended to burn the gate. 'Noice of ee vurmints to gather kindlin' for ee kitchen ovens, hurr!'

Gelltor stayed well back in the woodlands, issuing orders to a rat. 'Tell Ascrod and Predak to pull back from the north wall and meet me back here. Vannan, this is no time to be dozing. Liven yourself up, we've got to plan our next move.'

The vixen grinned maliciously at her brother. 'Oh, given up the idea of burning our way in, have we? What's the matter, didn't your good idea work?'

In the grey hour before dawn, Song came awake. All round her in the packed cave watervoles were snoring and snuffling in the hot stuffy atmosphere. The squirrelmaid shook Dann lightly. Startled awake, he instinctively touched his swordhilt to make sure it was still there. Song gestured for him to make his way outside, then prodded the sleeping Dippler. Rolling over, the Guosim shrew muttered drowsily, 'Mmm. Any o' that stew left, mate?'

Song stifled his mouth with a paw, whispering in his ear, 'Wake up, Dipp. We're going, if the boat's still there.'

Luckily it was. Dippler grumbled as they carried it to the water's edge. 'Wot's all the rush for? I liked it in there, that stew was nice.'

Dann tugged the shrew's tail sharply. 'Keep your voice down an' stop thinkin' of just yore stomach. Song's right, we'd best get goin' whilst the goin's good. I don't trust that ole grey watervole. He'd like it fine if'n he could hang on to both the Leafwood an' his boat. Those voles seemed friendly enough, but you never can tell.'

'Yiss yiss, y'could never tell, 'specially with a crafty ole beast like the Grey One!'

They whirled around as Burble emerged from the willows, carrying a sack of food and two extra oars. Dann eyed him levelly. 'Where d'you think you're goin'?'

Brushing past them, Burble slid the boat into the water and threw his gear aboard. He leapt in after it and held the vessel still by grabbing firm hold of overhead branches. 'Goin' wid you, yiss yiss, ain't livin' in some ould hole on a riverbank till I got grey whiskers like the rest of 'em. Stir yer stumps an' get in 'ere. We've got to get goin' quickish, afore the River'eads wake up an' find their *Swallow* gone!'

Dippler was about to debate the point when Song shoved him unceremoniously into the boat and thrust a paddle at him. 'Don't argue, Dipp, we haven't got time. Something tells me Burble's right. Let's get away from here. We can argue all you like as we paddle. I'll take this side with you, an' Dann, you an' Burble take the other side. Don't waste time, dawn'll soon be up!'

With the two oars already aboard the friends had an oar each. They steered their vessel out into the fast-flowing centre of the river, heading downstream. Wise in the ways of boats, Dippler praised their new craft immediately. Even with their limited knowledge, Song and Dann had to agree with him: the watervole's boat was a traveller's dream. The Guosim shrew watched happily as the boat responded to their paddles.

'Light as a feather she is, mates. This'n don't sit in the water, she skims it, like a bird. So that's why y'called 'er *Swallow*, eh?'

Burble nodded vigorously, casting worried glances behind. 'Yiss yiss, Dipp, now less o' the tongue an' more o' the paddle!'

Song peered suspiciously across at the young watervole, even as she took his advice and paddled harder. 'Burble, I've got a feelin' you haven't told us all. The way you talk, anybeast would think we stole the *Swallow*.'

Burble explained in part as the *Swallow* shot along the river like a glittering arrow. 'Ah well, y'see, missie, that Grey One is a real slybeast. The *Swallow* don't belong to 'im, she belongs to the River'ead tribe, but they all think Grey One traded his ole boat for yore Leafwood, an' he never told 'em different. They'll come after us soon, oh yiss yiss, sure as trout like mayflies. The River'ead'll want their *Swallow* back.'

Dann dug the paddle deep, his jaw tight with anger. 'So we're sailin' a stolen vessel. That ole watervole tricked us. He gets the Leafwood, but if they catch up with us we get nothin'!'

The prow dipped and rose beautifully, skirting a rocky outcrop poking from the river as they feathered their paddle blades. 'Rotten old swindler!' Song burst out, expressing her dislike of the Grey One.

However, Burble was smiling fit to burst, now that he

judged there was some distance between themselves and the Riverhead voles. 'Heeheehee! Don't git yore paws in an uproar, pals. Grey One thinks that 'cos he's old it makes 'im smart. But I'm younger an' smarter than 'im by a good stretch o' river. Yiss yiss!'

Song eyed Burble curiously. 'How so?'

The little fat creature shook with unconcealed glee. "Cos I tricked 'im! When that ole barrelbelly wakes up 'e'll find 'imself clutchin' a stew ladle in 'is paws, not a Leafwood. Yiss yiss, I pinched it back off 'im. Yore Leafwood is inside that sack o' grub I fetched wid me. Heeheehee!'

Song looked sternly at the watervole. 'That was very wrong, Burble. Grey One deceived the tribe, but we kept our part of the bargain. Now we're got double trouble!'

Dawnlight had begun filtering over the river in a pale wash of cerise and gold when a cry rang out faintly from behind them, echoing down the tree-shaded banks.

'Waaaaylaaahoooo!'

Burble's chubby face blanched with fright. 'River'eads! Paddle for yore lives, pals!'

'But I thought this *Swallow* could outrun anythin' on the river?' Dann called out as they wielded their paddles furiously.

Burble blew spray from his face. 'Mebbe, but they got eight rowers to a boat, an' River'ead voles know these waters a lot better'n you do, squirrel. They'll take every shortcut, fast current an' riverdodge the Grey One can think of. Look for a cutoff. We gotta get off the mainstream!'

Bending their backs, the four young creatures laboured at their paddles, mouths wide open as they sucked in air, every muscle and sinew of their bodies throbbing with strain. Behind them the cries of the Riverhead voles grew louder. They were getting closer, gaining on the *Swallow* with their riverskills and greater numbers. Shaking perspiration and riverwater from his eyes, Dann gestured

185

with his chin, nodding forward to a spot further upriver on the south bank.

'Looks like a sidestream ahead up yonder!' he gasped out.

But the watervole did not seem to fancy the idea. 'No no, not that 'un. 'Tis a dead end, I think, full o' slime an' gnats. 'Twould be stupid to go up there, Dann!'

'Waaaaylaaaahooooo! Death to boat-robbers!'

Song chanced a quick glance back up the river, her mind made up. 'Head towards that sidestream before they come round the bend and sight us. If 'tis a stupid idea to hide up a slimy dead end then mayhap they won't look there. Don't argue, just do it!'

As they cut across the stream, Burble scattered some supplies from his sack, bread and clay dishes, into the water. 'They'll find those in the rapids downstream. P'raps they'll think we was wrecked. Duck yore 'eads an' ship those paddles!'

Weeds, tall rushes and overhanging bush raked their backs as the *Swallow* glided into the cutoff. The water was dark, murky and fetid; gnats, mosquitoes and all manner of winged pests shrouded the four fugitives. Dippler grabbed some bulrushes and held the boat still. Sloppy green water vegetation swirled briefly on the surface and then settled again, as if no boat had ever disturbed it. Song's heart was pounding like a triphammer – she was sure it could be heard if anybeast passed too close. Fighting to get their breathing under control, they flattened themselves in the well of the *Swallow*. Dippler slapped at a large flying beetle that was trying to settle on his face. Dann shot him a warning glance, and then they heard the Riverhead tribe. It sounded as if they had a dozen or more boats out in pursuit. Old Grey One was in the lead craft, directing them.

'Waaaaylaaaahooooo! Straight ahead, they can't outrun us much longer. Bend yore backs, River'eads, keep t'the middle current!'

'Yiss yiss, but we ain't sighted 'em yet. Wot if they've shot off up'n sidewater, like that'n o'er there?'

'Arr, don't talk daft, vole, they got'n a Guosim shrew wid 'em. That'n 'ud know enough not t'do anythin' so silly. Cain't y'see, 'tis a dead end up there? Has bin fer many a long season!'

'Mebbe we'll overtake 'em at the rapids. Even Guosim shrews ain't so crafty when it comes ter rocks'n'rapids, eh?'

'Aye, y'could be right there. Wait'll I gits me paws on 'em, an' that liddle turnfur Burble. I'll beat 'is brains out wid the Leafwood afore I toss 'im into the rapids wid 'is thievin' friends. Yiss yiss!'

'Flamin' cheek of 'em, stealin' our *Swallow* like that!'

'Pirates, that's wot they are, matey, river pirates!'

'Well, mark me word, they'll suffer the same fate as any pirate would. Onward, River'eads, straight course ahead now!'

The shouts died away on the still air as the Riverhead tribe paddled downstream. Dann sat up and began slapping at the winged pests that assailed him. 'Gerroff! Leave me alone, you rotten villains!'

A big insect flew right into Song's eye, so hard that it caused her to see coloured stars. Dippler was tearing at his fur, moaning, 'We musta been mad comin' in 'ere to 'ide!'

The boat rocked as Burble performed a little dance. 'Ouchouch! I'm bein' et alive! Back out onto the river!'

Song squinched her eye, rubbing hard with a sweaty paw. 'No, we can't go out there. 'Twouldn't be long before we'd be running right into the back of them. Let's go a bit further up this creek. Maybe it won't be as bad farther along.'

Swatting and slapping at the insect hordes, they dug paddles into the muddy creekbed and poled the *Swallow* south up the vile-smelling inlet.

At mid-morning they called a halt. Though there were

still a few insects about, most of the myriad from the creek mouth had given up following the four friends. Shipping the paddles, they looked around. Fungus bedecked and pulp-soft, dead trees lay across the creek, preventing them from going any further. The water was black and peaty, with odd bubbles rising here and there, leaving a foul odour hovering in the air. In the bank shallows on one side there was a riot of blue flowers, bit scabious, brooklime, butterwort and skullcap sprouting thick. Dippler moored the *Swallow* midships to a slender sessile oak on the shaded side of the creek. Song and Burble unpacked apples, some scones and a flagon of cold dandelion and burdock cordial which had been stowed deep in her haversack. Wearily they hauled themselves on to the mossy bank and began eating, groaning as they stretched aching backs.

'Ooh, me paws'll never be the same again after grippin' that paddle so tight, mates. I can 'ardly pick me beaker up!'

Dippler winked at the watervole. 'Leave it there then, Burb, an' I'll drink it for ye!'

Dann polished an apple on his tunic. 'Whew! That was a narrow escape earlier. Those Riverheads wouldn't 'ave accepted any excuses. We'd be deadbeasts now if they'd caught us!'

Burble lifted the beaker in his cramped paws. 'Oh yiss yiss, that's true, pal. Ole Grey One's missin' both the *Swallow* an' 'is Leafwood. There'll be no mercy in that'n's 'eart!'

Song bathed her eye with a drop of the cool cordial. 'No, I don't imagine there would be. Why did you do it, Burble?'

The watervole made a derisory gesture with one paw. 'Yah, that ole Grey'n was far too big fer 'is coat. River'eads never 'ad one leader, just a council, but he appointed hisself 'ead of the council an' now 'e calls hisself Chieftain. 'Tain't right. Grey One was allus a cheat an' a liar. Bullied 'is way in, 'e did. Miss Song, 'ere's yore

188

Leafwood. Take care of it.'

The young squirrel caught the greenstone-topped stick Burble tossed to her. She looked at it pensively. 'All that trouble just for this. Strange, isn't it? Last night we were the best of friends with the Riverheads, this mornin' they're out for our blood. All because of a boat an' a stick.'

Dann made a pillow of his haversack and lay back. 'Great seasons, but 'tis warm hereabouts, heavy like. Ah well, if we must wait here till the coast's clear I'm goin' to get a bit of shut-eye. See if you can't keep yore debatin' down to a dull roar, will you, mates.'

Dippler tossed an apple core into the water. 'Good idea, Dann, but don't snore, it keeps me awake.'

Song flicked a drop of cordial at the young shrew. 'Listen who's talking, the champion snorer of Redwall!'

Dippler opened one eye, murmuring sleepily, 'Oh, spare me, missie, I'm only a Dibbun compared to you at snorin'!'

Before another half hour had passed, all four were curled up on the mossy bank, deep in slumber and snoring gently.

Raventail and his band of roving ferrets watched the four sleepers from their position behind the fallen trees across the inlet. Peering slit-eyed between a gap in the rotten trunks, Raventail slowly drew his scimitar, smiling wickedly at the scruffy rabble surrounding him. 'Kye arr, brethren. Don'ta dose lukky peaceladen a-lyin' dere? Crool crool shame 'twould be to wakeyup dem, dey on'y be younger beasters. Crool crool shame mesay!'

One of the ferrets slid a long knife from a sling at his back. 'Nono needter wakeyup dem. I makem sleeplong f'ever!'

Raventail's scimitar tip pricked the speaker's narrow neck. 'You do dat on'y when Raventail say so. Kye arr, I wanna much much fun wid younger beasters 'fore theybe deathstill!'

18

Brother Melilot and Gubbio Foremole had decided, war or no war, they were going to prepare the traditional Redwall Midsummer Feast. What else could fire their tired spirits? Their only problem was that Dwopple, Blinny, Wugger and several other rascally Dibbuns saw no reason why they should not help with the preparations. Foremole put the finishing touches to a great hazelnut and elderberry pudding he was creating, crimping the edges round the basin top with a fork. Brushing the pastry with a mixture of greensap milk and honey, the mole twitched his button nose with pride.

'Yrr, lukkit ee pudden, Bruther. Ee'm be a foine-lukkin' beast!'

Melilot left off preparing his apple and strawberry crumble to admire the mole's delicious-looking pudding. 'It certainly is a beauty, friend. You'd best light the back oven to cook one that size. There's plenty of wood and charcoal in the burner, just put a light to it.'

Gubbio lit a taper off a candle, shuffled across to the oven and poked the light underneath. It went out. He lit the taper and tried a second time. Still the light went out. Grumbling to himself, the mole lit the taper from the candle again. 'Hurr, they'm bain't makin' ee taperers loike they'm used to, burr no!' When he poked the lighted taper beneath the oven a third time, Foremole distinctly heard the puff of air, accompanied by a giggle. Throwing open the oven door he confronted the Dibbuns seated inside. 'Gudd job oi never loighted ee oven, lest we'd be 'aven baked Dibbuns furr ee party, hurr hurr!'

The mousebabe Dwopple dismissed Foremole with a wave of his paw. 'Go 'way, moley. Us'n's be's livin' in 'ere now. G'way!'

Brother Melilot came to his friend's aid, a big oven paddle in one paw. 'And what pray are you Dibbuns doing inside our oven?'

Dwopple wagged a small mixing spoon under the good Brother's nose. 'We maken a shrimberry pie. Don't asturb us, it very dissifult!'

Without another word, Foremole and Melilot exchanged glances. Between them they pushed the big wooden loaf paddle beneath the busy Dibbuns and slid them out on to the floor, bowl, mixture and all. Melilot sorted indignant Abbeybabes out from the ingredients. 'What's this? Dried watershrimp, blackcurrants, hotroot pepper, pears and radishes? You can't make a pie with that lot!'

The molebabe, Blinny, glared at him challengingly. 'Who'm sez uz can't? We'm h'inventerers, makin' et furr ee Skipper!'

Foremole advanced on them with a long baton loaf. 'Ruffians! Rarscals! Out, afore oi makes ee into a sangwich!'

The Dibbuns fled, hurling dire threats at both cooks. Rimrose and Ellayo passed them as they dashed from the kitchens. Rimrose shook her head, smiling as she watched the tiny figures scurry off.

'I remember when my liddle Songbreeze was like them. What a pawful that 'un was, I can tell ye!'

Brother Melilot bowed to them both. 'Ladies, we can always use some extra help down here. Would you be willing to aid us with Redwall's Midsummer Feast?'

Rimrose returned the bow with a pretty curtsey. 'That's what we came for, Brother. I was thinking of making a cheese and celery flan with sage and parsley trimming. My mother is very good at baking blueberry and almond turnovers. Oh my goodness, what's all this mess?'

Melilot threw up his paws in despair. 'Those wretched babes were inventing a pie with it, for Skipper.'

A slow smile crept across the face of Grandma Ellayo. 'Hmm, mebbe we'll finish the job an' serve it up t'that great lump of an otter. He's always puttin' ideas into the young 'uns' 'eads. 'Twill serve 'im right if'n y'ask me!'

Out on the south wall, Skipper was scanning the woodlands, in company with Janglur and Rusvul.

'Haharr, 'tis too quiet, mates. I don't like it, they're up to somethin'. I'd take me affidavit on that!'

Janglur twirled his sling idly, the longbow resting at his side. 'All's we can do is t'keep our eyes peeled, Skip. Ahoy, mister Florian, how're things over yore side?'

The Noonvale hare was guarding the east wall centre with Borrakul, both of them crouching down behind the battlements. When he heard the squirrel hailing him, Florian beckoned the three comrades over with a silent wave. Curious to know what was going on, they hastened across.

'Keep your heads down, you chaps,' Florian whispered. 'We've hit on a super wheeze. See this long pole? My troupe use it for their tightrope-walkin' act. Now pay attention. As y'see, me'n'the sturdy Borrakul have tied this dagger to one end. Matter o' fact, we've just finished sharpenin' the jolly old knife on the battlements. Feel that edge an' tell me what y'think.'

Skipper tested the blade, pulling his paw away and sucking it. 'Phwaw! That's wot I calls sharp, matey. Wot's the game?'

With a nod Florian indicated an unusually tall ash, growing not far from the wall. It was a huge, stately tree.

'See that ash? No, don't gawp an' stare like frogs at a fry-up! Merely take a peepette, quickly. Good. Now what did y'see?'

A peepette, as Florian called it, was all that the sharp eyes of Janglur needed. The squirrel saw it right away. 'There's a rope tied up there near the top!'

The lanky hare chuckled. 'Well done that squirrel! Let me tell you, I've been watching that since mid-mornin'. Blinkin' water rat climbed up an' tied the rope there. Hawhawhaw! Confounded oaf was slippin' an trippin'. Took the blighter an absolute age to get the bally rope fastened in those top branches. Now they've led it off, back a few trees. Good job you chaps've got me on your side, wot! I've twigged the whole blinkin' plan, of course – didn't take long for a great mind like mine. Now, lay low an' watch like good chaps. Wait for the fun t'start, wot!'

Three trees back, a rat named Stukkfur perched on the highest limb of an elm. Gelltor and Ascrod stood gripping the heavier branches below him. Gelltor called up to the water rat in a loud whisper. 'Is the top of the wall empty, nobeasts there?'

Stukkfur raised himself on tip-paw. He had a good head for heights. 'None that I can see, sire, though there's one or two shrews over on the west wall, but they're facin' the open ground in front.'

The Marlfox hissed impatiently. 'I'm not concerned with the west wall as long as the east wall is clear and empty. Can you see your way clear through to it?'

Stukkfur leaned slightly to one side, balancing capably. 'Aye, sire, I can do it from here. 'Tis a straight enough path.'

Ascrod did not like being so high off the ground. He clung tightly to the trunk. 'Remember, hold the rope as far up as you can. Just swing out and you should go in directly over the battlements. Don't worry if you can't make it first try – as long as it stays quiet you can have a few more goes if you don't manage first time.'

Extending his paws above his head, Stukkfur took a vicelike grip on the rope and drew in a deep breath, listening to Gelltor's final instructions for the risky plan.

'When you land on the walltop, pull the rest of the rope over, it's plenty long enough. Shin down it, open the wallgate bolts, then get clear and leave the rest to us. Do this right and you'll be well rewarded, Stukkfur, I'll see to that personally. Right, take off!'

From where they crouched below the battlements, Janglur saw the rope go taut. He nudged Florian. 'Looks like the fun's about t'start, mate!'

There came a swishing noise, like a wind through the forest, which increased in volume. Borrakul was watching between the battlements. 'Hoho, you was right, Florian. 'Ere 'e comes, flyin' like a bird!'

The hare stood up in clear view and leaned out from the walltop, with his long, blade-topped pole at the ready. Stukkfur could do nothing to stop himself. Whipped by small twigs and spitting leaves, he watched in horror as Florian lashed out, the razor sharp blade severing the rope at a single blow. Then the water rat really was flying free as a bird, not up, but down, though still travelling forward.

'Yiiiiieeeeeee!'

The immovable sandstone blocks of the east wall cut short his flight. Borrakul winced at the sound, but Florian's concern was not for the rat. 'Huh! Hope that chap didn't damage the wall, wot!'

From all around the walltop sentries came running to see what the disturbance was about. The Marlfox vixen, Predak, was waiting in the ditch near the west wall. The moment she saw the shrew guards desert their posts she made her move. Climbing stealthily from the ditch, she hurried to the base of the wall, unwinding a slim length of rope with a stone tied to one end. It took four throws before a satisfactory cast was made, but on the fourth try the stone soared upward and over the top of an ornamental spur jutting from the wall, just below the battlements near the northwest corner. Predak caught the stone as it fell. Now she held both ends of the rope in her paws, and she pulled each in turn, testing it. The rope ran free over the stone spur, backward and forward. Moreover, it could not be seen from the walltop unless a sentry were to lean out too far for safety. Leaving the rope with both ends touching the ground, Predak stole away, back to the east side, where Gelltor and Ascrod awaited her. The vixen radiated satisfaction as she made her report.

'Nobeast saw me, the rope's in place, and all we have to do now is get the siege ladder nearby in the ditch, wait for nightfall, then haul it up to the wall. How did the diversion go?'

Gelltor twirled the severed rope idly. 'Oh, it worked well enough, but they were on to us, more or less as I expected. That hare slashed the rope with a device he'd thought up. Stukkfur never made it over the wall, but it provided the decoy we needed.'

Predak inspected the shorn rope end. 'Stukkfur was a good soldier. A fool, but obedient. Pity he's gone.'

Ascrod interrupted her. 'Surprisingly enough, Stukkfur wasn't killed. He must have a head made of solid bone. Look, there he is.'

Stukkfur was wandering in a daze around the rats who were busy building the siege ladder. Both paws were still held high over his head, grasping a long piece of rope, which he stumbled over as he meandered willy-nilly. There was not a single tooth left in Stukkfur's mouth, and beneath the bulging lump on his brow both eyes were black and blue. Bumbling about, the water rat muttered to himself, 'Musht drop ober d'wallsh, ohben d'wallgatesh, musht do't!'

Bargle led his relief column of Guosim shrews up on to

the walltop, where Florian greeted him huffily. 'Well hoorah an' hang out the jolly old flags, relief at last, wot! A chap could fade from the famine, waitin' up here. Have a good night's sleep, did ye? No doubt you breakfasted well, early lunch too by the look of ye. Fiddle de dee, sir, tardy in the extreme!'

Bargle bated the hare unmercifully, yawning, stretching and patting his stomach. 'Slep' like a mole an' snored like an 'og, mister Florian. Woke to a wunnerful brekkist – honey, 'ot scones, fresh mint tea an' a little preserved fruit wid meadowcream. 'Fraid there's none left. Very partial t'meadowcream us shrews are. Mind though, we did ask the cooks to save yer some crusts, didn't we, Mayon?'

Turning his face to hide a grin, Mayon agreed. 'Ho yes. Why, I said t'the cooks meself, I said, You be sure'n save a crust or two for mister Florian an' 'is gallant sentries, a-guardin' those walls out there while the likes of us are sleepin' safe in our beds an' fillin' our stummicks!'

Florian Dugglewoof Wilffachop's ears stood erect with indignation. 'Cads the lot of ye, wot! Small spiky-furred grub-wallopin' bounders! Nothin' worse than a grub-walloper. Come on, chaps, form up in a line an' march off smartly. We're not stoppin' in the company of grub-wallopers an' tuck-scoffers!'

As Florian led his sentries off down the wallstairs, Bargle called cheerily to him, 'Grub-wallopers I don't mind, but tuck-scoffers is the worst kind o' beasts. You be sure an' 'urry back now, sir!'

Florian's whiskers bristled with outrage. 'Unmitigated impudence, sir, confounded brass-necked cheek!'

Deesum popped her head around the kitchen serving hatch to warn the cooks. 'Just thought I'd better tell you, mister Florian and the sentries are coming in from the walltops. They look pretty hungry, too!'

Brother Melilot clapped a paw to his forehead. 'Oh dear, so they should be! I completely forgot to send out their breakfast this mornin'. They haven't eaten since last night!'

Grandma Ellayo rescued her turnovers from the windowledge on which they were cooling, whisking them out of sight into a cupboard.

'Gracious me! If that ten-bellied hare is hungry we'd best hide everythin', or he'll eat us out o' house an' home, and there'll be no feast at all!'

Rimrose counted her cheese and celery flans. 'Florian must've already been here. There's one missing.'

Foremole removed his hazelnut and elderberry pudding carefully from the oven, shaking his head at Rimrose. 'Bain't no Florian tukk that 'un, marm. Ee Dibbuns beat 'im to et!'

Rimrose busily stowed the flans away, chuckling. 'Ah well, who could begrudge those liddle rogues a bite to eat? Hope they didn't burn their mouths, though, these flans are still hot. Oh, Brother Melilot, is that shrimpberry pie the Dibbuns put together for Skipper ready?'

Melilot pulled the pie from an oven. 'Done to a turn, marm!'

'Then why don't we serve it to Florian instead?'

Melilot grinned at the thought of Florian tackling the highly unusual pie. 'Why not indeed!'

Ascrod sat in the woodland glade the Marlfoxes were using as a siege camp, watching the water rats testing the ladder. It seemed sturdy enough for the purpose. Furrowing his brow, he tapped his paws distractedly on a nearby oak. Vannan slid into camp like a wisp of smoke and seated herself next to her brother, observing his mood.

'You seem out of sorts today. What is it?'

'Arrh, we're getting nowhere with this siege. We'll never get the best of those Redwallers – the luck's on their side every time.'

'So, what do you propose we do, brother?'

197

'Cut our losses and get out of here, back to the island.'

'Hmm, I only wish we could!'

'What d'you mean, sister? What's to stop us going?'

'Listen and I'll tell you, Ascrod. While you lot have been playing with ropes and foolish ideas, I took a trip back to see what was happening at our camp out by the river. Beelu was watching Mokkan for me, and I wanted to hear his report. But guess what?'

'What?'

'There's not a trace of anybeast. The camp was deserted, Mokkan and the rats we left with him all gone!'

'Gone? What about the tapestry we stole from the Abbey?'

'Hmph! Of course, that's gone also. Six shrew logboats we had, five of them are smashed to pieces on the bank there. That means Mokkan took the sixth boat, the rat guards, and our tapestry with him, bound for the island, I'll wager.'

'The traitor! I'd like to skin the deserter's hide from his back with my axe!'

'Aye, me too, brother, but it looks like we're stuck here for now. We can't go back empty-pawed.'

'So, what do you suggest we do, Vannan?'

'Only one thing to do. We put all our cunning into defeating Redwall. Once the Abbey and its treasures are ours, we can force the shrews to build us new boats. We'll fill 'em with treasure, and then play the waiting game. Then one fine day we'll start back for the island, when brother Mokkan's least expecting us, and then there'll be a reckoning, I promise!'

19

Martin the Warrior strode through Dannflor's dream. He pricked the young squirrel's footpaw with his swordtip, uttering only one word. 'Awake!'

Dannflor woke and sat up. The sword he had been holding loosely in his sleep had slipped free and nicked his footpaw. The first thing he saw was a big scraggy ferret, with a raven's feather braided to his tail, brandishing a scimitar, as he and a band of about twenty other ferrets crept up on the four friends. Dann shouted a warning to his companions. 'Look out, ambush!'

Dann had never been so frightened in his life. The ferrets had them outnumbered by five to one. Moreover, they were a savage, murderous-looking bunch, yellow-fanged, heavily armed and red-eyed with blood lust. He heard Song yelling, 'Run for it!'

Dann plunged off into the trees, pounding along as fast as his paws would go. He briefly saw the others begin to run. Song was fleet of paw. She ducked two of the vermin and fled into the thickets, but Dippler and Burble were not so lucky. Still sleepy-eyed, they were cut off and brought down by a group of the fastest ferret runners. Sobbing with fear, Dann ran as he had never run before, dodging round trees, dashing through nettlebeds, stumbling and tripping through roots hidden beneath deep, damp loam. Behind him he could hear the wild barbarous screeches of the ferrets, and their swords slashing at the undergrowth as they came after him. Chest burning, heart pounding, breath torn from him in ragged gasps, Dann blundered onward, still clutching the sword of Martin. They were getting closer, shouting now.

'Roundaround tharraway, we's gorrim nowsoon. Kye arrrrr!'

Desperately Dann looked about as he ran, then he saw it. A four-topped oak with thick limbs and an impenetrable profusion of leaves. Dann shinned up it, scraping his paws and barking his shins. Thrusting the sword between his teeth, he swung up through the thick boughs and stowed himself amid a clump of leafy twigs. Moments later his pursuers grouped below the oak, brandishing an ugly array of bladed weapons. They slashed at the bushes, hunting this way and that.

'Whereda squirl gotoo, you'va seed 'im?'

'Karrabah! Twoda squirls gerraway. Quickyquick, dose squirlers!'

'Gorra voler ander shrewbeast. Key arr, goodyerr!'

Scarcely daring to breathe, Dann lay flat on a limb, surrounded by oak foliage. He watched the jabbering ferrets, arguing and thrashing at fern and bush alike with their curved scimitars. When they had searched around awhile, one of them bared his stained fangs and pointed in the direction of the creekbank. 'Wego backnow backnow, lotsafun, voler, shrewbeast. Rabbagakk!' Screeching and whooping excitedly, they dashed off.

Half sliding, half scrambling, Dann came down from the oak on to the ground. Burying the sword deep in the soft earth, the young squirrel sank into a crouch, lowering his head into both paws and letting hot tears of shame flood down his face. Coward! His father had been right. He had run like a frightened Dibbun, leaving his friends to the enemy.

It was the sound of his fitful sobbing that led Song to find Dann. Rounding the trunk of the massive oak, she sat down beside him. 'Dann, are you hurt? What's the matter?'

Still weeping, he shook his head. 'I was frightened, Song, so frightened!'

Song angled her head so that she was looking upward into Dann's face. 'Goodness, so was I. I nearly jumped out of my skin.'

Dann thrust the swordpoint deeper into the soil. 'You don't understand. I've proved my father right. He called me a coward and I am. I deserted Dippler an' Burble, left 'em t'be captured by those ferrets. I was terrified, and I ran!'

Song gave him a hearty shove and sent him sprawling. 'Oh, I never. I stayed and got killed defendin' 'em!'

Dann shook tears from his eyes angrily. 'Oh, stop talkin' stupid!'

The pretty squirrelmaid smiled and clasped her friend's paw. 'I will if you will, Dann. We did the only thing we could do, we escaped. Imagine if we'd stayed and got gallantly slain, now that would've been a great help to Dipp and Burb, wouldn't it?'

Dann wiped his eyes with the back of a paw and sniffed. 'Didn't take much bravery to run away, though, did it?'

Song was beginning to lose her temper. She emphasized her words by prodding Dann in the chest with her Leafwood stick. 'No, it just took a bit of common sense, mate. We're still alive, y'see, and now we're going back there to be brave when we rescue our two friends from those dirty vermin. Come on, Reguba, there's other things to do with that warrior's sword than stab the earth!'

Dann stood up then, and pulled his sword from the ground. He wiped it clean on his tunic front, gritting his teeth. 'I'm glad I've got you for a friend, Song Swifteye.

Let's go an' deal with some vermin!'

Dippler and Burble were hanging upside down by their footpaws from a thick willow bough, swathed practically from neck to tail in vine ropes. Raventail stood in the *Swallow*, flicking his scimitar in front of their faces.

'Wellawell, likkle frien's, you likin' da drinkmore?'

At his signal, four grinning ferrets leaned down on the bough, causing it to bend so that Dippler and Burble's heads were forced down under the water, which amused the ferrets greatly.

'Givem lotsalotsa drink for longertime!'

'Kye arr, volers an' shrewbeasts be's much thirstynow!'

After a while they released the branch, and the two captives' heads came clear of the murky water. Both were coughing and gagging. Raventail flicked the scimitar closer to their faces.

'Tellame now when youbeasts got 'nuff drinkdrink, den Raventail cutcha loose . . . from you necks, from you necks!'

Burble spat out creekmud and wrinkled his nose at Dippler. 'Don't give us much choice, do 'e, mate?'

One of the ferrets by the bough suddenly sighed and flopped down for no apparent reason. Raventail cocked his head quizzically. 'Wotmarra wirra dat'n?'

Before he could enquire further another ferret went down. This time the thud of the slingstone was loud and obvious.

'Redwaaaaaalll! Regubaaaaaa!'

Even as the piercing warcries rang out from the cover of the trees, another two ferrets were laid flat by paw-sized river pebbles. Slingstones began thwacking in, hard and heavy, and the undisciplined remnants of the ragged ferret horde fled. Scrabbling and biting at one another, they clambered over the fallen trees which blocked the inlet and dashed off into the thick forest. Raventail stood swaying in the friends' boat, waving his scimitar and yelling at them, 'Kye arr! Getcherback, back 'ere, Raventail norrafraid!'

Then Dann came thundering across the bank, swinging his sword and bellowing like a badger in full Bloodwrath.

'Regubaaaaaa!'

There was no stopping the young squirrel. Like a bolt of lightning he flung himself on Raventail. The force of the impact was so great that both Dann and the ferret lost their swords and crashed into the water. Still hanging upside down, Dippler and Burble watched in awed silence as the warrior blood of Reguba rose in their companion's eyes. Spitting water and roaring, his weapon forgotten, Dann hauled Raventail almost clear of the creek and dealt him a fierce blow. Flinging the screaming ferret from him, Dann dived after his enemy, pummelling with all four paws, kicking, punching and baring his teeth as he thrashed the vermin unmercifully.

'Regubaaaa! Regubaaaaa! Regubaaaaaaaa!'

Song ran out to the bankside to watch the spectacle. She had never seen another creature take such a ferocious beating.

'Dann, leave him alone! He's had enough!'

But Dann was past listening. Grabbing Raventail, he hauled him over his head and flung him bodily into the marshy border of the creek's far side. Black with sludge and unable to stand, the ferret crawled away up the bank. Dann went after him but he stumbled and fell in the mud amongst clumps of blue-flowering plants. Swiftly Song untied the boat and leapt in, giving a hard shove against the willow trunk with her paddle. The *Swallow* shot smoothly out across the dark surface, slowing neatly as it nosed into the blue flowers surrounding Dann. Song passed him the mooring rope. 'Here, mate, grab this!'

Total exhaustion suddenly enveloped Dann. Gratefully, he held on to the rope and lay back while Song paddled back to the bank.

The Reguba warrior was hauled dripping on to the

mossy sward by Song, and sat shivering as reaction to his wild charge set in. Song found his sword in the shallows.

'Great seasons, what a fighter y'are, Dann. I never saw anythin' like that in my whole life. You were like a Badger Lord in Bloodwrath there – I was sure you were going to slay that vermin bare-pawed!'

'Yiss yiss, but are yer goin' t'talk about it all day an' leave us two pore creatures hangin' 'ere like apples waitin' fer autumn?'

Song turned to the two wet bundles hanging from the willow bough. 'Oops! Sorry, pals, I completely forgot you there for a moment. Hang on, I'll soon get you down.'

Viewing the scene from his upside-down position, Burble winked at Dann. 'Ah well, isn't that decent of the young missie now, she's gettin' round to releasin' us. If'n she don't put a move on with it we'll both have great fat purple heads with hangin' this way!'

The irony of the watervole's remarks was not lost on Song. Smiling mischievously, she crouched with her face level to Burble's. 'Hmm, then again I might just leave you to ripen and drop off like two damsons in the orchard. How long is it till autumn, Dann?'

Struggling upright, Dann swung Dippler in so that Song could cut his bonds, and together they lowered him on to the moss. The Guosim shrew had not said a word throughout his ordeal. Now he sat rubbing circulation back into his footpaws as he spoke. 'Sleepin' again, I was, same as last time when the Marlfoxes stole my tribe's logboats. Huh! Haven't learned much, 'ave I? Same puddle-'eaded beast as ever I was, that's me!'

When they had cut Burble down, Dann sat by Dippler and put a friendly paw about his shoulders. 'Don't blame yourself, Dipp. We were all asleep – it wasn't yore fault. Next time you'll be ready, wait'n'see. I think you'll surprise yourself when the time comes. I certainly did. After what took place here t'day I'll never be afraid of any creature livin'. What d'you say, Song?'

The squirrelmaid tossed her Leafwood in the air and caught it deftly. 'Don't think 'tis a question of you being afraid any more, Dann. In the seasons to come, any foebeast facing you will be the one who feels the fear, of that I'm sure!'

As the afternoon wore on the four friends sat on the bank discussing their next move. Burble was not happy about going back to the river. ''Tisn't the thing t'do, y'see. That ole Grey One an' the River'ead tribe'll scour that open water fer days yet. Yiss yiss, we'll only be like a butterfly flyin' into the mouth of a hungry crow, goin' straight inter trouble, so we will!'

Song glanced up from the scroll which contained Friar Butty's rhyme, which she had been studying carefully. 'You could be right, Burb, the river might be a dangerous place for us. You say we weren't far off some rapids when your tribe were chasing us, is that correct?'

'Oh yiss yiss, missie, the ould rapids are fast an' fierce. 'Tis a good job we never had t'face them so 'tis, yiss yiss.'

Song tapped the parchment thoughtfully. 'Hmm, it doesn't say anything in this rhyme about going over rapids on the river this early. All it says is:

'Just follow as I run away.
Discover the speechless hidden mouth,
Alas, my friends, our ways part there,
Go down green tunnel, bounden south,
Through trees with blossoms in their hair.'

Dann poured them the last of the dandelion and burdock cordial. 'So, what does that tell us, Song?'

'Think on a bit, Dann. Whilst we were following that river, did we see any streams or creeks running south before this one?'

'No, I'm sure we didn't. There wasn't a break in the bank until I saw this sidestream when they were chasing us. What are you getting at, Song?'

'Well, 'tis just an idea, but I think this is the speechless hidden mouth we were looking for. Dippler, you know about waterways, what's your opinion?'

The Guosim shrew scratched his whiskers. 'Mebbe so. The inlet does look a touch like a mouth, an' all that foliage makes it a proper green tunnel. So if yore poem says that's where our ways part, it must mean that is the spot where we part company with the river. Aye, I think yore right, Song!'

But Burble scoffed at the idea. 'Ah, will y'lissen t'the wisdom of 'em! 'Ow can words on an ole scrap o' parchment be right? This is a dead end, or is it meself is the only one can see it?'

Song shook the scroll beneath Burble's nose. 'Remember, though, this was written many many seasons ago. Couldn't this have been a proper stream before that? Mightn't it only have become a creek after those trees fell and blocked it?'

Dippler butted in. 'Ha! But y'forgot sumthin', missie. Aren't we supposed to be chasin' the Marlfox an' his crew?'

Song stood up and stamped about on the bank. She was fast losing patience with the whole affair. 'Look, I don't care which way the fox has gone, we can't follow on the open river with Grey One on our tails. Another thing, we know the Marlfox is bound for the secret island on the lost lake. This way we're sure to meet up with him. Burble, where d'you think you're off to?'

The watervole was already climbing over the fallen treetrunks which blocked the creek off.

'Don't git yore paws in a tizzy, bossytail, I'm just goin' to see if yore idea is right, yiss yiss. Well, are you comin'?'

They climbed over the trunks and inspected the ground. Among the clumps of agrimony, sawwort and saxifrage the old streambed was still identifiable by the narrow trickle of water filtering through the logs that had dammed it off. Song splashed about in it triumphantly.

'You see? I told you, this is the sidestream we're

206

supposed to take. Look, it's running south just like the rhyme said it would. What d'you say to that, fatty volenose?'

Burble had only one word to say. 'Porterage!'

They stared at him, repeating the word together. 'Porterage?'

'Yiss yiss, have ye not heard of porterage? Well, I'll tell ye, me fine-furred friends. It means that we've got to foller this liddle water trickle till it becomes a stream agin. Yiss yiss, a-carryin' the good boat *Swallow* upside down on our 'eads!'

Dann started climbing back over the treetrunks. 'Stands to sense, Burb. We'd never get anywhere tryin' to float the *Swallow* in that tiny dribble. Come on, porters, let's try a bit o' porterage. I'm game if you lot are!'

Fortunately the *Swallow* was a comparatively light craft. Shouldering their packs and placing the paddles flat across their shoulders, the friends turned her upside down, lifted her over their heads, then lowered her on to the outstretched blades. This meant that their heads were inside the upturned boat and one had to follow the other blindly. Dann took the lead, being the tallest, followed by Dippler and Burble, with Song at the rear of the line. It was hard going, hot and stuffy inside the boat, where they were visited by various winged pests. However, they pressed on stoically, trying to ignore the hardships.

Dunk!

'Yowch! Watch where yore goin' up there, Dann!'

'Sorry. 'Twas a big overhangin' branch, didn't see it.'

'Yiss yiss, maybe y'didn't see it, matey, but we felt it!'

'Well, so did I, so stop complainin', will yer!'

'Burb ain't complainin', he's debatin'. Creatures got a right to debate, watervoles as well as us shrews. Any'ow, how can y'tell if we're goin' the right way, Dann?'

'Pudden'ead! Because I'm walkin' in the liddle stream an' me footpaws are soakin' wet and soggy, that's 'ow! Song, will y'please sing a ditty or two to shut that pair up. Honestly, talk about gabby. Guosim an' wofflin' watervoles, spare me from them!'

Song liked the way her voice echoed inside the upturned boat.

'Oh how could a hedgehog marry a mole,
He's prickly prickly prickly,
An' live with a squirrel all in a great hole,
Very tickly tickly tickly.
An' what if an otter could dance with a trout,
He'd stay in the river an' never come out.
Pray tell me whatever they'd all think o' me,
Inviting a bumblebee in for its tea?
Why they'd come in and join us for goodness' sake,
For scones an' trifle an' blueberry cake,
Elderflow'r cordial an' strawberry pie,
Oh turn caterpillar to bright butterfly!'

Burble stubbed his footpaw on a stone, which did not improve his argumentative mood. 'Tchah! 'Edge'ogs'n' squirrels'n'bumblebees eatin' cake an' suppin' cordial together? Don't make much sense, do it? Yowch! D'yer mind not walkin' on the backs o' me footpaws, missie!'

'Sorry, Burb, and I'm sorry you didn't like my song. 'Tis only an old nonsense ditty my Grandma Ellayo used t'sing to me.'

The watervole trudged on unappeased. 'Ho yiss yiss, 'tis nonsense all right, no mistakin' that. Grr! Listen, mister wasp, keep away from my nose or I'll eat ye!'

Dann could not restrain himself from laughing at Burble. 'Chattin' to wasps now, Burb? Come on, you old grouch, let's see if you can sing us a song that makes sense.'

Burble sniffed. 'All watervole songs make sense. Lissen.

'A watervole grows like an ould bulrush stalk,
An' learns to swim afore 'e can walk,

Just give 'im a paddle an' lend 'im a boat,
There's nought as nice as a vole wot's afloat.
Go ruggle yore tookle an' rowgle yer blot,
Come floogle yore wattle an' pickle yer swot!
A watervole's clever'n'smart an' he's nice,
'E won't take a boat out onto the ice,
But 'e'll live all 'is life in a comfy ould cave,
An' when 'e dies it'll do fer 'is grave.
So twangle me gurdle an' griddle me twogg,
Right burgle me doodle an' frumple me plogg!'

Dippler tried to keep a straight face as he nodded wisely. 'Burgle me doodle an' frumple me plogg? Makes perfect sense. Wot d'you think, Dann?'

A deep booming voice that did not belong to Dann rang out. 'Hohohoho! Now I've seen everythin', a singin' boat! Hoohoohoo!'

The four friends whipped the *Swallow* off their heads to see who it was.

The hugest, fattest, most spiky hedgehog that any of them had ever seen was lying in an immense hammock, slung between a beech and an elm. Spikes and quills stuck through the coarse canvas of the hammock, making it look like a monstrous pincushion. He had two baskets, one on either side of the hammock, containing wild grapes and almonds. In his paw he brandished a giant mallet to crack the nuts with, and this he waved cheerily at the travellers.

'Good noontide to ye. Fancy some grapes? A few nuts, mebbe? Come sit an' rest yoreselves, pore liddle waifs!'

Song smiled and waved back prettily to him, commenting to the others, 'We could do with a rest. What d'you say, pore liddle waifs?'

With a grunt and a groan the big hedgehog heaved himself out of the hammock and bowed politely. 'I go by the name o' Soll. Full name's Sollertree, 'cos I'm the only 'edge'og in these parts. Now wot be yore given names, me liddle h'infants?'

Song introduced herself and her friends. 'I'm Song, he's Dann and that's Burble and Dippler. Excuse me, sir, but shouldn't your name be Solitary?'

The big fellow waved a paw airily. 'Solitary, Sollertree, wot difference, pretty one, save that Sollertree's the name I gave meself, an' I like it fine. Come, sit ye down on my 'ammock. A more comfy berth y'never found, eh?'

They sat on the hammock's edge, gently swinging back and forth. Apart from the odd spike which had to be removed from the canvas, they all agreed it was very comfortable. Soll smiled with pleasure.

'H'ideal, h'ideal! Now, you 'elp yoreselves to grapes whilst I crack some almonds for ye. Grow 'em all meself, nothin' better fer puttin' a twinkle to yore eye an' a point to yore spikes.'

The grapes were delicious, small but plump and juicy. Soll sat on a treestump, lining almonds up and popping them gently with his giant mallet.

'Isn't it lonely, mister Soll, living alone in the midst of the woods with nobeast for company?' Dann asked.

Soll passed them a great pawful of kernels, raising his bushy brows. 'Lonely, wot's lonely? Great shells'n'vines, 'ow could a body get lonely round 'ere, liddle bushtail? I got birds t'sing fer me, sunshine, showers, fresh breezes t'ruffle the hair o' my lovely trees, clear water t'drink . . . Oh, an' Croikle, too!' He reached down by the side of the stump and a small green frog hopped on to his platelike paw. Soll grinned happily. 'Croikle, these are me new friends. Bid 'em good noontide, will ye?'

The frog's tiny green throat bulged out. 'Croikle!'

This seemed to amuse Soll greatly. 'Hohohoho! 'Tis all 'e ever says. Croikle! An' who pray could argue wid that? Lissen t'this. Yore a great fierce beast who's slayed thousands, aren't you, mate?'

The frog gazed at him with its small golden eyes. 'Croikle!'

Soll laughed until his spikes rattled, and the four travellers could not resist laughing along with the simple-hearted giant. He passed them more almonds and grapes. 'See, my friend's never in a bad mood, never argues or grizzles. Go on, ask 'im a question.'

Dippler winked at the little frog. 'Soll tells me you ate four barrels o' grapes'n'almonds. True?'

The frog turned its gaze on the Guosim shrew as if it had heard his question and was considering the answer. Then it spoke. 'Croikle!'

Soll nearly fell off his treestump laughing. 'Hohohoohoohoo! 'E said it weren't four barrels, 'twas six!'

He encouraged the others to question his frog, commenting each time the tiny creature croaked. Song, Dann and Burble took turns.

'Tell me, sir, where d'you sleep at night?'

'Croikle!'

'Well I never. 'E said that 'e kicks me out o' my 'ammock an' sleeps there every night. Hoohoohoohoo!'

'Is it true that frogs like to swim in the stream?'

'Croikle!'

'Wot, swim, says 'e, never! I've got me own liddle boat, he says, mister Soll made it outta an almond shell. Hohohoho!'

'Sir, you look like a fine singer, would you sing us a song?'

'Croikle!'

'Did you 'ear that? 'E just sang 'is favourite song, the shortest one ever written. My my, wot a clever frog. Hohohohoohoo!'

The banter went back and forth until noon shadows began to lengthen. Song was enjoying herself, but she thought it was time they made ready to depart. Soll was busy crushing a grape, removing the pips and feeding it to Croikle as she explained it all to him, but he nodded his head understandingly. 'Fear not, liddle 'uns, 'tis all clear to ole Soll. You want to find the stream goin' south so's you can go a-sailin' in yore liddle boat. Now, 'twill take you best part o' two days carryin' the vessel, but lissen t'me, my dearies. I'll carry yore boat an' take you on a short cut that'll 'ave you onstream in a single day. So rest you now in my 'ome for tonight, an' we'll start out bright'n'early on the morrow. Yes?'

The reply was eagerly given by the friends. 'Oh yes please, mister Soll!'

The hedgehog's dwelling was a long jumble of stone slabs, timber, branches and mud chinking built into the side of a rock ledge. It was very homely and comfortable inside, once Soll had stirred up the fire embers and fed them with wood and sweet-smelling peat clumps. Evening cast its calm cool spell over all, and the four friends lounged round the fire whilst Soll stirred a cauldron of vegetable soup, which stood on a tripod over the glow. Keeping his soft brown eyes upon the task, he began telling of his life.

'I lived 'ere all me life. There were three of us, my goodwife Beechtipp, me liddle daughter Nettlebud an' meself. Ah dearie me, it do seem a long time ago now. Anyhow, it was on a misty autumn time, I'll never forget it. I'd trekked back t'the river seekin' russet apples, as there was none 'ereabouts. Thought I might get a russet saplin' to plant outside our door, so's we could grow our own. Well, on the second day out it came on to storm, when 'twas too far t'make it back 'ome. So I made a shelter on the riverbank below the rapids an' sat it out for three days. Then I returned 'ere, laden wi' apples an' a fine young saplin' tree.'

Soll paused, gazing into the glowing peat fire, his face wreathed by aromatic smoke. He sighed heavily. 'Aaaaaah, lack a day! Vermin 'ad raided my 'ome. 'Twas all ruin an' wreck, with no sign of the villains. Tracks washed out by storm, y'see. My pore wife Beechtipp lay slain. She were a gentle creature, couldn't fight t'save 'er

212

life. My liddle daughter Nettlebud was gone, taken captive by vermin. My name was Skyspike in those days, 'cos of me great size an' strength. But alas for me, I was never a warrior, couldn't raise my paw to 'urt no livin' thing. Be that as it may, I went mad with grief an' sorrow. Three seasons I roamed far'n'wide, always searchin', seekin' to find my darlin' Nettlebud. Questin', wanderin' o'er woodland, water an' moorland. But my pore baby was gone. Then one day in autumn, when leaves died all redgold an' small birds were flyin' south'ards to chase the sun, I found I'd roamed back to this place. I'll tell thee no lie, young friends, I sat 'ere an' wept for days, thinkin' on wot 'ad been. Then one mornin' I awakened to find the sun shinin' bright an' birds singin' joyous songs to it. A great peace came o'er me an' I no longer wanted to spend my life wanderin' about. That was when I changed my name to Sollertree an' decided to live out my seasons 'ere. I rebuilt my 'ouse, reared liddle Croikle from a tadpole I found in the tricklin' water, an' guess wot?' Soll pointed out of the doorway to a tree. 'That saplin' I'd cast away weren't no russet, 'twas a fine young almond tree. There 'tis yonder, see? So 'ere I am an' 'ere I'll stay, an' allow me t'say this. I'll never do another creature a bad turn if'n I can't do 'im a good 'un!'

Song smiled at the huge spiky beast. 'You're a fine an' rare creature, mister Soll!'

20

Mokkan was up to his usual tricks. As dusk fell, the Marlfox had ordered his crew to put in to shore and make camp, and now he sat in the branches of an elm listening to his water rats talking as they huddled in the lee of their logboat on the riverbank. From his tether in the stern of the vessel, Fenno was urging them to desertion or mutiny.

'Lissen, mates, now's yer chance, while Mokkan's away scoutin' downriver. Make a break fer it whilst yer still can, mates!'

A rat named Gorm stared dully at the shrew. 'We ain't yore mates, so shut yer trap.'

Fenno ignored him and carried on. 'See wot 'appened today. One of you was bashed agin' the rocks an' drownded gettin' over them rapids, the logboat was near wrecked an' we were almost lost altogether. But did yore Marlfox worry about that, eh? Ho no! All 'e was thinkin' of was that tapestry. Then Mokkan 'ad us breakin' our backs 'eavin' on those paddles to escape the vole crews. You there, I saw 'im whack you a belt wid 'is axe 'andle ter make you paddle faster. Wot sort of a leader is that, I ask yer?'

The rat he was addressing merely shrugged. 'We serve

214

the kin of the High Queen Silth. 'Tis no business of yores.'

Fenno curled his lip at the water rats scornfully. 'Huh! 'Igh Queen Silth! Look at yerselves, soakin' wet an' wearied t'the limit, crouchin' there on a damp bank widout a bite between yer or a fire to dry out by. You must all be crazy. D'yer think yore Queen cares the drop of a leaf about you lot?'

The rat called Gorm banged the side of the logboat to silence Fenno. 'All yore fine talk's doin' you no good, Guosim. Don't y'know that Marlfoxes are magic beasts? 'Twould do us no good at all tryin' to run from them. Where would we go? No creature can escape the magic of Marlfoxes.'

Fenno strained against the thong which bound him to the boat. 'Magic my whiskers! You water rats are really stupid!'

'Not half as stupid as you, shrew.'

Fenno actually jumped with shock. Mokkan was standing behind him, holding aloft a whippy branch he had cut from the elm with his axe. The shrew covered his head with both paws, crouching in a ball as blows rained heavily on him.

'Pain is the best teacher for stupid idiots. Marlfoxes are magic! Say it! *Say it!*'

'Aggh! Yeeeagh! Marlfoxes are magic, sire! Yaaargh!'

Mokkan threw the broken branch savagely at Fenno's head and kicked his sobbing prisoner brutally. 'You've learned a valuable lesson, oaf. We've got all night – shall I cut myself another switch to remind you of it, eh?'

Crouching in the damp logboat bottom, Fenno wept brokenly. 'Mercy, sire, please. Marlfoxes are magic! I won't forget, sire!'

Mokkan lost interest in his captive. Turning to Gorm, he said, 'Break out supplies and light a small fire. Keep it sheltered in the lee of the boat and don't let it smoke.'

The water rat bowed. 'It shall be done as y'say, sire.'

Mokkan stroked the intricately embroidered tapestry

roll. 'Keep this dry and in perfect condition. High Queen Silth would be angry if it were damaged.'

Queen Silth was distracting herself by paying the slaves a visit. As her palanquin was borne out to the rear courtyard she made small mewling noises of disgust as she watched the steaming mess of porridge made from maize and chopped roots being delivered to the bars of the pen. Hungrily the starving slaves grabbed pawfuls and gulped it down. Ullig cracked his whip and snarled, 'Be still in the presence of her Majesty, High Queen Silth!'

Immediately they quit feeding and huddled together in the darkness of the pen's back wall. Alarmed by the moody and unpredictable Queen's visit, they did not know what to expect. Athrak and his magpies strutted about in front of the bars, their wicked, beady eyes watching the pitiful prisoners. Rat guards stood stiffly at attention, the odd quiver of a spear denoting that they were as apprehensive as the slaves at Silth's unexpected appearance. All eyes were on the silk-draped conveyance. Servants hurried to place torches and lanterns all around the palanquin. The stillness was ominous, as if every creature present was afraid to breathe. Nothing moved in the awful silence except for the eerie dancing shadows cast by the flickering torches. Harsh and grating, the High Queen's voice rasped out from behind the silken veils.

'Are they working hard for the food we give them?'

Ullig, the rat Captain in charge of all slaves, replied stiffly, 'Yes, yer Majesty. Some in the fields'n'orchards an' others in yore workplace makin' things of beauty to grace yore chambers!'

There was a further silence, then Silth spoke once more. 'Hmm. Don't let them get fat and lazy, Captain. Remind them of the rules on my island.'

Ullig faced the cages and shouted out the rules, veins bulging from his thick neck as he did so. 'Work an' you live, an' remember there is no escape from 'ere! Disobey an' you get fed t'the Teeth o' the Deeps. This is the rule of 'er Majesty, 'Igh Queen Silth. You stay alive only by 'er mercy!'

There was a short silence, then the voice from within the palanquin called out petulantly, 'Take me back inside, to my chambers. I don't like it out here, there's only ugliness, nothing nice. I must be surrounded by beauty. Death will never visit where beauty reigns!'

Lifting the palanquin carefully, the bearers marched off with measured tread, halting suddenly as Silth screeched, 'Stop! There it is, at the upper chamber windows! Don't you see it, fools? The White Ghost! Captain, take a troop up there quickly and slay it. Hurry!'

Floating back and forth across the brightly lit window of an upper chamber, the fearful white apparition fluttered, howling.

'Queeeeen Siiiiiilth, Dark Forest awaits your spirit. Death is all you have left now. Oooooooooohhhhhh!'

Ullig clattered off at the head of his troops, knowing that the spectre would be gone when he reached the room upstairs. It was not the first time something like this had occurred.

Lantur stowed the 'White Ghost' in its corner cupboard and poured two goblets of plum wine. Sliding one across to the rat Wilce, the Marlfox smiled maliciously, listening to the guards hastening up the stairs.

'She'll have frightened herself to death by winter, Wilce, and then we'll prepare a deadly reception for my returning brothers and sisters. Give me a toast, Wilce!'

The female water rat nodded over the rim of her goblet. 'To High Queen Lantur, next ruler of this island and all the lake surrounding it. Long life and undisturbed sleep!'

Lantur quaffed her goblet's contents. 'Aye, I'll drink to that. After all, who could disturb my sleep? The White Ghost?'

Wilce topped up Lantur's goblet from the wine flagon.

'How could the White Ghost disturb my lady when 'twill be lying at the bottom of the lake, wrapped around ex-Queen Silth!'

'Heehee! Pour yourself more wine, Wilce!'

Cregga stumped her way downstairs to find out what had been going on in her absence. The few days she had spent alone in her room had been irksome. Now recovered from her wounds, the blind badger was eager for company, longing to be part of the daily hum of Abbey life. Her tread was slow and sure, and she kept to one side of the stairs, using the wall as a guide. Every joint and crack of the ancient red sandstone, each paw-worn stair with its own small dip or hollow, the Badgermum knew well. Redwall Abbey was her home, and she loved it so much that she felt every stone of it was part of her.

Reaching Great Hall, Cregga's sharp instincts told her things were not as they should be. She knew it was night time, and there were always Redwallers about this late in the evening. But now there was a hushed silence over everything. Moreover, her senses told her that candles and lanterns aplenty were lit, for she could feel their presence, the slight warmth, a guttering flicker, the odd drip of melted beeswax from a brimming sconce, the fragrant odour of pine resin. All was not right.

Moving silently into what she knew was the shadow of a thick stone column at the edge of the hall, the big badger felt about until her paw rested on the long pole of a brass-cupped candle-snuffer. Grasping it tight, she called out, 'Who's there? Speak if you know what's good for ye. I don't like creatures sneakin' about around me!'

From somewhere out at the hall's centre, a voice she identified as Friar Butty's whispered, 'One, two, three . . . Now!'

Music burst out everywhere, fifes, drums, and all manner of stringed instruments, with massed voices singing in harmony.

'Midsummer midsummer the solstice is here,
And now we give thanks to the day,
We joyfully sing like the birds on the wing,
For old winter is still far away.
The high sun of noontide smiles down on us all,
Sending warmth to the earth from on high,
Soon the autumn will yield, out in orchard and field,
Where the bounties of nature do lie.
Midsummer midsummer the solstice is now,
In the midst of this season so bright,
Yea we sing, aye we sing, hear our glad voices ring,
Far into this fine summer night.'

Dwopple and Blinny the molebabe dashed forward. Seizing Cregga's huge paws, they tugged her towards the feasting tables.

'Heehee! We frykkened you, Badgermum, but then us singed nice for ya!'

'Bo urr, marm, do ee cumm now, we'm got gurt 'eaps o' vittles furr ee, an' you'm can stay up late with us'n's!'

The blind badger allowed herself to be led to the festive table. Seating herself in the big Abbot's chair, she took both Dibbuns on her lap, joking with the little creatures. 'I must say, you did frighten me dreadfully, but that lovely song made me feel lots better. Thank you! Can we really stay up late tonight? Then I'll behave meself an' be extra good. Mmm, I smell blueberry an' almond turnovers. Pass me the dish, please. I'm so hungry I think I'll eat 'em all!'

Dwopple shook his spoon severely at the massive old badger. 'Tch tch! Thort you said y'was gonna be'ave. Friar Butty send y'back up to bed if you naughty!'

Outside the night was still, the day's heat still radiating from the sunwarmed stones of the walltop. A half-moon stood clear in endless plains of dark velvet sky. At the centre of the south rampart, Bargle stood talking to the shrew Mayon, on reluctant guard duty.

'Wot d'yer think the chances are of Florian an' his patrol comin' up 'ere to relieve us, so's we can get to the feast?'

Bargle shook his head at Mayon's simple and trusting nature. 'You got more chance o' sproutin' wings an' flutterin' away like a butterfly, matey! Imagine ole Florian an' Skipper pushin' woodland trifle down their faces, then sayin' all of a sudden like, "Better 'urry up, we got to go an' relieve the wallguards!" '

Mayon tried to imagine it, then sighed regretfully. 'Yore right, mate, 'twouldn't 'appen in ten seasons o' plenty. Oh well, mebbe they'll leave us some fer brekkist. I 'ope?'

The four Marlfoxes crouched in the ditch. Behind them, a contingent of water rats waited, holding the siege ladder between them. Gelltor hauled himself stealthily up on to the path. When he held his voluminous cloak still, he was almost invisible against the ditch edge and the path. At his signal the rats crawled out of the ditch, taking care to make no noise with the long rough ladder. Silently Gelltor fastened it to one end of the rope that had been left hanging from the protrusion beneath the battlements near the northwest corner. The ladder rose smoothly upwards as several rats hauled slowly on the rope's other end. When the ladder was raised to its full extent, Gelltor manoeuvred it firmly against the wall and nodded to the others waiting in the ditch. Vannan, Ascrod and Predak led the remainder of the water rats to the bottom of the ladder. Gripping his axe handle in tight-clenched teeth, Gelltor began climbing. When he was halfway up, Predak allowed the rats to follow.

The Guosim shrew guarding that area was looking over at Bargle and Mayon, not suspecting a thing. Swift and silent as a shadow passing across the moon, Gelltor slid over the walltop and slew the sentry. As the rats followed he gestured to the wallsteps in the northwest corner, whispering, 'Hide down there against the wall and wait for me!'

The first group of ten water rats padded softly down the stairs, into the grounds of Redwall Abbey.

Mayon yawned and stretched wearily. 'Let's 'ope that Friar Butty thinks of us an' reminds ole Florian that we're up 'ere, mate. Oooh! I dunno wot's gettin' to me most, 'unger or tiredness. Is that Fleggum over at the far corner there? Looks like 'e's gone asleep.'

Bargle stared over towards the shrew in question, who was lying prone. 'Sleepin' on the job, is 'e? Well, I'll soon . . . Rats! Lookit, mate, there's rats climbin' o'er the wall! Logalogalogalooooog!'

Roused by the Guosim cry, shrews pounded round from all sides of the walltops, following Bargle and Mayon to the northwest corner.

Gelltor cursed, grinding his teeth. 'Rot their lousy eyes, they've seen us!'

Bargle charged headlong across the ramparts, yelling out orders. 'Three to each wallgate! Mayon, take six an' secure the main gate! Stop those vermin openin' any gates. Splikker, bring the rest an' follow me. Chaaaaaarge!'

Gelltor was in a quandary. He could not fight off the charging Guosim, but neither could he climb back down the ladder against the stream of rats already on it, forging their way upward. Judging the situation hastily, he slipped quietly off down the wallsteps.

A water rat was halfway over the wall when he met a thrust from Bargle's rapier and fell back with a gurgle, plunging out over the heads of his upcoming companions. Bargle and three other shrews mounted the battlements, slashing with their blades at any rat foolish enough to attempt climbing further. Below on the ground Vannan, Ascrod and Predak knew that the plan had been discovered, but they urged their troops on.

'Come on, get up that ladder! You at the top there,

attack! Get on the wall and keep them shrews busy! Fight them!'

Bargle draped himself across the gap between two battlements, and by leaning down as far as he could managed to catch hold of the rope, still tied to the ladder top. The brave shrew hauled on the rope whilst his mates kept the attackers busy, until the free end was at last in his hand. Leaping up, he yelled out commands.

'Somebeast get over to the Abbey an' raise the alarm, there's nobeast in the belltower to warn 'em! The rest of ye, follow me!'

Bargle started running along the tops of the battlements towards the southwest corner, tugging the rope across his shoulders. Wily in the ways of battle, the other Guosim caught on right away to what he was doing. Climbing up to join him, each one caught hold of the rope and ran with it, pulling furiously. With a loud grating sound the ladder began heeling over sideways. Rats screeched in panic, caught in a jumble at the top of the ladder, unable to descend because of others clinging on in terror below them. Those lucky enough to be on the low rungs jumped for the safety of the ground, most of them landing on the heads of the bewildered Marlfoxes below. Unable to topple further, the ladder fell awkwardly, spinning out away from the wall, laden with screaming vermin. It thudded to earth with a sickening crunch, snapping at its centre as it hit the ground in a cloud of dust and carcasses.

Bargle jumped down from the battlements. 'Down into the grounds, mates, we don't know 'ow many got in!'

The shrew running for the Abbey to raise the alarm was brought down by an arrow. Mayon had his paws full defending the main gates against Gelltor and the ten water rats who had made it over the wall.

Gelltor was fighting for his life and he knew it. If he could not force Mayon and his six Guosim away from the main gate, there would be no help from outside now that the ladder had fallen. The Marlfox fought like a demon, snarling in the face of his enemies as he wielded his axe savagely. Three shrews were laid low as Bargle and the rest of his sentries came thundering up to join the fight. Gelltor and his rats saw them coming and dashed away for the south wallgate, where only three Guosim were on guard. The Marlfox's mind was racing. If he was fast enough they could lay the three low and escape. Bargle went after them, signalling Mayon to stay with his command at the main gate. One of the shrews running with Bargle was halfway across the lawn, whirling a loaded sling, when he tripped. The heavy pebble shot off into the night.

Smash! The stone took out a small windowpane in Great Hall. Janglur, Rusvul and Skipper were up and vaulting over the tabletops even before the final shards of crystal glass had finished falling. Borrakul was hard on their heels, blocking the doorway through which the trio had just exited.

'Friar, Deesum, Sloey! Git those Dibbuns to the wine cellars. Cregga, you an' the elders hold this door. Every other able-bodied Redwaller, foller me!'

Florian brushed past him in high indignation. 'Hmph! Just what I was about t'say m'self. Don't anticipate my orders in future. Thunderin' bad form, sir!'

Tragglo Spearback could not help raising his eyebrows as he patted Borrakul's back. 'Ho dearie me, you've got mister Florian really roused now, mate. I wonder who 'e's goin' to attack with that bowl o' pudden that 'e's carryin'?'

Gelltor had lost the fray. Bargle and his Guosim hurled themselves upon the water rats, with all the skill and ferocity of shrew Warriors. They took no prisoners. Gelltor was backed up against the wallgate, surrounded by a half-circle of rapier blades, when Janglur, Rusvul and Skipper arrived on the scene. Bargle staunched a leg wound grimly.

'Big ole ladder they 'ad, Skip, but I put paid t'that. I think this Marlfox 'ere is the last of 'em!'

Somebeast held up a torch, and Skipper studied the Marlfox in its glow. 'Florian, take yore guards up on the walltop an' secure it. We'll search the grounds an' make certain there ain't any more vermin prowlin' about. Janglur, bind this 'un an' lock 'im in the gate'ouse until we decides wot t'do with 'im!'

Gelltor flailed about dangerously with his axe. 'Put a paw near me an' it gets chopped off!'

The half-lidded eyes of Janglur settled on the Marlfox. 'Tough beast, ain't yer, fox? Yore the one who was goin' to execute me fer sendin' yore sister where she belongs.'

The Marlfox spat at the warrior squirrel and bared his fangs. 'Talk big with your army round you, windbag. You couldn't face me alone if I was bound an' blindfolded!'

Skipper smiled pityingly at the Marlfox. 'Oops! I think you jus' said the wrong thing there, matey.'

Janglur waved a paw at those surrounding the cornered Gelltor. 'Back off, everybeast. Do like I say an' stand well away.'

Rusvul shouldered his javelin and prepared to stride off. 'Best do like Janglur says. Where d'yer want us, Jang?'

Janglur's eyes never left the fox as he replied, 'Over yonder, out o' the way!'

The squirrel warrior nodded at the Marlfox's axe. 'You can keep 'old o' that thing. Now, let's do this proper. Walk past me, fox, about three tall treelengths, out on to the lawn.'

Gelltor was mystified, but he complied, feeling the squirrel's lazy eyes watching him as he paced off the distance.

'Right, that'll do, ye vermin. Stop there.'

Gelltor halted and turned to see Janglur whack the bolts back with two sharp movements and fling open the south wallgate. Janglur moved forward a few paces. Standing empty-pawed between Gelltor and the open gate, he addressed the fox. 'See, there's freedom – an open gate. All you got to do is get past me. Don't fret, nobeast will try t'stop yer, only me.'

Gelltor spat on his axeblade and swung it expertly, feeling lightheaded with confidence. What sort of fools were these Abbeydwellers, leaving only a fatbellied sleepy-looking squirrel between a Marlfox and his freedom? He ran a short distance forward, sprang into a crouch with the keen axe flat-bladed in front of him, and began stalking his prey.

Janglur waited until Gelltor was less than a pace from him. Then, as the axe swung, he dropped to the ground, kicking out sharply. Gelltor went down on his tail with a grunt of surprise. He had never missed a beast with his axe at that range. A sickening pain shot through his left footpaw and he scrambled upright, to find himself facing the squirrel whirling a stone-loaded sling. Limping, Gelltor took two sharp sideways chops at his adversary, snarling angrily, 'When I leave here I'll take your head with me, Redwaller!'

Janglur countered a blow, the stone in his sling ringing off the axeblade. He swung and caught Gelltor in the stomach. 'Save yore breath, bully. Are you goin' t'talk or fight?'

The Marlfox feinted to draw Janglur off, then swung an overhead slice directly between his opponent's eyes. But the squirrel was not there. Janglur had moved his position so that he was standing alongside his assailant. The momentum of the swing buried the axeblade in the earth, and the thwack of the stone-loaded sling echoed off the south wall as it struck Gelltor's skull.

Janglur took the axe from the slain Marlfox's limp grasp, passing it to Tragglo Spearback. 'This weapon's seen enough evil. Put it t'work in yore cellars choppin' up ole barrel staves. Skip, get those slain rats.' He hooked a paw in Gelltor's belt and dragged him outside the wallgate, where he dumped the dead Marlfox on open ground. 'Put 'em out 'ere wid their master. I told them they could bury their own when they started this.'

When the gate was secured, they started back for the Abbey, Skipper and Janglur supporting Bargle, who sported a makeshift bandage on his wounded leg. Rusvul ruffled the shrew's ears fondly. 'That's a wound to show yore grandshrews, mate!'

The tough Guosim limped forward with all speed. 'Hah! Never mind that! Is the feast still goin' good? Me'n'my crew bin waitin' on a relief since nearly noon, an' we're starvin'!'

Florian called down anxiously from the walltop. 'I say, old chap, if y'see a half-finished woodland trifle puddin', well, it's mine, so don't put a blinkin' paw near it, wot!'

'Righto, mate,' Bargle called cheerily back. 'I swear I won't touch yore trifle. Can't say the same thing for Mayon, though. 'E loves 'is trifle, that 'un does!'

'Cads! Trifle-burglars! Have you no sense of honour, sirs? Leavin' a poor creature up here in charge of your jolly worthless hides whilst you plunder his trifle, this'll go on your record, I warn you, great shrewfaced vittle-vulture!'

Mayon began ragging Florian ruthlessly. 'Are yer partial to mushroom and cheese flan, sir, or anythin' o' that sort? Jus' you tell us wot dishes are yer favourite, mister Florian.'

The hare's reply was tinged with hopefulness. 'Well, thank the seasons for a decent type o' shrew, wot! Yes, mushroom'n'cheese flan, that's jolly nice. Oh, let me see now, I like summer salad with hazelnuts, blueberry pudden, hot scones with meadowcream, lashin's o' the stuff! Er, apple pie, plum tart, heavy fruitcake with a wedge of cheese, anythin' like that!'

Mayon nodded, as if making a mental note of it all. 'Well, don't you fret, sir, we'll remove all that jolly ole temptation outta yore way, so that yore breeches'll still fit yer. Don't forget t'put that on our records, sir!'

They went inside chuckling, with the air ringing to Florian Dugglewoof Wilffachop's invective. 'Blisterin' salad-swipers! Confounded purloiners of puddens! You mop-pawed ragheaded bread'n'cheese bandits, I hope y'all scoff too much an' explode, see if I'll care? Hah, pish'n'tush I'll say, fiddledy hey an' serves 'em right! Why, I've a good mind t'go to sleep an' allow the flippin' place t'be overrun with water foxes an' Marlrats an' what have you . . . er, I mean, forterwoxes an' ragmats, yes, that's what I mean . . . er, no 'tisn't . . .'

21

Morning was high and bright by the time the travellers left Sollertree's dwelling with their guide. Song had the feeling that though the hedgehog giant professed to be happy with his lonely existence, he would dearly have wished them to stay longer. In normal circumstances the squirrelmaid would have liked to, but there was much to be done and now was not the time to linger. With their packs refilled from Soll's larder they trudged off, their big friend in the lead carrying the boat *Swallow* across his shoulders with ease. Dann figured that the path they were taking must once have been flooded by water, for thick fernbeds interspersed with clumps of marjoram, woundwort and hempnettle grew round the slender trunks of young rowan, elder and ash, which provided a veritable palisade on either side of the narrow path. Apart from the birdsong all around there appeared to be no signs of other creatures.

'Looks like we got the woodlands to ourselves, mates!' Dippler remarked airily.

Soll's reply caused them to look to their weapons. 'Not quite, me young dears, we're bein' watched. Now now, put not yore paws near blade or sling, 'tis nothin' a beast o' my girth cannot deal with! Follow me, look neither left nor right an' be not afeared.'

'Oh yiss yiss, keep close t'the big feller, though I don't see as 'ow he'll defend us,' Burble whispered to Dippler as they hurried to keep up with Soll. 'Yesterday 'e said that 'twas agin' 'is nature t'be a warrior or harm any livin' creature.'

Dippler kept close behind the hedgehog's broad back. He had confidence in Soll. 'Don't you worry, Burb, mister Soll will take care of us.'

Song's sharp eyes soon picked out the shapes flitting amid the screen of slim treetrunks. Whoever it was tracking them seemed well versed in stealth, using sunlight and shadow skilfully, slipping between ferns and bushes.

'Whatever kind of creature comes at us, I'm not afraid,' Dann murmured to her. 'This time they won't catch me nappin', I'll wager!'

The pretty squirrelmaid restrained Dann's swordpaw gently. 'I know you don't fear them, Dann, but let's do what Soll says, just follow and leave things to him. Look out, here they are!'

There were three of them, a stoat and two weasels. Their appearance was eerie and barbaric. Stripes of yellow clay and green plant dye swathed the trio from ears to footpaws, providing perfect camouflage for the type of woodland they hunted in. A mace and chain dangled from the stoat's paw, while the weasels brandished fire-blackened cutlasses. They stood on the path ahead, boldly blocking the way.

Grinning wickedly, the stoat twirled his mace and chain. 'Stay where y'are. This's our forest. Who said youse could walk on our path? I never, did you, cullies?'

The weasels were enjoying themselves. They shook their heads.

'Nah, we never gave 'em permission.'

'Trespassin', that's wot they're doin'.'

Soll unshouldered the boat, placing it carefully to one

side. His voice was calm and friendly. 'Me'n'my friends are travellers. We don't want trouble.'

The stoat turned to his weasel companions, putting on a mocking tone. 'Did y'ear that, buckoes? They don't want trouble. Ain't that nice?' Turning swiftly, he slammed the spiked metal ball of his mace and chain against a thin laburnum tree, tearing off a chunk of bark. His voice hardened as he shook the weapon at the hedgehog. 'Well, you've already got trouble whether y'want it or not. Now drop those foodpacks an' yer weapons too, an' leave the pretty boat where 'tis. Then run back the ways yer came an' I'll let yer off wid yore lives. But yer better do it quick!'

Soll held up a large paw. 'I hear you, friend. Let me have a word with these young 'uns first.' Without waiting for a reply, Soll turned and addressed his followers quietly.

'Steady now, me liddle dears. I know yore warriors an' you could deal with yon vermin, but why waste life? They're only bullies an' loudmouths, or they'd 'ave acted afore now. Leave this t'Soll.'

The giant hedgehog turned back then, and took a few resolute steps forward. Seeing the size of him reared up to his full height, the vermin trio fell back a pace. Soll's face was stern and unrelenting, and his voice rang like iron. 'Y'see those four young 'uns back there? Well, each of 'em is a Redwall Abbey Champion. They're born warriors. Any one of 'em could lay all three of you out!'

Both weasels looked apprehensive at this statement, but the stoat kept up his swagger. 'Yore lyin', 'edgepig. Those three, ha! I'll wager that four seasons back their mammas was still tuckin' 'em in bed!'

Soll raised his bushy eyebrows, widening his eyes until he began to look quite insane, and his voice rose to a roar. 'But I only keep my friends for special occasions, an' this ain't nothin' special, three painted popinjays like you. Yore all mine!'

Soll's powerful paws began clenching and unclenching, his eyes popped even wider and his voice swelled like thunder. "Cos you've left it too late to run away now! Y'must deal with me! I'm the son of a gutripper an' skullcrusher! Born in dark moon an' storm! My enemies don't 'ave graves, I et 'em all! First I'll bite off yer ears an' tails! Then I'll build me a great fire, a roastin' fire! I'll cut me a sharp green spit, one that can take three vermin at a time! Then I'll get my skinnin' sword an' I'll . . .'

But the vermin were gone, whizzing away through the woodlands like minnows with a pike on their tails.

Sollertree sat down on the path, placing a paw across his eyes and shaking his head woefully. 'Oh dearie me, grapevines'n'gravel! Dearie goodness gracious me!'

Song hurried forward and held his paw sympathetically. 'Mister Soll, whatever's wrong with you?'

The giant hedgehog waved her away. 'Leave me a moment, my pretty maid. I've gone an' upset meself with all that temper an' shoutin'. It had t'be done, though I don't like meself when I must resort to anger. Leave me, I beg you.'

Song went with her friends to sit a short distance from Soll. Dann's eyes were shining with wonder. 'Did you see him? Whew! Imagine what he'd 'ave done if the vermin'd stayed! I shudder t'think!'

Dippler had enjoyed the encounter immensely, once he was over the first fright of Soll's roaring tirade. 'Heheehee! Did you see their faces? I thought they was gonna break all their teeth, they was chatterin' so 'ard, eh, Burb?'

'Oh yiss yiss. Meself, I was hopin' that good ole mister Soll'd skin 'em an' roast the rotten toads, like 'e said 'e would. Yiss!'

Song tweaked the watervole's ear. 'You bloodthirsty little maggot, mister Soll wouldn't have done any such thing. He knew they were only bullies, so he outbullied them. Look at him, poor creature, he's quite upset.'

However, Soll's depressed state did not last too long. He sniffed quite a bit, wiped his eyes and stood up smiling broadly. 'Well, that's enough o' that, my liddle dearies. There's plenty o' creatures in this land to upset me, without my upsettin' meself. Life is given t'be lived happily, that's true enough!' Picking up the mace and chain that the stoat had dropped, Soll twirled it above his head until it was a humming blur, then he flung it up and out. They watched in awe as it sailed out of sight over the treetops.

About mid-afternoon Soll changed course slightly, veering off into an area where the trees were less thick, and small clearings and rocks dotted the land.

'I 'opes you don't mind, my dearies, but I got a liddle visitin' t'do. 'Twon't take up much of yore time.'

Dippler sniffed the air appreciatively. 'Ooh, lovely, scones! Somebeast's bakin' scones, I can smell 'em.'

Sure enough, a wonderful aroma of fresh-baked scones hovered elusively on the hot afternoon air. Soll halted and called out in a gentle singsong tone,

'Goodwife Brimm, are you at 'ome?
If'n you are 'tis only me,
Now you won't sit all alone,
'Cos I've brought some friends to tea!'

A voice, old and cracked through long seasons, answered him.

'If'n that's who I think it be,
Wot a din yore makin',
Seems to me I only see,
Yore face when I'm bakin'!'

Laughing uproariously, Soll hitched the *Swallow* further up on his shoulders and broke into a lumbering run, with the four travellers trotting in his wake.

Goodwife Brimm was a small, thin otter, incredibly old; her fur had turned a beautiful silver-white. Song had never seen an old otterwife dressed so charmingly, from her poke bonnet and puff-sleeved gown to the flowery pinafore with dainty lace edging. The goodwife's home was properly built from baked clay and mud bricks, walling in a flat almost square rock spur, which formed the roof. White limestones separated her vegetable and herb garden from a blossoming flower patch. The old otter left off gathering rows of scones from a window-ledge, where they had been cooling, and hobbled forward to greet her friend. Soll and Goody Brimm hugged and kissed fondly.

'My ole Goody Goody, prettiest otter an' best cook anywheres!'

'Soll, you big flatterer, yore singin' ain't improved none!'

'So it 'asn't, marm, but I got one 'ere can outsing larks!'

Soll introduced them, whilst Goody Brimm kissed their cheeks and squeezed their paws right heartily for one so frail-looking. 'Fortune smile on 'em, ain't they so young an' beautiful, Soll? My my, swords'n'slings'n'rapiers! Proper young warriors all. Come in and sit, I was about t'put the kettle on!'

Inside was the neatest, tidiest house they had ever seen. A brightly hued rush mat covered the floor from wall to wall, pottery ornaments graced the highly polished dresser, there were even embroidered linen headrests on the chairbacks. Goody Brimm put a sizeable copper kettle over the fire to boil, then, rolling mint leaves and dried burnet rosehips almost to powder with a long round stone, she tossed them in a fat blue teapot. Tea at Goody Brimm's house was very special. The travellers helped themselves to almond wafers and scones, spread with every kind of preserve from blackcurrant jelly to gooseberry and damson jam.

Soll hauled two bags from his pack. 'Brought you some grapes'n'almonds. Good crop this year.'

They explained their mission to the otterwife, who

listened, sipping her tea and nodding, whilst encouraging them to eat more. When they had finished their tale, the old goodwife spoke. 'The stream flows well not far from here. Soll will have you there by eventide, so don't gollop yore food an' rush off, now. Lack a day, young 'uns are always in a hurry. Slow down, 'tis better for you. Now then, pretty miss, with a name like your'n I think you should carry a nice tune. Do ye know one called "Mother Nature Dear"? 'Tis a great favourite of mine.'

Song answered without hesitation. 'Aye, I know it well, marm, my Grandma Ellayo taught it to me. 'Twas a long time ago, but I recall every word.'

Goody chuckled and winked at Soll. 'A long time ago, eh? Like as not two seasons back. When yore old as me, then y'can talk about long times, my beauty. Come, sing for me.'

Song began tapping her footpaw, and they all tapped along with her until the rhythm was just right to start singing.

'Who taught the birds to sing?
Why Mother Nature dear.
Who told the winds an' breeze to blow,
Rain to fall an' snow to snow,
Rivers to run an' streams to flow?
Oh Mother Nature dear!

Who coloured grass so green?
Why Mother Nature dear.
Who tells the moon, come out at night,
And teaches stars to shine so bright,
Then orders sun and clear daylight?
Oh Mother Nature dear!

Who makes the seaons change?
Why Mother Nature dear.
Who says the seas must ebb and flow,
An' tells each tree how tall to grow,

Then lets the days pass fast or slow?
Oh Mother Nature dear,
I see her plain an' clear,
She's all around us here!'

Song held the final note, letting it rise, holding it a touch longer, then ending with a double tap of her footpaws. Goody Brimm was smiling, yet she wiped her eyes with a small kerchief. 'I never 'eard that tune sung so sweet in all me days. 'Twas a rare treat jus' to sit'n'lissen to yore voice, young missie!'

Soll rose reluctantly. 'That's true, m'dear, but these young 'uns got a ways to go afore nightfall. We best leave now if'n we want to make it to the stream by twilight. So we'll be biddin' ye goodbye.'

Goody Brimm hastily started wrapping scones for them. 'Goodbye nothin'! I'll walk with ye as far as the stream. A stretch of the ole paws'll do me good!'

Afternoon shadows were growing long as they strode through the woodland in double file, chatting away animatedly. Dann watched the old otter, leaning for support on Soll's sturdy paw, both solitary creatures united for a short time. Song already had an idea of what Dann was going to say to her, but she let him speak his thoughts as they walked together.

'I can't help feelin' sorry for Soll an' Goody. You can tell they lead a lonely life, by the way they love company an' want us to stay an' visit longer. I think they'd be far better off livin' at Redwall Abbey. There'd be lots o' new friends there, an' things t'do. I bet they'd soon forget their loneliness at the Abbey.'

Song had already pondered this idea. 'Ah, but you must remember, Dann, they're solitary creatures by choice. I'll grant you that they like visitors, but if they were to live at the Abbey, perhaps they wouldn't be able to get used to constant company and living night and day without the solitude they've come to love so well.

235

Besides, Soll and Goody are old and set in their ways. I don't think they'd take so easily to a new life.'

Goody Brimm turned and winked at Song. 'Right, me beauty. You show great wisdom for one so young!'

The squirrelmaid felt her fur prickle with embarrassment. 'Oh, marm, I'm sorry. I didn't realize I was speakin' so loud!'

Goody's head nodded up and down as she chuckled. 'Heehee, you weren't. Sometimes my ole paws let me down, but these ears o' mine are sharp as the day I was born. What's more, when I hear yore voice echoin' round this great boat that Soll's carryin', it sounds a lot louder, I can tell ye. Heehee!'

Burble agreed with the old otter. 'Ah yiss yiss, missus, I carried that boat over me head wid these three fer nigh on a day. D'ye know, they near drove me mad wid their chatterin' an' singin' echoin' through me pore young ears. Yiss!'

Dippler stared at the watervole quizzically. 'Did I 'ear right, matey? Somebeast near drove *you* mad by chatterin'? Are yer sure 'twasn't the other way round, eh?'

Several rivulets joined in a small valley to form the stream. In the gathering twilight they heard the water sounds as they trekked through the trees towards it. Simple pleasure showed on Soll's heavy face. 'You see, me liddle dearies, I told you I'd get ye here afore dark, an' I was right, was I not?' Placing the *Swallow* onstream, Soll held it still whilst the four friends stowed their supplies, climbed into the vessel and took up their paddles. Then Soll and Goody Brimm bid them farewell.

'Go ye now, an' fortune sail with you, my dearies!'

'Aye, an' make them scones last well, 'twill be a long time till you taste any so nice!'

'Should you return safe from yore venture, be so kind as to call an' visit ole Soll again some sunny day!'

'You must all come an' see me too, but stay a bit longer

next time. Be careful now, go safe an' take our best wishes with ye!'

The *Swallow* cut her way out to midstream, with the four friends calling their goodbyes to the two good creatures waving from the bank.

'Thanks for everything, both of you. We'll come back, never fear!'

'Aye, a Guosim nose can scent scones bakin' anywhere, marm!'

'Yiss yiss, tell me friend Croikle to 'ave more jokes ready when we call back this way, sir!'

'Farewell, Soll, farewell, Goody! We'll never forget you, or the kindness you've shown us. Farewell!'

Watching the sleek craft slide downstream until it was lost in the nightfall, hedgehog and otter stood silent, tears dripping down their faces. Goody Brimm passed Soll her kerchief. 'They got a long an' dangerous way t'go, but they're young an' brave of heart. They'll make it.'

The giant hedgehog dabbed gently at his eyes. 'Wish they could've stayed safe with me'n'Croikle!'

22

Florian Dugglewoof Wilffachop struck his most noble
pose. Balancing high on the midwest battlements he
leaned forward, shading his eyes with a paw, back leg
stuck out straight behind, and his expression one of keen
and courageous intelligence as he peered searchingly in
all directions. The fearless commander, master of all he
surveyed. 'H'all cleeeeyaaahhh?' he called to the sentries
in his most authoritative voice. 'The enemy hath fled
from our gates! Nary a sign of one lousebound rat or
malicious Marlfox t'be seen in all this fair country, wot!'

Deesum clasped her paws together fervently. 'Oh,
thanks be to fortune, is the fighting over now?'

Florian blew out his narrow chest, placing a paw upon
his heart. 'The winds of war blow no more, madam, the
foebeast is vanquished, routed by our valorous efforts,
retreating in disarray, wot wot!'

The fiendish mousebabe Dwopple narrowly missed
the hare's tail with a stone from his sling. He scowled
ferociously. 'Worra 'im talkin' 'bout?'

Florian cast a jaundiced eye at his one remaining foe. 'If
you'd washed your pesky ears out you'd have heard first
time, O small and horrible one. Victory is ours! Toll the
bells! Strew rose petals round me paws and prepare a

great feast!'

Brother Melilot rolled his eyes skyward in despair. 'I had a feelin' he was goin' to mention food!'

The rest of the Redwallers sitting on the gatehouse steps looked to Cregga. Sister Sloey touched the badger's paw. 'What d'you think, Badgermum? Is the fighting really over?'

Cregga deliberated before giving her answer. 'It could well be, friend. Another Marlfox slain, and a good number of water rats. Perhaps they've had enough. They've not shown up today so far, and that must be a good sign.'

Gurrbowl Cellarmole jumped up and down with joy. She hated the notion, as most other Redwallers did, of continued strife. 'Oh, do saya ee vurmints be'd gone, marm. Ee foightin' do be's over, bain't it, do ee say 'tis.'

Cregga smiled. She could feel the hopefulness virtually radiating from the Abbeydwellers gathered around her. 'Oh, all right, if you wish, I think the war's over.'

Joyous pandemonium rang out over the grounds into the sunkissed morning.

'Victory for Redwaaaaaallllll!'

'Sound the bells! Sound the bells good'n'loud!'

'A feast! Let's prepare a great feast in the orchard!'

Florian strutted triumphantly down the wallsteps, bowing to all around in the most outrageous manner. 'Jolly well told you chaps, didn't I? Fightin's over, wot!'

Janglur sat on the northwest wallcorner with his friends, Rusvul and Skipper. They watched the cheering creatures pouring over towards the Abbey, eager to begin the preparations for the celebratory feast. Janglur's hooded eyes swept Mossflower woodlands north of the ramparts. 'Let 'em enjoy theirselves. I think I'll just linger round 'ere for a few days yet. No point in takin' chances, mates.'

Skipper tested a longbow that he had been restringing. 'Good idea. We're with you!'

*

Vannan's was the strongest personality of the three remaining Marlfoxes. She had ordered a retreat into the depths of south Mossflower. The vixen sat watching the water rats tend their injuries and cook food over an open fire, remarking noncommittally, as Ascrod came to sit beside her, 'We're fortunate there's no shortage of vittles hereabouts. Let 'em rest awhile. We need to use brains more than weapons now.'

Ascrod snorted scornfully. He snatched a roasted thrush from a passing water rat and sank his teeth into it. 'We need reinforcements more than anythin', sister. We've barely got a hundred an' twenty countin' me, you an' Predak.'

Vannan stood up, brushing her cloak off. 'Then we'll just have to use the ferrets, won't we?'

Ascrod spat a bone into the fire, wrinkling his face in disgust. 'What? You mean that scurvy bunch we rousted out of here last night? Raventail and his ragged crowd? They looked as though they'd seen enough fighting to last them many a long day. Anyway, ferrets have never served those of Marlfox blood. Surely you cannot be serious?'

Vannan adjusted the axe in her belt so it was ready to paw. 'I'm perfectly serious, brother. We can't be too choosy in times like these, and we need more soldiers. Those ferrets will join us, aye, they'll fight and die for us too, when I've put a bit of discipline into their backbones. You can come with me. Bring an escort of twoscore, well armed – Allag's patrol will do.'

Ascrod tossed the roast bird aside, wiping paws upon his cloak. 'But we chased them off. They'll be long gone by now.'

Vannan pointed to the telltale wisps rising above the treetops to the south. 'They're still hanging about over that way. I've been marking the smoke of their campfire since early morning. Are you coming?'

Ascrod signalled Allag's patrol and hurried to join his

sister. 'But there was no more than a score of them. What use is twenty ferrets to us?'

Vannan strode confidently onward. 'A score is all we counted, but I'll wager they can raise three times that number. Sixty extra soldiers is not something to be sneezed at. Let's go and talk to this Chieftain Raventail!'

When they reached the ferret camp, Vannan ordered Ascrod to stay concealed nearby in the woods with Allag and his patrol. Using all the considerable wiles of a Marlfox she made her way through the ferrets unheeded. Drawing as close to Raventail's fire as she could while remaining undetected, the vixen tossed a pawful of special ingredients from her belt pouch into the flames. Raventail shot up in alarm when the fire burst into a green sheet of flame, followed by a thick column of smoke. He was even more astounded by the appearance of Vannan, who materialized out of the haze. The ferret staggered backward, drawing his scimitar.

'Kye arr! Where comma you from, foxbeast?'

Vannan made a fearful sight, paws akimbo, revealing the axe she carried beneath her cloak, from under which the smoke still wreathed and curled. Her strange pale eyes narrowed as she glared at the ferret, calling out in a sepulchral voice, 'Be still and know that I am the Marlfox! The power of great magic is within me!'

Raventail wavered, not sure what to do next. He looked to an old toothless ferret, reputed to be wise, and the old vermin nodded his head vigorously. He too was impressed by Vannan's appearance.

'Yehyeh, meknow 'boutder Marlfoxes. Rakkarakka! Muchmuch magic!'

As if to confirm his statement, Ascrod stepped out from a tree behind Vanna, causing widespread consternation among the ferrets.

'Kye arr! See twobeast now! Shallakaaaah! Marlfox'n'Marlfox!'

Vannan's lips scarcely moved as she whispered to

Ascrod, 'Well done, brother. We've got these ignorant savages' attention.'

She raised a paw imperiously, pointing beyond to the woodland. 'Behold the warrior servants of the Marlfoxes!'

Allag and his patrol marched out of the trees in double ranks. The ferrets turned round to watch the smartly clad water rats. By the time Allag's soldiers arrived at Raventail's fire, both Marlfoxes had disappeared. Raventail circled the fire, utterly astonished. 'Kye arrrrrrr! Wherego Marlfoxes?'

Ascrod and Vannan had circled back to where Allag's patrol had been previously hidden. They emerged from the trees, walking very slowly and looking mysterious. The ferret Chieftain grabbed the paw of the ancient one he had consulted before.

'Yehyeh! Allmagic Marlfox be bigmagic!'

Vannan muttered out the side of her mouth to Ascrod as they approached the awestricken Raventail, 'Let's sit down and do business with this one, now that we've convinced him Marlfoxes are really magic!'

Florian was also impressing an audience at that moment. Armed with a soup ladle and a large wooden salad fork, he pranced about wildly in front of the Abbeybabes, performing a victory ode he had composed in which credit for the rout of the vermin was due largely to the fighting prowess of one Florian Dugglewoof Wilffachop.

'Armed to the dirty mangy teeth,
Ten of 'em came at me,
Hoho, me buckoes, here, sez I,
Only ten of ye?
So I boxed their ears an' blacked their eyes,
Then tied their tails in knots.
I kicked their bottoms o'er the walls
With javelins an' slingshots,

242

When suddenly behind me back,
Some foulbeast shouted "Charge!"
An' twenty-three came right at me,
Those villains were quite large.
So I got me trusty salad fork,
An' jabbed 'em here'n'there,
I left 'em weepin', full o' holes,
"Oh save us from that hare!"
Well I grabbed a fleein' Marlfox,
An' punched him on the snout,
Both his boots went flyin' off,
I gave him such a clout!
Those rats were dirty fighters,
Out came me old soup ladle,
The cowardly pack o' blighters,
Fled fast as they were able.
I chased 'em, laughin' bravely,
Haharr now off you pop,
I'm the warrior who saved Redwall,
An' me last name's Wilffachop!'

Unknown to the garrulous hare, Bargle and Mayon were watching the performance. The two Guosim shrews sat concealed by a berry hedge, observing Florian's wild contortions as he declaimed his outrageous ode. They were not sure whether to scowl or laugh.

'Modest ole beast, ain't 'e, mate?'

'I wonder who taught 'im t'dance, a mad caterpillar?'

'Even a scalded frog couldn't prance about like that. I've never seen a creature's paws, tail, ears'n'whiskers goin' so many different ways at one time!'

'Oh, haharrharr! Ole Florian's fell flat on 'is tail. I knew 'e would. Couldn't keep up a twirlin' jig like that!'

Sister Sloey, assisted by Rimrose and Ellayo, was checking up on Redwallers who had sustained injuries during the fighting. A line formed on the stairs to the Infirmary, the patients mainly shrews who had slingshot or arrow wounds which needed re-dressing. Rimrose finished neatly bandaging a Guosim paw. 'There you are, Splikker, good as new. Keep it dry now, that cut is healing nicely. Next!'

Ellayo and Sloey were applying a compress of wet herbs to the head of a mole who had been hit by a slingstone.

'Don't worry, sir, that bump is smaller than 'twas yesterday. Do you still feel dizzy at all?'

The mole touched a heavy digging claw to the swelling on his brow. 'Oi be foine now, thankee, marm. Doan't feels loik oi gotten two 'eads no more, hurr hurr!'

There was a commotion on the stairway. Florian was pushing his way to the front of the line. 'I say, make way for a warrior, you chaps, pish'n'tush! Load of scratches an' bumps, wot! A feller could be dyin' for all you flippin' lot care. Out o' the confounded way, sir!' He came barging into the Infirmary, but did a smart about-turn when he saw three females in attendance. 'Er, er, harrumph! Not t'worry, ladies, I'll come back another time. Extremely busy, lots t'do, wot wot!'

Ellayo and Sister Sloey cut off his retreat to the door.

'What seems to be the matter, mister Florian?'

'You never reported a wound. Sit down an' tell us about it.'

'Er, er, rather not sit down, Ellayo marm,' Florian blustered, backing up to the wall. 'Nature of the wound, doncha know, er, haha . . .'

Sister Sloey nodded understandingly. 'Oh, I see, you were wounded in the tail area. Why didn't you come here yesterday?'

'Er, well er, didn't feel so jolly bad then, you understand, just today though, been givin' me a bit o' gyp. Must've been a few arrows or a couple o' spears got me. Forgot all about it in the heat of battle, y'know. Chap doesn't like to cause a fuss.'

Rimrose began gathering herbs for a poultice. 'Oh, you

poor creature, you must have been in great pain!'

Florian turned sideways, showing his noble profile and devil-may-care smile. 'Oh, 'twas nothin' really. Stiff upper lip, wot!'

Winking and grinning at everybeast about, Bargle and Mayon entered the Infirmary. Each tossed a broken half of a wooden salad fork on the table.

'Mister Florian, sir, wot's Brother Melilot goin' t'say when he sees wot y'did to 'is salad fork?'

'Aye, I'll wager it smarted a bit when y'fell an' sat down on it like that. Must've give yer a nasty jab in yore backside, sir?'

Over the uproarious laughter from the shrews waiting in line, Ellayo gave the hare a piece of her mind. 'You great flop-eared fraud! Wounded by spears an' arrows durin' the fightin', eh? Yore a fiddle-faced fibber an' a trickster!'

The Infirmary door slammed before Florian could make good his escape. Guosim shrews crowded round the outside, peeping through the keyhole and pressing their ears to the woodwork, to witness what was taking place inside.

'Er, I'll come back t'morrer, marm. What're you doin' with those bally great tweezers? No, please, I beg you. Yaaaah!'

'Bargle, Mayon, hold him still, there may be splinters. Don't want to leave them in there, do we?'

'Ooooh! I say, go easy there! Yowchouch!'

'Is that water hot enough yet, Rimrose? I want to make a nettle poultice. Can't be too careful with tail wounds!'

'Yeeeek! Assassins! Help me, somebeast, they're torturin' me t'death! Owowowowowowwww!'

'So brave an' silent, ain't 'e, Mayon?'

'Whoooooooh! Fiends! Gerroff, lemmego! Oohoohooh!'

'Stiff upper lip, mister Florian, that's the jolly ole spirit. Chin up an' never say die, ole chap, wot wot!'

Brother Melilot and Runktipp were setting up the

banqueting board in the orchard. Gubbio Foremole and Tragglo Spearback upended a cask on to a trestle, and Tragglo knocked home a spigot with his bung mallet. He held a beaker beneath the tap, allowing a small quantity of sparkling pinkish liquid to flow into it. Melilot took the proffered beaker and sipped.

'Best strawberry fizz cordial I ever tasted!'

Runktipp sat on the ground, looping a thin wire about the big white celery cheese he was about to cut. 'Lend a paw 'ere, Brother, 'tis too much for me t'cut alone!'

Melilot clapped a paw to his forehead. 'Pear'n'chestnut flans! I've left six of 'em in the ovens!' He hurried off, calling back orders. 'Tragglo, help cut the cheese, will you! Foremole, send some of your crew to collect those oatfarls from the windowsills, they should be well cooled by now! Roop, Muggle, start loading the trolleys. Don't forget the salad – oh, and see if you can find my serving fork. I don't know where 'tis gone to. Deesum marm, would you be kind enough to top off the trifle? You'll find fresh chopped fruit on the big stone slab. Oh dear, I hope those flans aren't burnt!'

Tragglo and Runktipp pulled the wire smoothly through the large cheese, then lifted off the moist white circular slice and cut it into four wedge-shaped chunks ready for the table.

Runktipp glanced sideways at the berry hedge. 'We're bein' watched, mate. 'Tis prob'ly cheese-robbers!'

Tragglo took his barrel knife and cut a small piece from the cheese, held it up and called out to the hidden creatures, 'You can 'ave some cheese if'n you promises not t'slay us all afore our work's done 'ere!'

The fiendish Dwopple and his cohort, the molebabe Wugger, emerged from behind the hedge. Both Dibbuns were practically unrecognizable. Daubed from ears to tail with grey kitchen ash and flecked with black spots of charcoal, they wore grey blankets, purloined from the dormitory, as cloaks. Stumbling on the blanket hems, they leapt towards the cheese.

Tragglo struggled to keep a straight face. 'An' who might you turrible beasts be?'

Dwopple turned his most fearsome scowl upon the big hedgehog. 'Us be's Marmfloxes, an' y'can't see us, 'cos we be unvizzible!'

Tragglo caught on to the game right away. He looked strangely at Runktipp, who had also guessed what was going on. 'Did you say somethin', mate?'

Runktipp shook his spiky head vigorously. 'I never said a word. I thought 'twas you, mate?'

Dwopple sniggered gleefully as he and Wugger grabbed the cheese. 'It workin', tol' yer they cuddent see us, heehee!'

Wugger broke the cheese in two, giving half to his partner in crime. 'Hurr, vurry gudd. Us'n's best varnish naow, loike ee Marmfloxes!'

The heavy digging claws of Gurrbowl Cellarmole descended on them. 'You'm bain't a-varnishin' nowheres, rogues. Oi see ee gudd enuff t'know you'm be in gurt need o' a barth an' sound scrubbin'!'

Both 'Marmfloxes' were hauled off kicking and squealing by the dutiful molewife.

Added to the scent of the orchard, an aroma of wonderful food created an intoxicating atmosphere. Janglur, Skipper and Rusvul had been temporarily relieved by three good Guosim, and were sitting together with Rimrose and Ellayo. All around them the buzz and chatter of happy creatures added to the festive spirit. Even the vari-hued butterflies and bumblebees that hovered about the orchard seemed part of the enchanted afternoon.

Cregga Badgermum created an instant hush when she stood to speak. 'Friends, Redwallers, good creatures all, before we carry on to enjoy this sunny day, let me say a few words in the absence of either Abbot or Abbess. First, let us hope that the Marlfox threat has gone from

Mossflower country. Brave creatures lost their lives in defence of our Abbey, and we must remember them always in our minds and hearts. But also we must resolve never to yield to evil, whether it be Marlfox or any other vermin attempting to destroy the peaceful life of Redwall. Next, I feel we should give due thanks to our warriors. Janglur Swifteye, Rusvul Reguba, Bargle Guosim, Skipper of otters, Borrakul and all of you who defended the Abbey, our thanks to you brave ones!'

There was a mass murmur of agreement, which broke out into hearty applause. Cregga waited before continuing.

'Also we must live in hopes for the safety of Janglur's daughter Song, Rusvul's son Dannflor and the young Guosim Dippler. These, we now know, have gone to get back the tapestry, which is the very heart of Redwall. Fate and fortunes keep them well and aid them on their quest. Now, before we begin, is there anything that you wish to ask me, friends?'

Tragglo Spearback's voice rang out strong and clear. 'Aye, marm, I want to know why you ain't our Abbess. Everybeast wishes you were!'

Roars of approval and loud cheers echoed everywhere. Skipper was forced to whack the table with his rudder to get order. 'Ahoy, give marm a chance, will ye? Thanks, marm, the floor's yours.'

Cregga nodded gratefully in the otter Chieftain's direction. 'Well done, Skip! Redwallers, I once had command when I ruled Salamandastron, the great fortress by the sea. Now I wish to live out my seasons in peace. I can help and advise, but I will not rule, on that my word is final. So, if there are no more questions, we will start the feast!'

Bargle held up a paw, grinning mischievously. 'Beg pardon, marm, but could you tell us why mister Florian ain't sittin' down like the rest of us?'

Cregga's blind eyes turned in the shrew's direction.

'Isn't he? I hadn't noticed. Mayhap mister Florian can throw some light upon the mystery. Sir?'

Amid gales of laughter from all who knew what had happened, Florian glared daggers at the cheeky shrew. 'Flippin' spiky-mopped waterbeetle, mind your own business, wot! Chap has the right t'stand or sit as he jolly well pleases, without your bottle-nosed enquiries, flamin' fatbellied boat-bobber! Shove some salad down that great gob of yours an' give it a flippin' rest!'

'I was just about to do that, sir,' Bargle shouted cheerfully back, 'but I can't find the salad fork noplace. But we all trust you, mister Florian. You will find it!'

Adding insult to injury, Mayon roared out, 'Aye, you'll get t'the bottom of things, won't ye, sir!'

The outraged hare loaded two plates high with food and marched off, balancing a flagon of October Ale between the platters. 'A frog's feather for you lot. I'll go an' dine elsewhere. I'm not standin' here t'be insulted!'

'Then sit down if y'dare!'

Redwallers held their aching ribs, sobbing with laughter, as much at Bargle's parting shot as at the sight of Florian Dugglewoof Wilffachop, strutting off with a heavily bandaged rear end.

23

Late night turned extremely cloudy, leaving the four travellers paddling in complete blackness for long periods when the moon became hidden by heavy cloudbanks. The stream had grown much deeper – wider, too – and they could no longer feel the odd touch of paddle against streambed. Dann caught the first over-hanging branches that he could reach and hauled them in to the bank. 'That's enough for one night, pals. The stream may get pretty treacherous in the dark. Let's make camp.'

Pulling the *Swallow* up on to dry ground, they sat on a partially mossed rock shelf. Song peered about her, but could not make out much in the thick tree groves surrounding them. 'What d'you think, Dann? Shall we chance a fire?'

The young squirrel was busy digging food out of their packs. 'Hmm, I don't see why not, eh, Burb?'

'Ah yiss yiss, a bit of an ould blaze always cheers things up, an' we might see where we've landed. Yiss!'

Dippler went off to look for fuel, and was soon back, staggering under a load of wood. 'Found a stricken pine tree back there. Good dry stuff 'tis.'

Dann struck flint against his swordblade on to some

dry moss, and soon they had a bright crackling little fire. Supper consisted of a few scones, some almonds and raisins and a brew of Goody Brimm's mint and burnet rosehip tea. Only the immediate area of their camp was lit up; beyond that the woodland looked thick, dark and impenetrable.

Without warning a rock whistled out of the night and struck Burble a thudding blow between his shoulders. Dann and Song acted swiftly, dragging the watervole into the shadows, whilst Dippler scattered the fire into the stream with the flat of his paddle blade. A mocking voice called out of the woodland to them. 'Yah, y'ain't got yer big 'edge'og wid yer now. We're comin' t'get yez, me liddle buckoes!'

They recognized the voice immediately. It was the stoat whom Soll had chased off, and they had no doubt that his two weasel allies were still with him. He called out again. 'No use tryin' to 'ide from us, young 'uns, we'll get yer. Stand where y'are an' drop yer weapons. If ye do we'll make it quick. But move a muscle an' yore dyin'll be long'n'slow!'

Dann blinked his eyes hard, rubbing a paw into them to dispel the effects of the firelight. Song was already on the move. She launched the *Swallow* back into the stream, and then she and Dippler helped Burble into the boat. He appeared to be in considerable pain. Song pushed the craft clear of the bank.

'Burb, are you all right?'

'Yiss yiss, I'm fine, missie. Cummon, we'd best git goin'!'

But the pretty squirrelmaid had other ideas. 'Listen to me, Burb. Grab that branch hangin' down yonder. Hold the *Swallow* offshore an' wait for us. But if anybeast tries to get you or the boat, let go of the branch and drift off. We'll catch up with you downstream, all being well.'

Song and Dippler crawled back to where Dann hid in the shadows. The stoat was still calling. 'Naughty

naughty now, ye've moved. We'll 'ave ter punish yer fer that, me liddle friends!'

Song grasped her Leafwood stick, Dippler and Dann drew their blades.

'No use runnin' from them, they'll only follow us. Let's do a bit of punishin' of our own, mates. Remember what Soll said, they're only bullies and cowards. Split up and go three ways!'

Song crawled off into the trees, towards where the stoat's last call had come from. She heard the whirl of a sling close by and the whoosh of a rock hurtling off towards their former position. A voice then, whispering low; it sounded like one of the weasels.

''Tis 'ard to see in this dark. Mebbe they've got away?'

'Nah, they'll still be there,' the stoat replied, low but confident, 'terrified out their wits, you wait'n'see. You take the left, you take the right, an' circle in on 'em. I'll go straight in. We'll 'ave 'em on three sides wid the stream at their backs, and then fer a bit o' sport, eh, cullies?'

Song hoped that her friends had heard. She stood up silently behind the broad trunk of a sycamore and held her breath. Within a hair's breadth she sensed one of the weasels stalking by. She stepped out behind the dark shape and hit out with the greenstone-topped stick, slamming it square between the weasel's scraggy ears. He fell without a sound. Song placed her paw on his chest; he was stunned, but still alive. She hauled him into a sitting position, binding his paws behind him to the trunk of an ash with his own thonged sling. Then she undid the vermin's broad belt and gagged him with that.

Dippler lived by the code of the Guosim shrews, who seldom took prisoners. The weasel who had gone to the right met his end at the point of the young shrew's rapier.

Dann backtracked slightly, then stepped out in front of the stoat and took him completely by surprise. But the stoat was quick. He leapt to one side and began whining and pleading with the hard-eyed warrior with the deadly sword.

''Twas nought but a joke, mate. Can't yer take a joke? We was jus' 'avin a bit o' fun wid youse . . .'

Dann saw the stoat's dagger coming and dodged sideways. Then he leapt forward, striking down with the blade of Martin. The stoat fell with a shriek as Song and Dippler came charging through the trees.

'Dann, are you hurt, did you get him?'

Dann stayed the writhing stoat on the ground with his footpaw. 'I'm all right. Unfortunately my aim was bad in the darkness, or this scum would've been dead now.'

The stoat groaned, then spat viciously at Dann. 'You wounded me bad, y'stupid young fool. Couldn't yer see 'twas only a joke? We wasn't goin' to 'urt yer!'

Dann placed his sword edge on the side of the stoat's neck. 'One more word out o' yore lyin' mouth an' yore head'll be talkin' to y'tail. How's that for a joke, eh?'

Song nodded back into the woodland. 'Knocked my vermin cold and left him gagged an' bound to a tree. How did you fare, Dipp?'

Dippler wiped his rapier with a pawful of grass. 'Ole Guosim proverb, a dead enemy ain't an enemy no more!' Sheathing his blade he went to the boat, calling aloud, 'Burb, 'tis me, Dipp. Y'can bring 'er inshore now, mate.'

Dann took Song to one side. 'What do we do with the stoat?' he said quietly. 'I couldn't bring myself to kill him, and we can't just leave him here.'

The squirrelmaid watched the writhing, groaning beast as she sought for a solution. 'Go and get some rivermud. Leave this to me.'

Dann fetched a good glob of mud from the shallows. Song knelt by the stoat, who was wounded deep in his right side. She tore off a strip of his tunic, slapped the mud on his injury and placed the torn tunic in a pad on top of it. 'There, you'll live. Tomorrow you can free your friend – he's tied to an ash back there. Listen carefully to what I'm going to tell you, stoat.'

The stoat sneered and cleared his throat as if he were about to spit at Song. She gave him a quick hard cuff to the face. 'Spit at me and I'll leave you to my Guosim friend. You heard his rule about enemies. From now on you'll have to learn to live with yourself. No more bullying, stealing or villainy for you, stoat. With that wound you'll probably limp or walk bent for the rest of your days. My advice to you is to build yourself a home, grow your own food, or harvest it from the woodlands, fish, do what you will, but learn to lead a quiet honest life.'

When Song arose the stoat lay sneering at her. 'Leave me alone, squirrel. I knows 'ow t'lead me own life, see!'

Dann tugged her away from the wounded vermin. 'Leave him. Somebeasts never learn. He'll be an idiot all his life an' end up a dead fool!'

It was not wise to stay any longer where they had camped. The four friends paddled off downstream and chose a campsite on the opposite bank. Too weary to do anything further, they dragged the *Swallow* onshore, overturned the boat and slept under it for the short remaining time until dawn.

Morning brought with it another bright summer day. Eager to be off, the travellers breakfasted hastily. Soon they were paddling along in the centre of the wide stream. Sitting behind Burble, the young squirrelmaid could not help but notice the dark bruise at the base of his neck. 'Take a rest if you need it, Burb. We'll do the paddling.'

'No need fer that, thank ye, missie. I'm all right. Us River'ead voles are tough as ould oak trees. Yiss yiss, that's a fact!'

Dann shipped his paddle. 'No need for any of us to paddle, matey,' he called back to Song. 'See 'ow fast this current's runnin'. May's well sit back an' rest. We'll only need paddles to steer round rocks'n'things.'

By mid-morning the green tunnel of overhanging tree branches was showing signs of thinning out. When noon arrived they were sorry the shade had been lost, for there was little respite from the blazing sun as the *Swallow* shot along on the swift stream. Dry arid scrub and rockstrewn banks, with little shrubbery growing in the dusty brown earth, stretched before them on both sides.

Now they needed the paddles. The broad, deep stream grew treacherous, and sharp stone pinnacles began to appear, some with heavy drifts of timber, washed down by the water, piled up against them. On either side the stone sides of the banks rose higher, banded umber and fawn, worn smooth by the rushing torrents. The *Swallow*'s prow bobbed up and down as she sped between the steep walls of the gorge. There was little the travellers could do to arrest their furious progress. Dann and Dippler sat for'ard, plying their paddles this way and that to get the *Swallow* round the pinnacles, while Song consulted the rhyme Friar Butty had given her, speaking it aloud to Burble.

'Then when the sky shows blue and light,
And clear down to the bed you gaze,
Be not deceived by rainbows bright,
Beware tall stones and misted haze.'

Song turned her eyes upward. 'We're no longer in the green tunnel, so there's the sky showing blue and light. Is the water muddy or clear, Burb?'

'Ah, 'tis fast-runnin' as y'know, but still the stream's deep an' clear, yiss yiss, very clear, I see the bottom deep down.'

'Great seasons, lookit the size o' those rocks ahead!'

They looked in the direction Dippler was pointing.

Two enormous rock pinnacles, their tops thick with vegetation, reared out of the water further downstream like primitive sentinels. What lay beyond them was lost in a haze of mist formed by water spray shooting high as the stream divided three ways round the rock bases. The awesome spectacle was enhanced by a breathtakingly beautiful rainbow bridging the gorge.

Suddenly, Song seized her paddle, shouting out above the roaring waters, 'Bring her in to the side. Find somewhere we can stop. Quickly!'

Backs bent and paddles digging deep, they fought the headlong current. Tacking and veering, drenched to the skin, the four friends battled to bring the frail vessel towards the high rock wall which formed one bank.

Burble spotted a possible place. 'There, see, yiss yiss, there, where the rift is!'

Backing water madly, they checked the *Swallow* as she ran close to the towering cliff. All Dann could see for a moment was a wraithlike armoured mouse, hovering in the mist ahead, his hollow voice blending with the roar of waters.

'The sword, Dann, my sword!'

Leaning dangerously out from the prow, Dann whipped forth the sword and thrust it instinctively into the large crack running up the rock face. Throwing his weight forward against the hilt, Dann pushed hard. The *Swallow* hovered for a moment, then turned in a fast circle on the dashing waters until Dann found himself facing upstream. The boat had turned completely round. Straining against the mighty pressure, Dann held her firm.

'Song, do something quick! I can't hold her much longer!'

There was a ledge overhead. Song reached it the only way she could. With a bound she was on Burble's shoulders, thrusting herself into an upward leap. Her paws grasped the ledge and she hauled herself upward, scrabbling to find holds in the rifted stone. She pulled and struggled until she was lying flat on the ledge, hanging over the edge. She held out her paws. 'Burble, throw me the stern rope!'

The river vole threw the rope into her waiting paws, then made the other end fast by looping it round the rear seat. Song knotted the rope around a spur in the side of the rift while the others tossed their paddles up on to the ledge. Dippler was first up the rope. He and Song leaned over to help Burble, with Dann following in the rear. As soon as they were safe from the thundering waters, the four companions hauled the *Swallow* up to the rocky platform, with their supplies intact.

Dann sat panting, his back against the sunwarmed rocks. He patted the hilt of the sword. 'Whew! Thanks to Friar Butty's rhyme an' this sword we made it. See that haze down yonder, beneath the rainbow? I'd take me oath that I saw a vision of Martin the Warrior hoverin' there. 'Twas he told me to shove the sword into the crack.'

Song looked from the misted haze to the sword. 'I don't doubt that you did, Dann. That blade must be some powerful kind of steel to hold a boat and us four safe from those waters. I dread t'think what would've happened to us if we'd been swept away between those two big rocks. I wonder what's down that way?'

Dippler was setting out a makeshift meal of scones and fruit. 'Let's 'ave a bite to eat first. Then we'll foller these ledges downstream an' see where the current leads.'

Burble found a flask of dandelion and burdock cordial and swigged thirstily at it, massaging the back of his neck. 'Aye, you three go off an' explore awhile. Yiss yiss, I'll stay 'ere an' guard our gear. Me ould neck's a bit sore. You didn't 'elp matters by leapin' all over me head'n'shoulders to get up on this ledge, missie, you serpintly didn't!'

Song helped the watervole to rub his neck. 'Ah, poor old Burb. Never mind, mate, you'll live, but don't doze off now. Keep an eye on everything whilst we're gone.'

When they had finished eating, Song, Dann and Dippler took the rope from the *Swallow* and set off across the rocks to explore downstream. The grandeur of the scenery was awesome: hurtling water, towering stone and spray forever cascading through curtains of mist, over which the rainbow arched like a massive coloured bridge. Travelling in single file, they made good use of the rope to span places where there were gaps in the ledges. Sometimes they rested in sombre moss-strewn crevices where sunlight never reached. Other times they pawed cautiously over expanses of smooth banded stone, almost hot to the touch. Just beyond the two big rocks which stood centre stream, the mist cleared and they halted with gasps of wonderment at the sight.

It was as if they were standing at the very edge of the earth. Billowing, leaping, roaring, vast masses of water fell abruptly downward into the shrouding fog of boiling spray far below. Dippler clasped his friends' paws, eyes wide as he stared down into the hurtling chaos, his shouts almost lost in the reverberating din.

'Lookit that waterfall! Wooooooow!'

They sat on the rock edge, drenched with spray, watching the awesome majesty of the waterfall. Dann pointed to the far side, where the bank ran out a short distance underwater, forming an incredibly swift shallows. There was a great bird pacing up and down the bankside, watching the water intently.

'Great seasons, look at the size of that feller! What sort o' bird would you call him?'

Dippler had spent his life around waterways. Though he had only ever seen the species once before, it was unforgettable. 'That's a fishin' eagle. 'Tis called an osprey!'

The bird had a white crown of plumage, and its underparts too were snowy white. A mask, dark brown, almost black, stretched round its savage golden eyes, spreading back over shoulders and wings; it had a heavy hooked beak and fearsome talons. Silently they watched it prowling the bank. It struck once, but came back without any catch. Song was puzzled. 'Aren't they

258

supposed to fly and swoop on the fish, Dipp?'

'Aye, that's what they usually do. Aha, look!'

The eagle struck the water again, but could not catch the fish it was chasing. It gave a shriek of temper and charged awkwardly into the water, one wing flapping to retain its balance. Dippler nodded knowingly. 'It can't fly, see, keeps one wing close to its side. Musta been injured at some time, I reckon, Song.'

The pretty young squirrelmaid was full of sympathy. 'Oh, the poor bird. Imagine having big beautiful wings and not being able to use them. Oh, it's so sad to watch him!'

Dippler chuckled as he saw a brown trout leaping and squirming in the shallows as the osprey chased it.

'Pore bird? What about the pore fish, missie? Mind though, that trout's leadin' the eagle a merry dance. Mebbe it'll escape!'

As the Guosim shrew spoke, the trout gave a mighty leap and made it to deep water. The osprey was almost out of its depth. Squawking angrily, it stumbled and was swept into the wild lashing deeps.

Dippler put a paw over his eyes. 'Nothin' we can do to save 'im now. That'n's a goner!'

Before the words had left his mouth Song was in action. Tying the rope hastily around her waïst, she slung the end to Dann. 'Hang on to this. I'm goin' after him!'

Dann grabbed the rope instinctively, shouting, 'Song, no, you'll be killed!'

But the young squirrelmaid had already plunged into the roaring mêlée of waters.

24

During the night the White Ghost's eerie sighing and wailing echoed ceaselessly around the Queen's bed-chamber. Silth crouched in her bed, gaunt and hollow-eyed, her voice reduced to a hoarse croak from shouting for her guards.

'Oooooh Silth, come to me Siiiiiilth!'

There it was again. Silth buried her face in a satin coverlet, knowing it was not a dream. When she ventured to peep out, all the candles had sputtered and died. Only a single lantern remained burning on the bedside table. The room had become an ill-lit cavern of shifting shadows, draughts and breezes moving the silk wall hangings like fluttering shrouds. Silth's voice was a piteous whine. 'Guards, help me, where are my guards?'

Spectral tones answered her desperate plea. 'Gone, all goooooooone!'

Lantur beckoned Wilce out of the room from which she had been impersonating the White Ghost. 'That's enough wailing for now, rat. There's no reason for any of the guards to be up here since I dismissed them for the night. But just in case anybeast tries to gain entrance, you stay at the head of the stairs and keep them away. Tell them the High Queen is very ill and any creature coming up here against my orders does so under pain of death. Got it?'

Wilce nodded silently and went off about her task.

Lantur took up the tray she had prepared. It had two goblets upon it. One was Silth's own drinking vessel, beaten from fine gold, with her personal crest embossed on its stem. The other was a plain serviceable pewter type. Lantur made sure the Queen's goblet was on the far side of the tray as she carried it into the bedchamber. Silth cowered away from her, bunching the satin coverlet tight under her chin.

'Where are my guards? How long is it until morning light? The White Ghost has been haunting me again. Did you hear it? Well, did you? Speak, daughter.'

Smiling benignly, Lantur perched upon the bed, placing the tray next to the lantern on the table. Her voice was that of a true Marlfox, sweet as honey and deadly as an adder's bite. She removed the coverlet gently from Silth's chin.

'Don't upset yourself, Mother dear. I sent the guards away because I don't want them clanking and tramping about outside your door when you need rest. This White Ghost, 'tis all in your imagination. Sleep will cure all that. Things will look better in the light of day.'

Silth seemed to regain some of her regal composure. She chided Lantur sceptically. 'Sleep? How can I sleep? You haven't the slightest idea how I suffer. I order you to stay here for the rest of the night to keep me company through the dark hours. What's this you've brought, eh?'

Lantur held the tray out to her mother, taking care that she presented it so the Queen's cup was nearer to the royal paw. ''Tis a harmless drink, made from warm damson wine and special herbs. It will help you to sleep.'

Silth sniffed the goblet without touching it. 'I don't care what it is, I'm not drinking any!'

Lantur moved the tray closer to her mother. 'Now don't be silly, Mother. See, I've filled a goblet for myself. I'm going to drink, aye, and enjoy it.'

She picked up the plain pewter goblet. It was halfway to her lips when the Queen rasped out, 'Stop! Put that goblet back on the tray. I command you!'

With a look of long-suffering hopelessness, Lantur did as she was bidden. Silth smiled craftily at her. 'You placed the two goblets on the tray so that my personal one was closest to me, as if you wanted me to drink from it.'

Lantur smiled innocently back. 'But of course, Majesty. 'Tis your own cup. None but the High Queen would dare to drink from it.'

Silth pushed the royal goblet across to Lantur. 'Here's a better idea. You drink from my goblet and I'll drink from yours. What do you think of that?'

Lantur shrugged and picked up the golden vessel. 'A wonderful idea, Majesty. I've never taken wine from a Queen's cup. Mayhaps I'll get used to it!'

Silth snatched the golden goblet before Lantur could taste it. 'No you won't, that's mine. Now, let me see you drain the other one. Drink!'

Lantur's face blanched with fright. Her paw trembled as she picked up the pewter goblet. Silth cackled evilly. 'Drink it all, you wicked young schemer, or I'll have my guards feed you to the Teeth of the Deeps. Drink!'

Lantur was forced to swallow, her throat quivering fitfully, wine dribbling from the corners of her lips, her eyes wide with horror. Silth sipped at her own goblet, fully recovered from her former cringing self as she lectured her treacherous daughter.

'Did you think you could outwit a Queen of Marlfoxes, my dear? I knew that you would put the poison in your own goblet. You thought I'd think it was in mine, the silly way you offered the tray so that my cup was nearest to me. I saw through your ruse, Lantur, I knew you wanted me to drink from your goblet, suspecting that mine contained the poison. So tonight you learned your last lesson. Never try to outwit a Queen of Marlfoxes. Hee hee hee!'

262

Lantur had drained the pewter goblet. She put it aside and watched her mother, a smile suddenly beginning to play upon her lips. 'There, I've drunk it all as you commanded. Have you drunk yours yet, O High Queen?'

Surprised, Silth looked up questioningly. 'Only a few sips. Why?'

Lantur removed the golden cup from her mother's paws. 'One sip would have been enough. You did just as I gambled you would. Your Majesty outfoxed herself. The poison was in your cup all the time!'

Queen Silth's paws dithered helplessly for a moment, then her body flopped limply back. Lantur plumped up the pillow behind her head and folded the satin coverlet neatly under her mother's chin. The Queen murmured faintly through numbed lips, 'Guards, where are my . . .'

Lantur wiped away a dribble of wine from the corner of Silth's mouth. 'Hush now, your Majesty, go to sleep and remember your own words. Never try to outwit a Queen of Marlfoxes. I am Lantur, High Queen of all Marlfoxes, now!'

Silth blinked her dimmed, watering eyes. All power of speech had left her. Without a word she slipped silently into the deepest sleep of all.

Lantur washed the golden goblet out carefully, three times. Then she filled it with new damson wine and drank a toast to herself.

Morning sunlight flooded the island as Wilce the female water rat wandered down to the field where the slaves were husbanding fruit and crops. Seating herself on the ground, she opened a flask of damson wine and poured two beakers. Captain Ullig, the slave master, saw her from the corner of his eye. He cracked his long whip expertly over the bent backs in front of him. 'Keep those 'eads down, you scum, or I'll teach yer a lesson you won't forget the rest o' yore lives!' Satisfied that nobeast would dare look up, he joined Wilce. 'Thirsty work, eh? Wish I could lay me paws on more wine that tastes like this. Well, ye didn't come down 'ere fer nothin', Wilce. Wot news up at the castle?'

She poured more wine for Ullig, keeping her eyes fixed on the toiling slaves as she spoke. 'There'll be lots more o' this wine, much as y'want if you lissen t'me, Slave Cap'n.'

Ullig drained his beaker and held it forth for a refill. 'Oh aye? Wot is it now, another surprise inspection from 'er Majesty, or is the noise o' this whip disturbin' 'er royal peace?'

'Oh no, the royal peace won't be disturbed ever again, Ullig.'

'Wot d'yer mean by that?'

'High Queen Silth is dead, long live Queen Lantur, and her Chief Adviser Wilce!'

Wine ran either side of Ullig's mouth as he slopped it down and held out his beaker for more. 'Haharr! I'll drink ter that. So, you an' yore Marlfox friend finally finished off the old one. Clever, Wilce, clever!'

Wilce's paw was like a vice as she grabbed Ullig's, restraining him from lifting the beaker to his mouth. 'Keep talkin' like that an' yore a deadrat!' she hissed viciously. 'Queen Silth was slain durin' the night, by the White Ghost. I knew all along that White Ghost was the spirit of 'er mate returnin' to avenge hisself for the treacherous way she slew 'im. Right?'

A thin smile crossed Ullig's cruel features. 'Right you are, Wilce. Everybeast knowed that someday Silth'd pay fer killin' 'er mate. Lantur was 'is favourite daughter, so 'tis only fittin' that she rules the island now – wid you to guide an' advise 'er, of course, an' me to command the army.'

Wilce released Ullig's paw and allowed him to drink. 'Well spoken, Ullig. You catch on pretty fast. Now, there'll be a buryin' ceremony at the lakeside before long. What we need is for you to get everybeast yellin', "Long live High Queen Lantur!" '

Ullig tossed the empty beaker aside and tilted the flask to his lips as he toasted the conspiracy. 'Long live 'Igh Queen Lantur!'

Wilce gathered up the two beakers. 'Not so loud, friend. Nobeast's supposed to know she's dead yet!'

One of the slaves, a sturdy female hedgehog, whispered to an otter working alongside her, 'Did you 'ear that? Silth's dead an' Lantur's Queen now.'

The otter laboured on, not raising his eyes. 'Makes no difference to us, does it? One Marlfox is bad as another to a field slave.'

The news would have made little difference to Mokkan either. The Marlfox, following his own secret route, found himself attacked by lizards. He had deviated by mistake from the river into a watermeadow, which, half a paddle's depth beneath the surface, was swamp. Berating the rat paddlers and the shrew Fenno, he had them turn about, only to find that the way back to the river was blocked by a teeming horde of lizards, newts and toads. The first inkling he had was when a rat in the prow fell overboard with a gurgle, his throat pierced by a sharpened dried bulrush stem. Then the water came alive with reptiles swimming towards the logboat, whilst others hurled rush lances from the reeded shallows. Mokkan crouched low and shouted frantic orders to his crew. 'Use your paddles! Don't let them aboard or we're lost!'

The logboat rocked from side to side as Mokkan made his way to the prow, pushing past the paddlers. He seized the slain rat's oar and began wielding it energetically, making towards the twin tongues of land which formed the watermeadow entrance. Smashing a toad over the head with his blade, the Marlfox urged his water rats onward as they alternately paddled or hit out at the reptiles who attempted to board the logboat. In the stern of the vessel, Fenno gnawed on the thong like a beast in a trap. Slobbering and spitting, he chewed madly, straining the thong tight by pulling hard with his strong neck. The rawhide snapped as they were passing through the jutting landspurs. Fenno bundled himself ashore and lay still among the reeds and bushes, watching the cold-eyed reptiles hurrying by, trying to catch the vessel before it struck open water.

Mokkan felt the pull of the current. Knocking water rats aside, he dashed to the stern of the boat. 'Paddle for your lives! Keep to the centre stream! Go! Go!' Slashing left and right with his axe, the Marlfox slew a toad and a frilled newt who were clinging to the after end. Powered by panic-stricken rats, the logboat shot off downriver.

It was long after midnight when Fenno risked moving a limb. Shutting his ears to the horrible screams of a water rat whom the reptiles had captured, he crawled off stealthily through the undergrowth.

Mokkan forced his remaining nine rats to paddle all night. They halted at dawn on the bank of a dry sunburned field, but before he allowed them to eat, drink, or tend their wounds, the Marlfox had them spread the precious tapestry out on the grass. 'Clean it, brush the edges well and make sure the fringe isn't tangled. It must be kept in perfect condition for High Queen Silth. It is a thing of rare beauty!'

Mokkan posted two guards, then choosing a shady spot he spread his cloak and lay down to rest, thinking of Fenno and the fate he would suffer in the hold of the merciless reptiles. Mokkan felt slightly cheated. He had planned on killing Fenno himself.

Raventail surprised even himself. When he and his cohorts went out scouring the countryside to the north and east, they recruited nearly one hundred assorted vermin. Naturally, the Marlfoxes had promised Raventail anything his avaricious heart desired. Armaments, food, power, even the rule of a conquered Redwall. Vannan had assured the barbarian ferret that Marlfoxes had no need of the Abbey, because their home was in another place. She explained that the reason Redwall had to fall was because their creatures had murdered two of her kin. Raventail figured that there would be a catch to the agreement somewhere, but his overpowering greed got the better of him. Besides, he reasoned, with a hundred at his command he could always turn the tables on his strange allies. Raventail was not a stupid beast. He took note of the fact that Vannan had made a serious mistake in her talks with him. She had admitted that Marlfoxes could be slain.

Vannan, Ascrod and Predak sat surrounded by their water rat soldiers, watching the vermin horde dancing and chanting around a blazing log. Evening shadows, combined with the eerie flicker of flames, cast a wild and primitive air on the proceedings. Weasels, stoats and ferrets leapt and stamped, pounding the earth until a dustcloud rose around them, flinging their weapons high in the air and catching them expertly as they wailed their killing chants.

'Who be death? We be death!
Here's d'blade wot stop yore breath!
Kye arr rakkachakka whummwhummwhumm!
Plunder good! Slayin' good!
These d'blades wot shed yore blood!
Kye arr rakkachakka whummwhummwhumm!'

Over and over they repeated the chant, getting faster and louder as the tempo of their frenzied dance increased. There was a contemptuous, if slightly nervous, edge to Ascrod's tone as he viewed the primeval proceedings. 'Stupid savages. What do they think they're doing?'

The flames reflected in Vannan's pale, immobile eyes. 'Working themselves into a blood frenzy, of course, brother. Here comes Raventail. Don't refer to them as stupid savages whilst he's around. Greetings, Chief Raventail. You have done well, my friend, these are true warriors you have brought us!'

The ferret cast a swift sidelong glance at Ascrod, as if he had heard the Marlfox's insulting remark. Twirling his scimitar deftly he thwacked it into the ground a mere whisker away from Ascrod's paw. The Marlfox twitched. Raventail's red and black daubed face leered at him momentarily, then he turned away to address Vannan.

'Kyre arr, magicfox, desebeasts ready for warfight, muchslay muchkill, bettersoon we go fightnow, fightnow!'

Predak and Ascrod looked to Vannan. 'Now?'

The vixen stood, drawing her axe. 'Well, they won't get it done chanting and dancing here. What better time than now? 'Twill be full dark when we reach the Abbey. Our scouts report that they have been celebrating a victory. This is the time they'll least expect us.'

25

Abbey bells boomed softly on the still warm air over Redwall. Grandma Ellayo, in company with Sister Sloey, halted their evening stroll by the northeast wallcorner. Janglur turned from the battlements, a half-smile in his lazy eyes. 'Now then, ole Mother, don't ye go breakin' into a gallop down there. Supper'll be about ready, time ye get to Cavern Hole.'

Ellayo shook her stick at her impudent offspring. 'If'n my rheumatiz would let me climb yon wallsteps I'd tan yore tail for ye, Janglur baybelly!'

Skipper winked at Rusvul. He admired the feisty old squirrel. 'Haharr, that'd be a sight t'see, mate. Stop there, marm, an' I'll come down an' lend ye a paw. A spot o' tannin' wouldn't go amiss on this son of yores!'

Ellayo shook her head, smiling up at the otter Chieftain. 'Aren't you three comin' inside for supper? Me'n'Sister Sloey baked a great blackberry jam roly poly pudden this afternoon.'

Rusvul Reguba gnawed his lip regretfully. 'With pear'n'honey sauce, too, I'll wager. Trouble is, by the time we got down there, marm, ole Florian forkbottom would've scoffed the lot!'

Sister Sloey, normally quite a sedate old mouse, broke

269

out into hoots of laughter. 'Whoohoohoo! Florian forkbottom, that's a good 'un. Whoohoohoo!'

Ellayo turned Sloey in the direction of the Abbey, lecturing her with mock severity. 'Now now, Sister, that's not very nice. Don't you dare call that pore hare Florian forkbottom – leastways, not afore I do. Heehee!'

'Don't forget us three 'ungry beasts up 'ere, ladies,' Janglur called after the retreating figures. 'See if'n ye can get supper sent out to us, please.'

Ellayo waved her stick in acknowledgement.

Skipper turned back to the wall, leaning his chin on it. 'Hmm, it don't look like there's much doin' out there t'night, mates. Quiet as a butterfly's bedroom 'tis.'

Rusvul tested his javelin point lightly. 'Makes me nervous when it's this quiet. What d'ye say, Jang?'

'Y'could be right, messmate. I don't like it meself, too silent.'

Skipper was not a creature who favoured inactivity. Pacing restlessly up and down the ramparts, he checked his sling and javelin. Janglur and Rusvul were older than the otter, more used to biding their time throughout the long hours of sentry duty. Rusvul watched Skipper testing the longbow strings and counting the arrows for the second time that night. 'Skip, will you stop hoppin' about like you got a thistle under yore jerkin? What's up, matey?'

The big otter eyed Mossflower's vast thickness. Not even a leaf was stirring on the still air. 'There's somethin' brewin' out there, Rus. Me whiskers are startin' to twitch, an' that's a bad sign. My ole whiskers ain't ever let me down yet!'

Janglur's hooded eyes stayed intent on a new sling he was braiding. 'I know the feelin', mate. What are ye goin' t'do about it?'

'A quiet liddle look around out there wouldn't go amiss.'

Stretching the sling against his footpaw, Janglur

nodded. 'So be it, if'n that's what y'want. We'll let you out by the east wallgate an' keep our eyes skinned for ye comin' back.'

As the small door closed behind him the otter Chieftain slid off among the trees, armed with only his sling and stonepouch. He threaded his way southeast, using all his natural ability as a hunter, silent and capable.

Tragglo Spearback and Florian found themselves on dormitory duty. Tragglo was used to unruly Dibbuns, but the hare was losing patience with the wide-awake Abbeybabes. Stiffening both ears and squinching his eyes menacingly, he adopted his no-nonsense voice. 'Listen here, you confounded curmudgeons, get t'sleep immediately. One more flippin' squeak out of ye, an' I'll do a spot o' tail-skelpin', wot!'

'Hurr, wot be ee spotter tail-skelpen, zurr?'

'Never you jolly well mind, you young rip, just get t'sleep!'

'Will y'skelper my tail too, mista Florian?'

'Indeed I will, master Dwopple, double sharp if y'don't pipe down!'

'D'you skelper tails too, mista Tragg'o?'

'Hoho, I'm known fer it, young 'un, worstest tail-skelper in Redwall, that's me. Now git back into bed with ye!'

Immediately all the Dibbuns deserted their beds and clamoured around the two bewildered dormitory helpers, pleading with them to skelp their tails. It all sounded like great fun to them. Florian and Tragglo were completely overwhelmed, being new to dormitory duty, and the hare threw up his paws in resignation.

'It's all too bally much. How're we supposed to cope with this savage mob of infants, wot wot?'

'Just leave 'em to me, sir. I invented skelpin' naughty tails!'

At the sound of Cregga Badgermum's booming voice the Dibbuns hurled themselves into the little beds and pulled the blankets over their heads. Cregga strode into the dormitory. 'Right, let's get started. Any particular one you'd like me to skelp, mister Florian?'

The hare shrugged carelessly. 'Not really, marm. Mayhaps you could just dish out a good general skelpin' all round, wot!'

Cregga's huge paws felt their way around each bed as she recited:

'I'll skelp their tails I'll skelp their ears,
Then skelp some whiskers too,
Nobeast skelps like Cregga does,
An' I've skelped quite a few!
I love to see 'em turnin' pale,
Some'll weep or some'll wail,
Some'll grow up with no tail,
When I'm done skelpin' here!

So hush my naughty dear,
Go fast asleep till morn,
That's if you wish to waken up,
With tail unskelped by dawn!
One more word, just one more peep,
Woe betide those not asleep,
They will call out, Mercy! Help!
When the badger starts to skelp!'

Silence reigned in the dormitory, apart from one or two false snores, from those trying to prove they were really asleep. Tip-pawing out, Cregga closed the door. Florian gulped visibly. 'I say, marm, that did the trick, wot wot? I think a Marlfox'd take a swift snooze rather'n be skelped by you!'

Cregga smiled as she felt her way downstairs. 'Bless their liddle hearts, the only beast I'd skelp would be one who tried to put a paw near my Dibbuns. 'Tis the sound of my big voice puts 'em in their place, that's all.'

'So your roar's worse than your skelp, wot? Jolly

good idea!'

Cregga bared her teeth and growled menacingly. 'But only to Dibbuns. I come down extra hard on braggarts and salad fork wreckers!'

Florian Dugglewoof Wilffachop nipped smartly behind Tragglo, placing the hedgehog between the badger and himself. 'Indeed, quite right too, marm. Can't stand those types m'self!'

At the bottom of the spiral stairwell they met Bargle. The shrew was scratching his head. 'Did a mouse pass by you on his way upstairs?'

Tragglo shook his head. 'Which mouse? What was he like?'

'Well-built, strong-lookin' feller. Can't say where I've seen 'im afore, but 'e looked familiar like. Wearin' armour an' carryin' a sword, too, fine weapon . . .'

Bargle found his paw enveloped by Cregga's huge mitt. 'What did he say? Did he do anything? Speak?'

'Er, no, not really, marm. 'E smiled at me an' sorta nodded as if 'e wanted me t'foller 'im. Went up these stairs.'

Cregga pushed the shrew in front of her. 'Right, up y'go, let's see where your footpaws take you, Bargle. That could only have been the spirit of Martin the Warrior!'

On the floor above the dormitories Bargle halted, glancing down the passage. 'There 'e is, by that window. Hi there, matey!' He dashed off down the passage.

'Can you see him?' Cregga muttered to her friends.

The stolid Tragglo shrugged slowly. 'I don't see nothin', marm. Ain't nobeast there.'

Florian started after Bargle. 'Chap must be puddled, wot! Scoffed too much supper, I think.'

Cregga could not help remarking, 'Huh, if that were the case you'd be seeing visions day and night.'

The window was merely a long, narrow, unglazed slit in the wall. Bargle stood by it, rubbing his eyes and blinking. 'I'd a took me oath 'e was 'ere a moment ago,

273

an' now 'e's gone!'

Tragglo stepped up to the window. 'Well, 'tis clear that Martin wanted us to look out of this window. Why else should he lead us up here?'

It needed but a single glance through the window to see what Martin had wanted to warn them about. Torches and firebrands were advancing on the Abbey from the east, over two hundred of them.

Bargle felt himself pushed towards the stairs by Florian. 'Er, er, no need t'panic, old chap, just because the foebeast is back, wot! Dash on down an' get somebeast up t'the bally belltower, sound the flippin' alarm! Stand by to repel invaders, turn out the blinkin' troops! Er, er, what else? Oh, tell 'em t'pack me some tucker to keep me goin' up on those walls, wot! Nothin' elaborate, bowl of salad, basin o' trifle, er, er . . .'

Cregga's mighty paw stifled further babble from the excited hare. 'Hearken, go downstairs quietly, don't rush. Gather every able-bodied Redwaller and report to Skipper and his friends on the walltop. They'll know what to do. Above all, don't toll the bells. The vermin will know we've seen them if they hear an alarm. Go swift and silent, now!'

Ascrod laughed aloud with exhilaration as the whirr of blazing torches, carried by charging vermin, swept by him. Waving his own firebrand at Vannan, he called out, 'Tonight's the night we take Redwall, I know it!'

Pale eyes glittering in the torchflames, the vixen licked at her axeblade, as if she were already tasting blood. 'Luck is with us, I feel it in my bones, brother. One of Raventail's ferrets says he just slew an otter. A big male, probably a Redwall scout!'

Raventail was leading the front runners. His keen eyes glimpsed the unmistakable bulk of the Abbey ramparts looming up in the darkness. Waving his scimitar, the barbarian ferret gave vent to an eerie howl, which was taken up by his followers.

'Killslay! Kye aaaaaaaaarrr!'

Fearsome-looking vermin, their faces painted heavily for war, leapt forward. Thrusting their torches in the ground, they whirled grappling hooks on ropes and hurled them up at the battlements. Torches clenched in their fangs, the first wave began hauling themselves up the ropes to the parapet. The three Marlfoxes marshalled their archers in position, Predak herself taking a bow and calling orders. 'Shoot anything that moves on the walltops. Cover those climbing the ropes!'

Janglur stepped back as another grapnel flew over the battlements and latched in a niche. All along the east wall the three-pronged metal barbs were clanking and grating as they bit into mortared sandstone cracks. The squirrel warrior's hooded eyes watched them carefully. When he judged the time was right he signalled Rusvul and Bargle. 'They're all in place. Tell Melilot an' the others they can bring it up now, mates.'

Assisted by Rimrose, Ellayo, Sloey and all the kitchen helpers, Brother Melilot ascended the wallstairs. Each of them carried pan, pail, bowl or any other variety of large container they could lay paws upon. They came up the steps slowly, so as not to spill the contents of their vessels. Rusvul Reguba took a bucket from Sister Sloey's trembling paws, nodding politely. 'Well done, marm. Now stan' back down those stairs, you've done yore bit. Leave the rest to us.'

All along the wall Guosim shrews were taking the vessels from the kitchen helpers and setting them on the battlements anywhere a grapnel was fixed. Janglur took a swift peek over the walltop, moving immediately behind a battlement as a volley of arrows whizzed by. He nodded at Bargle and Rusvul. 'Their archers have the walls well marked – we'd best do it smart like. There's all manner o' scum comin' up these ropes.'

Rusvul steadied a large cooking pot with one paw. 'All

carryin' lighted torches, I 'ope?'

Janglur winked at his warrior friend. 'Aye, matey, pretty as a twinklin' nest o' fireflies. Let's give it to 'em. One, two, three . . . Now!'

On Janglur's signal, a blend of heated cooking oil, vegetable oil – used as lantern fuel – and any kind of waste oil or grease from kitchen or repair shop was heaved over the top. The outside of the entire east wall lit up with a tremendous whoosh as the hot oil met the battery of blazing torches. Both vermin and ropes went up in a crackling sheet of flame.

Janglur sat beside Rusvul and Bargle in the shelter of the ramparts, eyes streaming from the thick coils of black smoke wreathing about them. The squirrel warrior shook his head regretfully, raising his voice above the agonized shrieks of the vermin. ''Tis a terrible thing to 'appen to anybeast, mates, terrible!'

Florian came scuttling up to join them, bringing a jug of cold mint tea, which they passed from one to the other. The hare wiped his mouth with the back of a paw. 'Hmm, dreadful, I agree, but the blighters brought it upon themselves. I say, move over, you chaps, the vermin'll have somethin' else on their bally minds soon. Here comes Foremole with his stalwarts to chuck stones on 'em. Hah! Looks like my Noonvalers have joined 'em. What ho, Runk old lad, you taken to bein' a mole now?'

Roop and Muggle stifled giggles at the thought.

'Hurr hurr, 'twould take summ doin' t'be a spoiky mole, zurr!'

Runktipp helped the moles to lug large baskets of rock and masonry chunks over to the battlements. He winked at Florian. 'I'm as good a mole as the next 'un. We all are. Ain't that right, Borrakul?'

The otter nodded stolidly as he hefted a basket. 'Aye, we certainly are, matey, an' moles get better fed than performers, I can tell ye!'

Florian snorted. 'Cheeky bounder. Go on then, be

moles, all of ye, see if I jolly well care!'

Runktipp put on his best mole accent. 'Gurr, Foremole zurr, do us'n's be abowt ready naow?'

Foremole waved a digging claw to his crew and the Noonvalers. 'Hurr, moi 'earties, chuck umm o'er gudd'n'ard naow!'

On Foremole's command the joint crew of moles and performers grabbed the baskets and slung them forcefully over the parapet, scattering the contents on the attackers below.

Rimrose and others brought cool damp towels up to the defenders, who wiped their eyes and bathed their faces gratefully. Rimrose clasped Janglur's paw. 'Somebeast told me that Skipper's out there. Oh dear, I do hope he's all right. D'you think they've captured him?'

Janglur chided his wife gently. 'There y'go agin, worry worry all the time. First 'tis Song an' her friends, now it's Skipper's turn. I tell you, beauty, that ole riverdog's safe as a nut in its shell. He'd have a good laugh if'n he could see you now, frettin' an' fussin' o'er him. Skipper can take care of hisself better'n I can, believe me.'

Rimrose bathed Janglur's heavy-lidded eyes carefully. 'Well, if you say so I suppose Skipper's safe. I'm thankful that Song an' those two other young 'uns are well out o' this.'

The squirrel warrior squeezed his wife's paw lightly. 'Those three? Huh, I'll wager they're somewheres snug along a riverbank, feedin' their faces an' singing round a campfire!'

Rimrose smiled and nodded. 'Aye, an' our Song's the one who'll be doing the singin'. Oh, mister Florian, let me bathe your eyes for you, they look sore.'

Florian adopted his brave face, though his eyes were indeed streaming from the oily smoke. 'Most kind of ye, marm. Confounded little smudge in the corner of me left lamp here, p'raps you can get it. Nothin' like the thistledown touch of a pretty squirrel, wot wot!'

Mayon came from the south wall and reported everything quiet. Friar Butty, who had been watching the west wall, said the same. Janglur looked over to the north wall, where the Guosim shrew Splikker was stationed. 'Wot's wrong with ole Splikker? Looks like he's lissenin' hard over there. Go an' see if anythin's amiss, Bargle.'

The shrew slid off, crouching low. After a brief conversation with his comrade he came hurrying back. 'Splikker reckons there's a steady noise over that way, comin' from nearby. Sounds like they're choppin' at somethin'.'

Janglur and Rusvul went to the north wall to investigate. They crouched low alongside Splikker, listening to the steady ring of axe against timber. A leaf landed on Janglur's head. The squirrel studied it, then popped up to chance a quick scan of the woodland. He sat back down again, gnawing worriedly at his lip.

Rusvul looked at him. 'Somethin's wrong, mate. What're they up to?'

Janglur passed him the leaf. 'Oak! They're choppin' away at an ole giant three-topped oak. If'n it falls the wall could be breached, an' then we'd 'ave our paws full tryin' to stop 'em comin' in. We'll need t'get our thinkin' caps on, Rus. They could maybe fell a tree that size by tomorrer mornin' or midday.'

Somewhere in the depths of Mossflower Wood, Skipper gritted his teeth as he sat on a streambank, tugging a broken spear from his leg. As he pulled, the otter Chieftain was giving himself a good telling off. 'Uuunj! Puddle-'eaded ole rivergo, that's wot you are, matey. Fancy, a great big lump like yoreself gittin' caught off guard by a lousy painted varmint. Ooh! Easy now, messmate, out she comes. Aaaaah . . . there now! Ferret spear ain't made that could lay a decent otter low. That'll teach yer t'jump quicker nex' time, an' keep yore eyes peeled too!' He sorted through the plants he had garnered from nearby. 'Hmm, dockleaves, sanicle an' young burdock. That should do.'

Crushing them together with pawfuls of bankmud, he applied the cooling poultice to his injured limb and bound the lot with a strip from his jerkin.

'Liddle Sister Sloey'd 'ave a fit if'n she saw this sloppy job, but it'll have t'do fer now. Right, set sail, matey, in we go!'

He slid awkwardly into the stream. Once in the water, however, the otter swam slowly and gracefully away into the night, going in the opposite direction to Redwall Abbey.

Only two creatures at a time could chop at the great oak. At first Vannan had set four to the task, but they got in each other's way until two suffered axe cuts. Raventail snorted impatiently at the Marlfox. 'Kyre, arr, yousay bigtree be halfdead, no takelong. Yakkacha!'

Vannan regarded the barbarian ferret disdainfully. 'The tree is half dead, 'twill fall sooner or later. Patience seems to me a much better idea than charging in like your lot did. Screaming and yelling, with lighted torches to advertise your presence, what kind of stealth attack is that? They were ready for us long before we arrived at the wall.'

Raventail took a pace back, executing a scornful bow. 'Woah! Bigmagic fox be cleverer much much, scyoosee me!'

Vannan ignored the jibe, signalling to two water rats. 'You and you, take over chopping. I'll make it work this time!'

As the water rats stepped in to take over from the two ferrets currently wielding the axes, a big arrow from a longbow felled one of the vermin.

On the walltop, Janglur fitted another shaft to his powerful weapon. 'Ain't much to aim at, Rus, but 'tis all we can do to stop 'em.'

Rusvul Reguba sighted down the arrow on his bow, then let the string slack with a sigh. 'Tchaaaah! They could hide be'ind that oak an' chop away all season. Not much we can do about it, mate. The tree's goin' to fall sooner or later fer sure!'

The Queen's Island

26

As the pounding rush of waters enveloped Song she struck out wildly. Her world now consisted of a roaring, boiling mêlée, in which she was as helpless as a leaf in a hurricane. Water battered her eyes shut, gushing up her nostrils, down her ears and into her mouth. Without warning a powerful pair of talons latched on to her paws, like a drowning swimmer clutching a twig. Something hard struck her body: a jagged peak of rock, sticking up underwater. Heavy sodden feathers flapped slowly, embracing her. The squirrelmaid forced her eyes open for an instant and found herself facing a huge, hooked, amber beak. Then an eddy caught both Song and the osprey, whirling them around the rocky pinnacle like a pair of spinning tops. There was tension pulling at Song, from the rope tied about her waist, but then it slackened off with frightening suddenness. The side of Song's head thudded against the rock, knocking her senseless.

On the rocky edge of the waterfall, Dann felt the rope go slack. Numbly he drew in the line, stunned by what had happened. Behind him he could hear Dippler yelling hoarsely, 'Song, where are you? Sooooong!'

Dann sat down with a groan, covering his eyes with both paws, trying to blot out the awful realization of tragedy. Dippler slapped him hard across his face, shouting at him over the roaring noise of falling waters.

'Get up, mate! Keep an eye on the place where she went down. I'm goin' to get Burble an' the boat. Wait here!'

Galvanized into action, Dann sprang upright. He found a broken branch and tied it to the rope's end. As Dippler raced away he saw Dann throwing the branch out into the water cascade, roaring, 'Grab the branch if yore there, Song, grab the branch!'

Dippler clambered off over the wet stones, muttering aloud, 'Leastways he's doin' somethin' instead o' sittin' there in a blinkin' trance!'

Song twisted and turned. Grandma Ellayo was standing right in front of her, talking, but her voice sounded strange. Rimrose and Janglur had tight hold of Song's paws, and Ellayo was speaking to them. 'Rrrrrr! Should've threwed dem back in. Not fishes, rrrr no, only trouble. Glockglock!'

Now Ellayo was forcing Rimrose and Janglur to release their grip on Song, though her parents' paws felt unusually sharp and strong. Ellayo was speaking again. 'Rrrrr! Use ye beak, dumb duck, use ye beak. Rrrrrr!'

The squirrelmaid's eyes opened slowly. She could not focus properly and seemed to be viewing things through a haze. Small snakelike creatures with long narrow beaks surrounded her head. One pecked Song sharply on her nosetip. Song sat up, shaking her head, sending the creatures scattering. When her vision cleared, a big bird to one side of her was cackling, 'Gluck gluck gluck! Can't eat 'em, not fishes. Gluck gluck!'

The small creatures were not snakes, they were long-necked cormorant chicks. Her paws were freed by a full-grown male, obviously the father.

'Rrrrrr, we catch fishes, gluck gluck, you catch big eagle!'

The mother cormorant, whom Song had taken to be Ellayo, chanced a peck at the osprey. It did not stir.

'Glockglock, this bird deader'n deadfish, methinks!'

The male cormorant's strange blue eyes blinked scornfully. 'Rrrreek! Eagle alive as me'n'you, wait'n'see!'

Song lay recovering her senses as the two cormorants began an argument, hopping about and fanning out their wings, whilst the chicks scurried this way and that to avoid being danced on or batted by an outstretched wing.

'Rrrraahh! Eagle alive, squiddle too. Rrrrrr! Not in my nest thankee! Glock! They'll eat my eggchicks, gerrrrremout!'

'Gluckgluck! Don't be a daftduck, eagle an squiddle won't eat eggchicks, I saved their lifes. Rrrrr!'

'Rrrrr, glock! Shutcha beak, saved their lifes, rrrrrekk! I say gerremout, not stayin' in my nest, squiddles, eagles, chukk! Not stoppin' heeeeeere!'

Whilst the furious debate raged on, the little chicks never let up their ceaseless cries.

'Glick glick glick glick!'

Song took stock of her position. She was at the centre of a large untidy twig and grass nest sprawled atop a rock shelf, somewhere downstream. To her left she could vaguely see the falls and hear their distant roar. On other parts of the ledge were similar nests, all occupied by cormorant families. At odd moments one of the birds would plunge off the ledge into the broad deep stream, disappearing underwater for quite a while, then suddenly bobbing up a good distance away, usually holding a wriggling fish in its beak.

Beside her, the osprey opened one flecked golden eye. Immediately all activity ceased, the cormorants frozen in fear. The big fish eagle's dangerous beak opened wide. Song held her breath. It was a frightening sight, but then the osprey retched, spewing forth a fountain of water. Shaking its body vigorously, the big bird struggled into a standing position. Both the fierce eyes were open now, and Song quailed under their savage scrutiny. A heavily taloned claw placed itself lightly on her paw.

'Yerrah bonny beast, lassie, ye saved the life o' Megraw, an' ah'll no' ferget it. Whit name d'ye go by?'

Song shook the taloned claw warmly. 'I'm called Songbreeze, sir, but you may call me Song.'

Something resembling a smile hovered on the eagle's fierce face. 'Ach! Don't be callin' me sir, Song mah lass. Ah'm known by the name o' Mighty Megraw, but Megraw'll do jus' fain.' Then the eagle turned to the male cormorant, nodding politely. 'An' mah thanks to ye, guid bird, fer pullin' us frae yon water.'

The female cormorant averted her head, speaking as if to nobeast in particular as she hugged and plumped her feathers. 'Rrrrr! Squiddles'n'eagles can't stop 'ere. Gluck gluck, no!'

Megraw fixed her with a murderous stare. 'D'ye no say? Well, mah compliments to ye, marm, me an' mah guid friend'll no stay longer than the time et takes us tae walk away frae here. Though if ye look doon yer beak at us like that again, ah'll eat ye for sure an' give yer mate a bit o' peace. Good day to ye now. Come on, Song mah wee lassie.'

Song followed Megraw as he limped from the nest, nodding a silent and grateful farewell to the male cormorant as she went.

Making their way along the bank, they left the rocky area and sat to rest on a mossy sward. Night was beginning to fall. Megraw nodded his head in both directions. 'Well, which way noo, Song?'

The squirrelmaid looked back towards the waterfall. 'I have three friends, but I parted from them at the top of the falls when I jumped in after you. They'll be searching for me now, I expect. Perhaps we'd best stay here until they come along this way to find me. What d'you think, Megraw?'

'Aye, we'll do that, though ah'm powerful hungry the noo.'

Song undid the broken rope from about her waist, surprised that her Leafwood stick was still thrust into it. 'You stay there and rest, mister Megraw. I'll go and find us some fruit and berries. Should be some hereabouts.'

The osprey squinched his eyes up in disgust. 'Fruit'n'berries, did ye say? Ye'll poison yersel' fer sure, lass! You go an' search out yer ain vittles, an' leave me here tae fish. An' don't call me mister. The name's Megraw, d'ye ken.'

Song had not strayed far when she found blackberries and some fine apples. As she returned to the bank, Megraw averted his head politely and swallowed. 'A guid spot this, ah got mahsel' a plump wee grayling. But fear not, Song, 'tis gone now. Ah mind how the sight o' flesh-eaters can upset those who live on roots an' berries an' sich nonsense. Nae wonder they cannae fly!'

As night drew on the strange pair sat by the stream telling each other their life stories. When Song had told Megraw about the quest she and her friends were on, he perked up immediately. It turned out that the osprey was a wanderer. A lone, wide-ranging eagle, he had come down from the far northeast. In his travels he had discovered a big inland lake, where the fish were plentiful. All pike, but that made little difference to him, he was very partial to a big pike. But one night, when Megraw was resting in a partially constructed nest he was building on the lakeshore, he was ambushed by a mob of magpies. The birds took him completely by surprise and thrashed him. The osprey managed to escape with three things: his life, a broken wing, and a massively injured pride. He had travelled far from the lake, finally settling on the falls as a place where other creatures could not bother him. Megraw stared at the stream, his wild eyes glittering with the light of vengeance.

287

'Ah swear on mah mother's egg, ah'll find that lake again. Aye, someday ah'll gang back there an meet wi' yon maggypies tae settle mah score with them. Mark mah words, Song, they'll wish they'd ne'er been hatched when the wrath o' Mighty Megraw descends on 'em! Ach, but whit can a bird do wi' a broke wing? Can ye tell me that, Song?'

The squirrelmaid stroked Megraw's wing, which flopped uselessly at his side. She had come to like the big osprey immensely in the short time she had known him; he was fierce but well mannered, a true warrior. Also she loved the way he pronounced her name as Sawng.

'Well, you could come with me and my friends when we get together. We're searching for the lake too, you know. How would you like that, Megraw?'

The osprey blew out his chest to alarming proportions and winked slyly at his new friend. 'Ah'd like that fine, lass!'

Burble, Dippler and Dann did not rest that night. Each of them was convinced that Song was dead. Just one look at the mighty waterfall was enough. Nobeast could go over its edge and live, but none would admit it, so they kept up brave faces, reassuring each other. Now that Dann had snapped out of his despairing mood he was acting like a confident leader.

'Right, y'know what mister Florian would say, there's only one bally thing for it, chaps, wot wot! We'll scale down the cliff side, lower the jolly old boat on what's left of our rope, an' get to the bottom sharpish!'

Though Burble and Dippler felt as if leaden weights had been implanted in their chests at the loss of Song, they agreed with a great show of false optimism.

'Yiss yiss, an' I wager the first ould creature we find down there'll be the bold Song, eh?'

'Haha, right, an' she'll say, Wot took you lot so long, you should've come down the quick way like I did!'

It was the worst night of their lives, climbing down a spray-drenched cliff face, with the waterfall pounding along on their left side. Dann found that the broken length of rope proved invaluable. He would lower himself down, then have the *Swallow* lowered to him before guiding the other two safely on their descent. No easy task by night, even though the rocks on that side were not smooth. But with great good fortune, lots of rests on ledges and good co-operation between them combined with Dann's great climbing skills, they had covered halfway by dawn. Stopping on a small crag, they made a scratch breakfast.

Dippler peered down. He could see the pool below the falls through the misty spray. 'I'd say we could make it by midday, if things go all right.'

'Yiss yiss, midday, or even just before. We'd best save some vittles. Miss Song'll be about ready fer lunch when we arrive.'

Dann sighed heavily, but managed to force a smile. 'Come on, you two, let's get goin' instead of guzzlin'.'

About mid-morning Song confided her thoughts to Megraw on the streambank.

'Suppose they went right by us during the night? We didn't have anything to make a signal fire with, and my friends could quite easily have rowed past in our boat, not knowing we're here.'

Megraw flapped the useless wing at his side. 'Aye, ye could be right, Song. What d'ye suggest?'

The squirrelmaid stood up, pointing downstream. 'I think we'd do well walking slowly along the bank in clear sight. I'll bet they find us before the day's through.'

The osprey rose and walked along with her. 'Ach, anythin's better than squattin' in one place, or sittin' in yon fussy auld cormorant bird's nestie. Did ye hear her?'

Megraw could not help chuckling as Song imitated the cormorant.

'Rrrr! Squiddles'n'eagles not stay in my nest, glock no.

They not fishes, gluck gluck, eat up my eggchicks. Rrrrr!'

'Haw haw haw! Did ye mind the look on yon laddie's beak when I threatened tae eat his wife? He looked fair happy so he did!'

Mokkan could see the lake in the distance. The Marlfox stood on a hilly rise where the river flowed downward towards the huge body of water. He watched the wild rapids plunging down to the lake, thinking. Now he had come this far there was no point in having the logboat wrecked with himself and the tapestry aboard. He chose two of his remaining water rats.

'You and you, get in the boat and take it down to the lake. The rest of you, pick up that tapestry. Be careful with it. We'll walk along the bank and meet the boat at the lake's edge.'

Stolidly obedient, one of the two rats got into the logboat and picked up a paddle. However, his companion took one look at the pounding, rockstrewn rapids and stayed where he was, safe on shore. Mokkan patted him on the back reassuringly. 'What's the matter, afraid of a little rough ride?'

The water rat's eyes were wide with fear as he nodded dumbly. Mokkan shrugged, smiling at the rodent. 'You don't have to go if you don't want to. Stay here.'

The Marlfox's axe flashed in the sunlight as he slew the unfortunate beast with a single hard blow. Still smiling, he pointed to another water rat. 'Would you like to stay here with him?'

The rat leapt into the logboat and seized a paddle. 'No, sire, I'll take the boat down to the lake!'

Mokkan stowed the axe back in his belt. 'Good. We'll meet you by the shore!'

Dann and his friends reached the bottom of the falls at precisely midday. They searched the area as best they could until nigh on late noon. Dippler and Burble came back from their reconnaissance to find the young squirrel seated despondently on the ground, shaking his head.

'There's not a sign of Song or that osprey, not a feather, a scrap of rope, nothing!'

Ever the optimist, Burble nodded in agreement. 'Yiss yiss, that only means one thing, Dann me bucko. Song's alive an' safe somewheres. Yiss yiss, y'know wot they say, no news is good news!'

Dippler flung out a paw in the direction of the water. 'Then which way d'ye think she's gone?'

Dann was suddenly struck with an idea. 'The *Swallow* should tell us. Let's get away from this area to where the water's smoother. Then we'll launch her and see which way she carries us. The current goes the same way for anything on the water. Right?'

'Yiss yiss! Good ole Dann, yore right, mate!'

Finding a good spot, they launched the boat and sat in it, leaving their paddles shipped, so that the water could carry them along. When they were out in the mainstream of the wide swirling pool beneath the waterfall, Dann pointed off to his right. 'Look, there's a broad stream running off that way. Maybe that's the way Song went?'

Dippler watched the prow of the *Swallow* nosing along in the water. 'Maybe, but it ain't the way we're bound, pals. Look dead ahead.'

There was another high cliff in front of them. The water was running straight into a cave beneath the cliffs opposite the falls. The *Swallow* picked up speed, and they braced themselves. The current was sucking them towards the dark hole. Had they launched the *Swallow* on the other side of the pool they would have run into the stream, but the realization came too late.

Dann grabbed his paddle, shouting, 'Back water, try to turn her or we'll go right into that hole!'

But they could not fight the inevitable. Hard as they tried, the little boat was sucked into the dark gaping hole, despite their heroic efforts with the paddles. One moment they were sweating and striving in the bright sunlight, next instant they were swept into the black chasm and into another waterfall, which plunged straight down underground.

27

Tragglo Spearback and Friar Butty were in the kitchens making oatmeal scones for breakfast. Tragglo pulled trays of the hot scones from the ovens and laid them out in neat rows. Old Friar Butty followed him up, making a sloping slice into the top of each scone, until the whole batch was ready. Then Tragglo took an earthenware jar and a wooden spoon, and starting at the first tray he began filling the slice in each scone with a gob of thick, fawn-coloured honey. Friar Butty followed, placing a thin slice of crystallized plum in the honey. They worked dutifully and well, until Florian Dugglewoof Wilffachop sauntered into the kitchens, sniffing the air appreciatively. 'I say, you chaps, somethin' smells jolly good, wot!'

Tragglo menaced the gluttonous hare with his honey spoon. 'Them's for breakfast, mister Florian. You put a paw near our scones an' I'll raise a lump on it wi' this 'ere spoon!'

Florian managed a look of outraged innocence. 'Steady on, old lad, I'm no blinkin' scone-robber. I merely popped in, so t'speak, to see if you needed any assistance. No need to accuse a chap of felonious intentions on your scones!'

Friar Butty continued his work, keeping one eye upon the hare. 'Well, we don't need any assistance, so t'speak, thank you. I thought you were supposed to be up on the walltops defending us from vermin attack. What are you doing down here?'

Florian continued to sniff the aroma of fresh-baked scones, striding up and down the kitchens with an air of exaggerated boredom, getting closer to the cooling trays all the time. 'Doin' down here, me? Oh, this'n'that, y'know. Gets rather tedious standin' on a flippin' walltop all night, watchin' those vermin types choppin' away at a tree. Jolly borin', wot!'

Butty looked up from his work. 'Which tree? What's going on up there?'

Florian pulled a wry face at the stout Tragglo, who had placed himself in front of the scones. 'Over by the north wall, great old three-topped oak, half dead but amazin'ly thick. Those bally villains are hackin' away at it with axes. They want to fell it so that it'll fall against the wall an' provide a road into the Abbey for them. Fiddley dee! It'll take 'em all season t'chop that monster down. I say, what're you chaps smilin' at? Nothin' to be happy about, really. If that tree falls you'll have a mob o' vermin in here pinchin' your breakfast scones, wot!'

Tragglo put down his honey jar and spoon. 'Big half-dead ole three-topped oak at the north wall, d'ye say?'

'Rather, great blinkin' hunk of a thing. Must be nigh on a squillion seasons old!'

Friar Butty relinquished the crystallized fruit. Still smiling broadly, he wiped both paws on his apron. 'Tell me, how long have they been chopping at the old oak?'

'Oh, not too long really. Couldn't say for sure. Why?'

Tragglo was making for the door, a huge grin on his face. 'Come on, Butty, we got to see this!' The old Recorder followed him eagerly.

Florian pursued them, snatching two scones from a tray. 'Wait f'me, chaps. Ooh, ooh, these scones are scorchin' hot, wot!'

Janglur Swifteye paced the ramparts, arrow on bowstring, quivering with frustration. 'Can't see the scum to get a clear shot, Rus!'

Rusvul Reguba sat down, covering his ears with both paws. 'Chop chop chop. The sound o' those confounded axes is drivin' me mad, matey!'

Butty, Tragglo and Florian climbed the north wallsteps, with Cregga, Foremole Gubbio and his mixed crew of moles and Noonvalers following behind. Tragglo peeped over the battlements and laughed aloud. 'Hohoho! Any moment now they be in for a real surprise!'

Janglur looked at the Cellarhog strangely. 'I don't see nothin' funny in all this, mate. Neither'll you if that oak falls atop the wall!'

Cregga placed a placating paw on the angry squirrel. 'I'm sorry, friend. Let me explain. That old tree is rotted right through its middle due to big stinging termites. If it weren't night you could see the hive too, in the fork where the three tops meet. The largest honeybee hive in all Mossflower rests in yonder oak, but we've never been able to get at the honey because of the bees and termites. The bees guard their hive and the termites guard the tree. As soon as the vermin strike soft wood they're in big trouble!'

Foremole Gubbio shook his head. 'They'm bumblybees and turmiters be a-takin' ee arter solstice nap. Hurr, woe to 'e who wakes 'em up, zurr, burr aye!'

Borrakul peeped over the walltop, his curiosity aroused by the news. 'When can we expect somethin' t'happen, marm?'

Cregga felt about until she found somewhere comfortable to sit. 'As soon as the axes stop that hard chopping noise and hit the soft rotted wood.'

As Vannan watched two new axebeasts take the place of two weary ones, Raventail scoffed, 'Kye arr, we be oldbeasts bytime bigtree fall!'

The Marlfox ignored the jibe, listening to the steady ring of axeblades against oakwood.

Chop! Chop! Chop!

One of the water rats wielding an axe stopped suddenly, wincing as he rubbed furiously at his cheek. Vannan glared at him irately. 'What have you stopped for?'

'Something stung me, marm!'

'Idiot! Get back to work or my axe will sting your neck!'

Chop! Chop! Chop! Thunk! Whumph!

The Marlfox's pale eyes shone triumphantly. 'Ah, now we're getting somewhere. Swing those axes harder!'

As she spoke, Vannan drew in her breath sharply. Raising her left footpaw, she flattened the big termite that was biting her. At the same instant her right footpaw was attacked by several more of the angry insects. In no time at all, Vannan was hopping from one paw to the other, swiping at termites.

Raventail stepped back, laughing. 'Kyaahahaharr! Bigmagic fox dancin' lokka lokka!'

Both water rats had ceased chopping and were slapping their bodies all over, maddened by the fiery stabs of pain. An ominous buzzing filled the air. Raventail was still laughing as a swarm of bees descended on his head, where they went to work with a vengeance. Now the very air hummed and the ground was alive. Insects flooded from the three-topped oak, biting and stinging anything they encountered. The moment they felt the first stings, Ascrod and Predak fled the scene, leaving Raventail, Vannan and the waiting crowd of barbarians and water rats to their tormentors. The would-be invaders screamed and roared, some throwing themselves flat on the ground, unwittingly escaping the bees only to writhe amid the termites. Others tried to scale trees, driven almost crazy with agony as bees swarmed all over them. Those who fled were pursued by the bees, and they ran as if they were dancing some insane jig, slapping at the termites that clung doggedly on. Bushes were trampled, low-hanging branches snapped, and the night air rang with screeches and yells.

Tragglo Spearback began herding everybeast down from the wall, cautioning as they went. 'Go easy now. Don't 'urry, move slow an' stay calm. Those bees ain't flown up this 'igh yet, but they soon will.'

Dawn arrived in pale rosewashed sky, scattered with small cream-hued clouds. Cregga Badgermum stood in the Abbey doorway with Ellayo, listening to the massed chorus of birdsong resounding in the woodlands. Ellayo looked over towards the north wall. 'Birdies sound happy an' joyous this mornin', Cregga.'

'Aye, so they do. I hear thrushes, blackbirds, finches and robins too – all manner of our feathered friends. Do you know what they're doing, Ellayo?'

'Oh, yes. They're thankin' the vermin for givin' 'em such a fine breakfast of bees an' termites. Kind of the foebeasts, wasn't it?'

'Indeed it was, though I don't think they'll be bothered about birdsong right now. Mud poultices and dock-leaves will be more their concern this fine morning.'

'Let that be a lesson t'the rogues, I say. None of ours were stung, were they, Cregga?'

'Only one. That was Florian, who had a smear of honey on the tip of his nose. That'll teach him to steal scones!'

'Hush. Here he comes now.'

The hare looked a comical sight with his nose swathed in a poultice of dockleaf, motherwort and pond mud. He strode towards the pond in search of fresh mud, pursued by several Dibbuns and Tragglo, who had made up a little ditty about the incident, which he sang with evident gusto.

'Ho there am I, a liddle bee,
A-livin' in my ole oak tree,
When some bad varmint wid an axe,
Deals my 'ome a good few whacks.
Oh buzz, sez I, now wot's amiss,
Good gracious me, I can't 'ave this.
So buzz, buzz, buzz, I flies right out,
Wags my sting an' looks about,
Buzz buzz buzz, who can I sting?
Whoever did this wicked thing.
So right up in the air I fly,
An' there the villain I espy,
Buzz buzz buzz, the one I chose,
Had honey smeared all on his nose,
Buzz buzz buzz, aye, that's him there,
That 'orrible funny-lookin' hare.
Steal my honey, that ain't fair,
Yore goin' to pay the price, proud sir,
Buzz buzz buzz, so down I goes,
An' stings him hard upon his nose,
I made him leap an' howl an' wail,
An' that's the sting in my small tale.
Buzz buzz buzz, I tell you folk,
Stay clear o' my ole three-topped oak!'

Ellayo chuckled as she described the scene to Cregga.
'Heeheehee, the Dibbuns are dancin' round mister
Florian an' whirrin' their paws as if they was wings. Hear
'em makin' buzzin' noises? I won't repeat t'you wot that
hare's a-sayin'.'

Cregga smiled. 'You've no need to, friend. I can hear
him.'

Florian was stumbling over Dibbuns, holding the
poultice still and shouting at them. 'Away an' leave me in
peace, you pint-sized rotters! Get from under me paws,
vile infants! An' you, Tragglo sir, there's nothin' funny in
a warrior gettin' his hooter nipped by a confounded

buzzin' insect. Shame on you an' all your ilk, sir, you're a bounder an' a pollywoggle an' a dreadful singer t'boot, so there, wot!'

Tragglo retaliated by quickly composing the first line of a new ditty. 'I'll sing ye a ballad of a fork from a salad . . .'

Clapping both paws over his ears Florian dashed off, yelling, 'Yah, you great overstuffed pincushion, bad form! Addin' insult to injury. Go 'way an' leave me alone, y'fatty needle-bottomed cask-thumper!'

Rusvul joined the listeners at the doorway. 'Pore ole Florian. Don't 'ave much luck, does he, hohohoho!'

Ascrod and Predak were the least hurt of the besieging army. Raventail was unrecognizable, his head completely misshapen by stinging lumps, made uglier with a thick coating of pounded dock and stream mud. Vannan was so full of poison from termite bites that her footpaws had swollen like balloons.

Ascrod shook his head. 'Who'd believe it, sister, the injuries that insects can inflict. I took count a while ago. Six are missing, either stung to death, or run away after being driven mad.'

Predak viewed the scene in grim silence. After a while she gripped her axe handle resolutely. 'We're not going to be defeated, brother. This thing has gone too far. There has to be something simple, a thing that everybeast has overlooked. Redwall Abbey can be conquered, I know it can!'

Ascrod was impressed by his sister's fervour. 'I believe you, Predak, but what's the answer? Everything we've tried so far has failed, and two Marlfoxes are slain!'

Predak looked about her desperately. 'Leave these fools to nurse their wounds. Come on, we know that no creature alive can outwit a Marlfox. We're going back to Redwall. We'll lay low and study it carefully from every possible angle. We won't rush into any harebrained scheme. We'll stop and watch and listen, take note of everything, until we come up with a simple, foolproof solution.'

Ascrod stared levelly at the vixen. 'Yes, I believe we will, sister of mine. Remember that rhyme our mother used to recite when we were little more than cubs?

'The Marlfox cannot be bested,
Either in cunning or stealth,
Whenever there is power to be seized,
Plunder, land, or wealth,
When other minds are slumb'ring,
The Marlfox is wide awake,
Figuring how and where and when,
To deceive, to slay, to take!
Invisibly, by the magical guile,
Slyly, with less than a sound,
Count your paws, make sure they're yours
When the Marlfox is around!'

Like smoke on summer wind Ascrod and Predak vanished from the camp, into the thicknesses of Mossflower, back towards Redwall Abbey.

The mousebabe Dwopple and his partners in crime, molebabes Wugger and Blinny, had become Marlfoxes again. Daubed with flour and ashes and wearing grey blanket cloaks, they trundled into the kitchens and loaded a full plum pudding on to a cart. Believing themselves invisible they hauled the cart away, looking back over their shoulders and giggling. They made it safely out of the kitchens only to be halted by the javelin of Rusvul Reguba. 'Haharr, you didn't know that I'm the only beast in Redwall who can spot Marlfoxes, did yer? Now prepare to be slain!'

Dwopple blew a sigh of frustration and seated himself on the cart. Rusvul could not help smiling at the little fellow.

'Phwaw! Us allus gettin' catched, 'cos we not real

Marmfloxes I 'uppose. If'n you don't slain us we gives ya some pudden.'

Rusvul relieved them of the pudding and took it back to the kitchen. He gave them a candied chestnut apiece. 'It ain't nice to steal, y'know. If you want vittles you've only got to ask, for nobeast goes hungry at Redwall. Another thing, bein' Marlfoxes isn't good either. You'd do better bein' Redwall Warriors, like Martin on the tapestry.'

Wugger seated himself on a pile of floursacks. 'Yore Dann be fetchin' ee tarpesty back yurr, zurr, bain't that so? Oi speck Dann'll be back soon, do ee, zurr?'

The squirrel warrior seated himself beside the molebabe. A tear coursed down his craggy features, and he turned his head aside quickly, hoping the Dibbuns had not seen it. 'I 'ope he will, liddle 'un. If anybeast brings back the tapestry it'll be my Dann. He's a Reguba, y'know, bravest o' the brave!'

Dwopple popped a plum out of the pudding and munched it. 'Will Marmfloxes be back, mista Rusbul? Mista Florey say they'm all goed an' not come back 'ere no more.'

Rusvul stroked the mousebabe's head pensively. 'Mister Florian an' lots of others say they won't be back, and certainly nobeast in this Abbey wants to see that lot return. But you take my word fer it, liddle feller, there's a world o' difference between what we'd like an' what we get. Nobeast knows that better'n I. Take it from me, all of yer, those Marlfoxes'll be back, an' their vermin with 'em, I'm certain of it, sure as I'm sittin' 'ere talkin' to you!'

The Dibbuns shook off their blanket cloaks and began dusting themselves down.

'C'mon, Wugg, us gonna be Red'all Warriors. Wot does Red'all Warriors look like, mista Rusbul?'

Rusvul looked at the Dibbuns standing boldly before him. 'Just like you three, mates. Now go on with yer, off an' play!'

He watched them scampering off, thinking of his own

son Dann when he was their age, innocent, fearless and happy. Then Janglur peered around the kitchen entrance at his friend. 'Come on up on the wall, matey. There's somethin' I think you should see!'

28

Things happened so fast for Dann and his friends that it was difficult for them to recall the incident later. Clinging to the boatsides, paddles forgotten, they shot into the underground waterfall like an arrow from a bow. The *Swallow* was such a light craft, she was whipped over the torrent's edge and flung straight into the Stygian gloom. Noise like none had ever known echoed and reverberated around them; darkness was everywhere. Breathless and battered by heavy spray, the three companions felt their boat spin through the air, down, down, down. There was a sudden impact. The *Swallow* struck an underground ledge with a rending crunch. All three were flung from the boat, half stunned, into a whirling, sucking miasma of dark icy water, far below the earth's surface.

Dann felt himself rushed along on a mighty current, bumping into rocks and scraping against slime-covered side channels, being swept always on a downward path. His paws were bruised and torn from trying to grasp at passing objects – completely disoriented, he grabbed at anything. A shattered wooden spar met Dann's grasp, and he seized it, holding tight as he felt himself spilled over the top of another steep downfall. Striking the side, the spar flicked back at him, wiping out his senses with a sharp crack to his head. Darkness and silence enveloped the young squirrel.

Dann awakened gradually. Far away he could hear the muted roar of the waterfalls. It was cold and somebeast was anxiously patting his face.

'Dann, me ole mate, wake up! Y'can't die an' leave me here all on me own. C'mon, Dann, I'm beggin' yer, mate, wake up! If you die an' leave me down 'ere on me own I'll never speak t'you again, so there!'

Opening his eyes, Dann found himself staring into Dippler's tear-stained face. Despite his aching body, the squirrel smiled. 'You muddle-'eaded little ragbag, you'll never speak to me again if I die? That's a good 'un, mate!'

The Guosim shrew hugged his friend heartily. 'You know wot I mean, Dann!'

Dann clasped Dippler's paw. 'Of course I do, matey!'

Straightening up, they both took stock of their surroundings. The underground river flowed by on their right. They had been washed up on some rocks which skirted a huge pool to the left. Pale green phosphorescent light bathed the immense cavern, and stalactite and stalagmite formations decorated the far reaches of the pool's edge. However, they were of little interest to Dann and Dippler, whose eyes roved the strange place searching for the watervole.

Dippler voiced his thoughts. 'I wonder where ole Burble's got to?'

Cupping both paws around his mouth, Dann shouted, 'Burble, are you there, mate?'

Echoes of the call bounced back from all directions, but there was no reply, only the distant boom of the falls and a steady plip-plot of water dropping from the high cavern ceiling into the pool. It all sounded very eerie.

Dippler gave Dann a worried glance. 'Pore ole Burb. Wot if he's . . .'

The young squirrel placed a paw to the shrew's lips. 'Don't even mention it, Dipp. Come on, maybe he's been washed further downriver. Don't fret, we'll find him.'

Keeping close to the river edge, they pressed onward, sometimes wading waist deep, other times jumping from rock to rock. Dippler followed Dann. He was in a gloomy mood and took every opportunity to let his companion know it, voicing his thoughts aloud as they went.

'Huh, I've gone an' lost me blade. Wot sort o' Guosim must I look like, widout a rapier by me side? It's all right fer you, mate, you've still got that great sword slung over yore back. Pore ole me, I've got nothin' to defend meself with.' Dippler's voice re-echoed about the tunnel they were sloshing through after leaving the cavern. 'An' I'm so wet'n'cold that I don't think I'll ever get dry'n'warm agin. Blinkin' head's achin', too!'

Dann waded forward, trying to ignore Dippler's complaints. 'Proper little ray o' sunshine, aren't you, Dipp? Moanin' ain't goin' t'do us any good. One more word out of you an' I'll die an' never talk to you again!'

'Help! Gerroff me, y'dirty great hooligan! Heeeeeelp!'

Echoes of Burble's voice boomed all around the tunnel. Dann drew his sword, looking about wildly. 'It's Burb. Which way are those sounds coming from?'

Dippler pushed past Dann, stumbling and splashing ahead. 'Well, he wasn't back where we were, so he must be up thataway!'

The tunnel opened out into another vast cavern. Like the previous one, this also had a rockbound pool, but far larger than the first. They scrambled up on to the rocks and saw Burble.

The watervole was clinging fiercely on to a stalagmite at the shallow side of the pool, flat out in the water. He was caught by the tail, and a veritable monster of a fish was trying to drag him into the deeps. The fish was a barbel, white as snow and completely blind from living in the dark subterranean depths. It was a fearsome sight, with a head as wide as Dann was tall. Dippler hurtled into the shallows and grabbed Burble's paws as they

slipped from the smooth rounded stalagmite. He began a
tug of war against the barbel, with Burble roaring in a
panic, gripping the young Guosim's paws, trying to lever
himself forward as Dippler dug in, bending over
backward, grunting as he tried to heave his friend away
from the huge fish. The watervole felt his wet paws
slipping from Dippler's grasp as the monstrous barbel
pulled, dragging him further into the fathomless pool
with it.

'Don't let 'im get me, Dipp! Pull, pull! Dann, heeeeelp!'
he shrieked.

Dann dashed forward and tripped, cannoning into a
stalagmite, the limestone column snapping as he struck
it. Scrambling upright, the young squirrel hurtled
onward, booming echoes of his shouts ringing round the
cavern.

'Hold on, Burb, I'm comin'! Redwaaaaaalllll!'

Without thinking, Dann had seized hold of the broken-
off stalagmite, unconscious of its weight. Sloshing into
the shallows, he swung the cylindrical chunk of
limestone like a club, whacking the fish a mighty blow on
its jaw. The barbel's awesome mouth flew open and
Burble shot forward, collapsing in a heap atop Dippler.
Dann let go of the stalagmite and leapt to safety, landing
upon his two friends in a jumble of thrashing limbs. Like
a steel trap the barbel's mouth slammed shut, trapping
the stalagmite in its jaws. It slid backward, completely
stunned. Slipping from the shallow rock ledge, the
leviathan of the pool dropped back into the depths.
Slowly it sank from sight in the green translucent water,
leaving behind a spiralling trail of carmine from its
injured mouth. They lay exhausted, shuddering with
shock and fear.

Dann sat up first, massaging his limbs briskly, wide
eyes riveted on the still pool. 'Uuugh! What an evil-
lookin' monster. Are you all right, Burb?'

The irrepressible vole inspected his skinned tail

ruefully. 'Yiss yiss, 'twas a big 'un all right. Pity we couldn't 'ave dragged it ashore an' ate it. I'm starvin'!'

Dann burst into laughter at the gluttonous watervole. 'Hahaharr! Trust you, Burb, always thinkin' of yore stomach!'

Burble shook himself indignantly. 'Ah now, yer wrong there, bucko, I was thinkin' of the big fish's stomach, an' wot it'd be like livin' inside it. But thank ye, Dann, that's a useful ould club you swung there, yiss yiss!'

Dippler was in agreement with the watervole. 'Burb's right, though, I'm starvin' too. Wot I wouldn't give fer one of ole Goody Brimm's scones spread with honey an' cream!'

Dann took a glance at their surroundings. 'As for me, all I'd like to see is the sunlight shinin' on trees an' woodland again. This place gives me the creeps!'

The three friends lost all sense of night or day in the gloomy caverns deep in the mountain. They followed the course of the river, hoping that somewhere it might flow out into the open. However, there was always the dread in their minds that it would flow into ever deeper underground caves and keep going down. Hunger, cold and weariness pervaded their bodies, but they strove onward, knowing they could not afford to lie down and sleep in the bitterly low temperatures of the subterranean regions.

Dann began bobbing his head slowly from side to side as they progressed along a winding stone corridor. Dippler, who was walking behind him, grumbled. 'Keep yore 'ead still, mate. I'm startin' to feel dizzy, watchin' you shakin' it from one side to t'other all the time.'

But Dann continued moving his head. 'I can see a star shining up ahead. Leastways, it looks like a star, but maybe 'tis just a vision, I'm so tired.'

The shrew pushed his way in front of Dann. 'Let me take a look, mate. Hah! Yore right, there is somethin' glimmerin' up ahead, looks a bit like a star. Come on!'

307

Pushing their exhausted limbs, they stumbled ahead. The light grew larger, and then Burble shouted joyfully, 'Yiss yiss, I see it clear now. That ain't no star, 'tis a gleam o' daylight. It's daylight, I tell yer!'

Renewed energy flooded their bodies and they ran towards the light, laughing and rubbing their paws together like gleeful Dibbuns. Leaving the river course, they climbed upward over piles of stony debris, sliding back in the deep dusty shale. Dann used his sword, digging the blade in and hauling himself up until he reached the light. The young squirrel placed his eye against the hole and peered through.

'I can see the outside! We're on the lower slopes of the mountain at the far side. Stay back and I'll see if I can widen this hole with my sword!'

He stabbed at the hole and was immediately rewarded. A big chunk of rocky earth, with grass growing on it and a sprig of heather, tumbled inward. Dippler and Burble moved it out the way, and sunlight flooded in. They laughed and cried at the same time, letting the warm sun beam in on their dust-grimed faces.

'Yiss yiss, that's the good ould sun all right. Go on, Dann, give it a good dig wid yore blade!'

Several more stabs of the sword brought soil, rock, grass, scree and mountain herbage tipping in upon them.

Spitting soil and grit, they climbed out into the sunlit afternoon and sat blinking in the unaccustomed warmth and brightness. Behind them the mountain reared, high and forbidding, below was a woodland with a broad stream running through it.

Dippler pounded Dann's back, raising a cloud of dust from him. 'We did it, matey, we did it! Now fer some vittles. I'll stake me name there'll be fruit an' berries growin' aplenty amid those trees down there. Wot d'you say, Burb?'

'Oh yiss yiss, an' they'll still be there whilst we're sittin' about on our tails up 'ere lookin' at 'em. Come on, let's eat!'

Stumbling, rolling and scooting on all fours they bumbled their way down from the lower mountain slope into the peaceful green canopy of quiet woodland. Dann made a little camp on the streambank. He found flint in the soil and used dried moss with his steel swordblade to get a small fire going. Dippler and Burble were soon foraging about.

'Haha! Apples an' blackberries, loads of 'em!'

'Yiss yiss, I've found wild strawberries an' a plum tree too!'

They bathed in the warm stream shallows, getting all the dust and dirt of their ordeal out of their fur, drying off round the fire. Dippler shouted out with the sheer joy of being alive, his cheeks swollen with a great mouthful of apple and plum.

'Good ole Mother Nature.Thanks for the feast, marm!'

With the fire in front of them and the summer sun on their backs they gorged themselves shamelessly on sweet ripe fruit. Soon eyelids began drooping, and they tossed the mess of apple cores and plum stones into the stream and lay down gratefully.

'Dann mate, I'm glad you never died an' yore still talkin' t'me,' murmured Dippler.

'Oh, are you, Dipp? Well, that's nice. But let's remember there's someone missing. Poor Song. Will we ever see her again?'

For a moment the two friends were silent. Eventually, Dippler put his arm round Dann. 'Don't worry. She's a real warrior, that'n. I wouldn't be surprised if one bright morning she doesn't just come strolling by . . .'

Just then they were rudely interrupted. 'Will youse both be quiet. Yiss yiss. An' if y'don't go to sleep I'll kill the two of yer an' never talk to *either* of you again.'

Lying on their backs in the peaceful noontide the three weary travellers snored uproariously. It was the snores that betrayed their presence to a creature roaming the woods. Fenno!

Dippler was wakened by the point of a rapier pressing against his throat. The Guosim shrew opened his eyes to be confronted by his hulking former comrade. Fenno's brutal features split in an ugly grin, and he leaned close to Dippler, keeping his voice low. 'You an' yer mates snore too loud, Guosim. I 'ad a feelin' we'd meet up again someday. Quiet now, one peep outta you an' yore dead. We've got a score t'settle, me'n'you.'

Despite Fenno's warning Dippler managed to whisper, 'Promise you won't harm my mates?'

Fenno stared into Dippler's hard, unfearing eyes. 'I ain't promisin' nothin' to you, Dippler. Log a Log's liddle pet, 'twas you started all this trouble fer me. Now get up on yore paws. Make one false move an' I'll slay yer friends!'

Dippler rose slowly. Behind Fenno he could see Burble, still snoring loudly. But Dann had one eye open, and he winked at Dippler. Fenno kept the rapier point pressed to Dippler's throat, so Dann had to be careful of his next move. Rising silently behind Fenno, he suddenly grabbed the big shrew by both ears and pulled him roughly backward. Fenno could not keep his balance and fell flat on his back. Dippler's footpaw was speedily on Fenno's rapier paw, stopping him wielding the blade. The bullying shrew sneered up at him. 'So it takes two of yer, eh? Why not wake the other one, then all three could gang up on me, cowards!'

Dippler looked across to Dann, his eyes bleak. 'Stay out of this, mate. 'Tis my fight!'

Dann nodded his head, then drew his sword and tossed it over. 'So be it, friend. Here, borrow my blade.'

Burble sat upright, rubbing his eyes. 'Can't a beast get a bit o' sleep round here? What's goin' on?'

Dippler caught the sword, cautioning Burble, 'Nothin' t'do with you, Burb. Stay out of it. This is personal.'

Dann and Burble moved away from the two shrews,

and Dippler took his footpaw from Fenno's rapier. The big shrew sprang upright, swishing his blade.

'Now I'm goin' to slay you like I did ole Log a Log!'

Dippler was unused to the heavier weapon, but he levelled it at his enemy. 'You can't kill me like you murdered Log a Log. I'm facin' you, Fenno. You stabbed Log a Log in the back!'

They circled each other, blades flickering, each looking for an entrance. Fenno was a skilled swordbeast. 'I'll chop ye t'ribbons afore you can swing that clumsy thing!' he taunted.

Dippler parried his strike awkwardly and stood waiting for the next thrust, trying to accustom his paw to the blade. 'Yore a bully an' a murderin' coward, Fenno, you always were!'

Fenno swung and feinted. Bringing his rapier slashing down across the young shrew's footpaw, he grinned nastily. 'Bit by bit, I'll carve ye nice an' slow, young 'un!'

As he spoke he leapt forward, swinging sideways, aiming across his adversary's eyes. Dippler was ready this time, and he swayed backward, chopping the heavy blade down and breaking Fenno's rapier into two pieces. Fenno was quick, he jumped with both footpaws on the flat of the sword and headbutted Dippler. The young shrew saw stars, and fell flat on his back. Fenno grabbed the sword and dived at Dippler. Desperation and a quick turn of speed aided the younger shrew. He rolled over to one side, seizing the broken rapier and leaping upright. Fenno hit the ground in a cloud of dust. Dippler brought the broken rapier down forcefully with both paws as the hefty shrew rolled over. Breathing heavily and hardly able to lift his head, Dippler stood over the body of his enemy. 'Shouldn't 'ave let yer turn over, Fenno. I should've got you in the back, the way you killed Log a Log!'

Dann retrieved his sword. Kneeling, he examined the hilt of the broken rapier protruding from Fenno. 'Dipp, this is your sword. I recognize the hilt.'

The young shrew took a glance at it. 'That's my blade, all right. How did that scum come t'be carryin' it? I lost it back in the caves.'

Burble pondered a moment then held up a paw. 'Ah, I've got it, yiss yiss. Yore rapier wasn't a great heavy blade like Dann's, 'twill have been swept straight through yon mountain by the river into that stream. I'll wager that's where the big shrew feller found it, on the bed o' the stream shallows, yiss yiss!'

Dippler picked up the bottom half of the blade and flung it into the stream, where it sank and went rolling away with the current. 'Aye, per'aps yore right, Burb. Doesn't make much difference now though, does it? No rapier could stand up to the steel in Martin the Warrior's blade.'

Dann slung his sword over his back, into the belt that carried it. 'Right y'are, Dipp. The sword ain't been made that could best this blade!'

Later that afternoon they followed the streambank away from the mountain. The going was easy and they covered a fair bit of ground by nightfall. Dann was about to suggest they make camp when Burble gestured for silence. They stood quiet whilst Burble listened. He pointed to an ash. 'Stay there by that tree. I'll be back soon. Keep quiet now an' keep yore heads down while I take a look around.'

Dann caught Burble's paw. 'Hold hard there, mate. What is it? There's somethin' yore not tellin' us.'

The watervole sniffed the air, his nose pointing downstream. 'I've been smellin' a watermeadow up ahead for a while now. Yiss yiss, I'd know that heavy scent anywhere. But there's somethin' else, Dann, somethin' not very nice. I don't like it!'

The young squirrel unshouldered his sword. 'Well, you're not goin' alone, Burb. Whatever 'tis we'll face it together. Come on, stay together an' go quietly.'

Late afternoon was slipping into evening when they sighted the watermeadow on their right. It was landlocked on the nearside, though a narrow gap at its far edge filtered out into a river some distance away. The scent of water lilies, crowfoot and bulrushes mixed with the smell of rotting vegetation was heavy on the air. Dippler's voice sounded unusually loud in the sinister stillness which hung over everything. 'Yukk! So that's wot you could smell, eh, Burb?'

Burble glanced back at his friends as he pushed forward into a high fern thicket. 'Ah no, 'twas somethin' far worse than that!'

They navigated a path through the ferns, the ground squelching under their footpaws as they skirted the watermeadow. Burble steeled himself and thrust forward from the sheltering ferns. 'Smell's stronger now, somewhere around here . . . Yaaaaagh!'

He had walked straight into the half-decayed carcass of a water rat dangling from the limb of a crack willow, its grinning skull seeming to mock at them through eyeless sockets.

Dann froze. 'So that's what y'could smell . . .'

Phfffft ssssssstck! Two sharpened bulrush spears came whizzing out of nowhere, one burying itself in the earth alongside Dippler, the other narrowly missing Dann's head. Drums began pounding, and more spears came hissing through the air. Burble glimpsed the horde of lizards, newts and toads thrashing their way through the watery margin towards them.

'Oh, great seasons o' slaughter, run fer it, mates!'

Foul-smelling ooze squirted underpaw as they fled, flattening ferns and leaping over rotting treetrunks. A fearsome high-pitched wail arose from the reptiles pursuing them, and the drums throbbed louder. Dann made sure that whenever possible he kept hold of Dippler and Burble's paws as they ran across the marshy ground. Behind them could be heard the slithering and keening of the cold-eyed hunters, growing closer by the moment. Burble stumbled and fell flat in damp brown sedge, spluttering and coughing. 'Run f'yóre lives. I can't go no further!'

Roughly Dippler dragged the watervole upright. 'We're stickin' t'gether, mate. Move yoreself!'

Stumbling and gasping, they dragged Burble along with them. Two toads and a lizard, who had come from a different angle, leapt out in front of them, spears at the ready. Clasping paws, the three companions charged straight at them, tumbling them flat before they had a chance to use their weapons. Dann felt the toad's stomach underpaw, the breath whooshing out of the reptile as the young squirrel ran right over him. Into a grove of trees they pounded, dodging between the trunks, bulrush spears clattering off the branches around their heads. Dann knew they could not run much longer, but he staggered onward, looking wildly about for someplace to hide. There it was, a huge rotten elm trunk lying flat in a deep, leaf-carpeted depression, which had probably once been a stream.

'Down there, quick, under the fallen tree!'

They flung themselves under the dead woodland giant, quickly scooping out the thick sodden loam and building it around them. Dann pushed the other two further under, drawing his sword and fighting his way in alongside them. Surrounded by the nauseating odour, regardless of woodlice and insects that crawled over them, they lay, scarcely daring to draw breath, their hearts pounding frantically, hoping fervently that the hunters would not discover them.

Moments seemed to stretch into hours, then Dann heard the rustle of dry leaves. The drums had ceased and the reptiles had stopped their wailing. Now there were slithering sounds. The pursuers were in the disused streambed, searching for them. The three friends gripped one another's paws tightly, knowing that twilight had fallen over the area, giving them a slight hope that they might be bypassed. The watermeadow dwellers communicated with each other in a series of sibilant hisses and soft clicking noises, no language that the three friends could distinguish. Then they could sense the reptiles on the log above them. A bulrush spear probed into the hiding place, scratched Dippler's back and raked Dann's paw, poked about in the wet underloam, scraped against the log's underside, then withdrew. Dann, Dippler and Burble lay motionless, knowing that the streambed was swarming with toads, lizards and newts. The foul air was stifling, black mud and a soggy compound of long seasons' dead leaves pressed in on them. They were trapped.

29

Ascrod sat out on the flatlands in front of the Abbey. It
was a warm moonless night, the land was still and calm.
A shudder of delight shook the Marlfox. He had solved
the problem. Redwall's main gate was only held shut by
a long wooden bar set in open-topped holders, two on
either side of the double doors. One good push upward
by four strong creatures holding a spear through the
central crack between the doors would knock the bar out
of position. Ascrod had spent an hour at twilight, peering
into the crack, even testing the theory by quietly shoving
in his axeblade and pressing upward. The bar had
budged slightly. His plan would work! All that remained
was for Predak to return with the army. The Marlfox
listened to the warm toll of Redwall's muted twin bells,
softly ringing out the midnight hour. With any luck
Predak would arrive with Vannan, Raventail and the
others in the dawn hour, when all was quiet and the
Redwallers would still be abed, suspecting nothing.
Blending with the landscape so that he was almost
invisible, he lay flat and watched the night sentries idly
patrolling the walltop. By dawn, if they were not relieved,
those guards would be practically slumbering.

A single skylark began its lone song in the half-light as

the vermin army arrived. Under Vannan's directions they filed along the ditch which ran along the west side of the path outside Redwall. Ascrod slid into the ditch, gesturing towards the still figures of the shrews who were acting as wall guards.

'See, just as I figured, they're dozing nicely. I'll wager that apart from a few cooks that whole Abbey is still sleeping.'

Raventail pawed keenly at his cutlass. 'Besure you right dissa time, magicfox, kye arr!'

Ascrod shot the ferret a withering glance. 'Don't worry, my ragged friend, my plan will work. All you have to do is follow orders. Leave the thinking to Marlfoxes.'

Raventail licked the stained blade of his cutlass. 'Magicfox give order, me'n'mybeasts kill kill plenty!'

Predak gave a long narrow spear to four water rats she had personally selected, big, rough-looking beasts. 'Right, let's get it done. You four, follow me and Ascrod. Vannan, wait here until you see our signal, one wave of the spear. Then come quick, no yelling warcries and shouting to let them know we're here. Clear?'

Vannan's pale eyes scanned the waiting horde of bandaged and poulticed vermin, making sure they had heard the order. 'Just get the gates open, we'll come silently.'

Old Friar Butty had passed a restless night in the gatehouse. It was close to dawn when he guessed the reason he had only slept half the night: he had dozed off and missed supper. The Recorder never slept well on an empty stomach. He decided to have a good early breakfast, whilst helping in the kitchen. The ancient squirrel left the gatehouse and began walking across the lawn towards the Abbey, but he had scarce gone a score of paces when there was a dull thud and the gate bar hit the ground. Friar Butty turned and found himself peering through the half-light of dawn at six creatures, two Marlfoxes and four water rats, one of whom was waving

317

a long spear. Dark shapes poured out of the ditch and into the open gateway. Butty ran as fast as his aged limbs would carry him towards the main building, shouting, 'Attack! We're being invaded! Sound the alarm!'

Rusvul was up and about early, helping the breakfast cooks. He was coming out of the door with an apple basket in one paw, heading for the orchard, when he heard the cries. The water rat carrying the spear was chasing Butty, trying to cut him down before he reached the Abbey. Racing hard, he was barely a paw's length behind the old Recorder when he drew back the spear, ready to stab forward. Rusvul's apple basket caught him full in the face at the same instant that the squirrel warrior's flying kick struck his stomach. Rusvul grabbed the spear and flung it, bringing down a ferret who was leading the charge. Seizing Butty's paw, he dragged him headlong into the Abbey and slammed the door shut. Rusvul's roaring boomed through Great Hall as he shot home the bolts on the big door.

'Wake, Redwallers! It's an attack! They're inside the grounds!'

Janglur Swifteye came bounding downstairs, furious. 'First night we're not on watch, Rus, an' they're in!'

Guosim shrews, Redwallers and the Noonvale players came hurrying into Great Hall, some half dressed, others still in night attire. Janglur pushed them this way and that, yelling, 'Shove the tables over to the windows an' defend 'em! Tragglo, you an' Melilot get all the weapons you can muster! Florian, take yore creatures an' barricade the door, guard it! Sister Sloey, see the Dibbuns stay upstairs out of the way! Rusvul, get to an upstairs window an' see wot's goin' on out there, mate!'

Cregga Badgermum felt blindly about her until she touched Janglur. 'What can I do to help?'

Ellayo and Rimrose took the blind badger's paws.

'You come upstairs with us. We'll see what we can do from the upper windows!'

An argument had broken out on the front lawn between Ascrod and Raventail. Dawn was up, the rosy glow illuminating the two quarrelling creatures.

'Babarian oaf! I said to come silently when the signal was given!'

'Watch youmouth, magicfox, we came plenty plenty quiet. Oldmouse runnin' away didmuch shoutin', kye arr, that one shoutshout!'

Vannan interrupted the dispute. 'He's right, brother, we charged without a single sound. It was the old Redwaller who alerted them.'

Ascrod was not in a good mood at their failure to get inside the Abbey building. He turned on his sister, snarling. 'Who asked you? There were eight sentries on that wall, but the stupid ferret and his gang slew seven of them, so now we only have one hostage to bargain with. Perhaps you'd like to side with Raventail and slay him too?'

The Guosim shrew Mayon lay on the grass, wounded and bound. He kicked his legs, catching Raventail. 'Aye, go ahead an' slay me, slimesnout. I'm tied up an' you've got me outnumbered. Shouldn't be too 'ard for a hero like you!'

The barbarian ferret began kicking Mayon repeatedly. 'Kye arr, I kicka you plenty good for dat!'

Ascrod dragged Raventail roughly off the shrew. 'Idiot! You kill that shrew, an' I'll slay you!'

Raventail brandished his cutlass under the Marlfox's nose. 'Yakkachak! Dat'll be th'day. C'mon, magicfox, you wanta fight Raventail, mefight plentygood, kye arr, plentygood!'

Predak dragged them apart. 'What's the matter with you two? We should be fighting the Redwallers. Let's concentrate on getting inside the Abbey!'

Rusvul came downstairs grim-faced to make his report to Janglur. 'They're all over the place out there an' our main gates are wide open. Bargle's dead an' six other shrews who were on wallguard. They've got Mayon, he's still alive. What do we do?'

Janglur sat on the bottom stairs, gnawing at his lip. 'Well, we can't break out an' fight 'em, they've got us far outnumbered, matey. Then there's the old 'uns an' the Dibbuns to think of. Looks like they've got us boxed in.'

Florian was crossing the hall. Shards of crystal glass exploded on the floorstones around him and the hare dodged quickly to one side, his ears standing up with indignation. 'They're slingin' stones at the windows. Vandals! Wreckers!'

He sprinted across to one of the tables set by the windows. Leaping upon it, he began returning the stones that had fallen on the table. 'Scruffynecked bog-splatchers, take that, an' that too! Haha! I say, you chaps, I got one, right in the fizzog, wot!'

Janglur whipped the sling from round his waist. 'Well done, mister Florian! That's wot we can do, Rus, strike back at 'em. Let me at the scum!'

Redwallers lined the broken windows, slinging stones and hurling anything that came to paw at the attackers. However, the vermin fought back with slingstones, spears and arrows. Janglur stooped to help a mole who had been hit by a spear, only to find that he was dead. The squirrel warrior gritted his teeth, calling out to his friend, 'Rusvul, go an' get those longbows!'

Rusvul came hurrying back with bows and quivers. 'One of 'em's missin', Jang, I can only find two. Wish ole Skipper was 'ere to lend a paw. He could shoot a bow, that 'un!'

Janglur set shaft to bowstring and, standing tall, fired through the broken panes. From outside came a scream.

'So can I when I'm roused, mate, so can I!'

A dozen or more vermin lay transfixed by arrows when Ascrod decided to drop back a bit. He called a halt and ordered a large fire to be lit in the centre of the lawn. When it was blazing he stood boldly in front of it and hailed the Abbey.

'Redwallers, listen to me. You're surrounded. Come out!'

Florian Dugglewoof Wilffachop gave the answer. 'Come out? Nevah, sir. Why don't you come in an' get us, wot!'

'We could come in and get you if we wait long enough, but by then there'd be a lot of you dead and your young ones would be starving. If you don't come out immediately we'll kill the prisoner we took.' Without turning his head, he addressed his next remark to Vannan. 'Bring the shrew over here.'

Janglur sat on the table edge, looked at Rusvul, then placed his head in both paws. 'I don't want to see or hear any of this, mate. You know what they'll do to pore old Mayon.'

At a dormitory window the missing longbow was in the paws of the blind badger Cregga. Rimrose was amazed. She had never seen a longbow drawn so far back. The arrow was stretched to its very tip on the string. Cregga kept her face straight ahead, listening to Ellayo.

'Down a bit an' left, Cregga, now up a touch, just a mite, that's it, the shaft's well lined on that villain's head.'

The badger released the string with a mighty twang. The arrow carried on, straight through the fire, across the lawn and out through the open gates on to the flatlands, despite the fact that Ascrod was the first target it passed through.

Raventail snatched up a bow, and thrust a rag-bound arrow into the fire to set it alight. Tragglo Spearback ducked as the blazing shaft zipped in through a broken window. Raventail's horrendous message fell upon the Redwallers' ears as he screeched savagely, 'Burn Redwall! Kye arr! Burn, burn, burn!'

Cutting dark smoking trails, flaming arrows began whirring in through the windows. Foremole Gubbio alerted his crew. 'Hurr, get ee buckets o' water an' wetted sacks, 'asten naow!'

Rusvul stared ashen-faced at Florian and Janglur. 'They means t'burn this Abbey down with us in it!'

Another volley of blazing shafts came flying in. Redwallers dashed hither and thither amidst the smoke, dodging arrows and flapping away at burning tapestry hangings with wet sacks. Foremole and his crew were trying to set up a bucket chain from Great Hall to the kitchens, but the mole leader shook his velvety head in despair as he passed buckets of water. 'Hurr, lack a day, us'n's goin' to run short o' water soon!'

Cregga came pounding downstairs to hold a hasty conference with Janglur and Rusvul. They agreed with her plan immediately.

Janglur ordered the scheme into action, quietly and without fuss. 'Splikker, arm yore shrews. Tragglo, get all the able-bodied Redwallers together an' see they have weapons. Mister Florian, go t'the windows an' tell 'em we're comin' out.'

Florian leapt up on the table, calling to the attackers, 'Truce, you chaps, I say, truce! You can pack in tryin' to burn the old place, we're comin' out. Hold y'fire!'

Predak signalled the archers to cease firing, and called back to the Abbeydwellers, 'Come out unarmed, all of you, right now, or I'll order the archers to double their fire!'

Florian's head popped into the frame of a broken window. 'Keep y'shirt on, Marlfox, we've got wounded an' young 'uns to carry out. Just give us a tick an' we'll be there!'

A pitifully small group had gathered by the door, armed with anything that came to paw. Cregga placed her paws about Janglur and Rusvul. 'You're sure you want to do this, my friends?'

Janglur's hooded eyes gazed levelly at the big blind badger. 'Wouldn't 'ave it no other way, marm. You just hold that door an' stop 'em gettin' to those inside 'ere.'

322

Cregga's great striped head nodded solemnly. 'Never fear, Janglur Swifteye, I'll hold the door as long as Redwall Abbey stands. It has been a pleasure knowing you.'

Janglur bowed gallantly. 'The pleasure was all mine, marm. Open the door, Reguba!'

Raventail watched as the Abbey door opened slowly. No more than twoscore Redwallers filed out, but he saw the glint of weaponry as the door closed behind them. There they stood, facing the foebeast in the morning sun. The barbarian ferret grinned in anticipation. 'Kye arr, theybeasts come out to makefight!'

Florian Dugglewoof Wilffachop had momentarily forgotten all his dramatic eloquence and posturing. He raised a sharpened window pole and roared as he began to dash forward.

'Chaaaaaaarge!'

And charge they did, giving full voice to the time-honoured warcries as they hurtled towards the vermin army.

'Regubaaaa! Logalogalogaloooggg! Redwaaaaaallll!'

Vannan stood confidently, watching them come. The vixen drew her axe, remarking to Predak, 'So the day of reckoning has finally come. Now they will pay with their miserable lives . . .'

The Marlfox fell halfway to the ground, propped up by the otter javelin that had slain her.

Otter crews from far and wide charged over the Abbey lawns, headed by Skipper.

'Give 'em blood'n'vinegar, mates! Redwaaaaaaall!'

They flung themselves upon the foebeast like a mighty tidal wave, engulfing all in its path. Big brawny otters, both male and female, tribal tattoos decorating the sinewy paws which wielded sling, javelin and longblade. A rousing cheer rang from the Abbey's dormitory windows, as Dibbuns and elders shouted their heroes on to victory.

'Give um glugg'n'binnaga, mista Florey!'

'Come on, Janglur, me big fat son, show 'em yore a Swifteye!'

'Hurr, you'm give umm billyo, zurr Skip!'

'Rusvul matey, that Marlfox is sneakin' away. Quick!'

Predak had almost made it to the gatehouse when Rusvul came pounding up. The vixen slipped up the west wallsteps, shedding her cloak and causing the squirrel warrior to trip on it. She dashed along the battlements, straight into the waiting grasp of the otter Borrakul. He set his paws in a death grip round the Marlfox's neck. 'Now y'must pay for killin' my brother Elachim!'

Raventail fought like a demon, until he was backed up against the Abbey door. Florian could not resist stretching past the ferret Chieftain and striking the door with his pole. 'Vermin leader outside, come to call on ye, marm, wot!'

The door opened slightly. Raventail managed a whimper of fear as Cregga's paws shot out and snatched him inside. That was the last anybeast ever saw of the barbarian Raventail, alive.

Skipper dashed up to the walltop and waved his javelin. 'You vermin, throw down yer weapons an' you'll be spared. Right, mates, surround 'em an' pen 'em at the northwest corner. Slay any who still want t'fight!'

The remaining vermin hastily threw away their weapons. They were herded into the wallcorner, where they sat, paws upon heads. Skipper was about to come downstairs when he noticed Borrakul lounging against the battlements.

'Aye aye, matey, wot 'appened to yore Marlfox?'

The Noonvale otter shrugged, glancing over the wall. 'Vanished! You know the way Marlfoxes can disappear, Skip.'

Skipper knew it was a long drop from the battlements to the ground below. He nodded at Borrakul, straightfaced. 'Aye, I know 'ow Marlfoxes disappear!'

Friar Butty watched the apprehensive faces of the twoscore wretched vermin who had thrown down their arms. The Recorder's voice was stern. 'You have no need to fear. We at Redwall keep our word. Your lives are spared, which is more than you or your masters would have done for us, had you won the battle. We do not have prisoners or slaves at our Abbey, so you will be released. You will be split up into eight groups and let free at different times, five to go one way, five to go another, until Redwall is rid of your presence. Brother Melilot will give you each two days' provisions. That is all.'

Florian Dugglewoof Wilffachop, restored to his ebullient self, checked Butty. 'Oh no it ain't, beggin' y'pardon, Friar sir. Allow me a word with these malicious miscreants, will you? My thanks! Right, listen up, scurvy vermin types, pay attention at the back there! You will clean this Abbey an' its grounds thoroughly before I allow y'to leave, understood? All t'gether now, say yes sir.'

The reply was half-hearted. Florian wagged his cane at them. 'Not good enough, you villainous chaps. Now speak up or I'll come amongst ye an' liven your ideas up a bit, wot wot!'

Mayon stumped up, a poultice bandage on his shoulder. The tough Guosim shrew winked at Florian. 'I'll lend yer a paw, sir. I can see one or two rascals 'ere who aimed kicks'n'blows upon me earlier today. Now lissen t'me, you cowardly lot, I ain't tender-'earted like mister Florian, so if I gives you an order you'd best jump to it or I'll make y'wish you'd been slayed in the battle, understood? Let me 'ear you all say yes sir!'

The mass reply was crisp and clear, as if with one voice. 'Yessir!'

Janglur and Rusvul sat with Rimrose and Ellayo in the orchard, listening as Cregga explained everything to the Abbey Dibbuns. 'You are all safe now, my little ones, and so is Redwall – once again we can live in peace and good order. Bad creatures tried to take our Abbey from us and we had to do battle with them to preserve our way of life.'

Dwopple wrinkled his tiny nose. 'Tharra why mista Florey an' Jang an' Rusbul and T'agglo was slaydin' alla vermints out onna lawn. I no liked dat, I was frykinned. Good job Skip comed wiv all h'otters.'

Cregga nodded in the mousebabe's direction. 'None of us liked it, Dwopple, but we had to do it. Either that or let those evil creatures capture our Abbey. But now there is a lot of mending to do.'

Wugger the molebabe piped up helpfully. 'Us'n's do ee mendin', marm, me'n'D'opple get big 'ammer an' ee nailers, fix h'Abbey all gudd. Bangitty bang bang!'

Reaching out, Cregga took Wugger upon her lap. 'That's very kind of you, sir, but there are lots of different kinds of mending, broken hearts, bad memories, hasty tempers and departed friends. All of these need seeing to before the peace and the seasons grow upon us like soft moss and smooth all the edges of war away, so that you may sleep safe and calm in your beds of a night.'

Rimrose sat holding Janglur and Ellayo's paws. She sniffed, unable to check the tear which strayed from her eye. 'If only our Song were here. Where d'you suppose she an' her young friends are now?'

Cregga lifted her head in the direction of the squirrelwife's voice. 'I have dreamed that they will be back before the autumn leaves come down. Don't worry. Wherever your daughter and Dann are, and young Dippler too, I'll wager they're either impressin' somebeast with their good manners or giving a fine account of themselves. Those three are a tribute to their upbringing, wherever they are!'

30

It was night at the margin of the watermeadow. Dann lay crushed beneath the rotten elm trunk, listening to the noise above. It became so loud that he was able to whisper to his friends, 'I wonder what all the din's about?'

Dippler spat out dead leaves and grit. 'We ain't foolin' nobeast, mate. Our tracks lead right to this tree. I bet they're doin' some kind o' victory dance up there, prob'ly gettin' the cookpot ready fer us!'

Burble was inclined to agree with his shrew friend. 'Yiss yiss, sad but true, I say. Still, I think it'd be better gettin' captured by some ould reptiles than layin' under this rotten stinkin' thing all night. It's worser'n when we was hidin' up the creek from the River'eads. Wait, what's that?'

Dann listened carefully. 'Silence, that's what it is, Burb, silence. Maybe they didn't know we were here after all. What d'you think, shall we go out an' take a look?'

Dippler started scrabbling at the soggy loam to free himself. 'Anythin's better'n this. Lead the way, Dann!'

The dried-up streambed was deserted save for the carcasses of several reptiles. The three friends hurried off into the undergrowth, where they sat wiping themselves down and breathing the sweet night air gratefully. Burble tugged a woodlouse from his fur. 'Away with ye, wriggly thing, I ain't no rotten treetrunk. Well, 'tis thanks to whoever drove the reptiles off back there, yiss yiss, a thousand thanks!'

'Ach, save yer thanks, laddie, there may still be some o' they sleethery reptails aboot!'

An osprey emerged from the bushes. Surveying them with a distinct twinkle in his rather fierce eyes, he raised his beak and called, 'O'er here. They're sair bedraggled an' stinky tae, but they're o'er here!'

There was a lot of bush rustling and pawsteps, and then, unbelievably, a figure they'd lost hope of ever seeing again emerged from the undergrowth at a full dash and threw herself upon them, bowling them over in a laughing, joyful heap.

'Song!'

'Hahaha! So here y'are, you foul-smelling, lovely creatures!'

A fat, stern old squirrel and a big rough female hedgehog hauled Song swiftly off her companions. Dann, Dippler and Burble lay sprawled on the ground as the old squirrel wagged a paw at Song.

'No time for that now, missie. Let's get 'em out o' here. You can introduce us when we're downriver. Whew! An' downwind of 'em too. They smell pretty ripe!'

Song glanced at the muddy state she herself was in from embracing her lost friends, and turned to the old squirrel. 'Looks like I'll have to take a bath too, Grandpa.'

There were more hedgehogs, over a dozen of them, hulking, rough-looking beasts. They surrounded the friends as the party hurried off through the woodland at the watermeadow's edge. Dann trotted alongside Song, amazed by the turn events had taken.

'Did I hear you call that ole squirrel Grandpa?'

'You surely did. Soon as I saw him I recognized those lazy eyes. He's my father's father, Gawjo Swifteye. Take a look at him yourself. He's much older than my dad, of course, but you'll see the resemblance is unmistakable!'

Dann snatched a peep at Gawjo as he turned to converse with the leading hedgehog. 'Aye, now I see him properly the likeness is clear. Who's the big rough-lookin' hedgehog he was talkin' to?'

'I know you'll never believe this, Dann, but she's my aunt!'

Dann stumbled and almost fell. 'Your *aunt*?'

Song was still smiling as they trotted steadily through the night-shadowed woodlands. 'Aye, my aunt Torrab. It's a long and complicated story, but here's roughly what happened. My grandpa, Gawjo, was a prisoner on the island in the secret lake for many seasons, but he managed to escape, says he's the only beast who ever did. Anyhow, he made it back to the mainland, but he was completely lost. Then he stumbled upon Torrab and her band of friends, fourteen in all, half-grown young hedge-hogs from three different families. Their parents had been slain by Marlfoxes. Grandpa had lost his family too – he didn't know where Ellayo and little Janglur had got to. So he became their dad and has lived with them ever since, and Megraw and I just bumped into him yesterday. I still can't quite believe it.'

The odd-looking group had now reached the river on the watermeadow's far fringes, and they turned south along the bank.

Dippler looked back fearfully at the huge osprey hobbling in the rear, protecting the group's back. 'I 'ope that big fish eagle's on our side, Song.'

The young squirrelmaid winked at the apprehensive shrew. 'That's the Mighty Megraw. I have trouble understanding all he says, but since we went over the falls together we've become the best of pals. You'll like him, Dipp. You will too, Burb, once you get to know him.'

The watervole glanced back at the fierce-eyed Megraw. 'Ah yiss yiss, missie, I'm sure I will, 'tis a fine powerful bird he is. We'll have t'keep him well fed though, yiss yiss, I'd hate t'be around when that feller feels hungry!'

They halted before dawn at a hidden inlet, a screen of bushes and trees was pulled aside, and Dann, Dippler and Burble gave a delighted shout. 'The *Swallow*!'

The beautiful little boat was in the process of being repaired. It stood upside down on the wide-planked deck of a sprawling hedgehog raft. Torrab and the hedgehogs were about to dash aboard when Gawjo held forth a javelin, barring their way. 'Remember yore manners. We've got guests!'

Torrab made an impatient curtsey to the friends. 'Prithee, come ye aboard an' welcome!'

Once they were aboard, the hedgehogs charged on to the raft and fought to get through the narrow doorway of a big cabin built at the vessel's centre. Gawjo shook his head wearily. 'Back! Get back all of you. Now, what've I taught yer?'

Sheepishly the big spiky beasts stood away from the cabin door, the males bowing reluctantly to the females.

'Marm, I pray thee enter.'

Once Torrab and the other hogmaids were inside, the males began fighting each other in the doorway again.

Gawjo smiled. 'You'll 'ave to excuse 'em. They're fine hogs, but they love to fight. Huh, the trouble I 'ad rearin' 'em was nobeast's business. A squirrel dad with fourteen hedgehog sons an' daughters, who'd believe it. Still, I got me a pretty young granddaughter now, so things are lookin' up, eh, Song?'

Song hugged her grandpa, whilst Dann looked the *Swallow* over. 'How did y'find her, sir?'

Gawjo stroked the sleek resin-varnished hull. 'Swept downriver out o' the mountain she was, full o' holes an' almost broke in two pieces. That's why we were searchin' round the watermeadow. I figgered if'n you were still alive, then that'd be the place you'd land in. Enough jawin' now, you young 'uns. Time to eat, but first y'must jump in the creek an' wash the dirt off. Y'ain't comin' to my table smellin' the ways you do. Megraw!'

The osprey waddled up and dealt Song a buffet with his good wing, toppling her over the deckrail into the water. 'Ah ken ye'll get a guid scrub, lassie. Who's next, eh?'

However, before he could raise his wing again, Dann, Dippler and Burble had thrown themselves into the water.

'Ah now, ye've no need to be helpin' us in, sir, we'll be after scrubbin' ourselves, thank ye, yiss yiss!'

Morning sunlight streamed through the cabin's two unshuttered windows as they took breakfast with Gawjo Swifteye and the hedgehogs. The food was good: hot cornbread with hazelnuts and apple baked into it, and a salad of celery, lettuce, shredded carrot and white button mushrooms, with beakers of hot mint and dandelion tea to wash it down. Megraw took himself out on to the river for a fish breakfast. Gawjo peeled a fat pear with his dagger, outlining his future plans to the reunited friends.

'Everybeast I've come across has a score to settle with the Marlfox brood, meself, Torrab an' the family, Megraw an' yoreselves. So I've decided that the time's come when we travel over to that island. Queen Silth an' her offspring have come to the end of their bullyin', thievin', murderin' rule. I'm out t'clear the earth of their blight!'

Torrab stared at Gawjo over a steaming beaker of tea. 'Thou hast tried it before, Father. 'Tis too difficult.'

Gawjo tapped the tabletop with his dagger. 'Aye, we've always been defeated. Not by the Marlfoxes, but by the lake, a day and night's long sail, with the water teemin' with pike an' that Athrak an' his magpies patrollin' the skies. The Marlfoxes were always waitin' with their water rats once we'd been sighted by magpies, an' they could stand us offshore with arrow an' sling until we were forced to turn back. By the fur an' fang! If only I could get on to that island an' free the slaves, we'd overrun Silth and her forces. I never figured how t'do it, until my pretty Song arrived with 'er secret weapon!'

The squirrelmaid put aside her food. 'You mean our eagle, Megraw? But, Grandpa, he can't fly!'

Gawjo's lazy hooded eyes flickered. 'Are you sure, me young beauty? I've been watchin' yore eagle. There ain't a pinion feather missin' from his wing, an' 'tis not broken anywhere along its length, that wing. I've studied the way Megraw carries it, sort o' flopped down an' still. Now, I know more about fixin' injuries than mostbeasts, ask Torrab an' her crew. The fish eagle's wing's not broken, 'tis dislocated, where it meets the bird's body. I can reset the wing, put it back in its right place so he can fly again!'

'Do ye no say, Gawjo? Weel, ah'm willin' tae try et if it'll mek mah wing able tae fly again!'

Megraw had been standing near the cabin door, listening to what Song's grandpa was saying. He ambled in, his savage golden eyes flashing. 'Ah'd like et fine tae get mah beak an' talons intae yon maggypies whit did this tae me. So, tell us the rest o' yer gran' plan, ye auld treehopper.'

The creatures in the cabin crowded round the table as Gawjo Swifteye outlined his scheme, sketching on the tabletop with the point of his dagger. It was a risky proposition, calling for stout hearts and warriors who would not flinch from danger, but it was a good plan. Song watched her grandpa, the stern face and lazy eyes, deceptively quiet voice and perilous easygoing manner. Recalling Janglur Swifteye, her own father, she knew now where he had inherited his bravery and skill as a warrior. Pride flooded through the young squirrelmaid. Swifteyes were a breed of creatures to be reckoned with!

An otter and an aged mouse watched from the slave pens in the courtyard of Castle Marl, as the funeral procession of Queen Silth passed by. In the lead strode the Marlfox Lantur, clad in a purple velvet cloak, trimmed with silver. She wore a polished wood mask, with grieving features etched upon it. Behind her marched the elite guard, armoured in shining black, purple pennants hanging from their spearpoints and shield bosses, blacked with firesmoke. Next came the palanquin, draped with white silk curtains, inside which rested the body of the High Queen Silth, founder of the Marlfox dynasty, wrapped tight in the cloth that had once masqueraded as the White Ghost. The entire thing was borne on the shoulders of threescore paw soldiers with bowed heads and measured steps. All round and about the procession, Athrak and his magpies flew, carrying weeping willow twigs in their claws and cawing harshly over the sound of musicians playing dirges on flutes in time to a steady drumbeat.

The otter shook his head in disgust, whispering to the old mouse, 'Lookit that 'un walkin' in front, Lantur. Hah! She's laughin' behind that mask, matey, I'd wager a season's vittles on it. Wot a sham it all is! Everybeast on the island knows Lantur killed 'er own mother. Take my word fer it, cully, there ain't a beast walks under the sun wickeder'n a Marlfox!'

The aged mouse tugged his otter friend's whiskers. 'Stow that kind o' talk, pal. If Wilce or Ullig 'ears you they'll 'ave yore 'ead for sure!'

Banks of torches blazed on the plateau at the lake edge where the bearers set the palanquin down. Musicians ceased their playing and Athrak's magpies fell silent as they perched on the nearby rocks. All that could be heard were the fathomless waters lapping at the steep island sides and night breezes causing the torchlights to whurr softly. The water rat Wilce stepped forward and presented Lantur with a scroll, specially written for the occasion. The Marlfox unrolled it ceremoniously and read its contents in a voice artistically choked with emotion.

'No more on our isle will your presence be,
Or your voice sound like some silver bell,
Like summer smoke, you have gone from me,
My grief is too mournful to tell.
Great High Queen Silth we commend you,
With loving care to the deep,
May the guardians of waters attend you,
In silent depths of sleep,
Knowing that I, who rule in your place,
Draw all of my wisdom from you,
May show to all, a merciful face,
To your memory, always true!'

Ullig the former Slave Captain took three paces forward, signalling with his spearpoint to the bearers standing immediately behind the palanquin. They lifted the rear carrying poles slowly as the music started again. Tilting at a forward angle, the palanquin was raised above the bearers' heads. White silk hangings at the palanquin's front blossomed out, and Silth's wrapped body slid with a dull splosh into the lake. The body had been weighted with stones, and sank down into the dark waters. All was calm for a brief moment, then the long sleek glint of pike flashed in the torchlight as the ever ravenous predators rushed to the spot and shot down into the deeps, pursuing the grisly object. Lantur removed her mask, and spreading both paws wide over the waters she called out in a high-pitched whine, 'High Queen Silth is dead!'

Immediately, Wilce and Ullig shouted aloud, 'Long live High Queen Lantur! Long live High Queen Lantur!'

The cry was taken up by the attendant crowd of water rats until it became a chant. Lantur inclined her head to one side, smiling shyly as Ullig gestured for silence. 'What can I say to you, my loyal subjects? I accept!'

Ullig and Wilce were about to lead the cheering when the logboat nosed up to the plateau and Mokkan leapt ashore.

Mokkan had been watching, as usual. He never made a move without first studying the situation shrewdly. From out on the lake he had seen his mother's body being committed to the deep. Making for those he knew to be the two main conspirators, Mokkan seized Ullig and Wilce by their throats. They blanched in fear. Mokkan spoke in a low grating tone, so none but the two water rats could hear. 'So this is how you sell out behind my back. Shut up and listen hard. When I give you the nod, both of you get everybeast shouting. And here's what you'll shout . . .'

Lantur was beginning to feel uneasy. Of all her brothers and sisters, Mokkan was the slyest of Marlfoxes. She watched him carefully. He came to her, his face wreathed in smiles, and clasping her paws he shook them joyfully. 'My little sister, High Queen Lantur, what a happy homecoming for me!'

Lantur tried to break Mokkan's grip on her paws, but he was far too strong. He clasped her more tightly.

'What fortune, that I should return the very moment you are proclaimed Queen. Alas, I knew our poor mother's days were numbered, but she'll rest peacefully, knowing she has you to rule in her stead. But wait. I brought back a thing of great beauty for our mother; it shall be my gift to you, High Queen. Here, let me show it to you!'

Whilst he had been talking, Mokkan had manoeuvred Lantur to the edge of the rock plateau. He called out to the rats who were dumbly sitting in the logboat awaiting orders. 'Open the tapestry, spread it wide. Captain Ullig, tell your bearers to bring forward the torches. Let everybeast see the prize I have brought from afar to celebrate the start of High Queen Lantur's reign!'

The onlookers gasped in wonderment as the fantastically woven tapestry of Martin the Warrior was unrolled in the torchlight. All eyes were upon it when Mokkan made his move. With a quick flick of his paws he

335

pushed Lantur into the lake. She screamed once, thrashing about in the wet shreds of her mother's shroud, which were floating up to the surface. Had she remained still, Lantur might have been pulled to safety. But anything that moved in the waters was fair game to the pike shoals that hunted there. The lakewater boiled briefly as the heavy predators struck, then Lantur was gone. Mokkan nodded to Wilce and Ullig, and they shouted as though their lives depended upon it, which indeed they did.

'A sign, 'tis a sign! Mokkan is the rightful ruler! Hail High King Mokkan! Hail High King Mokkan!'

The last Marlfox of all turned to face his army, with a look combining tragedy, innocence and surprise. 'She slipped. I tried my best to hold on to her but she slipped! Alas, I could do nothing to save her. Lantur was taken by the spirit of the lake!'

Wilce and Ullig appealed to the crowd.

''Tis a sign, the lake judged her unfit!'

'Aye, Mokkan rules! Hail High King Mokkan!'

Soon everybeast joined in, shouting themselves hoarse until the din rang across the island.

In the slave pens the otter shook his head woefully at the aged mouse. 'So that one's back, eh? I wonder 'ow Mokkan murdered the murderer? I think I'd sooner be a slave than a Marlfox, you live a little longer.'

The old mouse shrugged, resting his head against the bars. 'Don't be too sure of it, pal. How long d'ye think we're goin' to last with Mokkan as King around here?'

31

Morning sunlight shimmered on the river. Megraw balanced on the rail of the raft, watched by everybeast aboard. The osprey flapped his reset wing experimentally, then, slightly doubtful, he set his fierce eye upon Gawjo. 'Mah wing still hurts. Are ye sure et's fixed?'

'Sure I'm sure,' the old squirrel warrior assured his patient. 'The wing's bound to hurt, 'tis stiff through bein' idle. Ye'll have to try usin' it. Go on!'

Megraw launched himself from the rail. Flapping madly, he flew a short distance, then crashed into the river. Torrab and Song extended a long punting pole to him, and Megraw grabbed it in his beak, allowing himself to be pulled up on to the bank. He stood shaking water from his plumage. 'Ach, ah kin fly, ah'm sure o' et, but ye lot are mekkin' me nervous, stannin' there watchin' me. Gang aboot yer bizness an' leave me tae mahself!'

'Sure I've seen everythin' now,' Burble muttered to one of the big hedgehogs. 'An eagle who's too shy to fly? Yiss yiss, that's the blinkin' limit!'

Dann threw a paw about the watervole's shoulders. 'Oh, let him be, Burb. Come on, Torrab an' the gang are goin' to show us how t'make hodgepodge pie.'

In the cabin the hedgehogs were tossing anything they

337

could find into a cauldron, which sat squarely atop a pot-bellied stove. The four friends had never seen anything like it. Torrab and her gang went at the business of making hodgepodge pie with wild abandon, singing in gruff off-key voices. What they lacked in melodiousness they made up for in volume. Gawjo had heard it all before, and he clapped both paws over his ears to gain a little peace.

'Oh you take an 'odge, an' I'll take a podge,
If anybeast asks us why,
Jus' tell him that some clever cooks,
Are makin' 'odgepodge pie.
We start with an 'azelnut an' a leek,
'Cos they're wot we likes best,
An' tho' they don't look much to speak,
Till we toss in the rest!
'Odgepodge 'odgepodge, good ole 'odgepodge,
That's the pie for me,
I'll scoff it 'ot at suppertime,
Or wolf it cold for tea.
Oh savage a cabbage, tear a turnip,
Rip ripe radishes too,
Chop up chestnuts, they're the bestnuts,
Chuck in quite a few.
Dannyline ransom, mushrooms 'andsome,
Beetroots nice an' red,
An' watercress, that's more or less,
With piecrust over'ead!
Oh 'odgepodge 'odgepodge, good ole 'odgepodge,
North west east or south,
You can shove it up yore nose, but I suppose,
'Tis better off in yore mouth!
Who loves an 'odgepodge . . . Hedge'ogs!'

Surprisingly enough, when it was served at midday, it looked good and tasted even better. Gawjo fought the hedgehogs off, rapping paws with his ladle and muttering darkly about manners. Then he dug through the thick golden piecrust and ladled out portions to them all, steaming hot and delicious.

Dippler scraped his platter clean and winked at Torrab. 'Great stuff. I'll 'ave to remember that recipe. Wot's it called, podgepodge pie?'

'Yaakaaareeeeeegh!'

A blood-curdling scream caused them to leap from their chairs. Gawjo went racing out of the cabin, dagger at the ready.

'Sounds like somethin' bein' torn apart by wildbeasts!'

Hustling and shoving, they piled out on to the deck of the raft. The wild cry cleaved the air once more, and a dark shadow fell over them, causing everybeast to duck as something large hurtled by. Song was knocked flat on her back, but she lay there pointing skyward, shouting with joy. 'It's the Mighty Megraw! Look, he's flying!'

With his tremendous wingspread stretching, closing, backing and flapping, the osprey flew as none had ever seen such a big bird fly. Soaring, wheeling, plummeting and twirling out of dives like a corkscrew, Megraw put on an exhibition of flight for his earthbound friends, sometimes skimming so low that his wing pinions clipped their ears. Song felt her heart soar with the eagle. She was thrilled that his wing was healed due to her grandpa's skill.

'Go on, Megraw, fly! Fly! Fly!'

And Megraw did just that. Winging up into the blue until he was a mere speck in the summer sky, he turned and did several victory rolls. Folding both wings tight to his side, the eagle dropped like a thunderbolt towards the raft, and for a breathless moment Song thought he would smash into the deck. But he spread his wings again, and the mighty talons shot out as he swooped and landed on the rail, where he stood with both wings spread to their extent. For the first time since she had met her friend, Song saw the fish eagle in his element. Filled with the

339

exhilaration of his own savage strength, Megraw flapped his wings, shouting aloud his challenge. 'Ah'm the eagle whit kin outfly a lightnin' flash! Mah egg was broken by the thunderstorm! Kareeeeeegha! Megraw rules the skies tae the world's edge! These talons o' Mighty Megraw cuid plough a field o' rocks! Oh weep, ye foebeast, there's a braw bonny bird a-comin' yer way! Karaaaaagh!'

Gawjo nodded in admiration of Megraw's brave display. 'I take it yore about ready to go to the lake?'

The fierce golden eye winked at him. 'Aye, laddie, ah ken ye'll be comin' wi' me?'

Gawjo Swifteye picked up a long raft pole. He nodded at Megraw and his crew. 'This very day!'

Out on the river it was broad and fast flowing. The hedgehogs would not let Song or her friends use the raft poles, so they worked on the *Swallow*, putting the finishing touches to their sleek craft. Torrab and the others formed two lines, port and starboard, and they punted deep with their poles. Gawjo sat on the stern rail, using a broad paddle as a rudder to steer the sprawling vessel. By mid-noon they were cruising free along a wide calm stretch, while the crew sat eating cold hodgepodge pie and drinking cider, watching the raft drift steadily downriver. Song joined her grandpa at the stern rail and showed him her parchment, torn, tattered and barely decipherable from the batterings it had endured.

'Grandpa, 'tis not very clear now, but there were a few lines of the rhyme here, let me see now. Ah, here it is.

'And should you live to seek the lake,
Watch for the fish of blue and grey,
Betwixt those two's the path you take,
Good fortune wend you on your way!'

Gawjo's hooded eyes scanned the waters ahead. 'Aye, the fish of blue an' grey, I know 'em well. You'll see those fish afore twilight. I'll say nothin', pretty one. See if'n you can spot 'em – yore young an' sharp.'

Twilight came as a relief after the long hot day, gold and crimson flakes of dying sunlight dancing on the waters. Song had positioned herself on the forward rail of the raft. She watched keenly from side to side, taking in all, searching for the signs. From the cabin window she could see Grandpa Gawjo and her friends observing her. The young squirrelmaid paid attention to the tiniest details. Rocks lining the banks, trees growing either side, any patches of bare earth. Then she sighted the fork ahead. A rock that was so large it was almost an island in midriver, causing the waters to part and run both sides of it. The left fork wound off sharply east, the right one curving slightly west, but further downriver straightening to flow due south. It was on the right fork of the island rock that Song spotted the fish. It was a natural spur of the greyish-hued rock, sticking out at an awkward angle, high up. Curiously, it closely resembled a trout, for the shrubbery growing atop it looked like the fish's small dorsal fin. Where the eye would be positioned there was a crack in the stone, with a thick spray of delicate blue-flowering wall speedwell growing out of it.

'Ahoy, me beauty,' Gawjo called from the cabin window, 'which course do we steer? Has the fish showed you yet?'

Without turning Song held up her right paw. 'Take the west fork an' sail due south, Grandpa!'

Gawjo chuckled as he emerged from the cabin to attend his steering paddle at the stern. 'Yore a born Swifteye, gel. West'n'south it is!'

Night had fallen when the lake came into view. The river was running steep and fast, with outcrops of rock poking dangerously from its surface. Gawjo gave the order to his crew. 'All paws on deck. Pole 'er over these rapids an' keep yore eyes peeled for those rocks. Lively now!'

Song and her companions found themselves standing alongside the burly hedgehogs, pushing and punting with the long raft poles. Burble was slightly tardy lifting his pole and was thrust up into the air, the raft rushing by him. Dippler saw him rise and shouted a warning. 'Watervole overboard! Er, I mean up in the air!'

Torrab and one of her burly sisters were aft. They snatched Burble and the pole, heaving them back on to the deck before he was left clinging to a pole in midriver as the raft went on without him. Song and her friends were laughing about it when the big craft began to buck and plunge. A hedgehog shot by, looping them all to the raft with a stout rope. Spray struck their faces, and Dann yelled above the din, 'Look out, here we go, mates!'

Song would have been frightened had it not been for the confidence she felt in the skill shown by her grandpa and Torrab's crew. Instead, a wave of exhilaration swept over her as the raft virtually flew down the rapids. Turning and heaving, sometimes head down, other times bow up, night-dark water crested with star-swept spray rushed by in a blur. Megraw balanced firmly on the for'ard rail, calling directions. 'Rocks comin' up aheid, swing tae yer left. Left! Left! Noo, awa' right a wee bitty. Hauld 'er steady, laddies, steady!'

Without warning a waterfall came up, and they shot straight over the top, right out into space. The breath was whipped from their mouths as they stood frozen, still holding on to the raft poles, water roaring at their back.

Wwwhhhhrrrrraaaaaaakkkkkkkkksssssshhhhh! The raft landed flat with an earsplitting splash. Gawjo wiped water from his eyes and shrugged carelessly. 'Well, this's the lake. We've arrived.'

Even in the darkness they could feel the immensity of a vast body of water, calm and smooth as a millpond in the warm summer night. Everybeast aboard collapsed into a sitting position, dog-weary and gasping.

Gawjo was first to recover, and he paced the deck sternly. 'Come on, me babies, up on yore paws, we're stickin' out like a bandaged ear if'n any foebeast shows up. Let's get 'er ashore an' into some cover. Jump to it, crew!'

They chose a spot further east on the lakeshore, where trees grew thick, willows on the fringes dipping their branches into the water. Waist deep in the lake, they levered the raft onshore with the punting poles. Burble stumbled and spat out a mouthful of muddy liquid. 'A proper ould slave driver that grandpa of yores is, Song. Yiss yiss, a right ould whipcracker!'

Gawjo's hooded eyes appeared over the stern, staring straight at the grumbling watervole. 'Wot was that you were burblin' about, Burble?'

'Er, ah, 'twas nothin', sir, yiss yiss, nothin'. We're all doin' a fine grand job down here, enjoyin' ourselves, yiss!'

Dawn was streaking the lake with beige and pink amid low-lying cloudbanks. The stillness was eerie; there were no sounds of singing birds over the far-reaching inland sea. From stem to stern the raft was covered with boughs and fronds, tufts of vegetation and shrubs. Song thrust a final willow bough into the cabin chimneytop and climbed wearily down to the deck. She threw her grandpa a limp salute. 'All covered, sir. Permission to sleep?'

A smile hovered around Gawjo's slanted eyes as he nodded at the exhausted crew. They had worked hard and well, 'Hmmm. Well, all right, permission granted. Y'can all sleep standin' on yore heads with one eye open.'

Dippler bit his lip with feigned emotion. 'O sir, yore too kind to us ungrateful wretches!'

Gawjo tweaked the shrew's ear. 'Aye, maybe I am, so I'll stay awake an' cut the throat of any crew member found snorin'. How'll that do ye?'

Dann sniggered. 'Better cut yore Song's throat right now!'

'Ooh, you listen, Dannflor Reguba, you're the snorer, not me!'

'Oh yiss yiss, Dann's a grand ould snorer, but I think the champion's got t'be me good mate Dipp, yiss yiss!'

'Hah! Stripe me blue, look who's talkin'. Anybeast out on that lake'd think it was a foghorn if you kicked off snorin'!'

'Who, me? Ooh, y'fibber, watervoles don't snore, 'tis a fact!'

Gawjo shook with laughter as he watched the indignant young creatures. The old squirrel cut short the dispute with a wave of his paw. 'Hah! Snore, you think you can snore? Now Torrab an' these hogs, they can snore! I'll be surprised if there's a leaf left on any tree within the area by the time they're done snorin'. Huh, you ain't heard snorers until you've slept in the same cabin as my family. I should know, 'tis me who's had to suffer these many long seasons!'

Torrab gave Gawjo an affectionate pat, nearly knocking him flat. 'Thou sayest the nicest things, ancient one!'

Song giggled. 'Give him another pat, Auntie Torrab!'

Whether through excitement or over-tiredness, the occupants of the cabin had difficulty in getting to sleep. Dippler propped himself up on a cushion. 'C'mon, Song, give us a little tune. Mayhap that'll help us to doze off. Yore grandpa ain't heard you singin'.'

Song recalled a ditty of her Grandma Ellayo's which reminded her of the joy she felt at watching Megraw fly.

'I sit alone and wish that I
Could be a bird up in the sky,
I'd join the breezes that do blow,
Whichever way they chanced to go,
Far o'er the waves, across the sea,
I'd drift along quite happily,
Or maybe out on field and fen,
I'd circle round some forest glen.
I envy bee and butterfly,

344

Maybe the birds could tell me why
I wipe a teardrop from my eye,
I sit alone, for I can't fly.'

In actual fact it was Gawjo who was wiping a teardrop from his eye, his mind wandering back over the seasons. 'Ellayo my wife used to sing that, almost as pretty as you do, Song. Of course, she was much younger in those days.'

Song stroked the old grey head of her grandpa. 'She's still young at heart, you'll see.'

Gawjo stretched out, closing his eyes. 'Maybe I will, if we live through what lies ahead, young 'un.'

Outside it began to rain, softly at first, increasing as a breeze sprang up over the vast reaches of the hidden lake.

One of Silth's ceremonial cloaks, held on the spear-points of two soldiers, provided cover for Mokkan against the driving rain. The Marlfox was in high spirits, far too cheerful to allow a wet morning to ruin his joy. Striding across a high-walled roof at Castle Marl, he peered over at the ground far below. 'Set it up here!'

With the aid of twelve slaves, Wilce and Ullig staggered forward, bent beneath the weight of Queen Silth's palanquin. Grunting and groaning they strained upward until it rested precariously atop the wall. Wilce and Ullig stood bareheaded in the rain among the slaves, awaiting King Mokkan's pleasure. He flicked a paw dismissively at them. 'You two, shove it over!'

It needed only a slight push, and then there was several seconds' silence, broken by a rending crash. The Marlfox giggled like a youngster as he stared over the walltop at the smashed palanquin on the ground.

'I always hated that thing. Tell somebeast to burn what's left of it when the weather clears up. Right, follow me, come on, come on, all of you!'

Wilce and Ullig exchanged apprehensive glances

before running in the wake of slaves and soldiers after Mokkan, down the winding slopes of the castle's corridors. The Marlfox rushed helter skelter in the lead, and arrived at the door of Castle Marl's main chamber smiling and exhilarated.

'What took you so long? Haha, getting too fat, Ullig, and you Wilce. Inside, all of you, step smartly now!'

A big carved oak chair had been set in the centre of the floor. Mokkan practically skipped over to sit on it. He banged his paws down on the chair arms. 'What d'you think? Not bad, eh? Of course, it's not a real throne, but it'll do until I have one made. The throne of High King Mokkan. Hahaha, I like that! If my fool brothers and sisters have survived they'll meet a fine welcome if they try to return.'

He waved imperiously at the two water rats who had been holding the cloak aloft with their spears. 'You've been with me since I left Redwall Abbey, right?'

The two stolid guards nodded silently. Mokkan leapt up, energy surging through him, and smiling and winking at the two dullards he clapped their backs heartily. 'Tell me your names. Speak up, don't be afraid!'

'Toolam, er, sire, er, Majesty!'

'Durrlow, your Majesty!'

The Marlfox paced a circle around both rats, looking them up and down approvingly. 'Good honest soldiers, faithful and obedient, just what a King needs. Durrlow, you are now my Personal Adviser. Toolam, I promote you to be Commander of my army!' Adopting a look of mock sadness, he nodded at Wilce and Ullig. 'Loyalty brings its rewards, you see. I always told you, never trust a vixen, and now look what Lantur has brought you to. Oh, don't look so glum. I've found an important job for you both, so cheer up!'

The two water rats managed to put on uneasy smiles. Mokkan winked mischievously at them. 'You can hang my beautiful tapestry for me. Hmm, let me see, that wall over there should do. Toolam, Durrlow, see to it that they hang it good and straight, use your spearbutts to chastise them if they don't. Ullig, I'm sorry, my old friend, I can't afford an untrustworthy Captain, so you're back to being a rank and file soldier again. Wilce, you've had it too easy for long enough, it's back into uniform for you I'm afraid. Right, that's that! I'm off to see what the cooks have prepared for my breakfast. I'm famished enough to eat a meal fit for a King. Fit for a King, good, eh? Hahahaha!'

Mokkan paused at the door and pointed to the slaves. 'You'll find that nothing escapes your new King's notice. Work hard and well, I may free you from slavery and promote you to be soldiers in my army, tell your friends this. And you soldiers, if I find you to be slow and lazy, then I'll take away your uniforms and make slaves of you, let your comrades know this. But remember this, all of you, even think of playing me false and you'll find out the lake still possesses teeth. Make sure everybeast knows that!'

The door slammed, and the self-proclaimed King Mokkan could be heard trotting off down the sloping passage, laughing at the echo of his own voice. 'I'm feeling hungry today, hungry! Hahahahaha!'

The slaves were left in a bewildered group by the door, murmuring quietly to each other.

'Never 'eard nothin' like that in all the time I been 'ere.'

'Aye, he's as mad as his mother was!'

'It must be the sudden power gone to his brain, I think.'

'Huh, I'd sooner be dead than serve a Marlfox as a soldier!'

'Crazier than his sister was, if'n y'ask me!'

'Who's bothered about wot we think? Nobeast asks a slave anythin', mate, they tells them!'

A water rat soldier prodded the speaker roughly with his spear. 'Stow the gab there. Silence, you lot! Back down t'the pens with yer, quick march. One two, one two . . .'

The hefty hedgehog maid, who had made the final

remark, muttered to her companion, a grizzled old shrew, 'See wot I mean, friend?'

Toolam gestured at the rolled tapestry. He felt nervous and unsure at issuing orders to creatures who had formerly been his superiors. 'Er, pick it up!'

Without any argument Wilce and Ullig bent to lift the tapestry. Suddenly Toolam was seized by a wave of confidence he had never felt before. Inflating his narrow chest, he realized that he really was Commander of the army. A slow grin suffused his normally expressionless features. 'Be careful y'don't damage it, you clumsy fools!'

Durrlow joined him, eager to exploit his new-found powers. 'Aye, or you'll feel our spear 'andles, you butter-pawed oafs!'

As Wilce and Ullig staggered to the wall with the tapestry slung carefully between them, Toolam and Durrlow grinned at each other and swaggered boldly behind the subdued pair. They had begun to realize that power was a mighty intoxicating thing to possess.

32

Grey afternoon cast its pall over the lake. Sheeting rain swept back and forth, causing the surface to spatter under a ceaseless bombardment of drops. When the raft had been poled clear of the shallows, Gawjo dropped a piece of trout, donated by the Megraw, into the lake. It drifted beneath the water for a moment, then two pike struck, dragging it under as they fought for possession of the morsel. Torrab watched over the old squirrel warrior's shoulder.

'Methinks 'tis time we sought out the bows, Father.'

Gawjo wiped fishy paws on his jerkin, nodding agreement. 'Aye, daughter, this is where the pike shoals start.'

Short bows with thin sharp arrows were fetched from the cabin. Torrab and six other hedgehogs notched shafts to their bowstrings and began firing arrows in a sloping direction at the water. Soon a pike was hit. It thrashed about close to the surface, vicious and hookjawed, a real lake monster. The arrow had wounded it, causing a blood trail in the water, and with terrifying speed it was attacked by a horde of other pike. The hedgehogs shot arrows furiously into the shoal, hitting the big fish indiscriminately, until Gawjo gave the order to stop firing.

Song had watched the whole thing from a cabin window. She did not like to see any living thing slain needlessly. The squirrelmaid questioned her grandpa as he stamped into the cabin, shaking rain from himself. 'Why were you shooting at the fish, Grandpa?'

Gawjo sat down at the table, wriggling a paw in his damp ear. 'All part o' the plan, me young beauty. This lake's swarmin' with pike. They've tried to attack us before now – you don't realize how big an' dangerous some o' those fish've become. So the plan is to shoot one. The pike are natural cannibals, they'll go for that 'un an' eat it. So we shoot a few more an' pretty soon they come far far'n'wide to feed on 'em.'

Song shuddered. 'Ugh! How horrible!'

Gawjo shrugged, pouring himself some hot mint and dandelion tea. 'Aye, 'tis not a pretty sight, but that's the nature o' pike. They fight o'er eatin' their own so fiercely that they bite each other, causin' more blood t'flow. Before you know it nearly all the pike in the lake are gathered there, snappin' an' rippin' each other to bits. Whilst their blood lust is on them they won't bother us or our raft.'

Megraw watched the rainy skies from the window. 'Whit a waste o' guid food! Nary a sign o' they maggypies oot on yon lake yet. Mebbe inclement weather's keepin' 'em close tae hame on their isle.'

Gawjo sipped his tea gratefully. 'The weather's on our side an' the wind's drivin' us towards the island. With luck we may make land by the morrow's dawn.'

Burble picked up a small stringed instrument from the corner where he was sitting and twanged it.

'Can anybeast be after playin' this thing? May'ap Song'll give us a ditty, yiss yiss?'

A huge male hedgehog relieved Burble of the instrument. 'Nay, rivermousey, sound doth carry far o'er waters like these.'

Song pulled a face at her friend. 'He's right, y'know,

rivermousey. You'll have to recite us one of your rivermousey poems, nice and quiet now!'

Burble's fur actually bristled with indignation. 'Sure I'll recite nothin' while I'm bein' insulted. If anybeast calls me rivermousey once more I'll fight 'em. Yiss yiss, so I will! I don't call you treewalloper, do I?'

Song laughed at her bristly companion. 'Call me what y'like, I don't care. Rivermousey!'

Dippler burst out laughing. 'Hawhaw haw! Rivermousey, that's a good 'un!'

Burble rounded on him with a wicked grin. 'Who asked you, boatbottom?'

The cabin became a verbal battleground as laughing and giggling they hurled insults at one another.

'Hohoho! Boatbottom, that's a great name for you, Dipp!'

'Ho is it now, Dannflower broomtail. Hawhaw haw!'

Gawjo joined in. 'Heehee, flopears is a better name for that 'un, or popplepaws. Heeheeheehee!'

'Popplepaws yoreself, ole baggybarrel-belly! Yahahaha!'

Torrab poked her head round the cabin door. 'Be there any within to relieve the watch this day?'

She was greeted with a barrage of impudent merriment.

'Go 'way, spikybonce!'

'Aye, push off, needlenose!'

'Out in the rain with ye, soggyhog!'

'Go an' watch yoreself, squelchspines!'

The burly hogmaid grinned and called to Megraw, 'What about thee, binnaclebeak?'

Dropping down from the window, Megraw spread his massive wings and glared about him savagely, raising a hooked talon. 'Whit was that ye callit me, marm? Nary a beast livin' meks sport o' the Mighty Megraw!'

A moment later they were all out on the deck, soaking in the rain, gazing at the locked cabin door.

Burble sighed. 'Sure, an' I wonder why 'tis that eagles don't have any sense o' humour at all. We had to run for our lives there!'

Megraw sat alone in the locked cabin, muttering darkly, 'Naebeast speaks ill o' mither Megraw's eggchick. Ye'll stay oot in the elements until ye apologize tae me!'

Apart from the skies louring darker a little, noon, twilight and evening remained virtually the same. Sheeting rain driving southward in heavy curtains over the lake surface as far as the eye could see, with a moderate wind spurring the raft ever onward towards the island. Megraw had been placated, but he deserted the cabin, choosing to stay on deck beneath a canvas awning, watching for sign of magpies. Gawjo lashed the tiller in position and joined his crew in the warm, cosy cabin, where a cheerful fire glowed within the pot-bellied stove.

He lifted the lid from a cauldron, sniffing the simmering aroma. 'By the seasons, that smells good'n' decent. Wot is it?'

Dippler checked the contents, sprinkling in a pawful of sweet ground arrowroot to thicken up the sauce further.

'That's a seagoin' recipe, sir, called skilly'n'duff. Log a Log used t'make it for the Guosim, when we followed the waters down to the great ocean.'

Torrab hovered about the young shrew impatiently. 'Twill soon be ready, I trust?'

Dippler added more of the arrowroot and stirred it slowly. 'Aye, soon now. The skilly is a thick sweet sauce with all manner o' good things in. That big pudden floatin' about in it is the duff, stuffed with wild plums, damsons, blackberries an' chopped chestnuts, all cased up in a ball o' spongy pastry, bit like a great dumplin'. Nothin' like it to cheer up a body on a rainy ole night, you'll see!'

The entire crew voted Dippler's skilly'n'duff delicious, some of the big hedgehogs noting down the recipe for use on winter nights. The Guosim shrew recalled a comic seagoing monologue concerning the dish.

'Aboard the good ship *Wobblechop*,
I sailed when I was young,
First in line an' feelin' fine,
When the dinner bell was rung.
Our Cap'n 'ad a fog'orn voice,
An' boots as big as me,
"Stand by, me lads, 'ere comes a ship,
'Tis a pirate craft!" cried he.
Whoa skilly'n'duff, that's the stuff,
To keep nearby when things get rough!

The pirate Cap'n was a rat,
His name was Itchee Scratch,
Upon his nose, why goodness knows,
He wore a red eyepatch.
"Haul to, ye dozy lubbers,
I'm fat'n'bad an' tough,
An' I smells plunder on the air,
Wot might be skilly'n'duff."
Whoa skilly'n'duff, that's the stuff,
Us waterbeasts can't get enough!

Well I tell you, me word 'tis true,
Our crew got quite upset,
To rob a sailor's dinner was,
The worst thing we'd 'eard yet,
So we put down our bowls'n'spoons,
Then armed ourselves with slings,
We slung at those ole pirate rats,
A dozen kinds o' things.
Whoa skilly'n'duff, that's the stuff,
To eat whilst fightin' searats gruff!

That pirate Cap'n he got shot,
By a barrel load of peas,
Wot blacked his eyes an' stung his thighs,
An' fractured all his knees.

We hit the crew with onion skins,
Big cabbage stalks as well,
With hardcrust pies an' 'orrible cries,
They splashed into the swell.
Whoa skilly'n'duff, that's the stuff,
When vermin crews you must rebuff!

As *Wobblechop* sailed away that day,
We sang a jolly song,
The bottlenosed cook with laughter shook,
As the dinner bell went bong.
I'm old an' fat with a greasy hat,
But this to you I say,
I must've scoffed a score o' bowls,
Of skilly'n'duff that day.
Whoa skilly'n'duff, that's the stuff,
When winter winds do howl'n'puff!'

High King Mokkan slept, though not peacefully or well,
that night. The Marlfox's dreams were a nightmare of
disjointed visions. Lantur, the sister he had slyly
murdered, kept trying to drag him into the pike-infested
lake, smiling wickedly at him and repeating a hollow
chant.

'Never trust a vixen, never trust a vixen!'

He turned to run, but was confronted by the brothers
and sisters he had deserted. Their faces pale and wan,
they pointed accusingly at him, murmuring, 'Blood for
blood, a Marlfox lies slain, somebeast must pay, blood
calls for blood!'

He fled from them and, seeking safety, found himself
leaping into his mother's palanquin. However, he was
surrounded not by a silk curtain, but by the tapestry from
Redwall Abbey. Stern-faced and fearless, the mouse
warrior figure stepped out from the tapestry and raised
his magnificent sword. Panic such as he had never known
seized Mokkan. With the blood in his veins like ice water,

he hurled himself from the palanquin. Time stood still, and the Marlfox stumbled slowly to the ground, only to find himself confronted by others. A grim-faced young squirrel wielding the same sword that the warrior mouse had brandished, a squirrelmaid armed with a rod tipped by a glowing green stone, a great black and white eagle, talons spread, beak open. Creatures he could not identify, a watervole, a shrew, hedgehogs, all gathered around him, and his mother's voice echoed mockingly in the gloom.

'Hail, High King Mokkan, last of the Marlfox brood!'

Grabbing his cloak, he hid his face in it and screamed, but the scream died to a whimper as the cloak tightened around his throat, threatening to strangle him. 'No, please, nooooooo!'

Mokkan woke on the floor of his bedchamber with a silken sheet, which had become caught on a bedpost as he rolled about trying to escape the dark world of fearful slumber, wrapped tightly about his neck. Throwing open the chamber door, he glared wildly at the two water rat sentries standing immobile in the flickering torchlight. They gazed back dully at the new High King, panting, dishevelled, with a bedsheet draped round his neck. Slamming the door, he retreated back into the bed-chamber, taking a deep draught of wine from a pitcher and tossing aside the sheet. Then he stood at the window, letting the rain cool his fevered brow, staring out into the dark wet night. What acts of murder and treachery had his own mother committed that she too always slept uneasily? Was this what it was like to gain the power of kingship?

33

Gawjo had taken the last night watch on deck. The rain slacked off to a steady drizzle before dawn when the old squirrel warrior returned to the cabin. Checking that the stove fire was burned down to white ashes, he unshuttered both windows.

Megraw stirred from his perch on a shelf. 'Ah ken et'll be a big day taeday, auld 'un?'

Gawjo Swifteye was still nimble and strong, despite his many seasons. He took down a short lance from the motley array of weaponry hanging from the wall. 'Aye, friend, 'twill be a big day, shorter for some than others before 'tis over. Come on, crew, stir yoreselves, the island of Marlfoxes is in sight!'

Song stared around herself in the half-light. Her grandpa and the hedgehogs were ready and armed.

Burble sat up rubbing sleep from his eyes. 'Well, wotever happens later can wait, yiss yiss, I'm hungry right now, so I am!'

Dippler and Dann were already at the table, helping themselves to warm fruit cordial and oatcakes that had been baked the night before.

Megraw hopped up to an open window. 'Nae use a-waitin' for yon maggypies tae find us, ah'm thinkin'. This time ah'll catch them nappin'. Guid luck, see ye later!' Launching himself from the windowsill, the great eagle sailed off into the rising dawnstreaked skies.

Gawjo addressed his remaining crew. 'Friends, you all know wot t'do. Dann, we'll give you an' Torrab until mid-mornin'. Is the *Swallow* ready?'

Dann strapped the sword across his back, nodding to Torrab and the other four hedgehogs he would be travelling with. 'She's ready sir, well stocked with weapons too.'

Gawjo shook the young squirrel's paw heartily. 'Luck go with ye, Dannflor Reguba!'

Song, Dippler and Burble pushed the boat out from the raft's port side. Sitting behind the hedgehogs, Dann waved his paddle. 'See you later, mates, I hope!'

The three friends waved to him silently, then stood by their poling positions at the side rails. Gawjo called out from the stern, where he sat plying the tiller, 'No time to waste, crew. Let's get there quick as we can!'

All eyes were fixed on the mysterious island looming up, dark and forbidding, with Castle Marl dominating its rocky landing plateau.

Owing to the previous day's events, when the rule of the island had changed so swiftly, the castle courtyards, front and back, lay silent. Mokkan had let the guards celebrate, and they were not yet up and about. In the slave pens the captives were beginning to stir. An old mouse stood with his face pressed to the bars. Behind him a grizzled otter hauled himself stiffly up from the damp straw which served them as bedding. 'Wot's 'appenin' out there, matey?'

The mouse was joined by a sturdy hedgehog maid. 'Well, it ain't brekkfist, that's for shore. Where's the guards today? Still sleepin', I suppose.'

'They'll appear all in good time. After all, we ain't goin' nowheres, are we?' called a squirrel slave from the back of the pen.

The mouse chuckled humourlessly at his dry remark. 'Right enough there, friend. We may's well make the best of our extra rest. Better'n toilin' in the fields drenched by that rain we had yesterday. I'm still damp all over.'

They sat in silence for a while, watching the clear dawn rise, thankful that the rain had ceased. The otter suddenly cocked his head on one side, listening. 'Wot was that noise? I 'eard a funny sound.'

'Prob'ly my stomach tellin' me mouth it's time to eat.'

Catching the hedgehog's paw, the otter silenced her. 'No, it wasn't that, mate. Lissen!'

Something metallic clinked against the back walltop, then clinked again as it fell back. There was a whirring noise, followed by a brief silence. A thick knotted rope flew down past the bars with a three-pronged grappling hook tied to its end which hit the courtyard stones with a ringing clank. Dumbfounded for a moment, they stood looking at it, then the hogmaid moved swiftly. Grabbing a piece of wet sacking, she lay flat and flopped it through the bars. It caught on the grapples, and she pulled it back in until the hook was in her reach. Her paws shook with excitement as she held on to the rope and the grappling hook.

The old mouse gazed at it in disbelief as the other slaves crowded round. 'Why'd anybeast want to throw that to us?'

Wedging the hook firmly between the bars, the otter gave the rope three sharp tugs. He too was shaking all over. 'One thing's shore, it ain't Marlfoxes, water rats or magpies. Whoever 'tis they must be friends. Let's 'elp 'em!'

Dann came shinning over the back wall. At the top he gave a swift look around, then signalled down to the hedgehogs below. A moment later he had dropped down into the courtyard and was staring into the pen at the emaciated slaves pressing forward to the bars. Unshouldering his sword, he flashed them a quick smile.

'Good morrow to ye, mates. I'm Dann Reguba. Anybeast fancy bein' liberated today?'

Raising the sword high, he swung it down energetically, shearing the lock from the slave pen door with one mighty swipe. Slaves stood gawping in amazement. Dann swung the door open as they found their tongues.

'Did y'see that? He chopped off the lock an' his blade ain't even nicked. By thunder, that's some kind o' sword, mates!'

'Dann Reguba, wot sort o' name is that?'

'I know, I've 'eard it afore. That 'un's a mighty warrior, I'm with him. Woe t'the beast who stands in the way of a Reguba!'

A shudder of pride ran through Dann. He strode into the cage and was surrounded by creatures trying to shake his paw, all of them with tears in their eyes at the unexpected arrival of help. Torrab followed with her hedgehogs, bundles of arms strapped to their backs. They passed out spears, slings, blades and javelins to the eager captives. An otter spoke for his fellow slaves as he loaded stone into sling. 'Just say the word, Dann. We're with you all the way, mate!'

Dann closed the door, hanging the broken lock back in place. 'Sit tight here, friends, you'll get the word soon enough!'

Overhead a harsh screeching of birdcall cut the morning air, followed by a mighty flutter of wings and the hunting call of an eagle. Feathers fell like a miniature snowstorm into the courtyard. Dann had no need to look. He knew the Mighty Megraw was wreaking vengeance upon his enemies. Magpies shrieked harshly with terror, more feathers swirled to the courtyard stones and floated into the pen. Slaves ran to the bars, clutching at them as they struggled to catch a glimpse of retribution being visited on the hateful birds, straining and craning their necks upward, pushing against the bars.

'An eagle, 'tis a great eagle up there, huntin' magpies!'

There was a thud on the pen roof, and the huddled carcass of Athrak rolled off on to the stones below.

'The eagle's slain Athrak! Look, look!'

From above, the osprey's warcry could be heard as he pursued magpies out across the lake.

'Remember me, mah bonny bairns, ah'm no half asleep an' helpless now, ah'm the Mighty Megraw, death on wings tae ye! Krrreeeeegaaaaah!'

Guards came tumbling out of their barracks, still sleepy-eyed, buckling on armour and stumbling over weapons. Dann kicked open the slave pen door, and hurtled out with an army of slaves brandishing weapons behind him.

'Chaaaaaarge!'

The raft thudded in against the rocky plateau. Song and her grandpa leapt ashore as mooring ropes snaked out behind them. Securing the raft, Gawjo was forced to duck as a small cloud of magpies sped low overhead, pursued by the Mighty Megraw. They fled out across the lake with the eagle hard on their tails like some avenging beast.

Gawjo gripped Song's paw as the sound of Dann and his slave army giving their battle cry rang out from the castle above. 'Stay by me, pretty one. The family'd never forgive me if anythin' happened to you. On the double, crew!'

They charged up the slope towards Castle Marl, slamming the gatehouse door shut as they passed and locking the half-awake guards inside. As they burst into the front courtyard, Song caught a glimpse of Mokkan at an upper chamber window. At once she remembered the original purpose of their quest.

'Dipp, Burb, there's the Marlfox. Come on, that's where the tapestry must be!'

For Mokkan it was like a continuation of his nightmare. There below in the courtyard of Castle Marl, the creatures he had fled from in dreams were staring boldly up at him.

Fear gripped the Marlfox and he looked about wildly, seeking an avenue of escape. The shrew logboat he had arrived in still lay moored to one side of the rock plateau which served as a jetty. That was it! Dashing from his room he motioned at the two guards posted outside. 'Follow me! Slay anybeast who tries to stop your King!'

They ran obediently with him, along the corridor sloping upward to Wilce's former room, which now belonged to Toolam, Commander of the army. Mokkan burst in on the slumbering rat. 'Rouse yourself, fool, foebeasts are at large in the castle!'

Toolam rushed to get his new armour on over a voluminous nightgown, then hefted his heavy spear. 'Er, sire, your word is my command, er, y'Majesty!'

'Muster the soldiers, every one, sweep these invaders from my island, slay them or take them prisoner! I will see you when this incident is finished. Fail me and you will go to serve the Teeth of the Deeps. Go now. You two, go with him!'

When they had gone, Mokkan dropped his heavily embroidered cloak of kingship and slunk swiftly down to the main chamber. There he donned his old cloak of dull brown and green weave. Immediately a transformation came over him, and his pale eyes glowed. Now he was a proper Marlfox once more, and everybeast knew that Marlfoxes were magic, invisible! Blending in with the stones of the wall, Mokkan slipped off down the back corridors.

Burble panted along with Dippler in Song's wake, staring around in puzzlement. 'Dipp, will y'look at this place, there's neither step nor stair anywheres, 'tis all slopes, yiss yiss?'

Song rounded on the pair and pulled them into a darkened alcove, beckoning them to silence as the sound of clanking spears against breastplates reached her ears. 'Somebeast dashing down to the courtyard. Stand by!'

Toolam and the two water rat sentries came into view,

hurrying clumsily down the slope. Song whispered, 'One each, wait until they pass!'

No sooner were the three vermin past the alcove than Song and her two friends hit them from behind. Amid a resounding jumble of weaponry and armour the three rats crashed headlong into the wallstones and slid down senseless. Song could not resist a slight giggle.

'Sounded like somebeast tripping into a broom closet at Redwall Abbey. Come on, the Marlfox's room must be somewhere up this passage. Go careful now, he'll have heard the noise.'

There were other chambers either side of the torchlit passage, but Song knew right away that the one with ornate double doors would be the chamber where the Marlfox had been sighted. Dippler and Burble had armed themselves with the sentries' spears. Brandishing her Leafwood stick, Song gave them a quick nod. They charged the doors yelling their battle cries.

'Logalogalogaloooog! Waylahoooo! Redwaaaaaalllll!'

The doors were not locked, in fact they were not even closed properly, and they slammed inward under the force of the charge. Song, Dippler and Burble exploded into the chamber, heads over tails in a mad jumble. The squirrelmaid was first upright, ready to do battle, but feeling rather foolish at the instant realization that she was facing an empty room. Dippler and Burble sat up, gazing around the chamber in awe. Silken hangings, burnished metal mirrors, incense burners and satin cushions were everywhere. The watervole scurried over to the large carved oaken chair which was serving as the High King's temporary throne and plumped down on it. 'Yiss yiss, this is a grand ould chair, so 'tis. I always promised meself one of these. I think I'll plunder it!'

Song and Dippler were not listening. They were staring at the great Redwall tapestry, hanging in all its glory. Martin the Warrior's likeness seemed to smile down on them both.

Dippler clasped his friend's paw. 'Wait'll Dann sees this, missie. You've completed yore quest!'

Pride flooded through Song. It had been a long and perilous journey, but they had completed it successfully.

Snapping out of her reverie, she rousted Burble from his plundered throne. 'Come on, cushytail, up with you, we need this chair!'

She and Dippler dragged it over to the wall where the tapestry hung. Climbing on to the seat, they began taking down the heavy object, with Burble hopping about protesting. 'Ah go easy now, don't scratch the woodwork, watch how y'treat me lovely ould chair, yiss yiss, be careful!'

Rolling the tapestry up, they stood it behind one of the doors. Dippler tore down a silk wall hanging and draped it over the prize, effectively hiding it from view. 'There, it should be safe enough here for the moment. What's up, Song? What're ye lookin' round like that for?'

'Where did the Marlfox go? There's another thing, too. Have you noticed that it's gone quiet out there?'

Burble looked up from the chair he was covering with drapes. 'Yiss yiss, y'right there, mate, there should be a grand ould battle ragin' round this castle by now, but there's not a single peep from outside. Well now, there's me plunder all wrapped up nice'n'tidy. Let's go an' take a look!'

As soon as Dann and his party had charged, the guards fled back into their barracks and locked themselves in. Torrab posted two hedgehogs and several freed slaves in front of the barracks, calling in a loud voice so the water rats could hear, 'Stay thou by here, slay any who come out!' She turned with a shrug to the bemused Dann. 'Mayhap yon vermin do not move without command from some Captain or Marlfox. They bear the look of beasts who be not overburdened with much intelligence.'

Dann took a parting glance at the dull-faced soldiers penned within their own barracks. 'Aye, I think yore right, Torrab. Let's go and see how Gawjo an' the others are farin' at the front entrance.'

Ullig and Wilce were in the main barracks, demoted to the rank and file. When they saw Gawjo and his small force enter the courtyard, both vermin grasped immediately their chance of being restored to favour. After a hasty conference together, they took up weapons. Ullig faced the horde of soldiers, who were lounging about awaiting orders from Toolam, who had not yet appeared. 'Arm yourselves, there are enemies within our gates. Hurry!'

The rats looked at him, but made no move. Wilce shook her spear at them, haranguing the indifferent vermin. 'You heard him, idiots. Pick up your weapons!'

One, bolder than the rest, sat down on his bed. 'You ain't officers no more, yore only the same as us. We ain't takin' no orders of'n yer!'

Wilce's brain was racing as she challenged the speaker. 'Us, common soldiers? Don't be stupid. Who told you that?'

Slightly unsure of himself, the water rat pointed out one of his comrades. 'Er, he did.'

Ullig did not hesitate. He slew the vermin who had been singled out with a sharp spear thrust. Turning on the rest, he shook his head pityingly. 'Him, what did he know about it? Barrack room gossip! You all know me an' Wilce 'ere. King Mokkan asked us to pose as common soldiers for a while, just to sniff out any traitors or rebels who was still loyal to the impostor Lantur. We're still in command 'ere, so pick up yer weapons an' follow us, or it'll go hard on you!'

Gawjo and his party were about to enter the castle when the main barrack doors burst open and vermin began charging towards them. The old squirrel warrior turned to face the foe, backed by his ten big hogs, and rushed the enemy with a bloodcurdling shout.

'Gawjoooooooo!'

Their quills bristling with the madness of combat, the hedgehogs threw themselves headlong into the water rat ranks, flailing out with long heavy clubs, smashing any spears that came close, hacking and thrusting with short broad cutlasses.

'Rollin' circle, form a rollin' circle!' yelled Gawjo above the mêlée.

The water rats did not fight with the same ferocity as their opponents, but they outnumbered them more than ten to one. Two of the hedgehogs were down before Gawjo succeeded in joining his small force into the rolling circle. Shoulder to shoulder, cheek by jowl they fought, facing the vermin horde, turning like a wheel, ploughing hither and thither into the foebeast ranks. A spearblade slashed down across Gawjo's paw as the hedgehog on his right side was overwhelmed by the crushing force of vermin. The old squirrel sighed as he slid in the blood flowing from his paw. They had underestimated the number of enemies. In a short time his column would go under.

'Regubaaaaaaaa! Strike for freedom!'

Dann and his slave army came charging to the rescue. They hit the vermin's flank like a tidal wave, changing the face of the battle completely.

Ullig and Wilce had fallen to the rear, careful not to be in the front line. Now, when the huge mob of reinforcements arrived, they saw defeat looming.

'That's torn it. Let's get out of here!' Wilce muttered to her companion.

A huge paw smacked down on Ullig's shoulder, and he was knocked flat by a burly hedgehog maid. She smiled grimly at him as she raised a loaded sling and spoke the last words Ullig was ever to hear in his life. 'Well well, if'n it ain't Ullig the Slave Cap'n!'

A crowd of slaves cornered Wilce. She had nowhere to run.

'Look, mates, 'tis madam 'igh'n'mighty, Lantur's ole pet!'

'Aye, she 'ad me beaten just for lookin' at 'er!'

'Remember she 'ad our rations cut when 'twas too cold for us to work?'

'I remember that was a hard winter. I vowed if ever I got the chance I'd pay 'er back someday. Now the time's come!'

Wilce's final shriek as they fell upon her was so piercing that it actually caused a lull in the fighting.

Song and her two friends emerged into the courtyard just as Wilce screamed. It was a critical moment. The water rats ceased fighting and dropped their weapons, an uneasy murmur arising from them at the sight of their two leaders lying slain. Taking in the situation at a glance, the young squirrelmaid tried a desperate gamble. Raising the Leafwood high above her head she strode boldly among the vermin, calling out, 'Surrender and you will not be harmed. The Marlfox has gone and your leaders are dead. Surrender, I command you. Surrender! Sit down upon the ground all those who want to live!'

Whether it was the authority carried by her voice, or the fact that the slow-witted vermin were conditioned to obey orders, Song never knew. She looked about, trying to hide her astonishment. Every vermin soldier was seated firmly on the ground, watching her.

Burble's outburst almost ruined the moment. 'All except you four, yiss yiss, yore fine big buckoes, I want y'to carry me nice ould chair down here an' . . . Yowch!'

Torrab had silenced the watervole by treading heavily on his footpaw. She glared at him ferociously. 'Seal thy foolish mouth, rivermousey!'

Meanwhile, Mokkan hurried along the damp rock passages that ran beneath Castle Marl, holding a small lantern. The tunnels wound many different ways in mazelike patterns, but the Marlfox kept unerringly to one passage, sure of his destination. It was a rusty metal door, small and set low at the rear of an alcove. Mokkan gritted his teeth as he prised with his axeblade, forcing the door to squeak in protest as it was wrenched open. He held the lantern ring in his teeth as he scraped through the doorway and began the long upward climb along a tunnel carved into the solid rock. At the top, he slid aside a flat slab and emerged into broad daylight. Tossing the lantern into the tunnel, he drew his cloak tight and took off along the boundary where the woodland grew down to meet the rocks. A sudden sound caused him to pause, then move silently back into the shade of a rowan and become almost one with it, using the Marlfox art of camouflage. Durrlow passed by him, glancing fearfully back at the high side wall of Castle Marl. Mokkan materialized behind the water rat and dealt him a sharp blow with his axe handle. Durrlow sprawled on the ground, one paw to his injured shoulder, the other held to his face as he cringed to avoid his master.

'I wasn't runnin' away, Majesty, I was . . . er . . . Don't kill me!'

Mokkan kicked him contemptuously. 'Get up, you whining oaf. Follow me and do as I say!'

Shortly afterwards, they lay among the loose rocks close to the plateau, Mokkan's axeblade pressed between Durrlow's shoulder blades as he whispered orders. 'Get down there fast and paddle that logboat over here. I'll be waiting for you. Hurry!'

Gawjo allowed Song to bandage his paw as they strode behind the vermin to the lakefront.

'Grandpa, will you keep still, please. This wound has to be bound, and I can't do it while you walk!'

The old squirrel warrior winked at her fondly. 'My liddle Song, the sweet voice o' reason. Time for all that when we've finished this job.'

At the water's edge the defeated rats were made to pile up their armour and weapons. Helmets, breastplates and shields in one heap, spears, slings, bows, arrows and swords in a separate array.

Dann took command of the disposal. 'You creatures have no need of armour. On an island such as this there'll be no need to attack or defend from this day forward. So step up smart now an' let's see ye sling all this gear into the lake!'

Gawjo admired his neatly bandaged paw as Song skimmed a shield out over the water. It skipped four times, then sank with the noon sun glinting off it. The old squirrel warrior watched as it disappeared from view, butted from side to side by the hooked snouts of curious pike.

'Well, missie, there goes the garments of war. That was a good idea of yours. 'Tis nice to 'ave a clever granddaughter.'

Song was as tall as her grandpa, so it was not difficult to throw an affectionate paw about his shoulders. 'Aye, and it isn't so bad having a good old grandpa!'

The weapons were next to go. Dann noticed that some of the vermin were actually enjoying it, laughing as they aimed their spears far out into the lake.

'Hoho, mate, mine went further'n yores!'

'Well, watch this fer a good throw!'

'Hah, last time I'll ever polish my spear fer guard duty. Remember 'ow Ullig used to 'ave us beaten for paradin' wid a dust speck on our spearblades?'

'Aye, curse 'is memory! This was 'is sword, I 'ope it rusts to nothin' in the waters!' The polished blade flashed in the sunlight, splashed into the lake and was lost to sight for ever.

Mokkan was concealed by high shelving rock at the side of the plateau as he climbed down to the waiting logboat with the laughter and cheers of his defeated army ringing in his ears. Durrlow crouched nervously at the water's edge, keeping a wary eye on the pike watching him hungrily from just below the waterline. He held the stern of the logboat steady for the Marlfox. Mokkan pushed past the water rat and jumped into the waiting

368

craft, which wobbled perilously for a moment and then settled. Seating himself, Mokkan readied his paddle, nodding to Durrlow. 'Get in!'

'I ain't goin' with you, sire.'

Mokkan stared at his subordinate in disbelief. 'What did you say?'

A look of stubborn resolution was in the water rat's eyes. 'I said I ain't goin' with you, Marlfox!'

A quiver of rage shook Mokkan. 'When this is over I'll be back,' he snarled. 'Mark my words, rat, you'll be screaming for death before I'm finished with you!'

Durrlow gave the logboat a hefty shove, shooting it out on to the lake, smiling happily at the irate Marlfox.

'Yore killin' days are over. Bad luck go with yer . . . Majesty!'

The last of the water rats' weapons had been cast into the lake when Mokkan hove into view, paddling furiously. Dippler was first to sight him, and hopped about wildly. 'Look, the Marlfox! There he goes!'

Mokkan paddled like a wildbeast to get out of weapon range. Dann ground his teeth in frustration. 'He's gettin' away. Gawjo, what'll we do?'

The old squirrel shook his head. 'We can't do anything, Dann. The Marlfox is out o' range. Nobeast could throw a spear that far.'

Suddenly everybeast leapt to one side. A whirring noise filled the air.

Whruuuuum! Whrrrrruuuuuuuummmm!

'Take this with ye, vermin!'

A former slave, the burly young hedgehog maid, raced forward to the rocky plateau brink. She was swinging an iron slave chain in both paws. Faster and faster she whirled it, until it became a blur. Song pulled her grandpa down flat, narrowly avoiding the broken manacles at the chain's end as the links thrummed louder and louder.

Whrrrruuuuummmm! Whrrrrruuuuummmm!

Whrrrrruuuuuummmmm!

The hogmaid released the chain and it whizzed out over the lake, a whirlwind of metal. She was carried forward by the mighty throw, slipping off the plateau into the water. Like lightning, Torrab and two of her brothers yanked her back, a pike clinging to her footpaw. Mokkan was just turning his head to look back as the chain struck him, wrapping round his neck in the blink of an eye and whipping him straight into the water.

The Teeth of the Deeps, the ravening pike shoals that preyed upon any living thing which was cast into their domain, closed in. Long silver bodies, bristling dorsal fins and ferocious ripping teeth, threshing the water to foam. So ended the reign of High King Mokkan, last of the Marlfoxes!

A mighty cheer arose from the freed slaves. The water rats stared blankly for a moment, then joined in wholeheartedly. The young hedgehog maid sat inspecting her footpaw and Song sat down beside her, eyes shining with admiration. 'That was a mighty throw, miss, you must possess great strength. What do they call you?'

'My name is Nettlebud.'

Song shook her paw warmly. 'I know your father well! He'll be overjoyed to see you!'

Burble scurried about, reassuring slaves and water rats as Megraw came swooping down to land on the plateau. 'Don't fuss now, me friend won't harm ye, he's on our side, yiss yiss, an' we're thankful for that!'

Folding his massive wings, the osprey nodded at Song. 'Weel, lassie, ah tek it the battle's o'er. Ye'll no be seein' maggypies round here nae mair!'

Nobeast doubted the fierce fish eagle's word.

Dippler eyed his logboat, floating empty out on the lake. 'I could take a dozen or so in the logboat when we gets it back to land. Anybeast want to come with me? I'm goin' home.'

Home!

The beautiful word meant everything to the creatures gathered by the lake's edge. Some of the freed slaves broke into sobs and wept at the thought of it. Gawjo was one of those who could not hold back a tear. Dann thought of Redwall and his father, and his own eyes filled.

'Look at 'em blubberin', Song,' Dippler whispered. 'Bet you can't start everybeast weepin' by singin' somethin' nice an' sad?'

Song tweaked the Guosim shrew's ear. 'You heartless little horror! Bet I can. Just give me a moment to dry my eyes.'

There on the rocks of the sunlit island the young squirrelmaid's voice rang out into the late summer afternoon.

'Please gaze round our garden, remember me there,
And always be faithful and true,
Then look to the sunset and know that somewhere,
'Tis I who'll be thinking of you.
Home, home, I will come home,
Back to the ones I love best,
Home, home, no more to roam,
My weary heart will find rest.

So leave the door open and keep the fire bright,
As I recall it was always,
It may be evening or dawn's welcome light,
I'll wander back one of these days.
Home, home, I will come home,
Ere the long seasons have passed,
Home, home, no more to roam,
Peace we will find there at last.'

In the hush that followed, Song noticed Dippler weeping.

34

Rimrose sat at the Abbey pond's edge with Cregga, Sister Sloey, Ellayo, Deesum and Gurrbowl Cellarmole. Between them they were candying nuts and fruit, shelling hazels, almonds and chestnuts, slicing apples and pears, removing stones from plums, damsons and greengages, and selecting berries. These they layered in pottery jars, pouring in honey, then sealing the tops with bark circles and beeswax.

Sister Sloey watched a crew of moles carrying ladders out of the Abbey. 'They've finished fixing all the window-panes, Cregga marm.'

The blind Badgermum nodded fondly. 'At last Redwall is restored to its former glory, and our beautiful tapestry will soon be back where it belongs. I can stand in the *centre of Great Hall and feel it, I know I can!'*

Gurrbowl placed another full jar to one side. 'Hurr, et be'd a long job awroight. This day's ee larst day of season *boi moi reckernin'.'*

Rimrose looked up from her work. 'The last day of summer? Surely not. You said that Song and her friends *would be back by then, Cregga.'*

The blind badger pulled the stalk from an apple and began slicing it expertly. 'That's what my dream told me,

Rimrose. Maybe summer has a few more days to run yet. Are you sure your calculations are right, Gurrbowl?'

The molewife nodded solemnly. 'Thurr bain't no mustakes in moi calyoocayshuns, marm!'

Ellayo reassured Gurrbowl hastily. 'Oh, we ain't questionin' yore reckonin', marm. Matter o' fact, summer does seem to have gone on quite long this season. Oh, by the way, has anybeast seen mister Florian an' the Dibbuns today? They was 'aunting us yesterday, pinchin' nuts an' dabbin' their paws in our 'oney, gettin' up to all sorts o' roguery they were. Wonder where they've gotten to?'

Deesum nodded in the direction of Mossflower Wood. 'Berrypickin'. I heard mister Janglur and mister Rusvul say at breakfast that they'd go along with Florian to keep an eye on the Dibbuns. Huh! Rather them than us, I say. Imagine having charge of that lot in the woodlands. I'll wager they come back filthy, with their smocks all snagged and ripped!'

Rimrose poured honey into a jar, chuckling. 'Mister Florian'll be glad to get Dwopple and his gang back here, I should imagine. Is that them now, coming in the main gate? Dearie me, just look at the state they're in!'

A band of Dibbuns charged across the lawn, stained red and purple with berry juice. Janglur and Rusvul followed, towing a cartload of baskets. Florian followed up, breathlessly trying to take a headcount of the Abbeybabes.

'Five, six, seven, be still, y'blighters, wot! Come back here, back I say, young sirs an' missies, line up correctly! Oh, confound the blighters, I've gone an' lost count again. Er, three, four, five . . . Stop dodgin' about there, Dwopple, I've gone an' counted you twice again. You should be five, or was it four? No, three, that's right. Now, three, four, five.'

Sister Sloey took a correct count as the Dibbuns ran towards her. 'Mister Florian sir, I've got a count, there's twenty-two in all. Is that how many you went out with?'

Dwopple swiped a strawberry and dipped it in honey. 'Course not! Twenny-two's norra right, us wen' out wiv twenny-free dis mornin', mista Rusbul counted 'em twice!'

Rusvul and Janglur took a swift count, which tallied with Sister Sloey's. They dropped the cart handles.

'One's missin', Jang. We'll have t'go back to the woodlands!'

'No, you stay 'ere, Rus. I'll go!'

Rimrose hurried past both of them. 'You two take a rest – I'll go. There's some cold mint tea setting in the pond shallows. Help yourselves – you deserve it.'

Florian Dugglewoof Wilffachop was first to the tea jug. 'Ah, jolly good, cold tea after a flippin' day chasin' those ruffians round bush an' shrub, nothin' like it!'

Rimrose found the Dibbun, a baby dormouse named Guff, with enormous ears. He had toddled right on past the main gates and was close to the end of the wall, going south. Rimrose caught up with him, though he started to run and she had to chase him. She swept the tiny fellow up into her paws. 'Where d'you think you're off to, my little button?'

Guff pointed a berrystained paw south down the path. 'Gunna zing downed durr!'

The good squirrelwife translated Guff's baby talk. 'Going to sing down there? Why'd you want to do that?'

The dormouse babe looked at her as if the answer was obvious. 'Cozz dat's whair alla singen be's!'

Rimrose did not doubt the Dibbun's word – his large sensitive ears could pick up sounds far better than hers. She stood there holding the little creature, listening for quite a while until her ears too picked up the noise. It came from many voices raised heartily as they came through the woods, roaring out an old ballad called 'Seven Seasons Gone'.

Rimrose felt her paws trembling as she lowered Guff back to the path. Excitement and many differing emotions crowded in on her, so that she could hardly put her words together correctly.

'Tell them Abbey, er, Abbey go, tell them Janglur, tell my daughter coming home. Quick Abbey!'

Guff nodded. He understood perfectly. Dibbuns spoke like that all the time, it was no problem. He trundled off towards Redwall while Rimrose dashed the other way, her skirts and aprons flapping as she yelled herself hoarse. 'Song, it's Song, my daughter's coming home!'

Soon the dustcloud was seen rising above the trees, tramping paws keeping up with the old marching ballad. Strung across four pikestaffs borne by Song, Dann, Dippler and Gawjo, the great Redwall tapestry provided a fitting banner as they bellowed the words.

'Seven seasons gone, oh seven seasons gone,
But now I'm comin' home, me dear ole mate,
Over valley hill'n'field an' me footpaws didn't yield,
Get some vittles on the table, I can't wait!
Go t'the left right left! Go t'the left right left!

Seven seasons gone, oh seven seasons gone,
Have the little ones all growed up big'n'strong,
Is me father in the chair, do his snores ring through
    the air,
Now I'm goin' to wake him up with this ould song.
Go t'the left right left! Go t'the left right left!

Seven seasons gone, oh seven seasons gone,
I've been fightin' roarin' marchin' all the time,
But I'm comin' home t'you, to give you a hug or two,
The moment that I've supped a jug o' wine.
Go t'the left right left! Go t'the left right left!'

Bong boom! Bong boom! Bong boom!

The bells of Redwall Abbey tolled out like melodious rolling thunder. Chores, rest, recreation and duty were forgotten. Redwallers poured out on to the path outside the gates to see the brave sight. Aprons waved and cooks' caps were flung into the air. Cregga seized Friar Butty and sat him upon her mighty shoulders, yelling, 'What do you see, friend, tell me what you can see?'

The old Recorder's voice squeaked with eagerness. 'I see Song, Dann and the young Guosim, wotsisname, Dippler! There's an old squirrel marchin' alongside them, looks like a seasoned warrior t'me. I see a rank of hedgehogs, biggest I ever set eyes on, must be close to a score of 'em! Right behind them there's squirrels, mice, moles – even some otters! They're smiling, laughing, singing, pounding the dust up high as they come. Oh, Cregga marm, did you ever see such a sight?'

Cregga chuckled at the thought of a blind badger seeing any sight, but she understood her friend's jubilation. 'No, I never saw such a sight, Friar. What else do you see?'

'I see Martin the Warrior! They've done it! They've brought the great tapestry home to Redwall!'

Rusvul grabbed his son's paws with a fierceness Dann could feel, dust settling on their faces as they stared intently at each other.

'Dann, that night, I'm sorry . . .'

Dann seemed to have grown taller and broader. 'Forget it, Reguba!'

Rusvul held his son at paw's length. 'No, Dann, yore the Reguba now. Let me look at the son who's made me proud t'see a warrior standin' before me!'

Janglur and Rimrose hugged Song so hard she could scarcely breathe.

'Oh, Song, Song, thank the seasons you're back safe!'

'Well, missie, I'll bet you've sung some songs an' been through a few adventures since you left yore ole dad'n'mum. Haha, yore even prettier'n when y'went away!'

Song found herself looking over Janglur's shoulder at her grandpa and Ellayo, staring at one another like two creatures in a dream.

'Gawjo Swifteye, is it really you?'

'Aye, 'tis me, Ellayo me dear, older an' greyer, though mebbe none the wiser. Bet I'm a sight t'make sore eyes sorer, eh?'

'Oh no, Gawjo, you look 'andsome, all silver-furred an' well.'

'Aye, but not half so pretty as you, Ellayo. You've not changed a single hair. Wait, is that our son Janglur?'

'You could wager on it, Gawjo. That apple never fell far from the tree! He's the breath out o' yore mouth. Go to him!'

'Thank ye, I will. Oh, Torrab, bring yore crew over here. Ellayo, I want you t'meet yore other sons an' daughters.'

The old squirrelwife looked up at the big hedgehogs surrounding her and shook her head in amazement. 'My sons an' daughters? Great seasons! You there, you look too big to be anybeast's son.'

The giant hedgehog bowed, his face wreathed in smiles. 'Hoho, marm, I ain't yore son, I'm just a visitor. My name's Sollertree an' this is my daughter Nettlebud an' our friend Goodwife Brimm. She's a fine cook, I can assure ye, marm.'

Dippler found himself chatting to many Guosim friends. 'Poor ole Bargle. That's another Log a Log we lost, mates. Who's Chieftain o' the tribe now? You, Mayon? Or Splikker maybe? I'm sure you've chosen another Log a Log since I've been gone?'

Mayon shook his head ruefully. 'No, mate, Bargle was only actin' Log a Log. We can't make a new Chief until we catch up with that murderin' Fenno.'

Dippler looked puzzled. 'Fenno? Surely ye weren't thinkin' o' makin' that blackguard into a Log a Log?'

'Oh no. But Guosim law states clear that a new Chieftain can't be appointed until the old one is avenged,' Splikker explained. 'The Guerilla Union rule is that when

377

a Log a Log dies by the paw of a Guosim shrew . . .'

Dippler interrupted him, as shrews invariably do when debating. 'Lissen, matey, you've no need to go huntin' Fenno. I caught up with that murderin' scum an' slew him with my own sword, even though it was snapped in half. He's deader'n last season's grass an' good riddance to the villain!'

Everybeast turned as the shrews threw up their paws and pointed their snouts towards Dippler, setting up a shout.

'Logalogalogalogalogaloooooooog!'

The young Guosim shrew stood totally embarrassed. 'Ahoy, mates, steady on there. Wot's all the shoutin' about?'

A venerable old shrew named Marglo came forward, carrying something wound in barkcloth.

'Yore only a young 'un. Stands t'reason y'not expected to know all of the Guosim law, so I'll quote some to ye.

'The paw of the shrew that slays the beast,
Who made our Chieftain fall,
Will wield the sword of Guosim,
And be Log a Log over all!'

Marglo unwrapped the barkcloth from a short rapier. Dippler recognized his dead leader's blade straight away. The oldster presented it to him ceremoniously. 'From this day forth yore name is forgotten in our tribe. Take the Chieftain's blade. Hail, Log a Log of all Guosim!'

Everybeast on the path in front of Redwall set up an earsplitting cheer. Skipper waved them to silence. 'Would y'like to say a word to yore tribe, Log a Log, me ole mate? Come on, don't be shy.'

The new Log a Log thrust the rapier into his belt. 'Ahem, now let me see . . . er . . . yes. Guosim! I'm only young but I'll try to be as good a Log a Log as our old 'un was, fortune smile on 'is memory. But I been thinkin'. No more logboats fer us, we're goin' to build new vessels, light an' swift an' easy t'carry overland. Soon now I'll take ye to see me friend Chief Burble, boss of the River'ead watervoles. He's the bucko who'll show us 'ow t'make boats like the *Swallow*, neatest liddle craft ever to sail a stream! Oh, an' there's another thing. I won't stand t'see any young 'uns in our tribe pushed around or bullied or made fun of! Er . . . that's all fer now, but I'll think of more to say to ye later.'

Dann strode over to congratulate his friend. 'Well said, Log a Log. I think you'll be a great Chieftain!'

Cregga's searching paw reached Dann. 'What about you, sir Reguba? Have you got any plans?'

'Who me? Er, no, not really, marm. Oh, I'm sorry, here's yore sword back. Sorry I borrowed it without permission.'

Janglur's lazy eyes flickered as he murmured to Gawjo and Rusvul, 'Just watch young Dann's face when Cregga tells 'im the news!'

The blind badger's paw closed tightly over Dann's, holding the sword there. Everybeast heard what she had to say.

'The sword of Martin is yours now for as long as you shall defend this Abbey with it. Dannflor Reguba, I name you Champion of Redwall!'

Before the cheering could start anew Skipper's paw shot aloft. 'Belay the roarin', mates, there's more t'come yet. Now, is there a Songbreeze Swifteye among us t'day? Well, if there is you better get yoreself over 'ere smartish!'

Willing paws ushered Song forward until she was standing alongside Dann in front of Cregga Badgermum. Looking slightly bemused, the squirrelmaid whispered to her friend, 'Hope they're not going to ask me to sing. My mouth's full of dust from that long trek.'

Ellayo tweaked her granddaughter's ear. 'Manners! Stop whisperin' an' lissen to wot the Badgermum has to say to ye, missie!'

A hush had fallen on the crowd. Curious onlookers at

379

the back stood on tip-paw to see and hear what Cregga was about to say. She did not keep them waiting. 'Song, you are to be the Abbess of Redwall!'

The crowd went wild with delight. It took Skipper, Sollertree, Torrab and several stout hedgehogs to restore order and a degree of quiet. The pretty squirrelmaid sat down upon the dusty path, completely dumbfounded, as Cregga continued, 'Redwall Abbey needs someone like you, miss, young, bright and courageous. Dann is our Champion, and he will have his father, Janglur and Skipper to advise him. You, as Abbess, can always look to your grandma, your mother or to me for help. We will happily assist you in your decisions '

Song stood up slowly, her eyes searching Cregga's face. 'But why me? There are many Redwallers who have lived here far longer than I have, Sister Slòey, Friar Butty, Tragglo Spearback. It is an honour far beyond my wildest dreams, marm. Tell me, why do you choose me as Abbess?'

The blind badger gave her reasons readily. 'Whilst you were gone I was visited in my dreams by Martin the Warrior. This is what he told me.

'Four Chieftains from the isle return,
But one with his own tribe will stay,
Three will return, back to this place,
On summertime's last day.
The riverbeast to rule his kind,
Where once his errors were maligned,
But this to you I say,
Look to the young two went from here,
A-questing for my tapestry,
The Reguba and Swifteye's maid,
Champion and Abbess they shall be!'

Florian Dugglewoof Wilffachop bent a leg, twirled his floppy hat and produced the most elaborate bow anybeast had yet witnessed. 'Truth will out, my deah companions, ah yes. Who among us would doubt the words of Martin the Warrior? Splendid chap, absolutely first rate, wot wot! Ahem! Would you kindly bestow upon these rustic creatures a few pearls of new-found wisdom from your rosepetal lips, O Abbess Song-thingummy?'

A puzzled look crossed Song's face, and Friar Butty muttered, 'He wants you to say a few words, missie – sorry, Abbess.'

Song was lifted on to the Noonvale Troupe's cart. She looked down at the expectant faces gazing up at her and took a deep breath. 'Would you like a feast?'

A roaring cheer arose. 'Yes, yes, a feast!'

Holding up her paws for silence, the young squirrelmaid smiled sweetly. 'Well, you'll just have to wait. 'Tis autumn tomorrow and the harvesting must begin. As Abbess of Redwall I'll have no idle paws or gluttonous faces about me whilst there's work to be done around my Abbey. Dann Reguba, I give you as Champion permission to liven up any slackers – tug of the ear, swift kick in the tail, that sort of thing. And you visitors, we'll see if we can't find you some useful chores, washing pots, scrubbing floors and what not. Oh yes, you'd better watch out when you hear the swish of this Abbess's robe!'

Song stared solemnly at the crestfallen faces staring up at her, and then she gave a hearty giggle. 'Heeheehee! Stop looking at me like frogs at a funeral! What's the matter, can't you take a joke? Listen – here are my first four official words to you as Abbess of Redwall. On with the feast!'

Cheering and laughing, they pushed the cart across the lawn to the Abbey. Florian, bringing up the rear, chatted away to Rimrose. 'Whew, marm, greatly relieved, that's what yours truly is. I thought we'd voted in a right young terror t'run the jolly old place, wot, a proper new-brush-sweeps-clean stickler! Good job your pretty daughter was

381

only jokin', wot wot! Nothin' like a sense o' humour I always say, chap should always be able t'take a joke or a bit o' ribbin' . . . Yowch!'

A pebble from the fiendish mousebabe's sling clipped Florian's tailbob. The hare dashed off after Dwopple shouting threats. 'Assassin, rapscallion, figdoodle, pollywoggin' savage infant! Yes, you, sah! I'll kick y'little tail ten times round Great Hall if I catch you! I'll chuck you in with the flippin' apples an' trample you to cider! I'll . . . Er, now now, put that sling down, there's a good little chap . . . Heeeeelp!'

Florian flew in behind the merry cavalcade and slammed the Abbey door shut.

Epilogue

Extract from the records of Redwall Abbey, written by an Apprentice Recorder under the direction of Friar Butty.

What a feast we had that day, and the three days following it. My word! I thought mister Florian could clean a platter, until I watched those big rough hedgehogs tucking in. 'Twas a good thing there was more than enough, for Redwall lived up to its name for providing lavish hospitality to everybeast within its gates. Abbess Song's First Feast was a rousing success! I declare, there never was such an array of food, ten kinds of cheeses, twelve different breads, all crisp and fresh. Cakes, puddings, flans, trifles, tarts and crumbles in abundance. Oh, those scones! Goody Brimm baked batches of them, assisted by the giant Sollertree and his long-lost daughter Nettlebud. Sollertree is the jolliest of creatures now that he has his daughter back. He brought with him a sack of almonds and a basket of dried grapes as a gift to our Abbey. There was a Last Summer Salad at the feast which had to be balanced between two tables because of its size. October Ale and strawberry fizz were very popular, but then, so was every other drink. Have you ever tasted skilly'n'duff? The Guosim made pans of the stuff, it is very delicious and difficult to stop eating. However, the serious trencherbeasts, Skipper, Florian, Tragglo and some others, went on to sample the moles' famous deeper'n ever turnip'n'tater'n'beetroot pie and the otters' formidably spicy hotroot soup. Excellent entertainment was provided by the Noonvale Troupe, though our poor Abbess was called upon to render ballad after ballad. I thought they would never let her sit down to eat. Martin the Warrior's tapestry was hung in its former position amid all the jollity. That feast! Redwallers will tell of it in song and story for generations to come.

It was a strange and exciting adventure our travellers had to relate. We listened eagerly to the tale of how they quested to bring back our stolen tapestry. Dibbuns sat wide-eyed as Gawjo told them of the lost island at the centre of the great lake and of how it was conquered. He said that now it was a place inhabited by water rats who live there peacefully in the castle, learning to farm the land for their food. All the slaves were freed, some to return to their homes, others being part of the force that came back to Redwall. Now that the curse of the Marlfoxes was lifted from the island it was a pleasant place to be, ruled over by a great fish eagle, whom all spoke well of. Abbess Song said that the bird's name is Mighty Megraw. She wanted him to come to the Abbey with her, but he refused. We laughed at the curious speech of Megraw, and our Abbess herself has written down his parting words to her. This is what he said. 'Leave mah island? Ach, awa' wi' ye, lassie. Ah'm King o' this place, d'ken. Atop yon castle is mah perch, a bird would be oot o' his mind tae leave a fine braw lake, full o' bonny pikefishes, so easy tae catch an' guid tae eat. Ah'll bid ye fareweel, go an' awa' back tae yer Abbey an' eat all manner o' dreadful fruit an' veggibles. Mebbe ah'll gang aroond tae see ye wan day!' I had great difficulty understanding this, but Dwopple and the Dibbuns didn't. Often we have to bring them down from the walltops, where they stand watching for a visit from the one Dibbuns call 'Mig'aw h'eagle'.

It is mid-autumn now, and the trees shed tears of brown and gold as their leaves fall softly to the quiet earth. We gathered in the last of our orchard's russet apples yesterday. Mister Florian and his troupe decided to travel on, it was a sad parting, but after all they are strolling players. Well, scarce half a day's journey down the path their cart fell entirely to pieces. Since they had eaten all the provisions they had been supplied with, Florian traipsed boldly back at the head of his troupe and enquired if dinner was ready (wot wot)! So the Wandering Noonvale Companions are installed in Redwall once more. Abbess Song was informed by Florian that it might take a season or three to build a new cart. We are all very fond of the old rascal, he may stay with us as long as he pleases.

Log a Log has taken his shrews off to see the Riverhead watervole tribe, where they will learn how to construct a new fleet of boats, lighter and faster than their old logboats. I hear Burble, the Riverhead Chief, is a very odd and humorous young watervole. His full title, I am told, is Chief Burble Bigthrone, Holder of Leafwood and Commander of the boat *Swallow*. Dann could hardly tell me for laughin', of how Burble plundered his throne from the Marlfoxes' castle and insisted on bringing it back home on Gawjo's raft, polishing it the entire trip. We look forward to a visit from both Riverheads and Guosim at our Midwinter Festival.

What more is there to tell? Redwall's harvest is in, days grow short and birds are flocking together in the trees for their long flight to the sunny places. Skipper and his otter crew are hauling in dead treetrunks from Mossflower Wood, fuel for the Abbey fires. I dearly love a good fire, particularly on some cold winter night when snow is driven by howling winds outside. We sit around a cheery blaze in Cavern Hole, roasting chestnuts, singing songs and telling tales, happy together in the warmth and safety of our beloved home, Redwall Abbey. They say our bells can be heard from afar at any time of day or night.

If you are travelling 'cross the flatlands, through the woods, or along the path, you may hear our twin bells. They will be calling you to come and join us, and we would be pleased to see you. Do call in someday, you will be made welcome by all who dwell within our walls.

Rimrose Swifteye, Apprentice Recorder to Friar Butty at Redwall Abbey in Mossflower country (and never too old to learn new skills).

Curtain!

NB
This narrative has been edited by Florian Dugglewoof Wilffachop, Actor Manager Impresario. Who insists that the entire tale is a drama, which he will be later performing as a play. Hence the three parts being named as acts, rather than books. We crave your indulgence for this deviation.

ABOUT THE AUTHOR

Before he started writing books for children, Brian Jacques' life was as full of adventure as the stories he creates. At the age of fifteen he went to sea and travelled the world, before returning to his home town of Liverpool, where he still lives today. He has worked as a stand-up comedian and playwright and now hosts his own programme, *Jakestown*, on BBC Radio Merseyside. For twenty years, his bestselling Redwall books have captured readers all over the world and won universal praise.

For more information about Brian Jacques and his work please visit his website **www.redwall.org.**

BRIAN
JACQUES

LORD BROCKTREE

Salamandastron, ancestral home of the Badger
Lords, is under threat from the wildcat Ungatt Trunn,
whose power seems absolute and whose evil knows
no bounds. The mountain's only hope is the badger,
Lord Brocktree, who is drawn to the fortress by
an undeniable sense of destiny.

**'Not since Roald Dahl have children filled
their shelves so compulsively'**
The Times

978 1 862 30145 0

BRIAN JACQUES

SALAMANDASTRON

Redwall slumbers in the summer sun, unaware
that the mountain stronghold of Salamandastron lies
besieged by the weasel army of Ferahgo the Assassin.
Or that danger is also creeping towards the Abbey
in the form of the deadly Dryditch Fever . . .

**'Not since Roald Dahl have children filled
their shelves so compulsively'**
The Times

978 1 862 30141 2

NEWS FROM REDWALL ABBEY

JOIN NOW!

The official REDWALL READERS' CLUB with news of upcoming books, Redwall merchandise plus a free Membership Pack!

Important!

To join the club please send £3.50 (UK), $12.00 (USA) or £6.00 (Everywhere else) with your application form. Cheques or International Postal Orders made payable to REDWALL ABBEY CO LTD.

This fee covers the cost of postage and packing of your membership pack plus two further mailings over an 18 month period.

Write to:
Redwall Readers' Club
P.O. Box 57
Mossley Hill
Liverpool, L18 3NZ
UK

www.redwall.org

APPLICATION FORM

NAME _____

ADDRESS _____

_____

_____

POST/ZIP CODE _____

COUNTRY _____